RAINEY
NIGHTS

RAINEY NIGHTS

R. E. BRADSHAW

Published by
R. E. BRADSHAW BOOKS

USA

•R.E.B.BOOKS•

RAINEY NIGHTS

R. E. Bradshaw
© **2011 by R. E. Bradshaw. All Rights Reserved.**
R. E. Bradshaw Books/AUG 2011
ISBN: 978-0-9835720-3-9
LCCN: 2011911869

http://www.rebradshawbooks.com
Rebecca Elizabeth Bradshaw on Facebook

For information contact rebradshawbooks@gmail.com

This novel is entirely a work of fiction. The names, characters and events portrayed in it are the work of the author's imagination. Any resemblances to actual persons living or dead or events are entirely unintentional.

From the Author

I am writing this on the one-year anniversary of uploading my first novel. I was finally pushed into this dream by the people around me who were tired of being guinea pigs and said, "Publish!" I did and what an amazing ride it has been. I owe a gigantic thank you to many people, but most important are the readers. Thank you for giving me a shot at a dream. Your constant encouragement keeps me at the keyboard.

Lynne, Dawn, Linda, Henriette, Terry – you ladies simply rock!

Kaycee, you are a savior. I am lucky to have such a patient editor.

Gayl, what can I say? You were a blessing sent from above. Thank you for everything.

My four-legged editorial team, I thank you for hours of company and for listening to me read. More treats are coming. Yes, the chicken jerky kind. (The real Freddie Krueger, the model for Rainey's bobbed-tail black cat, lives at my house and is a constant source of entertainment and consternation.)

Mom and Dad, thanks for being there. Like the Sugarland song says, "Remember me in ribbons and curls, I still love you more than anything in the world, Love, your baby girl."

Jon, you're the best son ever. Kendra, you are the best daughter-in-law ever.

Deb, as always – you are my inspiration. Thanks for the gallons of coffee, bringing me food when I was too wrapped up in the story to remember to eat, sleeping alone for nights on end while I wrote into the wee hours of the morning, and not minding when I slept away the next day. Thank you for all the little things that mean so much. You are the reason I believe in love at first sight.

About the book...

RAINEY NIGHTS is the second novel in the Rainey Bell Thriller series. This a stand alone book, but if you want more background on former FBI Behavioral Analyst Rainey Bell, read RAINEY DAYS to see how the series began.

In RAINEY NIGHTS, the reader is given a glimpse into Special Agent Rainey Bell's former life, where she is unaffected by the tragedies that later derailed her career and changed her future, (detailed in RAINEY DAYS.) This glimpse into her past gives perspective to the challenges Rainey faces, starting a new life with Katie Meyers. This is not a coming out story, it is a coming to terms story. At the beginning of any relationship, there are adjustments and compromises to be made. In Rainey's case, her past shapes her decisions and often complicates the situation. It may end up getting them both killed.

Above all, RAINEY NIGHTS is a thriller. It is not a romance, although Rainey and Katie's relationship provides the backdrop for the story. This book is not for the squeamish or weak of heart. Fair warning; RAINEY NIGHTS contains violence of a sexual nature. For those of you that choose to proceed, do so with the doors and windows locked and the lights on all over the house. As one reviewer said, "Don't assume you know how this story is going to end."

PART I

"No one who, like me, conjures up the most evil of those half-tamed demons that inhabit the human breast, and seeks to wrestle with them, can expect to come through the struggle unscathed." ~ Sigmund Freud

CHAPTER ONE

Saturday, May 5th, four years ago.

Botetourt County, Virginia

Tears mingled with the cold water dripping from her body. The drops fell to the ground, streamed down the hill, and slid off the embankment just a few miles south of Iron Gate, Virginia. The James River headwaters swirled by, carrying the tears away on a meandering journey across the Commonwealth to the Chesapeake Bay, where they would slip into the Atlantic and out to sea. In the deep-green valley created by the Blue Ridge Mountains on the east and the Appalachian Mountains on the west, a mother began to worry. The two ancient mountain ranges nearly touched in Botetourt County, separated only by the little town of Buchanan and the James River. This lush land was an ideal place to be born and, as it turned out, a very lonely place to die.

Crystal Lynn Granger, like the James River, was born in these majestic highlands. She grew to be a dark haired beauty with big brown, soulful eyes. A long legged, gifted athlete, Crystal was a two-sport star, playing basketball and tennis. She was also very popular among her peers, voted Class President all four years of high school. She would graduate Valedictorian of her class in a month and head off to college in the fall. Crystal Lynn was destined to follow the James River out of the valley and on to greater things.

Raised by God-fearing country folks, Crystal was very active in the youth ministry at her church. Jesus played a big part in her life. It was to Him that she prayed, as she looked up into the deep black night at the stars twinkling through the treetops. The waning moonlight could not erase the surrounding darkness. Though Crystal could not see down the embankment, she knew the James River gurgled below her. Her sense of sight was useless, but her hearing was keen. What she heard made her pray even harder. She did not pray for herself. She prayed for the family she was about to leave behind. She prayed that God would help her devastated parents and friends, and see them through the grieving. Crystal closed her eyes and prayed her Lord would end her suffering soon.

From behind, Crystal heard the snapping of twigs, as he moved closer. Some time ago, he had slipped into the blackness, leaving her tied to a tree. She wasn't sure how long ago he left. Time had no meaning, now. Crystal knew he was coming back for her. He told her he would, right after he taped her hands into praying position, tied a rope around her neck, and fastened her to the tree on her knees. His final act was the duct tape on her forehead that held her head up, so she was forced to look at him, while he ranted and raved in front of her, and then he was gone.

Crystal was glad to be left tied there. At least he wasn't hitting her anymore. He beat her black and blue, before viciously raping and sodomizing her for the last two hours. The more she fought him, the more he seemed to enjoy it. Finally, she submitted to stop the beating. After the sexual assault ended, he tied a rope around her neck, and threw her in the river. She repeatedly lost her footing on the slick river rocks and nearly drowned. Laughing, he pulled her up, only to let the rope go slack so she would fall again. She screamed when she had the breath, but no one could hear her over the rushing rapids this far away from the road. At least the freezing water had eased some of the pain in her brutalized body. Crystal was sure, however, that he was not done with her. She knew he was going to kill her. She knew who he was, or at least she thought she knew the blond haired young man with the kind blue eyes and handsome smile.

Crystal found him waiting by her car when she finished work. Surprised and flattered that he came to see her, she felt her face blush with excitement. His invitation for a quick cup of coffee was thrilling. She understood when he told her not to tell anyone, because the other girls would be jealous, and she wouldn't want that either. Crystal didn't call home, because her strict parents would not let her go out with a boy they had not met. It was just coffee. "No harm, no foul," she thought.

He promised to have her back in time to make her curfew. He already had the coffee, prepared just as she liked it, waiting in his truck. He drove to a place where they could sit and watch the river. Crystal was not nervous or apprehensive about being alone with him, because of what he said he stood for. In fact, she felt safer with him than some of the boys her parents vetted. He was so handsome and charming, he seemed a dream come true, the perfect boy. When he leaned over and kissed her sweetly her heart fluttered, but as she returned his kiss, everything changed.

The light from his small battery operated lantern illuminated the area in front of the tree again. Through eyes that were nothing but slits from the swelling, Crystal saw his feet first before he raised the lantern, bringing his full body into view. He was completely naked. During the earlier assault, she closed her eyes, but she knew he didn't use part of his body to rape her. He had not removed his clothes. Now, she could see him standing before her with his penis in full view. She had only seen a nude man in a picture a friend showed her. She wasn't sure, but something didn't look right. He saw where she was looking and the look in his eyes sent lightning bolts of terror through her body. Shaking uncontrollably, Crystal searched for some place to take her mind, some place to find peace, so she wouldn't be there, alone, with him. She wasn't sure where the inspiration came from, but she began to sing softly. Through bloody, split lips the words came out in a whisper and they stopped him in his tracks.

"Jesus loves me, this I know…"

He froze only for a second and then a wicked smile crept across his face. The last thing she saw was that evil sneer and the flash of light reflected from the thin blade slicing through the air. She felt nothing, as her soul and body separated with the first swing of the sword, nor did she feel the second slash disembowel her. Crystal Lynn Granger's blood flowed down the embankment and into the James River. Her soul followed the flow of the river out of Botetourt County for what she had always been told and knew in her heart was a better place.

4

CHAPTER TWO

Thursday, May 10, five days later.

Southeast of Eagle Rock Gorge, the James River formed a small island. On the east embankment facing the island, the dark trail of dried blood was still visible five days after the murder. Bloody bare footprints ran up and down the hill, forming a macabre choreography along the crimson trail. Rainey's eyes followed the stains to the rapidly moving water below and then back up to the naked, headless body attached to the tree. The hands were still duct taped together in prayer. Rainey pulled on the latex gloves she had been squeezing tightly in each fist, trying to distance herself from the pain and horror the victim experienced. She turned from the rotting smell of the corpse and took a deep cleansing breath, before she walked back up the hill to join the others by the tree.

FBI Supervisory Special Agent, Danny McNally, his broad muscular shoulders in stark contrast to the wiry mountain men, towered over the two local detectives. His red wavy hair was wildly out of control. He had not tried to tame it since they ran out from under the helicopter blades, jumped into a waiting SUV, and rushed to the crime scene. Rainey's experiences with helicopter blades and the thick mass on her head were not good ones. Before leaving this morning, she captured her unruly chestnut locks in a ponytail that stuck out the back of her FBI baseball cap.

Rainey and Danny were here to try to make sense of a series of brutal murders along US 220, from the Blue Ridge Mountains down through the Piedmont area of North Carolina. They left the National Center for the Analysis of Violent Crime, or NCAVC, on the campus of the FBI Academy, just after seven a.m. Using the twenty minutes of flying time to go over the files prepared by the Behavioral Analysis Unit, of which they were both members, Danny and Rainey were now analyzing the most recent crime scene. The BAU2, as it was known, was tasked with understanding evil the average person could never fathom. Her unit concentrated on violent criminal acts like serial murders, mass murders, spree killers, unusual murders of all types, along with sexual assaults and kidnappings targeting adults. The nine murders tied to this particular unknown subject or UNSUB certainly met the criteria of violent and unusual.

Danny turned to Rainey, as she approached, and made the introductions. "Detectives Blaine and Martin, this is SSA Rainey Bell."

Rainey ignored the hands extended toward her. She held up her gloved hands to show the officers she didn't want to contaminate them. She simply nodded and acknowledged each with, "Detective."

Danny began to fill her in on what he found out from the locals. "Blaine here says the body was discovered just before dawn by those two scared boys over there. They were huntin' a new spot to do some fly-fishing, found a path, followed it, and stumbled on her. They're going to have to wash out those waders when they get home. No sign of the head, but they're pretty sure this is the Granger girl that went missing last Saturday."

Rainey walked over and studied the body without touching it. "What makes them so sure it's her?"

Blaine answered, "That 'WWJD' tattooed on her ankle is exactly like the picture her folks gave us. They weren't too happy she had a tattoo, but it helped us identify her. We'll know positively when we get the hands un-taped and compare prints. We hope the scavengers left the thumbs under the tape untouched. The M.E. thinks the tape may have preserved the skin well enough to rehydrate. She was printed at one of those safe kids things at the mall, so we have a comparison set. If we can't get a print, then we'll have to wait for DNA, but I'm pretty sure it's her."

At that moment, a small white haired man in blue coveralls came toward them. He made eye contact with Rainey. A huge grin enveloped his face, curling the ends of his white mustache upward. "Agent Bell, how nice to see you again. Sorry it's under these circumstances, but then we always seem to meet over a dead body."

"Dr. Patrick, I'm glad to see you. I was hoping it would be you on this one," Rainey said, and then added, "Her hands... they are the same. Can we see if she's holding anything before you bag her?"

"Let me get something down so we can lay her over and then we'll see what the tape could be hiding," Dr. Patrick said, as he and his assistant moved a plastic sheet into position beside the body.

Rainey squatted in front of the putrid, blackening remains. Rainey wasn't "used to" the smell, but she had learned to block it out and breathe properly. Still, she had to fight the gag reflex trying to overtake her. Detective Martin moved closer.

He spoke behind a handkerchief, held over his nose and mouth. "Did he beat the others this badly?"

"It's hard to tell what's bruising and what's lividity. The animals and insects didn't do us any favors," Rainey answered, dispassionately.

She had to be detached. How else could she deal with the torturous images she saw almost daily? She spent the last seven years researching serial killers, rapists, sadists and the like, by reading about them in reams of reports, interviewing them in prison, cataloguing their behavior, and going out into the field to help catch the new ones. It took time to develop the expertise needed to become one of the eight members of Rainey's team. In conjunction with their extensive field experience and accrued wisdom, she and her coworkers had studied an extremely large volume of cases. An average law enforcement officer would pursue maybe one serial killer in a lifetime. Rainey's team averaged twelve serial investigations a year.

Criminal behavioral analysis developed based on the idea, a person's behavior directly resulted from that person's thought processes. The repetitions of behavior in his or her crimes became recognizable. By comparing types of criminal behaviors and the people who committed those offenses, it was possible to classify the type of person who would most likely commit a crime with similar characteristics. In other words, Rainey Bell spent her days and most nights submerged in human depravity. Today would be no different.

Rainey stood up and moved back as Dr. Patrick approached. He removed a cross, suspended on a gold chain, from what remained of the neck. He placed it in an evidence bag and handed it to Rainey. She studied the cross while the doctor and his assistant cut the ropes fastening the victim to the tree, careful to leave the knots intact. Slowly, they lowered the body onto the plastic sheeting. Once all the bindings had been bagged and tagged, the doctor moved to the hands. He cut the tape with a scalpel only enough to see inside. Prying the hands open slightly, he reached in with tweezers and removed a small piece of folded paper. He placed the paper, stained with body fluids from decomposition, in another evidence bag and handed it to Rainey. She looked at the paper, unable to see what was written on it, but she knew from the way it was folded what it would say.

Detective Martin moved in to get a look at the contents of the bag. "I don't remember seeing anything in the reports about a note in the previous victims' hands."

Danny spoke up. "We kept that out of the reports. We need one piece of evidence that only the killer knows. We would very much like to keep it that way."

Rainey was glad Danny didn't give Martin all the information about the notes. The fewer people that knew certain details the better.

"Sure, sure," Martin replied. "So you don't think this is a copy cat? This is the real deal?"

Rainey looked down at the body, trying to see the smiling face of Crystal Lynn Granger from the missing persons report. She said quietly, "Yeah, this is the real deal."

#

Later in the evening, Rainey and Danny were shown into an empty conference room at the county sheriff's office. They spread a stack of files across the long table in the center of the room. They just arrived from the morgue where Dr. Patrick confirmed that Crystal Lynn Granger suffered almost identical wounds as the first eight victims. The doctor had the unfortunate experience of recovering, now, his third victim in the case and had reviewed the other victims' autopsy reports. He concluded that all of the women were victims of the same killer the media had nicknamed, "The Praying Hands Killer," in reference to the victims' final pose.

Crystal most likely died within hours of when she was last seen on the previous Saturday. Like the others, the retraction of her neck muscles indicated decapitation was the cause of death. Crystal's body was in advanced decomposition when she was found, but there was still enough evidence to link the cases. All of the young women were bound, choked, beaten severely, savagely raped, and sodomized. The instrument used to behead the victims appeared to be consistent with a long, thin blade, possibly a sword or machete. The same weapon also made the cut to the abdomen. No semen was found and Dr. Patrick seemed to think all the rapes had been carried out with a large phallus or similar instrument. There was no sign of the head. It was assumed to be in the James River. Several of the other victims' heads showed up weeks after the bodies were found, downstream from the scene of their murders and always in a river.

Rainey set about taping pictures of the known fatalities on a white board placed in the room for that purpose. Nine times she reached into a file folder and pulled out a picture of a teenage girl, full of life. Nine more times she taped a picture of each girl's mutilated body beneath their corresponding smiling faces.

"Damn," she said, under her breath.

Danny looked up from the corner where he was concentrating on pouring a cup of coffee. "What?"

"Nothing," Rainey responded, then added quickly, "They were all so young with their whole lives ahead of them. Look at their faces. These are confident, athletic, beautiful girls. How does he get a girl like that to go with him willingly?"

"The news media all up and down 220 warned about this killer, but he has no trouble getting control of them," Danny said.

Just that quickly the two analysts began the process of working the Granger murder case without an official pronouncement. They brainstormed, shared ideas, and formed hypotheses based on the evidence at hand and the knowledge they gained studying similar murderers. Back at Quantico, Rainey, along with the rest of the analysts, already generated a profile of this serial killer. Rainey and Danny were sent to evaluate the latest murder to see if the profile still applied. An hour later, they emerged from the room ready to give the local detectives their opinions on the case.

Often asked to work together, they made a good team. Rainey was always happy to go into the field with Danny. They were Academy classmates and joined the BAU at almost the same time. She never let him forget she was a full member of the team first. At thirty-nine, Danny was just two years older than Rainey. They had an almost sibling relationship on and off the job. He sometimes made her crazy, but she loved him anyway. He could always make her smile when his cherubic, freckled cheeks dimpled up in a grin. Rainey's work didn't allow her to smile often. Danny took her mind off the human misery they witnessed. She appreciated it more than he would ever know.

Rainey followed Danny into the squad room where the detectives and other officers had gathered. She was used to the way local law enforcement stared at them. It was as if she and Danny were magicians about to reveal the secrets behind a trick. Most people did not understand what the BAU did. Behavioral analysts were not psychics, but rather a group of people who were trained to recognize the undercurrents that link various criminal personality types. Rainey couldn't tell them exactly who the perpetrator was, but she could tell them what kind of person to look for. It wasn't magic. It was hard, life consuming work.

Rainey's most recent and longest standing relationship, with Bobby, a cop in Arlington, had fallen victim to the job. He wanted to marry her, but he also wanted a wife he would find at home, not one he had to wonder when or if she was coming home. Rainey chose the job and they parted amicably, but she missed him. She missed his companionship most of all. He was her best friend. She didn't have time for many friends. In a sad way, Rainey was glad to have this case to occupy her mind while her personal life fell apart. She needed a vacation, but she was determined to find this killer before taking time off. For now, she buried her needs and focused on the young girls whose pictures she had taped to the board.

With all eyes in the room on her, she began to speak. "The UNSUB in this case has now taken the lives of nine young women that we are aware of. You are looking for a white male between the ages of twenty and thirty. He will be above average to very good looking, with no outward physical deformities. He will be well liked and appear non-threatening. The young women this UNSUB takes are pretty, self-confident, in good physical condition, and live very low risk lifestyles. We think these women go with him willingly, with no resistance. They are comfortable and feel safe with him. If they felt threatened, these girls would have fought back. There is no evidence of a struggle at the scenes where we think he coaxed them into his vehicle."

Danny jumped in. "The victims were all good girls, smart, popular, with strong ties to their churches. This type of girl does not go with a stranger willingly. She must have known the UNSUB, if only casually. You are looking for a man that travels Highway 220 for some reason. He gets off the highway and comes into these little towns, picks a victim, and then leaves again without anyone suspecting him. We know he travels this route frequently, going both north and south. He has a totally innocent reason to be here, to meet these girls, and then returns to take them at his pleasure."

Rainey added, "We're encouraging all the other law enforcement agencies involved to re-examine the victims' history for any possible connection to traveling salesmen, businessmen, service technicians, etc. You should also check out local hotels for men fitting the profile, who stayed in hotels near the crime scenes, around the time of the murders or when the bodies were found. This guy would probably hang around a few days to watch the cops."

Danny rejoined the conversation. "Due to the remoteness of his kill sites, he could have committed crimes we are unaware of. With that said, we think the first murders happened up here in Virginia, then he traveled south to North Carolina, and now he's back up north. Highway 220 is significant to him for some reason. We have no evidence that he's committed a crime like this anywhere else, but don't be surprised if more bodies turn up near here. This is his territory."

"We think he lives on this highway, maybe even close by," Rainey said, pointing at a map of the area on the wall behind her. Nine red pushpins marked the places where the victims were found. "He is familiar with local trails into the woods and secluded areas where he takes his victims. He needs time to do what he does and he must know he will not be discovered there. He has studied each of these communities. He knows the habits of people in these rural areas, what the locals do for fun, and where to catch these young women alone. He most likely stalks them for some time to establish their routines and takes them when he knows they are most vulnerable. He probably watches more than one victim at a time. People have seen him with these young women, but like Agent McNally said, he had a legitimate reason for being there."

Detective Martin asked, "That could be anybody. How do we know what to look for?"

Rainey answered, "The guy you are looking for would be appealing to these girls. Remember he is probably good-looking and charming. I believe he is in his early twenties or appears younger than he is. That's young for this type of killer, but he has to be attractive to these teenage girls. He is also probably in good physical condition. These were not tiny girls and he would have to be large enough to gain control over them. There will be no reason to suspect him and that will be your first clue. This is not an outwardly disturbed person. He will fit in socially. He will not be awkward in any way. He possesses above average intelligence. He is organized and planned his crimes for years. When you question him, he will show the appropriate emotional concern for the victims. He may even offer to help with the investigation."

A uniformed cop in the back said, "This guy has to be insane to do what he does to these girls. How can he hide that?"

It was Danny's turn to answer. "He's not insane in the legal sense of the word. You are not looking for a mental patient. This guy is a true psychopath. Outwardly, he has learned to mimic normal human emotions. These guys learn the words but not the music, so to speak. The music of emotion has no power to move him. He has learned to mask his true personality and desires, in order to get what he wants. Above all, he sees nothing wrong with his behavior. He has no remorse, no guilt."

Rainey continued, "He may have exhibited psychopathic behaviors at a younger age, but often these behaviors are misinterpreted as common 'boys will be boys' situations. He may have been caught peeping in a window, or accused of going too far with a girl, but through charm and maneuvering, he escaped punishment. Some psychopathic behavior is thought of as simple alpha male assertiveness and applauded in athletes or successful businessmen and women. Not all psychopaths are murderers. What you need to look for is a guy who can talk his way out of or in to anything. This type of UNSUB is a master manipulator."

Another officer spoke up. "What about the crosses and the praying position? What does that tell you?"

"Because it took three to five days to find his victims, the distance he travelled with them, and the fact that he doesn't want them found right away suggests a controlled killer," Danny answered and continued, "He brought ropes, a weapon, and instruments to torture the victim. The planning, stalking, and his obvious social skills all point to an organized offender. This also backs up the theory that he may appear younger than he really is, because his maturity as a killer is fairly advanced."

Rainey completed Danny's answer, as they often did for each other. One could pick up the other's thoughts in mid-sentence and never miss a beat.

"This type of serial murderer gets off on controlling his victim, instilling as much fear as possible. He is sadistic in that his reward is his victim's terror. He may be impotent, substituting her fear for his sexual gratification. The posing of the victim and the religious connotations we believe are this killer's attempts to make us look for a disorganized, mentally ill person, a smoke screen as it were. The beating these girls took might indicate a disorganized killer caught up in a rage, but it may just as well indicate how hard he had to fight these girls to control them. He must dominate them and get them to submit. He picks victims he knows will fight. He gets off on that. He takes the cross from one victim as a trophy and places it on his next victim. This act has strong meaning to the UNSUB. It is his signature. He wants us to know it's him, but beyond that, he is no 'hand of God' killer, not a mental patient who hears messages from God. He does all of this to fulfill his narcissistic fantasies. He may belong to a church, but his real deity is himself."

A young female deputy, Rainey guessed not more than five years older than the victims, read from the notes she had taken. "So, I'm looking for a good-looking, well built, charming young man with a narcissistic personality. Sounds like my boyfriend."

The room erupted in laughter.

Without cracking a smile Rainey said, "It could be. Where was he on the night Crystal went missing?"

The laughing ceased.

Danny reiterated Rainey's point. "That's what we're telling you. This guy is slick. He moves among you without notice. Do not discount anyone. You've probably already talked to him or someone that knows him."

Detective Martin stood up and began giving assignments to the officers. Rainey went back to the conference room to pack up the files, while Danny stayed behind to give Martin their written suggestions for how to proceed with the investigation. Rainey was looking forward to getting back on the helicopter for home. She already made up her mind that this was the last case she would work until she took a much-needed rest. She was drained of energy. It had been a long day and a longer year. Re-charging her batteries was in order.

The young deputy stuck her head in the open door. "Hey, I'm sorry about the boyfriend comment," she said.

Rainey looked up and smiled. "Sorry to be so hard on you. It's just that's the point really, this guy is the last person you would suspect and that makes him exceedingly dangerous."

"Yes, ma'am."

The ma'am made Rainey feel old. She knew it was simply a sign of respect. She heard it at the academy often, but it stung just the same. She deserved the "ma'am" because of the tone she was using, her instructor voice reserved for the wayward trainees. In a much friendlier manner she asked, "How long have you been in uniform?"

"It'll be a year in July. I went to UVA, got my Bachelors in Criminal Justice, and then I signed up here. I grew up just a few miles out of town. I knew Crystal's family. I go to the same church, when I go that is."

Rainey pulled out a chair and sat down. She motioned for the officer to join her. "Well, it's nice to meet a fellow Cavalier," she paused, peering at the nametag on the other woman's shirt, "Deputy Knox."

Knox pulled out a chair, saying as she lowered herself to the seat, "Please, call me Gillian. You went to UVA?"

"Class of '93. I went straight into the Academy after graduation."

Gillian brightened. "That's my goal, to do what you do. I know I have to get some experience under my belt, but I've applied already. I'm just going to keep trying until I get in."

Rainey had this conversation often. In almost every place she visited, someone wanted to be a Behavioral Analyst. She had the spiel down to a few sentences. "Once you're in the Bureau, you'll need at least five years of field service. Your time here could count towards that, depending on what types of investigations you experience. Then it's back to the Academy for sixteen weeks and up to two more years of mentored training before you can work in the unit. Be aware that there are few positions exactly like mine, but working within the NCAVC is a challenging and rewarding assignment in itself."

"You sound like you've said that a few times," Gillian said, grinning at Rainey.

Rainey couldn't help but return the grin. "Yeah, it's a pretty frequent topic when we hit the road."

"You can't blame us for wanting in the BAU. You guys are rock stars."

Rainey's smile slipped. "Just remember, there is a price to pay for being a rock star. This job is not for everyone. You will make sacrifices. People who love you will make sacrifices. Make sure the person you become romantically involved with in the future, and I'm assuming you'll be dumping the narcissist, knows what your career goals are. It takes the right kind of relationship to make it work with this job."

Rainey felt the pain of losing Bobby once again. She heard it in her voice. She didn't usually open up to people as she was with the young deputy. Rainey kept her life in mental boxes, only opening the ones she needed to function at the time. It was the only way to survive a job like hers. Something about Gillian made Rainey want to warn her about the losses she might suffer. Rainey was tired, emotionally raw at the moment, and her boxes were opening without her consent.

Rainey gathered her emotions in, pushed the box lids back down and stowed them away, as she usually did. There was no room for self-pity or regrets in Rainey's life. In the young deputy's enthusiasm, Rainey recognized the fledgling cop she had once been. Silently, she wished Deputy Knox a happy life far away from Quantico and the losses a career in the BAU would bring her. Instead of saying what she was thinking, Rainey pulled the picture of Crystal Lynn from a folder and slid it across the table to Gillian.

"What can you tell me about this girl? You said you knew the family. Did you know Crystal personally?"

Gilliam looked down at the picture, studying it, and then looked up at Rainey. "I'm five years older than she is… was, so I was out of high school before she got there. I remember seeing her and I knew who she was, but we didn't travel in the same circles. I know that she was very active in the church youth group."

Rainey prodded Gillian. "What was your impression of her? Just tell me what comes to mind, anything you can think of."

"Well, like I said, she was heavily into the youth group. I was at church the Sunday before she went missing. She stood up during the service and told everyone about the youth revival scheduled for… I think it would have been tomorrow. I don't know if they're still having it. Anyway, she was very sweet and enthusiastic. I remember thinking she looked like a kid going places, you know. Self-confident and very pretty, she just seemed to have it all together."

Rainey added what she knew. "She had a job cleaning the church on Saturday nights. That's where her parents found her car when she didn't come home."

Gillian nodded in agreement. "Yes, I was the one who answered the call. I went to the church and checked out the car. I didn't touch anything, but I did look in the windows. The car was locked. Nothing indicated she was taken by force."

Rainey already knew that. She wanted to know more about Crystal. She needed to know why a girl like Crystal would get in a car with this guy. "What did you see in the car?"

Rainey watched as Gillian closed her eyes, trying to recall the scene. This cop has good instincts, Rainey thought to herself. Officer Knox probably would make a good agent, in time.

Gillian began to speak. "I saw Chapstick in the tray on the console, with some change, and a few colored hair ties. One of them was yellow. There was a box, like a Kinko's box you get copies in, on the passenger seat. A sheet of paper was stuck on the top of the box. I know now the box contained abstinence pledge forms the kids were going to fill out at the lockdown."

Rainey was intrigued. "Do you have one of those copies here?"

"Yes, there's a copy of one in the squad room." Gillian started to stand.

Rainey stopped her. "Wait, we'll get that in a minute. What else did you see?"

Gillian refocused on her memory of the car. "I remember thinking how clean the car was. She took really good care of it." The deputy paused to think. "Oh, and there was a dress hung up in the backseat... and a pair of black pumps on the floor. She attended the athletic banquet before she went to work. Her mother said Crystal changed clothes at the high school. The church doors were locked and her keys were missing. I had the preacher open the church and we searched it thoroughly. No sign of her anywhere. It looked like she just evaporated."

The religious angle of the UNSUB's signature and the fact that all the victims were extremely active in their churches made Rainey's skin crawl. When she got that feeling, she knew she had to keep digging. The answer was near, if she could just put the pieces together.

Rainey continued her inquiry. "What do you know about this abstinence pledge and the lock down?"

"I attended a few lockdowns in high school. It's just what it sounds like. They locked us in the church overnight with a few adults. No one could leave or come in after the doors were closed. We played games and ate food. Some religious stuff went on, but not much. It was basically something we could do to be away from our parents overnight with their approval."

"And the abstinence pledge?" Rainey asked.

Gillian laughed. "I had to read up on that one. Certainly didn't take that pledge myself."

Rainey laughed with her, putting the younger woman more at ease.

Gillian visibly relaxed back against the chair. She went on, "That last time in church, Crystal said she visited a youth council where she'd taken the pledge. After that, she arranged for a representative of the group to come here for the lockdown. She was so excited about signing up more kids in the congregation."

Rainey could see the sadness begin to creep across the deputy's face and decided it was time to wrap it up. Although she didn't know her very well, Crystal's death had shaken Gillian. Rainey knew the facts would begin to blur when the emotion entered an interview like this, and that's what it had been, whether Gillian realized it or not. Rainey had one final question.

"Is there anything else that comes to mind? Let your instincts do the work. Close your eyes. What do you see?"

Gillian obeyed and shut her eyes. She squirmed in the seat a little, and then her eyes popped open. "The ring. She wore an abstinence ring. She held up her hand in church to show us. I saw the autopsy report. The ring was not on her hand."

Rainey jumped up. She shuffled through several folders, scanning the information rapidly. Without looking up, she spoke to Gillian.

"Go get the copy of the pledge and tell Agent McNally I need to see him." Gillian didn't move. She seemed stunned at Rainey's sudden change. Rainey looked up. "Now, Knox. Get moving."

"Dammit! How did I miss that?" Rainey grumbled aloud. "Dammit!"

She pulled out her cell phone and hit a button, speed dialing the Communication and Information Technology Unit, CITU, in Quantico. She waited for the familiar voice of Melatiah Brooks to pick up on the other end. After four rings, a harried voice answered on the other end.

"Rainey Bell, you hold right there. Don't hang up, I'll be right back."

Rainey waited for the hold message to begin. Melatiah was famous for her messages that changed frequently, as did her mood. Agents either sang her praises or shrank at the mere mention of her name, a name so difficult to say, everyone just called her Brooks. Pronounced Mel-ah-TI-ah, it meant 'one whom Jesus has set free,' at least that's what she told Rainey. As round as she was tall, which wasn't very tall at all, Brooks certainly felt free to speak her mind. Rainey, at five feet ten inches, towered over her, but that didn't stop Brooks from intimidating Rainey, at first. They became great friends over the years. Brooks was the daughter of a wealthy African American family from New York. She was educated at the best schools and found her niche in building hacking programs, which got her thrown out of the best schools and into the FBI academy. Brooks was no holds barred with attitude, but she could take it too, which is why she and Rainey got along.

Today the hold message was a rant about the fact that everyone thought that his or her case should be a priority. It was a running monologue on the distinction between wants and needs, and how few of the agents actually understood there was a difference. It was quite hysterical, probably the only reason she had not been forced to remove it. Once instructed to delete the message, she would, but within a few days another would surface. Rainey usually found the messages entertaining, but she was anxious to find the answer to her question. Brooks was fabulously good at her job. If the information Rainey sought were out there, she would find it.

Brooks clicked on just as the message was about to begin again.

"Okay, Rainey Bell, you're next." She always called Rainey by both her names. "Where are you and what do you want?" Brooks sounded pleasant, but wasted no time getting to the point of the call.

Rainey knew this tone. It indicated the short round woman was up to her ears in agents' requests for information, some of which were life and death questions. What she could tell an agent could break a case and save lives. She was under a lot of pressure to get it right.

Rainey answered quickly, "I'm in Botetourt County, Virginia, with Danny. We're on the Highway 220 cases. I need you to find out what you can about the abstinence pledge people. Specifically, whom do they send out as representatives to local churches? Concentrate on anyone who's been near the locations connected with these murders."

"Got it," Brooks said quickly, and then asked, "How fast do you need it? Of course, I know the answer to that is as soon as possible."

Rainey smiled into the receiver. "Yes, that would be the answer. Did I tell you how much I appreciate how hard your job is and how much I admire you?"

"Don't try to schmooze me, Rainey Bell. I know your tactics. I'll get back to you within the hour. Be safe out there."

Rainey didn't get the chance to say goodbye. Danny entered the room in a hurry. His face was a bit flushed with the excitement. Deputy Knox clearly got the message to him that Rainey needed to see him right away.

"What is it, Rainey? What did you find?" He asked, coming around the table to stand next to her.

"This last girl, Crystal, she wore an abstinence pledge ring, a simple gold band. It was not on the body. I remembered reading that at least two other victims were missing a gold band. I think we have the link to all the victims. We need to talk to the families again. Find out if their daughters had any connection with these abstinence pledge people. I have Brooks looking for information on any of them that could have come in contact with the victims."

Danny looked down at the table strewn with victim files. "What are you thinking here, Rainey?"

"It doesn't necessarily have to be one of the people associated with the Pledge. It could be someone who goes to these events, trolling for victims. Think about the different bible verses he's left us."

Rainey shifted files on the table until she found the one she was looking for. She pulled a sheet of paper out of the file and handed it to Danny. The paper contained the bible verses they were able to recover from some of the bodies, the ones discovered before decomposition destroyed the paper. There were five verses, including the one they found today.

Psalm 45:14 She shall be brought unto the king in raiment of needlework: the virgins her companions that follow her shall be brought unto thee.

Isaiah 47:1 Come down, and sit in the dust, O virgin daughter of Babylon, sit on the ground: there is no throne, O daughter of the Chaldeans: for thou shalt no more be called tender and delicate.

24

Jeremiah 14:17 Therefore thou shalt say this word unto them; Let mine eyes run down with tears night and day, and let them not cease: for the virgin daughter of my people is broken with a great breach, with a very grievous blow.

Lamentations 2:21 The young and the old lie on the ground in the streets: my virgins and my young men are fallen by the sword; thou hast slain them in the day of thine anger; thou hast killed, and not pitied.

Ezekiel 23:8 Neither left she her whoredoms brought from Egypt: for in her youth they lay with her, and they bruised the breasts of her virginity, and poured their whoredom upon her.

Rainey pointed out, "We talked about the virgin theme, but this puts it in context. Crystal was planning a big Pledge drive at a lockdown for the youth in her church. We need to know more about that."

Deputy Knox came in with a copy of the pledge document from Crystal's car. Rainey took it and read it quickly. There was no official logo from any organization on the paper, just the simple pledge to abstain from sex until marriage. It also had places for the name and address of the pledger, plus a space to write something about themselves. It was a stalker's dream come true; all the information he would need to find them and wait for his moment to strike. Rainey knew in her gut this pledge had something to do with the case. She handed the paper to Danny. He began to read it.

Rainey turned back to Gillian, reverting to official names in front of Danny. She knew how important it was for a female officer to retain a professional air around other officers. "Deputy Knox, would you find out if anyone from the church is available to meet with us there? Also, ask Detective Martin if he could join us for a moment."

Knox started moving. She didn't need reminding to respond to Rainey's request swiftly. She was almost out the door when Rainey's words made her pause.

"Hey, clear it with your supervisor so you can go with us to the church."

Knox almost smiled, but gathered it in quickly. "Yes, ma'am." She left on a mission.

Danny looked quizzically at Rainey. She answered his unspoken question, "She's a member of the church. I think she can help us. She's the one that mentioned the missing ring."

"I think she's got a crush on you," Danny said, chuckling.

"Shut up, asshole."

Rainey wasn't really angry. It wasn't the first case of hero worship she had to deal with, and at least this one was cute. She and Danny teased each other mercilessly. It eased the tensions of the job. To an outsider it may appear callous to stand over a table full of horrible images joking, but it was never disrespectful of the victims. They both needed the coping mechanism.

"Are you sure she has a boyfriend?" Danny wasn't letting up.

"I don't have one," Rainey shot back. "What does that make me?"

Danny patted her on the shoulder, his dimples showing, as he said, "A lonely old woman, ma'am. Maybe you should try the other team. You're not doing too well with the boys."

It was too new, too raw. Danny just never knew when to stop. He was older, but he acted more like an annoying little brother sometimes. Rainey stiffened under his hand and turned her green eyes on him with a glare.

"With you as an example of what I have to choose from, it doesn't sound like such a bad idea."

Knox entered the room, saving Rainey from Danny's retort. Sure there was going to be one, Rainey was thankful the young officer had shown up when she did. Rainey wasn't in the mood to exchange pithy banter with Danny. She wanted to solve this case and take a vacation. North Carolina was calling her home. She had not seen her father in months, or Ernie, the woman who practically raised her and managed her father's Bail Bond office. Rainey saw her real mother only on holidays when she couldn't escape without repercussions she'd rather avoid. Her wealthy, pretentious mother had not been a part of her day-to-day life since Rainey was fourteen and deemed uncontrollable. She had been handed over to her Vietnam veteran, real father, whom she had only learned about at age ten. It was the best thing that ever happened to her.

Deputy Knox burst into the room, almost breathless, saying, "The pastor's at the church. They're going ahead with the lockdown. The church secretary said they thought it was best to let the kids grieve together. Pastor Morrell is in the education building setting up. Detective Martin is on his..."

Martin entered the room before Knox could finish the sentence. He asked, "What did you find?"

Rainey didn't want to blow her hunch out of proportion. She said, "We aren't sure, but there may be a connection to the abstinence pledge found in Crystal's car and at least two of the other victims. We want to go to the church and speak with the pastor. He may know something and not realize it."

"Okay, what do you want me to do?" Martin asked.

Danny, who had stacked all but three of the files in a pile, pointed at them. "We need to contact each of these families. Find out if any of the victims took the abstinence pledge, or were involved in a group that may have attended a meeting, a rally, even a church camp where it could have come up. Also, were any of them missing a ring, a gold band?"

Martin looked confused.

Knox explained, "Crystal had a gold band. She got the ring when she took the pledge. It wasn't on the body."

Rainey picked up Crystal's file from the three Danny held back. They already knew the other two victims' rings were missing. She added a request. "Ask Crystal's family if they have the ring at home. We're going to go talk to the pastor."

Rainey started to leave. She turned back to the young deputy. "Well Knox, are you coming?"

"Yes ma'am."

Rainey heard Danny chuckle behind her.

#

The Rose of Sharon Church sat just off Highway 220, north of Fincastle, just five miles from where Crystal's body was found. The soaring steeple of the old white clapboard church reached high into the sky above the blue-gray slate covered roof. Against the deep green forest background, it looked like a Thomas Kincaid painting. Azalea bushes surrounded the church with so many blooms the building glowed pink just above them. Bright yellow tulips lined the walkway in well-attended beds carved out of the carefully manicured lawn. On the other side of the parking lot, out under the big Hickory trees, picnic tables were placed near a large brick barbecue pit. Deputy Knox pulled her cruiser to a stop just beyond the doors of a newer looking, flat-topped annex attached to the back of the church. Rainey and Danny followed in a black SUV.

When they were out of the vehicles, Deputy Knox said, "That's the education building," pointing at the modern addition. "That's where the secretary said the pastor was."

Rainey surveyed the parking lot. The only vehicle, other than the SUV and the deputy's cruiser, was a large, four-wheel drive truck, with a snap down cover over the bed. There were no markings at all on the truck. Everything on it was painted shiny black, even the rims. The windows were as dark as legally allowed. The only color on the truck was the Virginia license plate on the back. She couldn't see it, but there should have been a corresponding plate on the front bumper. It was an impressive ride. Danny stared at it with desire in his eyes. What red-blooded man, who grew up in the country, didn't want a truck like that? Danny was, after all, raised a farm boy. This particular truck, however, was not a vehicle she would associate with a pastor.

"Is that the pastor's truck?" She asked Knox.

"No. He lives next door, so he leaves his car there."

A drooling Danny said, "Well this doesn't belong to a church secretary."

Knox laughed. "No, Miss Mary's husband drops her off and picks her up. She never learned to drive. I don't think I've ever seen this truck before. I'm pretty sure I would have remembered it. That's a nice truck."

"Using a word like nice to describe a truck like this is a sin," Danny quipped.

He reluctantly left his daydream about driving the truck and followed the two women to the door of the building. Rainey let the deputy lead the way. She learned a long time ago that a familiar face helped get locals to open up to them. Besides, she was growing fond of the blond young woman walking in front of her. This would be good experience for Gillian. Rainey remembered her first year as an agent, having to fight for chances to gain field experience. It was better now for women, but young Miss Knox had a long road ahead to gain her colleagues' respect. Rainey hoped this show of support from the visiting FBI agents would help the novice deputy on her way.

They entered the building and made their way down the hall lined with classrooms on the left and a day care room on the right. At the end of the hallway, they came to a large meeting room that appeared to double as a gym and game area. In the middle of the room, a tall, slender man, with graying temples was setting up a Ping-Pong table. A young man with a head full of blond curls was assisting him. Both men turned as Rainey, Danny, and Deputy Knox came into the room.

The older man spoke first. "Ah Gillian, Mary said you were coming."

While Rainey and Danny got out their credentials, Deputy Knox took over the introductions. "Good to see you, too, Pastor Morrell. I can see you're busy, but could you give us a few minutes? This is Agent Bell and Agent McNally from the FBI. They would like to talk to you about Crystal."

"This has been so devastating to the congregation. Such a tragedy," the pastor lamented. "I can't imagine why anyone would hurt such a beautiful child of God."

Rainey extended her hand and shook the pastor's. "Yes, it is a tragedy. Thank you for talking with us."

Danny shook the pastor's hand, as well, saying, "We're very sorry for your loss."

Pastor Morrell repeated, "Such a tragedy." Then suddenly seeming to remember the young man, he said, "I'm sorry, I forgot my manners. This is Dalton Chambers. He volunteered to help me set up for the kids tomorrow. He drove up here today from Roanoke. Crystal invited Dalton to help her with the abstinence pledge drive she had planned for this lockdown."

The curly haired blond stepped forward. The hair framed his handsome face. He looked to be in his early twenties, with chiseled good looks and a dimple on his left cheek when he smiled. Rainey figured him to be six-foot-three, at least. He was built like an athlete and appeared to be in terrific shape. He probably lifted weights. His blue eyes were piercing when he made eye contact with Rainey. Immediately the hair stood up on the back of her neck.

Dalton stepped forward and extended his hand to her, which Rainey shook and felt the strength in his hand. A hand she was sure had been around Crystal's neck five days ago. She watched as Danny shook the young man's hand to gauge his response. Maybe she was over-reacting, because she wanted her theory to be correct. While Dalton shook the deputy's hand, Rainey got her answer when Danny gave her a look that said he thought they found the killer, too.

Dalton said to all of them, "It's a pleasure to meet you. I hope you're making progress to find this guy. I'm up and down through here all the time, and I tell you the girls on 220 are scared."

"They have good reason to be," Rainey said, making eye contact with Dalton again.

This time she saw his right eye twitch when he held her gaze just a second too long. Dalton had a "tell," a signal to a keen observer that he was under stress. They needed to be careful. Rainey wanted Dalton to talk to them, but she couldn't let him in on her suspicions. She turned her attention back to the pastor, while at the same time glancing at Knox. Gillian was sizing Dalton up, as well. Rainey hoped the young officer would keep her composure while she and Danny questioned the two men.

"Pastor Morrell," Rainey began, "we're trying to locate a ring Crystal may have been wearing. It was not found with her. Do you think she could have lost it or left it here while she was cleaning?"

"Mary would be a better person to ask that question. All the lost and found things get turned in to her."

Dalton chimed in. "Are you talking about her pledge ring? I know she would never have taken that off voluntarily."

"Why do you say that?" Danny asked.

"Because it really meant a lot to her. I remember her talking about how the ring made her feel closer to God. It symbolized her promise to him to remain chaste. We talked about it the last time I spoke to her. She said she never took it off."

Rainey saw an opening. "When did you talk to her last?"

Dalton pretended to be trying to remember. "I think it was the Friday before she went missing. She called me to make sure I was still able to come for her pledge drive."

Nobody forgets the last time they spoke with someone who died tragically. Dalton was trying too hard to appear uninvolved.

Danny jumped in. "You drove up here from Roanoke. So you're not from here. How did you meet Crystal?"

Dalton's eye twitched again. Danny was pressing too hard. Rainey was afraid this guy was going to bolt, or worse, make this his last stand. At that moment, Rainey's cellphone rang. She pulled it out of her jacket pocket and saw that it was Brooks calling back.

"Excuse me. I need to take this call."

Rainey stepped back out in the hall away from the others and flipped her phone open.

"Tell me you have some names for me," she said, without saying hello.

"My, aren't we a bit tense today," came the reply.

"Oh God, you have no idea. I need a name and I need it now."

Brooks laughed. "No honey, you need to get laid. You're so wound up, you're liable to just blow a gasket any day."

"Brooks, I could be standing in the same room with a serial killer, as we speak. Tell me you have this guy's name."

Suddenly serious, Brooks began to speak rapidly. "What I found is these pledge folks do not have employees that travel a route like you're looking for. They train people at retreats around the country, but there are no representatives that actually go from church to church like you said."

Rainey let out, "Shit," just a little too loud.

She looked through the doorway to see if anyone was watching her. Dalton was answering Danny's questions. No one heard her.

Brooks went on, "Now, hold on. I did get a list of churches requesting information and materials to hold their own pledge drives. I pulled the ones in your geographic area. There are quite a few. Don't these people know sexual experimentation is a healthy part of growing up? Lord honey, I tried out a bunch before I found the one that rocked my world and then I married him. Anyway, each of your victims lived in or near a town where one of these pledge travesties took place."

Rainey sighed. "But no names."

"I tried to get a list of trainees, but they don't keep that information on computer. That ought to tell you how backward these folks are."

Rainey was suddenly hit with inspiration. She backed slowly out of sight of the others, and then broke into a trot down the hall and out of the building. Once outside, she ran to the front of the truck. Virginia was one of those states requiring tags on the front and back of vehicles.

Breathing faster now, she rushed out her words. "I need you to run a license plate for me."

"Okay, shoot."

Rainey read the plate off and then added, "It should come back to a Dalton Chambers. See if he has any traffic violations that correlate with the dates of the murders, credit card receipts too, and run a background check on him. I'm going to stay on the phone with you."

"You do know I will call you right back, don't you?" Brooks quipped.

"Well, since we don't know how he's going to react, if he knows we suspect him, I'd rather stay on the line."

Brooks let a whispered, "Shit," escape into the receiver, before she said, "Okay, you stay with me. Let's see what one Dalton Chambers has been up to."

After a few seconds of keys clicking on a keyboard, Brooks began to speak. "Your boy is from Acredale, Virginia. He is twenty-five years old. He drives a Ford F150, black, four by four. He has no criminal convictions other than a few traffic tickets. I'm running his credit card receipts through a program, looking for matching dates. That will take a few minutes. He was charged once in a sexual assault, let's see, at age seventeen, but those charges were dropped and should have been expunged from his record, but the wheels of justice do turn slowly."

Rainey needed more than that. She pressed, "Where and when did he get the tickets? Can we tie him to a murder site?"

"No, these tickets were all before the killing started... Wait... There is an article here. Damn, somebody beat the shit out of your boy a few years back."

"What? What?" Rainey almost shouted.

"It says Dalton Chambers was savagely beaten his senior year, by unknown assailants, so severely that he spent several weeks in the hospital. Evidently, he was a star baseball player and the beating ended his career. The head injuries gave him chronic vertigo, so he couldn't play anymore... Hang on... It says, 'he credits God with his recovery and knows that he has a better plan for him...' This is your guy, Rainey. From what I've read of the files, he's a Jesus freakazoid, or at least pretending to be."

Rainey had a hunch. "Can you access his medical records?"

"I'm already doing it, but it looks like I need to make a phone call. Do you want to stay on hold, or should I call you back?"

As badly as she wanted to hold on, Rainey knew she couldn't leave Danny in there alone much longer.

"I'll hang up. I'm going back in the building. I'm sure Danny is running out of dance moves by now."

"Okay Rainey Bell, you be safe and Big Momma Brooks will be right back to you."

The line went dead. Rainey flipped her phone shut and put it back in her pocket. Just before she turned away, she glanced up at the windshield. By law, it could not be as dark as the other windows. Suspended from the rearview mirror, a gold chain glinted in the sunlight. Rainey saw at least a dozen gold bands dangling from the chain. Dalton kept his trophies where he could see and touch them. If she asked him about the rings, he would claim that they were just trinkets to hand out to others. Rainey had a gut feeling DNA testing would prove that to be a lie.

She walked back into the room with the others, forcing herself to remain calm. They were within inches of a serial killer, she was sure, but they had no evidence to take him in.

They could ask him to come with them, but he was too smart for that she thought. Of course, he could be one of those killers that liked playing games with the police. Dalton struck Rainey as the type who would disappear, as soon as they lost sight of him. He would reinvent himself somewhere else and start killing again. He was intelligent enough to pull it off. Ted Bundy did it and took his dirty deeds all the way across the country. They could not let Dalton Chambers leave here today, not without some kind of plan to keep track of him.

Rainey rejoined the group. She looked at Danny. "Sorry, that was my mother. I had to answer it or she would just keep calling."

Danny knew it wasn't her mother. Rainey avoided answering her mother's phone calls at every opportunity. He feigned concern. "Is everything all right?"

"It's my little brother. He's gotten himself in a bit of trouble."

Danny also knew Rainey was an only child. "Is there anything you can do?"

Rainey needed him to know Brooks was looking into something and that they had nothing so far, except the rings. She thought the rings were the answer. Now, they just needed enough probable cause to get a search warrant. "I told her to call a lawyer and then call me back. I don't know what she thinks I can do from here. My hands are tied."

Pastor Morrell spoke up, "May God be with your family during this trying time. Thank goodness he never gives us more than we can bear."

Dalton added an, "Amen."

Rainey wanted to pull her gun and put this guy in cuffs right then, but they could not jeopardize a conviction by moving too quickly. She needed evidence beyond the churning in her gut.

36

Danny began to fill her in on what she missed. "Dalton has been telling me what a wonderful young woman Crystal was. He met her at a retreat last fall in Roanoke."

"Oh, is that where you're from?" She wanted to catch him in a lie.

Dalton was too smart to fib about something she could check so easily. "No, ma'am." He poured on the charm. "I'm from a little town about a hundred miles south of here called Acredale, but like I said, I travel a lot."

"All in the service of God," the pastor chimed in. "Dalton is on a crusade to help our youth make the right decisions, ignore peer pressure, and follow the Lord."

Rainey looked at the pastor. "So, you know Dalton through his work?"

"No, I just met this fine young man today," the pastor answered. "He's been filling me in on his mission. We discovered that he has been to many of the churches of pastors I'm very familiar with. It does my heart good to know the youth have a positive role model to look up to. This young man has traveled from Rockingham, North Carolina to Iron Gate, Virginia and back, all to the Glory of God and..."

Rainey watched Dalton, as he listened to the pastor. His body language suggested he wasn't comfortable with the preacher continuing to speak. His eye twitched again, just before he interrupted.

"Pastor Morrell, thank you for those kind words, but these folks want to know about Crystal's mission, not mine."

"No, I'm very interested in your work," Rainey said to Dalton. His veneer cracked just a little, so she decided to push him. "I'd love to hear more about this abstinence ministry. I'm also curious as to why you only travel 220 on your quest. Surely there are bigger audiences in larger towns, more souls to save."

Dalton regained his composure, answering, "There are already abstinence programs set up in most of the big cities. These kids out here need me more than the ones in the city do. This is the kind of place I grew up in and I know we needed it when I was in high school."

"Since you minister at churches along this road, you may have come in contact with some of the other victims. Do you know if you were in one of the churches they could have attended? We're researching any tie the victims may have in common. We think they may all have signed an abstinence pledge."

Rainey wanted to watch Dalton squirm. She just told him they were connecting the dots. He had to be thinking it wouldn't be long now until they had proof of his involvement in the case.

He answered, "No, I don't think I met any of the other girls. It's hard to tell from the pictures in the paper."

The pastor started to speak and Dalton visibly lost the color in his cheeks.

"Well now, Dalton, you told me you were at Pastor Wells' church and I think one of those girls went there. Maybe you did meet her. And I know one of them went missing from Pastor Smith's congregation in Rockingham. You were there last September you told me. That was a while before the girl went missing, but if she signed the pledge, I'm sure you must have met her."

Dalton tried to recover. "I'm sorry, Pastor Morrell, but I meet so many girls. I'm sorry to say they all start to blend together after a while."

She knew they had him. She could now tie him to at least three locations where the victims were killed.

Rainey probed even harder. "And yet, Crystal stuck out among all those other girls. You seem to remember quite a lot about her."

Dalton Chambers stared at her, at a loss for words for the first time.

He was saved by Pastor Morrell's comment. "Oh, Crystal would be hard to forget. She made an impression on everyone she met."

Deputy Knox, who had been silent up to now, began to speak. "Yes, Crystal was a special girl. The man who killed her is a coward. He's not a man at all. He had to use an instrument to do his dirty work, couldn't get it up probably. Sorry, Pastor."

Rainey would have hugged Knox, if she could. The young deputy's understanding of what they were dealing with was uncanny. She obviously paid attention in psychology class. Question this guy's manhood and he would come unglued.

The pastor went on talking, oblivious to what was happening around him. "It's okay Sister Knox. Our anger can sometimes make us speak plain. I just pray that the villain is captured soon and brought to justice."

Danny joined the party. "Which in Virginia means the bastard gets the needle."

Knox added, "Those creeps always make a deal to save their skins."

"Vengeance is mine sayeth the Lord. God will punish the wicked. It is not man's place to pass the ultimate judgment," Pastor Morrell commented.

He was about to get up on his pulpit. Rainey quickly steered him in another direction. "Do you think you could supply us with the phone numbers for these pastors you mentioned, the churches where those two victims went?"

"Sure. I'll need to go to the office. Would you like to follow me?"

Once again Deputy Knox was right on cue. "I'll go with you. I need to say hello to Miss Mary anyway. I'll ask her about Crystal's ring."

"Is there anything else I could help you with before I go?" The preacher asked.

Danny answered, "No, I think that just about does it. Thank you for your time Pastor Morrell."

He shook both Rainey and Danny's hands and then went off with Deputy Knox, through an archway that led into the church. Just when they were almost out of sight, Dalton surprised Rainey by moving to go after them.

He said, "Hey, wait. I need to make a call. My cell battery is dead. May I use the office phone?"

The pastor turned back and smiled. "Why of course you can. Come on."

Knox looked stricken. Rainey thought quickly. She and Danny couldn't stop Dalton from going. They needed a minute alone so Rainey could tell him what she knew. If she tried to hold Dalton without cause, other than a hunch, he could walk away. Knox looked back over her shoulder at Rainey, after letting both Dalton and the pastor go ahead of her. Rainey put her hand on her weapon and nodded at Gillian. She hoped she understood the unspoken message, "Watch your back."

She called to the deputy, "We'll be in the parking lot when you're ready to go."

As soon as they cleared the doorway into the hall, Rainey and Danny broke into a run toward the exit. They needed backup and they needed to watch Dalton's only escape route, his truck. He could run into the woods, if he found another way out, but that truck was his lifeline. Rainey suspected he was like many of the sexual sadists who were driven to travel great distances. Jon Barry Simonis, a serial rapist, traveled over eight thousand miles in ten months across twelve states. Jon Barry stated to one of the original Behavioral Analysts, Roy Hazelwood, that it gave him a freedom from responsibility. It was a myth that all serial murderers travel and operate interstate. Most of them had a defined geographic area, but they still may drive endless hours. Rainey believed, as did some psychologists, it was a need for stimulation provided by the constantly changing scenery pushing the sadist to keep moving. Dalton would need his truck.

There was also the possibility the truck contained more evidence, other than the rings, which Dalton could not explain away. He wouldn't want the cops going over his truck. No, Rainey was sure he was going to come out of the church any minute, hop in, and drive off. They had to stop him. This might be their only chance. If he got out of sight, Rainey was sure he would leave the area, but he wasn't about to stop killing. Once she and Danny were outside, Rainey pulled out her phone. Danny already had his out.

Danny asked, "Do you think that deputy will be alright?"

Rainey looked at the church. "Yes, I think she can handle herself."

"You know that's him, right?" Danny asked

Rainey pointed at the windshield of the truck. "Look what's hanging on his mirror."

Danny looked up, saw the rings, and immediately started punching buttons on his phone.

"I'm waiting for Brooks to call back," Rainey said. "Chambers was arrested at seventeen for sexual assault, but charges were dropped. I'm sure there are probably more things that fit the profile, but guys like that get away with so much by just talking their way out of it. He suffered a severe beating his senior year of high school that ruined his athletic career. He dedicated his life to God after that. I want more details on his injuries."

Danny held his phone to his ear. "I'm calling Martin for some backup. He can start the search warrant process for the truck."

"Right now, it's all circumstantial, but I bet that truck has physical evidence in it, no matter how much he cleaned it," Rainey said.

Rainey's phone jangled in her hand. She answered, while Danny waited for the detective to pick up.

Brooks started talking as soon as Rainey said hello. "Okay, baby girl, you got your dirt bag. I got nothing from his credit cards, so I ran his parents' cards, and bingo! There are records of purchases near each site on or around the dates of the murders and when the bodies were found. Bastard used his mother's accounts to finance his sicko tour."

"Hang on," Rainey said. She filled Danny in on what Brooks just told her. It would help with the search warrant. Then she put the phone back to her ear. "Okay, and what about the medical files?"

"Wow. No, 'Thank you, Magic Brooks,' for that case breaking input."

Rainey answered swiftly, "No time. This asshole is about to walk out of this church and drive away."

"Oh shit," was followed rapidly by, "he was a messed up boy. Whoever beat him paid special attention to his genitals. He was effectively castrated. I found the police report. There was some thought that this was retaliation by some brothers of a girl Chambers was suspected of raping. Chambers claimed he didn't know who did it. No charges were ever filed in either case."

Rainey saw it all fall into place in her mind. Chambers' sordid history laid out in front of her like a movie leading to this moment.

"Thank you so much. I owe you dinner," Rainey said, anxious to hang up and tell Danny. "I have to go."

Brooks signed off with her usual, "Rainey Bell, you be safe."

"Always," came the reply.

Rainey hung up and got Danny's attention. He was still on the line with the detective, explaining what to put in the warrant request. He told the detective to hold on and listened to Rainey.

"It's him, Danny. No doubt about it. He was beaten and castrated for raping a girl when he was eighteen. That's his motive. Revenge on all the virgins. We have receipts placing him at the scenes."

Danny responded, "More cops are on the way. Watch the doors, I'm going around back."

Danny returned his phone to his ear and began talking fast, as he moved around the building. Rainey undid the snap on her holster. She walked around the truck so that she was partially hidden from view. She removed the FBI issued, Sig Sauer P220, semi-automatic pistol from her waist, made sure she had a round chambered, and re-holstered it. Rainey hoped she wouldn't have to use it, but these guys were unpredictable when cornered. Hopefully Chambers would come down for questioning, without any fuss. She highly doubted it.

Rainey heard a door open. Looking up she saw Deputy Knox and the killer coming out of the education building together. She stepped around the truck and back into view.

"I was just admiring your truck. It's quite impressive. Looks like you keep it spotless," Rainey said, as nonchalantly as she could muster. She felt the adrenaline beginning to quicken her heart. She hoped it didn't show in her voice. She needed to buy time.

Dalton smiled his practiced grin. It wasn't genuine. These guys were consummate actors. "Yep, that's my baby. I spend a lot of time keeping it detailed."

Deputy Knox's eyes were locked on Rainey. She was looking for a sign as to what to do next. Rainey didn't have a plan. She was hoping a host of police cars would come sliding into the parking lot about now. She needed Dalton Chambers to feel too outnumbered to try anything.

Dalton looked around. "Where's your partner?"

"He went inside to use the restroom," Rainey answered.

She could see that Dalton was sizing up his situation. She thought he must know they weren't going to let him leave. This type of killer would think he was smart enough to wiggle out of anything. He was making a mental plan of action. He turned to look behind him and that's when Rainey saw it. Chambers was wearing a blue polo shirt. All three of the buttons at the neck were undone. When he turned, the sun caught the gold cross around his neck and Rainey recognized it as the one custom made for Crystal. She wore it in her smiling picture. Rainey's hand went slowly to her weapon. Knox's eyes followed Rainey's hand. The young deputy stopped walking, freezing beside Dalton who saw the movement, too.

Rainey smiled, thinly. "I like that cross, Messiah." She drew her weapon quickly, shouting, "Freeze!"

The instant Rainey pulled the Sig, Chambers made his move. He grabbed Knox and pulled her tight to his body. Rainey had no shot. She kept her weapon trained on Dalton, but all she could do was watch, as Chambers grappled with the deputy for her gun. In seconds, the stronger man overcame Knox. He held her in a chokehold with one arm and put the barrel of Knox's nine-millimeter against her temple with the other. Rainey slid behind the truck bed, putting it between her and the serial killer, now brandishing a weapon and threatening to shoot a cop. Not good. The truck wouldn't stop the bullet, unless she was behind the engine block, but at least it would slow it down.

Rainey had not expected to run into the UNSUB. Unlike on TV, her unit was almost never involved in the actual hands on apprehension of a suspect. Their job was to tell the local investigators where and whom to look for. She had been involved in arrests before, but she always had on protection, and usually followed a SWAT team in. This time she wasn't wearing a vest. There was no SWAT team in sight, no sirens coming in the distance. She looked into Knox's terrified eyes and spoke as calmly as she could, even though her heart was about to beat out of her chest.

"Okay, Dalton, you need to just drop the weapon and we'll talk."

Dalton glared at her. "You drop *your* weapon and then we'll talk."

"You know I can't do that. Drop the weapon. You know how this ends, if you don't."

Knox struggled to get free, having regained some strength after the initial battle for her gun. The handsome face of Dalton Chambers transformed before Rainey's eyes. He tightened his grip around Knox's throat, enjoying the smaller woman's attempts to pry his arm from her throat. Knox gasped for air. Dalton chuckled and smiled at Rainey. He narrowed his glare and spoke in an almost jovial tone.

"Yes, I do know how this ends. The deputy and I are going for a ride. She's a little old for my taste, but damn, she's a fighter. Look at her go." Knox kicked at his legs. Dalton laughed and then narrowed his eyes at Rainey, his voice now pure evil. "And if you try to stop me, I'll blow this bitch's head off."

Rainey was not only an FBI agent trained in tactical weapons, negotiations, and critical response, she was the daughter of a man who survived several Special Forces tours in Vietnam. He taught her to shoot, but more importantly, he taught her to survive. She knew she had to keep Dalton focused on her. Rainey hoped Knox would understand her next words.

"When she put on that badge this morning, she knew she might not make it home tonight. It's the nature of the beast. You might shoot her, but then I'm going to drop you like a sack of potatoes. No trial, no publicity, just a dead killer and a hero cop. They'll write article after article about the deputy and her tragic death. You, you'll be a footnote in the story."

Dalton started dragging his captive toward the driver's door of the truck. Rainey thought fast. She took a step back, dropped her aim, and fired. The right rear tire went flat. That got Dalton's attention and hopefully Danny's, too. She quickly reacquired her target, the only part of Dalton that was exposed, his head.

Rainey laughed. She needed Dalton off his game. "Wooo. That's gonna cost you. Bet those tires run over three-hundred dollars a piece."

Dalton said, through gritted teeth, "You bitch." He changed directions and started for the SUV.

Danny had a bad habit of leaving the keys in the ignition. Rainey could not let Dalton get to the vehicle. She dropped her aim again and fired at the back tire of the SUV. Bam, whoosh, the air left the tire.

"Now, that's gonna cost the government. Guess we'll put it on your tab."

Dalton was losing his composure rapidly. "Crazy bitch. I'm gonna drop this cop and then I'm gonna fuck you up."

Rainey was waiting for him to aim his weapon at her. If he pulled the barrel away from Knox's head, Rainey would not hesitate to shoot him. Still, Rainey kept the truck bed in front of her, in case he got off the first shot. She doubted he would. Rainey was the best shot in her class and had every confidence that she would drop him where he stood. She would shoot now, but Knox could move the wrong way and catch the bullet, or he could spasm at the time of death and kill Knox. The truck was so tall she couldn't see in front of it, where Danny should be by now. Rainey had no choice, but to keep talking and hope Danny was creeping up behind Dalton.

"Come on Dalton, drop the weapon. You have no way out of this. My partner heard those shots. He'll be coming soon. Nobody's hurt, yet. Let's just calm down and put the weapons away, before he gets the wrong idea and shoots you in the back."

Rainey saw the door to the education center begin to open. It creaked just enough to draw Dalton's attention. He turned quickly and fired, believing it to be Danny coming out of the church. Pastor Morrell hit the ground, crawling for safety. Dalton wheeled his arm back around and fired at Rainey. She hit the ground, too. The round hit the truck bed, where she had been standing. Instantly she sighted her gun on one of Dalton's legs and fired. At the same time, she heard Danny's weapon go off in front of the truck. Dalton crumpled, still holding on to Knox, but he lost his grip on her. She elbowed him in the ribs, rolled over, and jumped to her feet.

Knox kicked the pistol from Dalton's hand, the adrenaline coursing through her veins causing her to scream, "Motherfucker!"

Rainey scrambled to her feet and ran around the truck. Danny appeared from in front of the truck. He had evidently been watching the whole time, waiting for a shot. Neither Dalton nor Rainey knew he was there.

"Everybody okay?" Danny asked.

Rainey kept her weapon on Dalton who was writhing on the ground, moaning in pain. "I'm fine. You okay, Knox?" Rainey asked the freaked out deputy.

"God dammit!" Knox was pissed. "I can't believe I let him grab me. Fuck!"

Rainey smiled. "You're all right. Just breathe. Pick up your weapon."

Dalton moaned louder. Rainey could see he was shot twice. Her bullet shattered his lower leg. Danny got him in the butt. Neither wound was life threatening. Anyone who says they don't feel fear when confronted with a weapon is a liar. Through training, Rainey learned to channel that primal instinct into hyper alertness in order to reduce or stop the threat. Now that the danger had passed, her fear turned to anger. Rainey went over to Dalton and stepped on his injured leg.

"How's that feel, asshole? You like pain don't you? Isn't that what gets you off?"

"Get off me bitch. I'll kill you."

"I doubt it," Rainey said. "You have a date with a needle Mr. Chambers. Look up at the sky. The next time you see it will be through razor wire."

Rainey reached down, rolled him on to his stomach, slapping a pair of handcuffs on his wrists. "You're going to prison Mr. Chambers. You just shot at a federal agent."

Danny started reciting the Miranda Rights. "To start with, Dalton Chambers, you are under arrest for the attempted murder of a federal officer. You have the right to remain silent.

Anything you say or do can and will be used against you in a court of..."

"I know my fucking rights."

Danny continued the recitation of the rights, ignoring Dalton's outburst.

Dalton kicked at Rainey with his uninjured leg. "I'm going to kill you, bitch. I'll hunt you down and kill you."

Rainey stepped back. She looked over at Knox and smiled mischievously. "Hey, Knox. You want to help me hogtie this uncooperative prisoner?"

Knox finally regained her composure and smiled back. "Yes, ma'am. It would be my pleasure."

CHAPTER THREE

June 25, fourteen months later.

Wise County, Virginia

A transparent blue mist blanketed the mountain range passing beneath the helicopter. The only sound Rainey could hear was the muffled plop-plop of the blades through the air. No one spoke on the headsets, as the sleek black chopper cut through the haze that gave this mountain range its name. They were closing in on the target destination. Surrounded by ridges of thick, green forest that opened onto multicolored fields of wild flowers, the beauty of the Blue Ridge Mountains was lost on the muted passengers. From behind dark sunglasses, Rainey glanced down at the fence and razor wire sparkling in the morning sun. She was making her final "descent into hell," as she had begun to call this part of the trip.

A few minutes later, a tall, very large, prison guard motioned for them to follow. "Right this way, agents," he said, while sliding a key card through a slot and then punching a code into a control pad on a heavily armored door. A loud "thunk" signaled the release of the bolt and the door slid open.

Danny and Rainey entered the front gate of Red Onion State Prison, a super maximum-security facility housing the worst criminals the state of Virginia had to offer. From that moment on, they were never alone within the confines of the prison. A guard escorted them to the main intake area where they presented their identification to another blue clad guard behind the glass. It was a formality that seemed unnecessary since they had been there a dozen times in six months. Rainey and Danny removed their weapons and slid them into the security drawer, where they were pulled back out of sight. Rainey took her hair down from the ponytail she was wearing and shook it free, to fall across her shoulders. This was part of the game she had to play here. The guard behind the glass smiled at Rainey and motioned them to step through the opening gate, while he raised a phone receiver to his ear. The guard spoke into the phone and more locks clanged open. Two more guards appeared to escort them through the maze of halls and security checks of "The Onion."

Heavy steel doors ground opened, metal on metal screeching as they moved. The bolts banged shut instantly behind them, as they passed. Loudspeakers barked orders and reverberated off the prison's concrete block walls. The sounds of ankle chains clanked in the air, keys jangled from the guards' Sam Browne belts, blurring with the roar of humanity from inside each pod. The din grew and dissipated as they made their way through the labyrinth of hallways to solitary confinement. Rainey endured the vile calls from inside the cells. The deeper they went into the prison where the worst offenders were held, the more abusive the taunts became. Men masturbated openly, trying to rattle her. She kept her eyes focused ahead, not giving them the satisfaction of looking. Buried beneath the prison walls, where he would never take another free breath, Dalton Chambers waited.

At the end of a long hallway, they turned left to face a single, heavily guarded room. The reinforced glass and steel wall allowed them to see inside the high security interview area. Two guards stood watch by the door, two more in riot gear a few feet away. Five guards, dressed in Prisoner Removal Team gear, stood outside the door. With extra armor and helmets, they were prepared to make the prisoner comply, forcefully, if necessary. A few of them wore an eager expression, apparently hoping for a chance to use their unique skills.

Dalton's wrists were cuffed and attached to a chain connected to a belt at his waist. His leg restraints glinted under the table. A guard stood watch in the corner of the room, holding a black box in his hand. Rainey recognized the box. It operated an electronic custody control stun belt, also around Dalton's waist. At their last meeting, Dalton became furious, lashing out at Danny. It took three guards to restrain him. They were taking no chances this time. If Dalton so much as twitched, Rainey was sure the guard would not hesitate to send 50,000 volts coursing through his body.

Their escort spoke into his radio. "Control, open on twelve."

The door in front of them slid open. Danny entered first, a stack of file folders in his hand. He walked straight to the table. Tossing the files down, he glared at Dalton.

"I'm not going to have any trouble with you today, am I?"

Dalton ignored Danny. He looked around him at Rainey as she entered. "Why Agent Bell, you look beautiful."

Rainey woke up on, what her dad would have called, "the wrong side of the bed." She was in no mood to pretend to like

Dalton, but she had to. Her part in the investigation was to appear sympathetic to Dalton's situation. She pulled her hair down, because he liked it that way. Rainey didn't want Dalton to be attracted to her, but her looks distracted him. Their tactics were for Danny to push and prod, while she coaxed and cajoled the information out of this sadistic rapist murderer. In his plea deal, to avoid the death penalty Dalton was given six consecutive life sentences, without the possibility of parole, in exchange for the location of other victims' bodies tied to him after his arrest. Nothing he said about his Virginia crimes after the deal could be used to prosecute him further. He had been careful not to mention any unknown crimes in North Carolina.

Once again, television and movie portrayals of behavioral analysts were wrong. The BAU did not like to interview serial killers until after incarceration, because they had reason to lie before trial. Dalton had no reason to be anything but honest about his Virginia crimes, now. He was under the mistaken impression that once he was locked up for life, North Carolina would not be interested in spending the money to continue their investigation or hold a trial there. Rainey certainly did nothing to dispel this belief. In total, Dalton admitted to sexually assaulting and murdering eighteen young women over the course of three years and two states. It made Rainey sick to her stomach to feign interest in his long rambling descriptions of his crimes. She interviewed dozens of sadistic criminals and never felt the disgust she did for Dalton Chambers, but they needed to study him. What they learned from him could one day prevent or help solve future crimes. It was her job, but she didn't have to like it. Today, she especially loathed being there.

Rainey produced a smile and took a seat at the table. "How are you? Are you eating enough? You look tired."

Dalton sneered at the guard in the corner. "These fuckers won't let me sleep. Rousting my cell in the middle of the night and I haven't had my hour in the yard in a week."

Dalton's muscular body had actually increased in size since his incarceration, partly due to getting and taking his medication on a regular basis. On the outside he saved his meds and took them in bunches, instead of daily as they were prescribed. The rage brought on by the exploitation of steroids was evident in his crimes. The drugs did not cause his actions. He simply used them as a tool to enforce his already sadistic fury. Now, he had nothing to do but exercise within his cell, where he was locked down for twenty-three hours a day, more if he misbehaved. He was allowed to shower three times a week and was supposed to get one hour in the tiny enclosed exercise yard every day, but that could be withheld if he broke the rules. Dalton had been misbehaving.

Rainey knew Dalton was approaching that time in a prisoner's life when the futility of his existence and the permanence of his situation set in. This time was usually accompanied by acting out. With no way to release his anger on his choice of victim, he demonstrated it by being less than a model prisoner. Rainey read the discipline reports during the helicopter ride from Quantico. Since she saw him last, two weeks ago, he had attacked a guard while being led to the shower, thrown feces at the doctor who came to check on him after the guards had to use physical force to remove him from the shower, and exposed himself to the facility nurse charged with administering his synthetic testosterone treatments. Rainey thought the testosterone should have been withheld, but the court ordered it for health reasons produced by his traumatic castration.

Rainey answered Dalton's whining with, "I'm sorry. I'll see what I can do about that."

54

The guard in the corner of the room let out a short laugh.

Dalton reacted. "See, these assholes are just looking for a chance to fuck with me. One of them told me I killed the warden's cousin. Is that true? Was one of those girls kin to him, cause if that's the case, then you guys better get me out of here."

The guards were having a joke at Dalton's expense. Rainey tried not to laugh and instead answered, "No, I don't think that's true, but I'll look into it just to make sure."

Danny snickered, drawing Dalton's attention away from Rainey. He glared at Danny, momentarily showing his true colors. "Fuck you, McNally. You're lucky I didn't break your neck the last time you were here."

Danny smiled. "And you're lucky the guards stepped in, because I would have saved the Commonwealth a lot of money keeping you alive for however many years you have left, before one of these other fine upstanding citizens in here shanks your ass."

The muscles in Dalton's neck tensed, his temples began to pulsate, and his right eye twitched. He glanced at the guard with the black box. Rainey knew Dalton was contemplating what he could do to Danny before the voltage took him down. He relaxed back against the chair, after a moment, turning his attention back to Rainey. This was all part of the plan her team had come up with. Danny would get nowhere with his questions, but Rainey, who had gained Dalton's trust, would. Evidently, he had forgotten his threats to kill her, or more likely, his psychopathic personality was trying to win her over, completing his need to make her a victim of his charm. The angrier he got with Danny, the more he reached out to her. Rainey took her cue.

"Dalton, don't make things worse." She turned to Danny. "Agent McNally, maybe you should step out and compose yourself."

Danny made a show of being livid. He pushed his chair back violently and stormed towards the door. The guard on the outside spoke into his radio again and the door opened. Just before leaving, Danny turned back around.

"We've got everything we need from this asshole. Don't play his games, Rainey."

That was just it; they didn't have all they needed. They had the how and why of his crimes, but they were sure not all of his victims. From the information they had so far, the team decided that Dalton fit the anger excitation rapist's profile developed in the 1980's, by some of the original behavioral analysts. Dalton got his sexual gratification from the victim's suffering. He got off on inflicting excessive physical pain and psychological terror. He used a planned con game to gain his victim's trust, initially charming and intelligent, only to become hostile and violent once he gained control. Like others who committed similar crimes, he often asked, "Do you like that, bitch," while using bondage and torture during the prolonged sexual assaults. He was lethal after his initial years of maturation into a full-blown methodical, ritualistic murderer. Escaping this type of rapist was almost impossible. The women who encountered Dalton were doomed from the moment he met them. There were more similarities to the profile and Rainey knew them all.

What they needed to know were the facts surrounding the first murder, a much younger victim than the others. The BAU was positive he committed the brutal slaying, but could not get him to admit it. Dalton had a good reason not to tell, whether he realized it or not. This murder occurred after his lengthy recovery from his own brutal beating. The crime scene photos showed a thirteen-year-old girl beaten beyond recognition, her body mutilated. Dalton had lost complete control of his anger with her. Even if she couldn't get him to admit to the murder, Rainey was charged with finding out why that crime changed his behavior. Something about the murder shook him. It was followed by a two-year period where he seemed to have lost his nerve for killing.

A string of unsolved sexual assaults ensued with no more bodies discovered. The victims reported being attacked from behind, stunned, and then beaten. The perpetrator wore a ski mask and became extremely violent when he could not complete the rape. While Dalton had no testicles, he did have a penis, although it was a bit malformed from the surgeries he had to endure. He could obtain an erection, but with great difficulty. When he began killing again, at age twenty-two, he used a dildo to complete the rapes. These crimes showed a criminal with much more control and the use of extensive planning. He was a mature killer at an earlier age than most serials. Since his injuries kept him from pursuing other distractions, he had nothing to do but fantasize and plan his crimes. He did not work. Instead, he lived off his moderately wealthy parents, who were just thankful he survived his own attack. They encouraged his work with the young Christians he claimed to be trying to save from the dark path of sin and debauchery, happily funding his "mission."

Rainey needed to be sure he didn't actually commit murders during his two years of apparent down time. There were missing young women, but none they could tie specifically to him without his confession. Still, the families of the missing girls wanted answers. So did Rainey. Why did he modify his behavior during the later rape/murders? If he committed the assaults after he killed the first one, why did he start killing his victims? What changed? That was the question she most wanted answered.

Rainey knew she might never find out. Besides his unwillingness to talk about it, the fact was, this was her last trip to see Dalton at "The Onion." They had already spent more time on interviews with him than most of the serial killers in the FBI database. Rainey remembered reading that John Douglas, one of the original Behavioral Analysts, said, "When you tell me we should keep someone like Bundy alive to study, I say, fine, keep him alive six hours longer; that's all I need. I really don't think we're going to get much more beyond that."

When their supervisor told them that she and Danny would not be going back after today, Rainey was secretly elated. She'd had enough of Dalton Chambers to last a lifetime, but she couldn't let him know that. Once Danny was out of the room, she began her final attempt to get some truth out of Dalton about the young girl and any of the other murders he was suspected of committing. If he admitted to the rapes, well, that was just icing on the cake.

"Dalton, he's gone now. Just focus on me. Don't give the guards a reason to hurt you, okay?"

Dalton took his focus from Danny in the hallway and moved his blue eyes back to Rainey. She watched his face reform from murderous intent to charming. In another life, he could have been a movie actor. He had the looks and the ability to transform into whatever he wanted others to see. Dalton was an actor of sorts, playing out his fantasies, as star and director of his own sick plot.

Dalton smiled easily. "I don't know how you work with that guy. You're much too nice to have to deal with that every day and a whole lot better looking."

"Thank you, Dalton. It isn't easy. He loses his temper so often, I wonder if he should be doing this job." Rainey knew Danny could hear her through the speaker in the hall.

Dalton made a show of deep concern. "You should ask to be given a new partner. You shouldn't have to put up with him."

"I'll do that. He really is a pain in the ass," Rainey said, chuckling.

"So, what do you want to talk about today, pretty lady?" Dalton was pouring on the charm, as if they were going to talk about the weather, not the heartless murders and rapes he committed.

Rainey pretended that she was being forced to ask the questions. "I don't really want to bring this up, because I know you don't like to talk about it, but my supervisor insists that I get the answers to some questions. He said that if I didn't get answers today, he is going to take me off the case."

"I don't want to talk to anyone else. Tell him, I'll refuse to see them. I requested you from the beginning, remember. The only reason I let McNally come today is because you were with him."

"I appreciate that, but I'm afraid it won't do any good. The Special Agent in charge says there is no reason to send me back here, if I can't get what he wants."

"If I answer just a few of his questions, will they let you come back? You're the only person who comes to visit that I really want to see."

Rainey saw the opening and jumped. "What about your parents? Don't you enjoy their visits?"

Dalton displayed his uncanny ability to mimic real human emotion. Psychopaths could feel fear, anger, even sadness in the moment, but not remorse or guilt for what they've done or are about to do. He dropped his head, trying to appear ashamed. "I hate to see them. They are so hurt by this. I can't stand to see my mother cry like that."

"You told me your relationship with your parents was good when you were growing up. Don't let your mistakes ruin that." Trivializing Dalton's crimes as mistakes almost made Rainey choke. She tried to move the conversation toward her goal. Rainey lowered her voice and said, softly, "If we could just move on from this confession stage, put it behind you, and start the healing part of your recovery, I think you would feel better."

She saw his eyes measuring her. He whined, "If I tell you everything, you won't come back. You would have no reason to come see me."

Rainey laughed faintly. "Oh Dalton, we will be studying you for years." Which wasn't a lie. They would study him, but they had nearly everything they needed and wouldn't need to interview him anymore. She continued, "People will always want to come see you and ask questions. You're one of the youngest, most successful serial murderers we've ever encountered. People want to know what turned such a nice boy into a killer. There will be thousands of words written about you. You are special."

This puffed Dalton's ego sufficiently. "I would like to help in any way I can. If studying me helps prevent this from happening, at least I will have done some good. I don't know why I turned out this way. I think my brain is wired differently than normal people."

"No question about that," Rainey thought silently. Dalton didn't give a rat's ass about helping anyone. He was in it for what he could get out of it personally. She kept her feelings covered by saying, "I know, deep inside you are truly remorseful. You wouldn't have helped us this much if you weren't. I hope that we can help you come to terms with what triggered the change in you, so we can help you move on."

If Dalton truly loved anything, it was talking about himself. He responded, eagerly, "I've been thinking about that. My dad made me help slaughter cows at the ranch. Do you think that had anything to do with it?"

Cattle ranchers slaughter cows every day and don't turn out to be serial killers. Rainey knew Dalton was looking for an excuse to blame his behavior on someone else. She ignored his question with her own.

"Did it excite you sexually when you participated in the slaughter?"

"No, that's sick. I didn't like it. Too much blood."

Dalton was lying, again. Rainey interviewed his parents and siblings after his arrest. They reported that Dalton asked to participate at a very early age. He always got excited during slaughter time. He was extremely happy and agreeable afterwards.

"But Dalton, your murders were bloody. Why do you think the blood didn't bother you then?"

Rainey watched as Dalton began to reminisce about his crimes. He visibly became more relaxed, sliding down in the chair, getting comfortable. He looked beyond Rainey, acquiring a glazed over quality to his eyes. Rainey knew he was reliving some young woman's death, reveling in it, becoming sexually excited as he did. She had no choice but to let him.

After a moment, Dalton began to speak. "When you chop off the head, the heart still beats for a while. It's just a muscle. Without the brain, it has no idea that it's supposed to be dead. The blood pumps out of the neck in spurts, like the body's gettin' off, you know. It settles down to oozing in just a minute or two."

Rainey didn't react. He was trying to get her to show fear or horror, his favorite emotions from a woman, but that would turn the game they played. He would then focus all his energy on terrifying her and be less likely to tell her anything of value that she and her team didn't already know.

In the same tone she would use in a casual conversation, Rainey asked, "Did you do anything with the blood? Your mother told me she found you with blood smeared on your face and hands after a slaughter. You told her it was something you saw on TV, some ancient ceremony to thank God for his gift of the beef. That wasn't true, was it?"

Instead of being upset that Rainey knew this about him, Dalton smiled. "She came up after I had put my clothes back on. I was twelve. I had been running naked in the pasture, covered in blood from head to toe." He laughed at the memory and then continued, "I was walking to the river to wash off my body when she found me. I had to make something up. She's so religious, if I told her it was in the glory of God, she would have let me cut *her* head off."

Rainey carefully worded her response. "So, what you said earlier about there being too much blood, that wasn't true either. Come on, Dalton. I thought we were beyond your lying to me. I want to help you, remember?" Rainey paused, and then began again. "You were the All-American kid, with the idyllic life. Tell me when it changed. When did you know you were different, special?"

Rainey was leading him to the first murder. Dalton no more wanted help than he wanted to be in prison. If he could, he would leave today and begin killing tomorrow. A true psychopath, when asked if he would like to be cured, would say, "Cured from what?" Dalton didn't think there was anything wrong with him. He couldn't care less about the victims or Rainey. They were all the same, just things that crossed his path. Remorse was a foreign concept to Dalton. His ego, however, was inflated. He believed himself to be smarter than anyone he met. He believed he was steering the conversation he was having at the moment. Rainey let him think that and fed his ego, keeping him off balance enough to show her his real thoughts.

Dalton took the bait. "I knew early that I was smart, around nine or ten, I think. I found out pretty young that I could talk my way out of stuff. People are really stupid, you know. Like my mom, I could tell her anything and she believed me. Dad wasn't so easy to get around, but then mom would convince him he was wrong. I kept my secrets to myself, so no one ever suspected me."

"Your secrets, like why you covered yourself in blood?"

Dalton was distracted by his own thoughts and answered without thinking. "I did that with the girls, too."

This was new information. Rainey took advantage of Dalton's willingness to talk about it. "So this part of your ritual came to you early, before you actually started killing the women you raped?"

"Yes, the blood on my skin felt empowering. It did the first time I saw myself in the mirror after we killed some cows. I didn't want to wash it off, but they made me. It looked like war paint, you know."

"Did you smear your first victim's blood on you? Was it more powerful than the cows blood?"

With his guard down, he answered her question. "Yes," he said enthusiastically. Caught up in the rush of just thinking about the blood, Dalton wanted to talk about it now. "You have no idea how it feels to let someone's blood pump out onto you. It was like electricity, cranking me up to a high I could not have imagined."

"Is that when you got your sexual release, when their blood spurted on you from the neck?"

Dalton showed just a touch of his true sadistic self. His eyebrows lowered, he stared into Rainey's face. His right eye twitched. "Yes," he said, and that was all.

Characteristically, when they got to his activities after the beheading he grew cautious, evasive even. Rainey suspected he did things to the bodies after the girls were dead, but they couldn't prove it.

She asked, "Then why did you gut them, as you call it? If you had your release, why do that?"

Dalton's voice was cold, when he answered, "That's what you do to cows."

Rainey felt the color in her cheeks begin to rise. She couldn't let him focus on her steadily growing anger and disgust. She said quickly, "And you were completely naked, as I recall from your previous statements. You then took the head to the river and went 'swimming with it,' you said."

"Yes, but you don't actually swim in rapids. I tied a rope to a tree and around my waist. I waded out to let the water wash the blood off, then threw the head in."

"Why did you throw the head in the water? Was it to make the ID more difficult?"

The darkness crept across Dalton's face. "Yes."

Rainey pressed. "You knew there were other ways to identify them easily. So, there had to be another reason."

Dalton just stared back. His eye twitched again.

Rainey didn't press. The way he looked at her, she knew he threw the head in the water to get rid of the evidence of what he did with it after he killed the women. She wanted to crawl across the table and rip off what was left of his sexual organs. Instead, she changed the subject. Dalton was more likely to give her something else, just to keep her from bringing up his necrophilia. These guys would admit to revolting crimes, but most didn't want anyone to know about what they did to the bodies after death. Even a psychopath knows those acts are unspeakable.

"Okay, I won't ask you about that. Let's go back to when you began to use the sword and the bible verses. You didn't do that with the first girl."

Dalton, so distracted by her interest in his post murder activities, slipped up. "I just lost it with her. I didn't intend to kill her, but she pulled my mask off and recognized me. Then she started saying how she knew me from being her church camp counselor and she knew about my...my not having any balls and I just lost it."

"So, are you now admitting to killing Janelle White?"

Dalton realized an instant too late what he had done. His face flushed red. He glared at Rainey. His eye began to twitch. He glanced over at the guard with the black box. Rainey got Dalton's attention.

"Are you also admitting to being the masked rapist for the two years after that?"

Dalton continued to grow angrier. Rainey knew it was time to pull back.

"Okay, you don't have to answer that, but I have to tell you, if you talk about the rapes and how you went from sexual assault to serial killing, people will want to listen. It'll buy you more visits from the BAU." Silence. "Well, what about the bible verses? Will you talk about that?"

The Dalton that spoke next was the scary Dalton, the pretty boy turned evil killer. In a flat tone, he said, "They claimed to be virgins. Virgins don't get in a truck with a stranger and go necking in the woods. They were sluts. I gave them a chance to ask for forgiveness and then ended their lives before they could sin again. Isn't that what you want to hear?"

"No, that's what you want me to think. What I think is you specifically hunted virgins in retribution for those brothers who beat you half to death for raping their sister. Was she a virgin, Dalton?"

Dalton shouted, "I didn't rape that cunt. She wanted it. They all wanted it."

The guard in the corner took a step forward. Rainey put her hand up to stop him and kept at Dalton.

"Okay, we won't talk about that girl either. Calm down so the guard won't have a reason to push the button on his little box." She waited a second then continued, "After Janelle, you went two years without killing. Why? What made you change your methods?"

Dalton breathed heavily, his eye steadily twitching; he was close to losing control. He didn't answer her.

"Was it the blood, Dalton? Did the blood from Janelle excite you? Did it scare you for two years, that you liked the blood, and then you couldn't resist the need anymore? The rapes weren't enough. You needed the blood for the sexual release, didn't you?"

Rainey didn't care about the rapport she spent six months building with this creep. She hoped he rotted in hell. She was on a roll and couldn't stop herself.

"Or was it screwing her dead head that did it for you? Or maybe it was because she was the same age as your little sister. Did you fantasize about your little sister, too?"

Dalton leaned forward. "I think about your blood on me when I masturbate, now. It's the only way I can cum."

Rainey didn't flinch. Instead, she laughed. "I assure you I'm not a virgin. Probably wouldn't do a thing for you."

With a spine-chilling smile, Dalton spewed out, "I fantasize about taking your head over and over. The look on your face...what I'd do to that pretty mouth... It's what gets me through my days."

Rainey knew they had reached the end of their conversation. Dalton was beyond answering questions, now. Something snapped inside Rainey, and with the knowledge that she would never have to see him again, she stood up. Her supervisor would reprimand her for jeopardizing any further communication with Dalton, but it did not stop her from telling him just what she thought. This was going to cost her a week's suspension and a trip to the Bureau psychiatrist, but it was worth the price.

"Dalton, before I leave there is something I've always wanted to say to you. I hope North Carolina gives you the needle. I know what you did to those women. I know why you did it. You are not special. You are a run of the mill sadistic psychopath and I will make sure that everything you've said will be evidence enough to put you to death. I especially will derive pleasure from telling the jury about your taste for dead body parts. Everyone is going to know exactly what kind of miscreant you are, Dalton Chambers."

Rainey gathered up the folders on the table. Dalton's expression changed to pure hatred. He screamed after her, as she began to leave, "If they take me there, I'll find you. I already know where your father lives. That's a nice little place there on Jordan Lake."

Rainey stopped and turned around.

Dalton continued his rant, "Yes, that's right. I have fans and they tell me things. I know all about you Rainey Bell. I'll get to you, one way or another."

Rainey gave Dalton her best smile. "The next time I see you will be at your trial, followed by your execution, at which I will most definitely be in attendance."

"They can't prosecute me there. My deal covered all my Virginia murders and the ones in North Carolina, too."

Rainey laughed. "Ah, therein lies the rub. You just told me you killed Janelle White. You took her from just across the North Carolina line. You may have killed her in Virginia, but the kidnapping occurred in North Carolina. You never admitted anything about the murder until today. It wasn't covered in your deal. North Carolina can indict you for felony kidnapping that resulted in rape and murder."

Dalton yanked at the chain around his belt. Rainey didn't flinch.

"Why wouldn't you admit to that one killing? We all knew you did it. Was it because she was so young? You knew your supporters would dump you if you admitted to killing a child. She was a young innocent girl, just barely thirteen, who did nothing but cross your path. If the guys in here know you killed a child, the target already on your back is going to grow exponentially. Dahmer lasted, what, nineteen months? You're going to die Dalton, one way or another. Too bad they don't use the guillotine anymore, it would be so fitting."

Dalton lost all semblance of control. "I told you I was going to kill you the day you shot me. You thought I forgot about that. I keep my promises. One day when you least expect it, I'm going to send someone after you. You're going to be looking over your shoulder for the rest of your life. When you close your eyes at night you'll see me. I'm going to haunt your dreams..."

Rainey signaled the guard on the other side of the door that she was ready to be let out. He spoke into his radio and the door began to slide open.

Dalton continued to scream behind her, "You'll never forget me. I'll get you one way or another, you can bet on that, bitch. I have fans right now that want you dead. You're going to die just like those other whores."

Just before the door closed behind her Rainey looked at the guard in the corner. She nodded. The guard smiled. Rainey walked down the hall with Dalton's screams echoing off the walls, his body writhing in pain, as 50,000 volts jolted him from his chair.

Under her breath, she said, "Give it your best shot, asshole."

PART II

"When I let go of what I am, I become what I might be." ~ Lao Tzu

CHAPTER FOUR

Monday, April 4, present day.

Raleigh, North Carolina

"Cease fire! Cease fire!"

Rainey shouted, but to no avail. The two women in front of her continued to pull the triggers of their respective weapons. The rounds came fast, one behind the other, disappearing toward the black silhouettes in their sights.

She tried again, louder this time. "Cease fire!"

The blonde stopped firing first. She turned her eyes back to Rainey just as the other woman fired her last round.

"That's it!" Rainey continued to shout, because she hadn't yet taken out her ear protection. "You two will not be shooting semi-automatic weapons. You are staying with the revolvers I gave you to begin with."

Katie pointed to Rainey's ears and then removed her own earplugs. She grinned like a kid at Rainey. "Oh, but that was so much fun."

Ernie laughed. "You could blow a hole in a bus with that thing, before you knew what was happening."

"Exactly my point," Rainey said, letting the earplugs drop to dangle around her neck. "Now, take out the clips like I showed you and clear the chamber." Rainey was all business until the weapons were safely out of Ernie and Katie's hands.

Katie prattled on while she did as she was told, still giggling from the thrill. "That was amazing. I wonder if I hit the target? After that first pull, it just got easier, but you're right. I think I need to be able to actually control the damn thing, if I'm going to shoot it."

"I tried to tell you both that I had given you the weapon most suited for you, but no, what does a trained FBI agent know about shooting?"

Rainey's sarcasm was not lost on Ernie, who practically raised her, and didn't take the smart remark without a comeback. She placed her hands on her hips, her gray head bobbing, as she said emphatically, "Former FBI agent."

"And you're making me miss it more and more every minute," Rainey shot back.

Katie came up behind her and wrapped her arms around Rainey's waist. "Don't lose your patience. That was fun. Finish up with Ernie and I'll go out and talk to Gary at the front. Take your time." A quick peck on the cheek and Katie walked off the firing range.

Rainey watched the petite blonde, still mesmerized by the sheer energy Katie cast out around her. She had taken Rainey's breath the first time she saw her, standing at the gate of her old home in Chapel Hill. Now, nine months later, she took it no less frequently.

"Ain't love grand," Ernie said snidely, drawing out the syllables in each word.

Rainey's face broke into a grin. "Yes, yes it is."

"All right, lovey-dovey, let's wrap this up. I got shows to watch."

Rainey removed her father's Smith and Wesson .45 semi-auto from the shelf in front of Ernie. She double-checked that it was unloaded and placed it on the table behind them. She talked while she did this, returning with a smaller .380 revolver, and placed it, cylinder opened, in front of Ernie.

"Now, when we get here tomorrow, what are you going to do? Go through it step by step."

Ernestine Womble, the sixty-seven year old office manager of Bell's Bail and Bait, wanted to qualify to carry a concealed weapon. With their clientele and what happened last summer, Rainey didn't really blame her. The nature of the bond business was bad enough. In addition, through her time as a behavioral analyst, Rainey was involved in some of the worst serial murder cases in the last decade. The fact that some of those cases remained unsolved kept Rainey's Glock tight to her side. Knowing there were so many more out there, roaming undetected, kept Rainey in a constant state of vigilance. She paid dearly the one time her guard was down. That was never going to happen to Rainey Bell again.

73

CHAPTER FIVE

"Rainey, did you see this article about the missing woman from Durham?"

At 7:45 a.m., Tuesday morning, Rainey stepped out of the bathroom wearing nothing but a towel wrapped around her waist. She was using another towel to dry her thick hair as she walked bare-chested into the room. Last April, Rainey wouldn't have been caught dead without a shirt on, but that was before Katie Meyers took over her life. Rainey no longer felt self-conscious about the scar slashed across her chest and torso by a madman. None of that mattered anymore.

Rainey smiled at the sight of Katie seated at the computer wearing a terry cloth robe. She still had a hard time believing this was her life, now. Rainey had never been in love with a woman before, but then she never met a woman like Katie. During the previous July, Katie's marriage ended abruptly, and the "Y-man Killer" that scarred them both met his maker. Katie moved in with Rainey immediately. Since then, life continued to get better every day.

Rainey, towel draped over her shoulders, stepped up beside Katie who was intently reading from the computer screen. Rainey put her hand on Katie's shoulder and leaned down to kiss her on the top of her head.

"What did you say?" Rainey asked.

Katie slid her arm around Rainey's toweled waist without looking away from the computer screen. "This woman from Durham is still missing. Today's the fifth isn't it?"

"Yep, it says so right there on the screen."

"Don't be a smartass," Katie said, popping Rainey on the butt. "That means she's been missing for a week."

"Really? Who is she?" Rainey peered at the monitor. A picture accompanied the article Katie was reading. It showed a smiling woman with short dark hair. She was attractive, but in a rugged, outdoorsy way.

Katie turned to look at Rainey. A smile spread across her face. "I didn't realize there was a naked woman standing beside me."

Katie stood and stretched her five feet-six inch frame, reaching up to wrap her arms around Rainey's neck. The four-inch difference in their heights forced Katie to stand on her tiptoes, until she could reach Rainey's lips with her own. Katie melted into Rainey's arms, kissing her slow and long. She could kiss Katie all day, every day, but alas her job beckoned and it was getting late. She pulled back from Katie's lips and whispered against them, "Don't start this now, or Ernie will be over here knocking on the door, wondering where I am."

"You started it, walking in here naked," Katie said, kissing Rainey again.

As hard as it was to tear away, Rainey really did need to hurry. She tried a different tactic when Katie let her up for air. "Don't you have a doctor's appointment this morning?"

Katie released Rainey from her grasp. She looked down at the clock on the computer screen and flew into action. "Oh God, I need to hurry. I was so lost in that story, time got away from me." She playfully pushed Rainey away. "Go away, you. I need to get dressed."

Katie took off toward the master bedroom with Rainey hot on her tail. Katie giggled in front of her, skipping out of Rainey's grasp. She caught up and tackled Katie onto the new king sized bed. Katie giggled louder. She brought out the playful, carefree side of Rainey, the part of her that slowly faded into the background during her years with the BAU. She smothered Katie with kisses, while Katie lost control of her laughter. Then just as quickly as she had thrown her onto the bed, Rainey released the squirming Katie and stood up.

"Okay, that should hold you for a bit." Rainey said, while grinning down at the love of her life.

Katie smiled, raising a hand for Rainey to help her stand. "Have I told you I love you today?"

Rainey grinned and winked. "No, I don't think you did."

Katie winked, accompanied by a sexy smile. "I love you, Rainey Blue Bell."

One more kiss on the cheek, before they began to dress. Rainey chose her standard black jeans, black shirt, and gun holster. Katie assumed her classic Chapel Hill, thirty-something, wealthy housewife persona in navy blue slacks and a white Peter Pan collared, short-sleeved, cotton shirt. Rainey dressed quickly, then stopped to watch with fascination as Katie stood in front of the mirror putting on makeup. Katie was beautiful without it, and she didn't wear much, but she was gorgeous when she did. Rainey only wore makeup when she was forced to and that was a very rare occasion. Katie winked at her, knowing Rainey was still captivated by the sight of her. She checked her hair in the mirror one more time.

Rainey leaned on the door jam. "You're beautiful."

Katie brushed past Rainey, pecking her on the cheek. "Thank you, darlin'."

They made it to the front door without further delay. Rainey swiped her finger on the biometric pad of the gun safe. Katie insisted Rainey install the safe after she moved in. The door popped open. She liked the ease of the fingerprint lock, but in case the biometrics failed it had back-up keypad access, and a battery for power loss. Katie's prints were stored there, too. Should Katie need a weapon, more than enough surrounded her, and Rainey was making sure she could use them all.

Katie didn't like to see the guns around the house, though she knew they were there and why. Rainey kept the weapons in the bedroom in a new larger gun vault built into the wall, but they were within arm's reach and one finger swipe from being in her hands. Katie said the guns were a daily reminder of the danger Rainey believed they were in. Katie liked to think if she didn't acknowledge the threat it would go away. Rainey knew different, but agreed to put the weapons in the safes. Rainey secretly kept a small pistol hidden in a secret compartment in the bookcase. Old habits were hard to break.

Removing her Glock 19 and holstering it, Rainey closed the safe door. She covered the offending weapon with a lightweight black jacket she pulled from the coat rack, by the door. Once they were ready to leave, Katie leaned up attempting to kiss Rainey on the lips.

"No you don't," Rainey said, pulling back. "You're going to kiss me and smear lipstick all over me."

Katie grinned. "Come here, I'll be gentle." She rose on her toes and pecked Rainey lightly on the lips. Stepping back she looked at Rainey's mouth and ran her thumb across Rainey's lips. "See, no harm done."

Rainey hugged her and then opened the door. She let Katie out first and then set the alarm. Freddie Krueger, stalker of all things small, Rainey's bobbed-tail black cat was waiting to escort them down the cottage steps. He left the cottage every morning at sunrise to hunt and terrorize local wildlife. He returned about this time each day to walk Rainey to the office, before entering the cottage through his doggie door for a snack and a nap.

At the bottom of the stairs, Rainey parted from Katie. Walking backwards toward the office, she said, "Call me when you're done with your appointment."

Katie waved. "I will. And hey… I wouldn't worry so much about the lipstick on your mouth, but I'm sure Ernie's going to love that full set of lips on your cheek."

Rainey's hand shot to her face. She rubbed the spot where Katie had kissed her cheek and then looked at her hand. A smudge of pink glistened faintly on her fingers. "Damn, you did it again," she said, but she was laughing.

Katie opened her car door. "See you later. Be safe."

Rainey smiled and waved to her, giving her standard answer, "Always."

After watching Katie drive away, Rainey headed toward the office at the bottom of the hill. It was a bait shop and tiny grocery on Lake Jordan when her father inherited the property. She smiled at the old hillbilly Mountain Dew sign she still preserved in her father's memory. He faithfully painted it with a protective clear coat every year he lived there. He built the cottage next door up on stilts, mirroring one from his memory down at Nags Head. Rainey looked around and out over the lake. She had a good life now, and even though she was without her father, she had never been happier. The pain and loss she experienced before Katie no longer weighed her down. The clouds had parted and Rainey could see the sun again.

#

The toe tapping on the lavender high-heeled pump belonged to Ernie, who was never late and expected those with whom she worked to hold punctuality as dearly as she did. Since Katie moved in, Rainey faced many mornings like this. Ernie loved Katie and accepted her into the fold with open arms, but that didn't let Rainey off the hook when it came to the business. Rainey prepared for Ernie's wrath, as she closed the office door behind her and turned to face the petite gray-haired woman in the lavender power suit.

Rainey smiled. "Can we at least say good morning before you light into me?"

"Good morning," Ernie said, still tapping her toe. "You do remember that we have an appointment this morning?"

Rainey crossed to the coffee pot, filling the mug that waited for her there, while she talked. "Yes, I remember. We still have an hour. Are you going dressed like that?"

"What's wrong with the way I'm dressed?"

"Well, Ernie, most folks don't wear power suits and heels to qualify at the firing range." Rainey tried to control her childish giggles and hid behind the coffee mug. Giggling was something Rainey had forgotten how to do, but Katie had reminded her.

Ernie, hands on hips, stated, "Since this is how I dress on a daily basis, and this is how I'll be dressed if I ever have to use the damn thing, I suppose I should qualify in my usual attire."

"Well, all right then. I guess you've got a point there," Rainey answered, but she was still chuckling behind the cup.

A black Escalade pulled in front of the office, interrupting the debate over proper clothing at the firing range. Miles Cecil McKinney, Rainey's business partner, had arrived. Mackie, to those who knew him, unfolded his gigantic, six-foot six-inch, in excess of three hundred pounds, frame from the vehicle. He paused to put his oiled buffalo hide, black Outback hat on top of his massive head. Mackie was as dark as night, in stark contrast to his blazingly white teeth. Like Rainey, he was dressed all in black, a long leather coat adding to his intimidating appearance. Mackie's broad shoulders cast an impressive shadow, not to mention how scary it was to walk up on him in the dark. He smiled when he entered the room, shutting the door behind him with a loud thud.

Ernie flinched and then lit into him, "Mackie, I'll bet your momma tanned your hide for slamming doors. How in the hell a grown man doesn't know his own strength is beyond me."

Rainey remained hidden behind the coffee mug, snickering at the tiny Ernie and the cowering giant man. Mackie spotted her and saw his chance to avoid Ernie's wrath.

His rumbling bass voice filled the room. "Why are you still here? I thought you told me you and Rainey would be gone before I got here this morning."

The ruse worked. Ernie turned on Rainey again. "I've been waiting on love-struck over there. Look at her. Still got lipstick on her cheek."

Rainey stopped laughing and reached for a napkin on the counter. She went into the bathroom, leaving the door open, so that Mackie's laughter echoed into the little room.

Rainey called out to her office mates, "Y'all are just old and have forgotten what being in love is like. Besides she does this to me on purpose, just so you two can have a laugh."

Ernie answered, "You ain't been worth two cents since that girl got a hold to ya'."

"You got that right," Mackie said, followed by more rumbles of laughter.

Rainey came out of the bathroom with her left cheek rubbed red where she had removed the offending lipstick. She

knew they were secretly ecstatic that she was no longer
moping around and her nightmares had quieted. She played
along. "Okay, okay. You've had your laugh at my expense.
Now, aren't we supposed to be going somewhere?"

Ernie headed for her desk, saying, "Since you're here,
Mackie, take this paper down to the state office and get your
bond ID and license renewed."

Mackie reached out with a giant paw and took the papers
Ernie held extended. "Thank you. I'll go as soon as I answer a
few messages. Junior's 'bout found that Simpson boy. I think
we'll get him this evening."

Rainey's father started Billy Bell's Bail and Bait, after he
and Mackie came home from the Vietnam War. With Mackie
as his partner, Billy built a healthy bond business. When he
was killed, two years ago, Rainey inherited fifty-one percent of
the business. Shortly after, she took medical leave from the
BAU and came to work in the office full-time.

Ernie turned to Rainey. "Do you have your paperwork in
the car?"

"Yes, ma'am," Rainey answered obediently.

It might be Rainey's last name on the sign outside, but
Ernie was most definitely in charge. She ran the business for
the last thirty-five years and saved them more than once when
the money got tight. She was the mother figure in Rainey's
life. After all these years, and more than one near death
experience, Rainey depended on Ernie for much needed
support and guidance. On the other hand, Rainey went out of
her way to avoid her real mother, Constance Herndon.

"All right then, let's get going," Ernie said, grabbing her
matching lavender handbag.

"Where's your pistol?" Rainey asked.

"In my purse."

"Is it loaded?" Rainey asked, retreating instinctively.

"Yes, I'll unload it before we go in. I have to buy the bullets at the range anyway," Ernie answered, as if this statement negated the illegality of her actions.

"Ernie, you can't carry a concealed weapon, yet. Take it out and put it in the gun case I gave you."

"Who's going to know? No one would suspect I was carrying a gun," Ernie shot back.

"Why, because you're dressed so nicely?" Rainey said, sarcastically.

"No, because they'll be looking at that cannon strapped to you," Ernie answered, and then started out the door. "You are no longer an officer of the law, so shut up, and get in the car."

Mackie chuckled. "You heard her. Get going."

Rainey followed Ernie out the door, fussing at her as they left. "Don't call me when you get arrested. Hope you know a good bail bondsman."

#

Several hours later, Rainey and Ernie left the firing range with Ernie's newly endorsed concealed carry training certificate. Although she tried to cover her excitement, Ernie was beaming. She completed an eight-hour training class a week ago and passed the firearms proficiency portion with flying colors, today. Now, Rainey had to take Ernie to be fingerprinted and turn in her application to the Sheriff's office. Rainey was about to unleash a legally armed Ernie on the world. God help them all.

Cell phones had to be turned off on the range. Rainey checked her messages on the hands free device as soon as she was inside the 2010 Dodge Charger, her dream car. Rainey loved the sound of the 5.7-liter, V-8 engine roaring to life. This was no ordinary Charger. It was customized with dark tinted armored window glass, ballistic panels in the doors, wireless network access, digital video cameras, run flat tires, and a sweet weapons vault welded into the trunk. Everything a person could need to fight the boogey man. Rainey had fought him and won, but she knew there were more just like him out there, and that made her love her car even more.

She also loved the woman whose voice was coming through the speakers of the car. Katie had left a message only minutes before.

"Hey, good lookin'. Guess you're still on the range. Don't call me back. I have to turn off my phone. Everything went fine, but I'm going in for a quick ultrasound, if there is such a thing as a quick medical anything. Then I'm going by the school to see some old friends. I'll see you back at the house. Love ya'."

Rainey hit the button on her phone to erase the message. The next message played.

"Hey, it's me again. Be home by five. I'm cooking your favorite. Bye."

"Aww, now isn't that just the sweetest thing," Ernie chimed in mockingly. "You are the most lovesick two people I have ever witnessed."

Rainey blushed and hung up the phone. Ernie was right. They were absolutely gushing and Katie appeared not to care who noticed. Rainey had always been much more reserved when it came to romantic emotions, but Katie was a force to be reckoned with. They came together in a clash of heat and loneliness that shook both their worlds to the core. Katie turned out to be irresistible and broke through any of Rainey's wariness with unbending faith that it was the right thing to do. Rainey never loved anything or anyone the way she loved Katie. She hadn't known she was capable of loving that deeply. Although Ernie and Mackie, but mostly Ernie, teased her mercilessly, Rainey wouldn't change a thing. This was it, the happiness everyone was looking for. Katie made Rainey's life complete.

Rainey sighed and shrugged her shoulders. "I can't help it, Ernie. She fascinates me."

Ernie patted Rainey's hand. "I know, honey. I'm glad you're happy, but you two are sick'nin' sweet. I hope it wears off some before long."

Rainey grinned over at Ernie just as she turned the key in the ignition. She depressed the accelerator several times, making the big engine rumble. She winked. "I don't."

Ernie examined Rainey for a moment before she spoke. "I really am happy for you and I'm sure your father would be too..."

Rainey pulled the car out of the parking place and headed for the street. "I hear a 'but' in there."

"You're moving really fast, Rainey. You went from broke down and worn out to rapture pretty quick, don't you think? You're a behavioral analyst, how would you advise someone like you?"

Rainey turned the car out onto the street, heading for the Wake County Sheriff's Department offices, in downtown Raleigh. She thought about what Ernie was asking her before answering, "I assume you're talking about the baby thing."

"Not just the baby thing, and good lord that's enough, but you're also building a house. You changed your sexuality about a minute ago and you and Katie haven't even had time to deal with that. You were both traumatized when you found each other. That's not usually a recipe for a long-term relationship. These are life changing steps you're about to undertake and they are happening at a record pace, in my humble opinion."

"Ernie, you've never had a humble opinion in your life," Rainey said, laughing, unable to be offended by the older woman's prodding.

"Don't be a smartass. You know I'm right," Ernie shot back.

Rainey reached over and patted Ernie's leg. "Okay, okay, I know you're just worried. Look, I appreciate that this all appears very fast and I do recognize that Katie and I met under less than ideal circumstances. This whole falling for a woman thing took me by surprise, too." She shook her head and chuckled. "I mean, come on, this was the last thing I thought was going to happen to me."

Ernie's voice came out softer when she said, "Is it because of what that man did to you? I mean, I wouldn't blame you if you never wanted another man within a mile of you."

Rainey returned her hand to the wheel and gripped it a little tighter. She rarely thought about the attack, but when she did the rush of emotion would often overwhelm her. Not this time. She held the flashing pictures in her mind at bay. She took her eyes off the road just long enough to make eye contact with Ernie, who looked sincerely worried.

"No, Ernie, that is not why I'm with a woman. I'd be foolish to say that having a relationship with a man after that would not have had its challenging moments, but I hold no animosity towards men in general. A man didn't do what happened to me; a monster did. Believe me, there is a distinct difference. My being with Katie has more to do with who she is than what sex she is. I don't know that I would be attracted to other women like I am to Katie. It just feels right. It feels permanent."

Ernie didn't let up. "Okay, but this having a baby is a huge step."

Rainey considered her response carefully. "I'm not going to sit here and tell you that I haven't had moments of doubt. Not doubts about Katie and me, but I've worried that we were rushing into this, that I was caught up in glow, and so eager to please her that I said yes without thinking."

"That's what I'm saying," Ernie interjected.

Rainey waved a hand and cut her off. "Wait, I'm not finished. I fully believe whether she was with me or not Katie would still be doing this. Losing the baby last year just made her want a child even more. If this is that important to her, how could I not say yes? I promised to support her in this decision and that's what I'm going to do. Katie is a package deal."

Ernie turned in the seat to face Rainey. "How do you feel about becoming a parent?"

"Katie is just going through the process of preparing for the procedure. The actual attempts to get pregnant will come later. The doctor just wants to make sure she's fully recovered from all the trauma she went through last year."

"Rainey, that's not what I asked you. Are you ready to be a parent?"

Rainey smiled at Ernie. "This is going to surprise you, but yes I am. I can't imagine anything more satisfying than having a family with Katie."

"It's a lifelong commitment," Ernie said, adding, "You do realize you can't just put food on the floor and let it in and out a doggie door?"

"I was thinking of using a shock collar and an electric fence. Is that too much?" Rainey grinned and winked, making the turn toward the Capital. She wasn't looking at Ernie when she casually added, "Besides, Katie's the mother."

Ernie burst into loud howls of laughter. "You think Katie is going to handle all the child stuff and your life is going to go on just like it is. You think about this moment when you're rocking a screaming child at two a.m., smelling like vomit and dirty diapers, while Katie is passed out trying to grab just a few minutes of sleep. Honey, your life will never be the same."

The image was too real for Rainey. She shook her head and tried to make a joke. "I'll have to use all those great parenting skills I learned from my mother."

It only egged Ernie on. She started a different tack. "And you're going to build a house this year, too. Which comes first, the baby or the construction?"

"We meet with the architect next Monday. Should start building in a month or two. In a perfect world, it will be done by the end of summer, but I'm guessing fall probably. I don't know how long it will take for Katie to get pregnant." She paused and glanced at Ernie, before continuing, "Hey, I was going to build a house on that land anyway. That's what Dad and I talked about."

Ernie shook her head. "I'm just worried about you... and Katie, for that matter. I hope beyond hope that all your dreams come true, but be careful." She stopped talking and stared ahead. Then she added softly, "I don't know that you can take another heartbreak."

CHAPTER SIX

It had been a very wet fall and winter in the Raleigh-Durham area of North Carolina. The lakes and rivers swelled beyond their banks, receding slowly back to normal levels only recently. The drought stricken region needed the moisture. The barren trees of winter siphoned the water into their roots, filling out with new growth, as the warm spring days grew longer.

Today was just such a day. The cool of morning gave way to temperatures in the low seventies. Although it was overcast, the warm air brought people outside for their first forays of the spring. While Rainey and Ernie ate lunch in downtown Raleigh, a young couple decided to take a canoe ride along the Eno River, northeast of Durham.

The students, from the nearby university, escaped the cramped walls of dorm life for fresh air and sunshine. The previously high waters left behind fishing lures, odd items of clothing and trash, among other things, tangled with logs and branches bunched against the bank. Paddling along the shoreline, the couple came upon a large object, tied in thick black plastic, and partially submerged beneath a logjam. The young man poked it with his paddle. Not satisfied, he pulled out his pocketknife, and began to cut the plastic.

"Stop it, Jeremy. It's probably a dead animal, a deer carcass or a dog... just leave it," the dark haired coed said to her boyfriend.

"I want to see what it is. It could be a body or something," her companion answered.

"Great. If it is a body, you're destroying evidence and if it isn't you're going to get deer guts or some crap on you and then want to get back in my car. No way!"

The boy inside the young man would not let him leave a potential glorious find. He sliced at the wrapping, pulling back several layers.

The girl covered her mouth and nose. "Oh my God, it smells horrible."

The boyfriend turned to look her, his left hand still gripping the last layers of plastic.

"Are you ready to see what I've discovered?" he asked in a mock mad scientist voice.

He started to chuckle, but swallowed the laugh when his girlfriend's face went pale. He turned back to the plastic cocoon and nearly fell backwards out of the canoe from the shock, before he started slapping the water frantically with his paddle, backing the boat away as quickly as he could.

Shriveled black fingertips, protruding from hands wrapped in duct tape, extended out from the blackness of the package. A primal scream finally left the girl's mouth after seconds with no sound but the panicked paddling efforts of her boyfriend. The young man paddled faster, leaving the horror behind them. Neither would soon forget what they had seen.

#

Rainey clicked on the blinking box at the bottom of the monitor screen. The news alert distracted her from the mundane paperwork that occupied her afternoon. Rainey had been at it since she and Ernie got back from lunch, around one o'clock. Being in the bail bond business was not all "Dog the Bounty Hunter" excitement. There was far more desk duty involved than would make for a good reality show. She spent the hours since arriving back at the office trying to put a dent in the files piled on her desk. She made phone calls, sent emails, did a bit of cyber searching, and filled in the blanks of countless forms, which was quite a feat since she hated sitting still. She was ready for a distraction when the alert caught her eye. She clicked on it.

When the page loaded, the headline read, "Body of Woman Found on Eno River."

Remembering her morning conversation with Katie, she scanned the story. The headline said all there was to say at the moment. The body was discovered by some college students and reported to the police a little after noon today. Other than the couple's story of being a bit shaken by the experience, the article had few details. The body was recovered and transported to the Medical Examiner's Office. The police spokeswoman did say they were not ready to link the body to the missing woman from Durham.

Rainey looked at the digital clock in the corner of the screen. She had fifteen minutes to shut down the office for the day and be home for dinner by five. Rainey glanced out the wall of windows overlooking the docks and the lake beyond. There were still a couple of more hours of sunlight left. Maybe Katie would go fishing with her after supper. She closed the open files on her screen and shut down the computer. Last spring she would have stayed in the office and then gone out with Mackie to track a bail jumper, arriving back at the office in the early morning hours to collapse on the couch and drink herself to sleep. Katie changed all that.

Rainey had the rules of the FBI to live by for the past fifteen years. Before that, she had a demanding college career and her father to keep her on track. When she lost both her father and her career, all that structure disappeared. Although Ernie and Mackie tried their best, they could not stop the train wreck that was Rainey's life before Katie.

Katie quickly determined she didn't like spending so many nights home alone. They couldn't plan anything, because Rainey would tear off after a bail jumper at a moment's notice. She put her pretty blond head to work and came up with a solution. Rainey smiled, remembering that she was holding Katie against her naked body, at the time of the conversation that changed the way they ran the business.

"Rainey, I realize that you do not have a nine to five job, but you have to set aside time for your personal life," Katie said, about a month after they settled into their new life together. "You need to get on some kind of regular schedule. It's not healthy to work the hours you do with no breaks."

"Criminals don't take breaks. I have to go when I know where they are."

Katie rested her chin on Rainey's chest, her blue eyes locked on Rainey's.

"Why can't you and Mackie let Junior do more of the staking out? Put him on full-time. He can use a few of those contract guys and then call you and Mackie if he can't handle it. You wouldn't have to sit in the car all night just waiting."

Rainey ran a hand through Katie's hair, brushing the stray strands from her face. She asked Katie, "What would Mackie and I do then?"

"Concentrate on catching them in the day time."

It sounded simple enough, but Rainey thought Katie was just being naïve. Even so, Rainey would have agreed with anything said by the woman in her arms, but Katie had turned out to be wise, too. They added Junior to the staff. Rainey and Mackie worked out a schedule that suited everyone, including Katie. Ernie was the only one of them that kept a regular schedule up until that point. Since the new hours went into place Mackie and Rainey's health and attitudes had improved dramatically, not to mention how much their significant others were enjoying them being at home more. The business had not suffered at all. Rainey had to admit she liked this arrangement much better. It was the closest thing to regular job hours Rainey ever had.

Ernie's head popped into the doorway, breaking Rainey from her thoughts. "You about ready to call it quits, today?"

Rainey took one last look at her desk, cut off the lamp, and stood up. "Yeah, I better get moving. Can't be late for supper."

"Boy, she's got you wrapped around her finger," Ernie said, poking fun at Rainey.

Rainey started for the door, laughing. "It's not that. She cooks these amazing meals and she times everything out. If I'm late it won't be perfect and she'll be disappointed."

Ernie patted Rainey on the back as she passed through the doorway and followed her into the main office. "Well, bless your heart. Aren't you just the sweetest thing?"

Rainey answered, laughing, "Yes, yes I am."

Rainey took the daily ribbing from Ernie with the intention it was meant. Ernie loved her and she thought the world of Katie, but she earned the right to poke at Rainey. Ernie had nursed Rainey through some of her darkest days and any perverse pleasure she got out of tormenting the now gloriously happy Rainey was well deserved.

Rainey stopped at the exit to wait for Ernie to grab her purse and turn out the lights. She glanced up at the cottage. Her heart quickened just knowing she would see Katie in a few minutes, for what appeared to be an important dinner. She forced herself not to go home when Katie called earlier to say she was back. It was hard to concentrate on work when Rainey knew Katie was so close. Most days Katie came down to the office and helped Ernie with filing and things. Rainey discovered she liked having Katie at work with her. They even did a few stakeouts together. When she wasn't around, Rainey counted the minutes until she would see her again. Ernie had every right to pick on Rainey. She was "love-struck."

Rainey often wondered how long she was going to walk around in this state of perpetual bliss. It had to end. Rainey was a realist. It would be impossible to sustain this level of romance forever. In the future, the chemicals that surged during the beginning stages of a love affair would settle back to more reasonable levels. It was nature's way of assuring procreation and then maturation. Rainey knew all the science of it, but never having experienced a love of this magnitude, she had been unable to predict how it would change her. After all those years of hiding emotions, Rainey was delighting in just letting go for once.

Rainey pulled the office door closed and locked it. She walked Ernie to her car door. "If I didn't know better, I would think you are secretly excited about getting that concealed carry permit," she teased Ernie.

Atypically, Ernie snickered before saying, "You know, I really am, I'm now a legal pistol packing momma."

Rainey held the car door while Ernie climbed in. "Not quite yet, but your license should be here in about a month."

Ernie smiled up at Rainey. "Well, what they don't know won't hurt them."

Rainey leaned down and kissed her on the cheek. "I guess you'll have to be nice to me, so I don't tell on you."

"I'll skin you alive, if you do." Ernie started her car. She looked back up at Rainey and said, "Goodnight, sweetheart. See you in the morning."

"See you tomorrow. Drive safe," Rainey added.

Just before the door closed, Ernie got in her last little jab. "I still say she's got you wrapped."

"She does, Ernie. That she does."

Rainey turned the handle on the front door of the cottage and was disappointed to find it unlocked. How many times did she have to tell Katie to keep the door locked? She walked in ready to deliver a reprimand, but was interrupted by Katie's appearance in the archway to the kitchen, wiping her hands on a dishtowel.

"Before you say anything, I saw you coming. I just unlocked it."

Rainey flushed all over. It was impossible to stay mad at Katie, especially when she looked like she did at the moment. All the lights in the cottage were turned down low. She could see the candles lit on the table in the kitchen. They didn't have a dining room, but Katie went out of her way to make the small cottage as romantic as possible on some evenings. "Special Occasions," she called them. Katie was wearing jeans and a Carolina blue, sleeveless mock-turtleneck that fit her form tightly. The blue reflected in Katie's matching eyes. The sparkle in those eyes told Rainey that this was indeed going to be a "Special Occasion."

Rainey put her Glock in the safe and re-armed the alarm. She turned back, crossed the floor quickly, sweeping Katie into her arms and kissed her deeply.

"Wow!" Katie gasped when Rainey finally let her go. "Was that for locking the door or are you just glad to see me?"

Rainey grinned. "Both. So, what did the doctor say?"

Katie went back to the kitchen, answering over her shoulder, "I'll tell you in a bit. How was your day? Did Ernie qualify?"

"Yes, she will soon be legally carrying a weapon, as opposed to her current illegal status."

Rainey entered the kitchen. She saw the table set with Katie's good china and silver serving dishes. Her investigator's mind said either the doctor's appointment went very well or Katie wanted something else added to the architect's plans for the new house. She came up behind Katie, who was busy at the stove, and placed her arms around the smaller woman's waist, nuzzling into her neck. Katie turned off the gas under the pot she was stirring and patted Rainey's hands on her abdomen. She leaned back into Rainey, relaxing into her arms.

"I missed you, too." She turned to face Rainey, smiling. "But hold that thought until after we eat. It'll be ready by the time you wash up."

Rainey reluctantly let Katie out of her arms. "Okay, be right back."

Rainey left the kitchen and went to the master bedroom to clean up. Her shirt smelled like gunpowder, so she took it off and tossed it in the hamper. Her holster went on the bedside table. Rainey was washing her face when she heard Katie's voice in the bedroom.

"Anything exciting happen at work?"

Rainey thought about the news alert. "Did you see they found a body today?"

"Yes," Katie said, now leaning in the bathroom door. "I wonder if it's that missing woman."

"It's hard to tell sometimes. They may have to wait for DNA results. Depends on how long she was in the water." Rainey answered and then thought how detached she sounded. This wasn't someone in law enforcement. Katie wasn't used to seeing the things Rainey had seen. Rainey needed to be more sympathetic to that. She added quickly, "Sorry, you didn't need that graphic image."

"I watch crime shows when you're not here. I can take it."

Rainey dried her face. "Be careful. You're going to become as paranoid as you say I am watching that stuff."

Rainey hunted for a shirt. Before Katie, she would have just grabbed the first tee shirt she happened upon. Now, she cared about how she looked, especially since it appeared Katie planned a special night. Rainey's mind wandered while she looked for a shirt. Rainey began thinking like the FBI agent she used to be. The family dynamics would be the first thing her team would look at in a missing person's case. She wondered if the BAU was involved. A pang of... what was it? Loss, isolation... the knowledge she would never again be what she spent her life becoming.

Katie tapped her on the shoulder. When Rainey turned around Katie was holding the soft white, button up blouse she bought for Rainey. It was just a casual cotton shirt, but the first time Rainey wore it Katie beamed with delight. She evidently liked the way it looked and Rainey had reaped the benefits. Remembering, Rainey smiled and took the shirt. Although they were talking about a missing woman and a dead body, both their inner thoughts were heading in the same direction. It was all Rainey could do to put the shirt on without just throwing Katie in the bed behind them.

Katie slipped away, evidently sensing how close she was to being the victim of a pounce. She walked toward the doorway. Getting back to the subject at hand, she said, "Didn't another woman go missing about a month ago?"

Rainey buttoned the shirt. She left the top two buttons undone. The small white trail of long healed stitches peaked out of her cleavage. She no longer wore a tee shirt under everything. The scar was just a part of her now. It did not define her. It happened to her, but it didn't hold the power it once did.

She answered Katie's question, "Yes, but she was from Chapel Hill."

"That's not so far from Durham. Do you think they are connected?"

Now dressed, Rainey followed Katie back to the kitchen. "I don't know enough about the cases to draw that conclusion. Why do you ask?"

"I was just wondering if maybe it was a serial case."

Rainey smiled. Katie wasn't too good at hiding her motives. "No, I haven't been contacted by the police to help."

Since resigning from the FBI, Rainey consulted with local law enforcement needing a profile for an UNSUB. She had only done it once since Katie moved in. It was a one-day affair involving a series of rapes. She delivered the profile and was done, before Katie became too nervous. Rainey chasing bail skippers made her crazy enough. The little blond was having difficulty getting used to being a cop's wife.

Rainey sat down beside Katie and surveyed the table. Katie had poured them glasses of wine and prepared Rainey's favorite, Cheese Ravioli, with fresh baked bread. Her stomach growled at the sight.

Katie touched Rainey's hand. "I don't care if you want to consult on this. I know you miss the investigative side of your job. I just don't want the nightmares to come back."

Rainey's vivid night terrors more than once sent Katie scrambling out of bed. Katie made the mistake of putting her hands on Rainey, the first time she experienced one of her blood curdling screams in the middle of the night. Rainey awoke just before she was about to punch Katie's lights out. They agreed afterwards that the best course of action was for Katie to get out of the bed and talk calmly, until she was sure Rainey was fully awake.

"I haven't had a bad dream in months now. I think you cured me," Rainey said, smiling, and then changed the subject. "Is this meal a bribe for something?"

Katie's grin lit up the room. "Maybe."

Rainey leaned over to kiss Katie on the cheek. "Whatever it is, the answer is yes."

"I have something to show you after we eat." Katie beamed, while serving the ravioli.

Rainey took a sip of wine, and then asked, "Have you been reading those lesbian romance novels again?"

"Why do you say that?"

Rainey chuckled. "Cause every time you read one, you have to show me what you've learned."

Katie took a drink of wine and looked at Rainey seductively. "I haven't heard you complaining."

"Oh, far be it for me to discourage your lesbian edification," Rainey cracked.

"I think you've benefitted from my research, don't you?"

Rainey smiled broadly. "Oh yeah, I most certainly have."

Rainey and Katie had learned a lot about each other in their short time together. Katie moving in had gone nearly seamlessly. It was as if they had known each other forever; still there were some adjustments. Rainey was subject to leave things lying around. Katie picked up after her without much complaining. There was a fair amount of teasing, but no fussing. Katie adjusted to Rainey's obsession with NCAA basketball, by reading books while Rainey shouted at the TV. Rainey, who wasn't much for going out, gave in to Katie's need to see a movie in the theatre, when she'd really rather wait for the DVD. Katie learned how to just kick back and not be busy. She could now sit quietly on the dock beside Rainey, listening to the sounds of nature. They compromised and laughed and somehow made it all work.

Rainey winked at Katie. "What are you reading these days?"

Katie broke the bread and handed Rainey a piece. "A story about a hot bail bondsman and her new girlfriend."

Rainey savored the big bite of Ravioli she had in her mouth. Katie was a self-taught gourmet and learned very well. Rainey swallowed and smiled. "Does she have to run extra miles cause her girlfriend is a fantastic cook?"

"Yes, but she doesn't mind. She's healthier than she's been in a long time and did I mention she's hot?"

Rainey laughed. "She's probably grateful for the food and the attention."

"Oh, she is and she shows the girlfriend how much quite frequently."

"I think I like this book," Rainey replied, grinning.

Katie winked. "I thought you might. I'll change the subject, so you can finish eating." She paused, pouring them each some more wine. "I went by my old school today."

Rainey sipped her wine. She knew how difficult it was for Katie to walk away from her job as a first grade teacher, but it had been Katie's decision to do so. She reached out and touched Katie's hand. "I know that had to be hard for you."

Katie nodded affirmatively. "I have to admit my heart did beat a little faster before I walked in, but once I was there the panic went away. I thought I would be hit with so much remorse for resigning. That's not what happened at all."

Rainey relaxed and picked up her fork. "So, things went well?" She resumed eating, while she listened to Katie.

"I miss the kids. I miss spending time with them every day, but I don't miss the politics or paperwork. Those teachers looked so tired. I wonder if I looked like that."

"I saw you when you were a teacher and you did not look tired. You looked like you loved it, from what I could tell."

Katie continued, "Oh, I did, but Chelsea is doing a great job with the kids. Do you remember her? She took over for me when I had to take leave."

"Yes, I remember her from the day we packed your stuff."

Katie smiled. "She told me her sister is part owner of Feme Sole, a lesbian night club in Durham. She said we should go."

"Do you really want to?" Rainey asked, honestly having never thought about going to a lesbian club.

Katie grinned broadly. "I've been dying to go."

Rainey stopped eating and looked at Katie's excited face. She laughed at the pretty blonde. "Why didn't you say anything?"

"I don't know. I guess I didn't want to seem too eager to meet other women."

Rainey cocked her head. She teased Katie, "Hmm, I hadn't thought about that... Maybe I should go by myself and check it out first. See if it's safe to turn you loose on the unsuspecting lesbians of Durham."

"No way. They're always all over the hot cop or P.I. in these books I'm reading. You're not going to a lesbian bar without me."

Rainey continued the tease. "What? So now you don't trust me."

"You're the one that said I couldn't go. Who has trust issues?"

Rainey laughed. "I just had no idea you'd be so interested in going to a gay bar."

Katie's smile slipped a little. "Are you worried about being seen with me in a lesbian bar?"

Rainey had guarded their privacy over the last nine months. After the initial stories broke in the paper, she and Katie could go nowhere without someone taking their picture and posting it on the web or in the paper. Maybe Katie had the wrong idea about why she did that. It certainly wasn't because she was embarrassed to be with a woman. Rainey had reasons beyond Katie's knowledge not to want her personal life made public.

Rainey reached out and took Katie's hand. "No, I am proud to be with you. It's just, I'd rather not have our pictures splashed all over the web, again." Rainey saw the disappointment in Katie's eyes and added, "Maybe we're old news by now. It has been nine months. Surely, no one is interested in the two of us anymore."

"Oh please take me, Rainey. I want to see all those women just having a good time with each other. I want to dance with you."

"Honey, I hate to break it to you, but I don't dance. I'm a wall flower."

"Then we'll just watch. I know you can slow dance. We've done that here. Come on, Rainey. Who knows, you might even have a good time?"

"I always have a good time with you. Okay, I'll take you to a lesbian bar."

Katie leapt out of her chair and landed in Rainey's lap. She hugged her with excitement and then asked, "When can we go?"

Rainey kissed Katie's lips and said, "I'm on duty Friday night, but I'll see about Saturday, after your father's party, okay?"

Katie was so excited she jumped out of Rainey's lap and did a little happy dance.

Rainey laughed aloud, as she said, "If I had known it would make you this excited, I would have taken you to a bar much sooner."

Katie hugged Rainey again and then sat down. Katie was too wound up to eat. She chattered away while Rainey continued to devour her favorite meal.

"Well, anyway, I'm not sorry I left the school. I'm glad I went and faced everyone. I'm sure, between all the publicity from this summer and moving in with you, I was the talk of the teacher's lounge for a while. It felt good to hear people say I never looked happier."

A smile seized Rainey's lips. Of all the things in the world that Rainey wanted, the most important was for Katie to be happy. "I'm glad you went then. And you know you can always go back to teaching when you're ready. I'd hate not having you around as much, but anyone who ever saw you with those kids knows you were born to it."

"Oh, I'm going to be too busy for a couple of years, at least."

Katie said this so nonchalantly that Rainey almost missed it, but her investigator's ears caught the implications. Yes, they had discussed having a baby. Rainey said she would be a willing participant in the parenting, but it still made her nervous. Katie was so sure of what she wanted and was prepared to be a parent. Whether Rainey was in Katie's life or not, there was going to be a baby. Katie had been very clear about that before they began their relationship. Rainey wished she were as positive that she could be a good parent. She wanted to have a family with Katie. She just feared she would screw it up somehow. Her own family history wasn't exactly "Ozzie and Harriet." Katie's statement hung in the air, while they ate.

After a moment, Rainey said, "So, are you going to tell me what the doctor said or not?"

"I wanted to wait until we'd eaten, but okay. He said everything was fine and I could start the procedure whenever we're ready."

Rainey, finished with the food on her plate, sat back, holding her wine glass. She looked at Katie, not commenting. Katie cocked her head to one side, wiped her mouth with her napkin, and sat back, as well. Silence fell over the room. Rainey had known this moment was coming, but now that it was here, she was unable to say anything.

Katie rescued her by saying, "This is all so fast; are you sure you want to go through with it, or are you just trying to please me?"

"Ernie asked me the same question today." Rainey took a sip of wine.

"Well?"

"Yes, Katie, I'm trying to please you." Rainey leaned forward. "I can't tell you it doesn't frighten me. I've barely gotten my feet back under me and this life with you is so new. I don't want to make a mistake here. On the other hand, I can't imagine life without you, and life with you means children. So, there you have it."

"Children." Katie's eyes sparkled. "Let's try for one and see what happens."

"Well, we need to know if we're building a three or four bedroom house."

Katie stood up without answering and started cleaning off the table. Rainey reached out and took her hand, pulling the smaller woman down on her lap. She kissed Katie sweetly on the lips and said, "Thank you for the wonderful meal and all the preparations. Now, tell me what's going on in that pretty head of yours?"

"I'm being selfish. Forcing this on you. You told me you never thought about having a baby." Katie said.

"I also told you that none of my relationships ever went that far and my job took precedence over everything else. I just never had the time to think about it before, but I know I want children with you."

"There you go, with that children word again."

Rainey laughed and pulled Katie to her, hugging her tightly. "Honey, you would have a whole classroom full if you could. I know that. I'm thinking three would be more reasonable, but I'm about to turn forty-one, so we need to get started."

"I love you, Rainey Bell," Katie said into Rainey's neck.

"I love you, too," Rainey said, feeling her body wake to Katie's touch. She pulled Katie's mouth to hers and kissed her thoroughly.

Katie's cell phone rang and vibrated on the kitchen counter. She pulled away from Rainey. "I have to get this. It's my mom."

"Really?" Rainey said. Katie's mother could wait, as far as Rainey was concerned.

Katie went to the phone, turning to Rainey before answering it. "Don't pout. It's not attractive. This will just take a minute."

Katie answered the phone. "Yes, mother. I do remember your number," Katie said into the receiver. She listened and then replied, "What time do you want us there? ... That early? Let me talk to Rainey and I'll get back to you.... I love you, too. Bye."

Katie's mother was throwing a birthday party for her father and Rainey was expected to be there, along with Katie's two sisters and their significant others. This was to be their third full-on family gathering. Rainey's experience with the sisters portended a lively family discussion, with Rainey as the main topic. Katie was the darling youngest daughter and the last person anyone in her family expected to begin a lesbian relationship. All the money had been on the middle sister, Helena, to do something so shocking.

Maria, the oldest sister, was the most vocal about her dismay. Was it homophobia or Maria's fear of what people might think of her having a lesbian sister? Rainey had not decided. Katie's mother, Melanie, as it turned out, knew Rainey's mother and stepfather. It made her accepting Katie's sudden shift in sexuality a bit more palatable, but she still seemed mystified by the whole thing. Katie's father had long since given up any semblance of control or understanding of the women in his life. Katie's family was handling her leap into this relationship, each in their own way. No one was openly hostile to the idea, but the astonishment really hadn't worn off. Rainey was not looking forward to another outing with the Meyers clan.

"Rainey, my sisters are coming in Friday night and Mom would like us to come for brunch at ten thirty on Saturday, before the party that afternoon. I know that makes for a very long day with my family, but we are so rarely all in the same place. I want them to get to know you better."

"I'm not so sure I can last that long in the same house with all three of you sisters. Christmas was almost a deal breaker, or have you forgotten Maria asking me which one of us was the boy?"

Katie started whipping herself with laughter. "I loved it when you said, 'Depends on which day of the week it is, but Katie is kinda attached to that role so I let her wear the equipment, know what I mean?' When you winked at her I thought she would die right there."

Rainey chuckled. It was not her finest moment, but she's had a few drinks and Maria just got on her nerves. She said, "Besides, I don't know how your parents did it. It's so noisy. Remember I was an only child."

Katie laughed. "Do what my dad and Maria's husband do, drink and watch sports on TV."

Rainey laughed. "So I'm relegated to the husbands' room to smoke cigars and drink brandy."

Katie put the phone on the table and stood in between Rainey's legs, her arms draped over Rainey's shoulders. "You can drink scotch or bourbon, if you prefer. Let's face it, Rainey, you're not one of the girls. You have more in common with my second-amendment-loving father and brother-in-law, than with my Hollywood sisters and globetrotting mother. By the way, are you going to wear your holster this time?"

Rainey grinned. "It depends. Is Maria going to wear a muzzle?"

"Oh, don't worry. You and I are old news. Helena is bringing a boy toy that is the same age as Maria's oldest daughter. He's twenty. Remember Helena is forty-two. It's making Maria crazy."

Rainey would never get used to the way these sisters went at each other, only to join ranks if attacked by an outsider. Rainey learned quickly that she was not one of them. She measured her words carefully when speaking of the sisters. She was genuinely surprised the muzzle comment hadn't met more resistance, but Maria could be a bitch, and this afforded Rainey a little leeway.

"Now, that might be worth going to watch," Rainey said, chuckling.

Katie pecked Rainey on the cheek and started clearing the table. "Maria called this morning ranting about it. I told her to be careful, her moral superiority was showing."

Rainey laughed. "I am delighted that Helena's new boyfriend now tops the list of things Maria thinks are her business."

Maria vacillated between total disbelief and quoting scripture, to mild acceptance of Katie's relationship with Rainey. In the meantime, Maria kept them informed of her every thought on the subject. Hell, Rainey didn't understand how it happened anymore than Maria did; she just didn't spend every waking moment trying to figure it out. For once in her life Rainey walked straight into the unknown willingly, giving her heart freely to a woman she barely knew.

Rainey was helpless to do anything else. If it made Katie happy, then what choice did she have? She smiled up at Katie. "Whatever you want to do is fine with me."

#

"Katie, come on. Open the door."

Rainey had been pacing up and down the hallway for five minutes. Jesus, how could she have been so stupid? Now she was faced with a locked bedroom door and a very angry woman on the other side. Katie locked her bedroom door before, but not to keep Rainey out. She used this tactic on her husband. Rainey was experiencing this particular form of dismissal for the first time.

She knocked again. "Katie, this is childish. Open the door." Something hit the other side of the door loudly. Perhaps chastising Katie had not been the best approach. She tried apologizing, pleading, and downright begging, but none of that had worked. Katie was pissed. There was no use trying to kick the door open. After the gunfight that nearly destroyed the place in July, Rainey had to replace the doors. She planned never to be afraid to fall asleep in that room. She closed in the wall where the sliding glass doors to the deck had been, and replaced the exit with a metal door and high security dead bolt lock. It wasn't as nice a view but she slept well. The interior door blocking Rainey's path was solid oak, complete with a sturdy lock and reinforced frame. Rainey never envisioned the lock being used to keep her out.

She tried again to make some headway with the irate woman on the other side of the door. She spoke softly, calmly, trying to become the voice of reason Katie might hear.

"Katie, I know what I said upset you. I am truly sorry. Please open the door and talk to me. This isn't going to just go away and I can't fix it if you won't talk to me."

Nothing. Not a word. Rainey gave up. She'd try again later, but right now all she wanted was a drink. She had only taken two steps down the hallway when the bedroom door opened behind her. She turned, hopeful that Katie had finally given in, only to see Katie's arm slipping back inside the door, having dropped a blanket and pillow on the hall floor. Freddie ran into the bedroom before the door closed quickly. Rainey heard the lock slide into place.

"Traitor," she called after the cat. She felt bad, but bad was turning to angry, pretty swiftly. She shouted at the door, "Good night to you, too!"

Dammit! How had a romantic evening with so much promise turned into such a disaster? Rainey went back to the living room, pulled a bottle of bourbon from the liquor cabinet, and sat on the couch. She didn't drink much anymore, but this situation called for some real soul searching, and she happened to need a drink to get through it. Rainey's demons reared their heads at some of the most awkward moments. Tonight they got out and she didn't rein them in fast enough.

Earlier, when they finished playing grab-ass in the kitchen and went out to the main room, Rainey was ready to skip the surprise and head straight to bed, the couch, the floor… she wasn't picky. Katie had other plans. She made Rainey sit on the couch beside her and placed a file folder in Rainey's lap. She kept her hand on top of the folder so Rainey couldn't open it yet.

"Before you look in here, I have to ask," Katie paused and then added, "when you said you were afraid to make a mistake earlier, what did you mean? Are you talking about us? Are you afraid this might be a mistake?"

"No, Katie. Not us. I'm afraid I won't be a good parent. I didn't have the kind of home life you did. My family just wasn't normal. I know nothing about raising a kid. I don't want to screw it up."

"Oh Rainey, no one knows how to raise a kid. You just do the best you can. Between the two of us, I think we can manage." Katie lifted her hand from the folder and touched Rainey's chin, pulling her eyes into focus. "But I'm telling you now, you have to teach the sports stuff."

Rainey grinned. "How do you know he or she will be into sports?"

"I'm stacking the deck so to speak." Katie tapped the folder. "If not athletic, the child will at least be coordinated."

Rainey opened the folder. Once again she was faced with a stack of profiles, only these weren't of serial rapists or murderers, they were sperm donors. Rainey surveyed the information available. It flooded at her from the pages and pages of facts and interviews. A lump formed in her throat. She couldn't help but look for the information she knew wouldn't be there.

Katie prattled on in her ear, "These are longer than the initial donor profiles. These contain all the general information about the donor's main characteristics, like hair color, eye color, height, weight, education, blood type, ethnic origin, plus a three-generation medical and genetic history - their religious affiliations, whether they are athletes, what their interests are, hobbies, stuff like that. I picked these because they look like you. So we'll look like a family."

Rainey was sure she was supposed to respond positively to the last comment, but at the moment her mind was occupied with the forms in front of her. Each donor's file contained extensive interviews, essays, even a childhood picture accompanied a few, but what caught Rainey's eye were the psychological exam results.

Katie had gone quiet when Rainey didn't respond to her declaration to have the child's donor look like her. Rainey turned without thinking and asked, "Who gave these psych tests? Are they legitimate? Most psychos can pass a simple standard test. Do you know we had documented cases where sociopaths donated sperm to reputable places? Can you imagine finding out your sperm donor was a serial killer?"

Katie stiffened. "What if he was? Would you give the child back?"

Rainey tried to defend her comments. "Of course not. I'm just saying you have no way of knowing who this person really is. Whether you believe it or not, genetics can play a big role in some of these malformed personalities."

"And you don't think environment has something to do with how these 'personalities' are formed? You don't think that a loving home with responsible parents plays a bigger role in how a child turns out?"

Rainey was seeing the error in her bluntness, but she couldn't stop herself from saying, "Yes, it can play a very large role, even bigger than genetics, but if the building blocks that make up emotion are not there, they cannot be created by just loving the child. I've looked at many a parent that had no idea that little Johnny was a stone cold killer."

"You just made my argument, Rainey. Those parents were normal and loved their child and it turned out badly. You're basically saying it's a crapshoot. You're never going to find the absolute perfect donor, if you look for every possible sign of defect."

"It's better to look at them hard now instead of be sorry later."

Katie stood up suddenly. "What if it's not a psychological defect? What if the child has autism or a physical disability? And if you were sorry, who would you blame, the donor or me? Have you profiled me yet, Rainey?"

Rainey tried to calm Katie. "Wait a minute. Don't get upset. I just want to be careful. We can't rush into something and not know what we're getting."

"We'll never know for sure, Rainey. I believe babies are born innocent and we shape them through love and education."

"Yeah, and you believed you knew who your husband was, too."

Rainey couldn't imagine why she said that. She wanted the words back so badly. It was too late. They hit their mark dead on.

Katie's hands flew to her hips and her face flushed bright red. "You know, you're right, Rainey. You probably would screw up a kid. I certainly don't want to sit around and watch you profiling our children, waiting for one of them to turn into a monster."

Katie stomped off and slammed the door. Now on the couch, about to spend the night alone, Rainey's own words echoed through her brain and she could not for the life of her figure out why she had said them. She finished her second drink and poured another. She had royally fucked up this time.

She heard the old radio show voice in her head. "Who knows what evil lurks in the hearts of men?" Rainey did. Why couldn't she leave that life behind her? One of the things she loved most about Katie was her eternal optimism. Rainey needed that in her life. So why was she hell bent on making sure Katie remembered that evil existed? Katie knew it. She'd seen it up close and personal, yet she chose to look for the good in the people. Rainey still suspected the worst and was never surprised to find it, especially after her own dance with the devil.

Rainey reached down and lifted the file folder. The contents spilled across the coffee table. She sipped her bourbon, slowly being drawn to certain words on the pages; chestnut brown hair, curls, green eyes, tall, sports, law enforcement, computer science, honor, valor. A single theme began to emerge. Katie saw these traits in Rainey. The things she wanted to see in her child, their child. Katie had obviously spent many hours searching donors and these were the files she had chosen for Rainey to see. Rainey read each profile thoroughly.

When finished, Rainey had a much better understanding of what Katie saw of value in her. Beyond their physical attributes, these men were intelligent, self-confident, trustworthy, and loyal. All were men of good character. The interviewers mentioned feeling comfortable and safe with them. Katie considered all that she could with the information she was given, and she did a lot of it with Rainey in mind.

Rainey shuffled through the pile of papers once more. Katie slammed the bedroom door around seven thirty. Rainey looked at the clock on the bookshelf; it read "1:45 a.m." She pulled out three sheets of paper, looked them over again, and then put the others back in the file folder. Carrying the papers with her down the hall, she tapped on the bedroom door lightly, and then slid them under the door. She waited.

When Katie opened the door she simply said, "I'm tired and I don't want to fight anymore. Come to bed. It seems I can't sleep without you."

Rainey followed Katie into the room, slipped out of her clothes, and crawled into bed. Katie spooned into her, pressing into her body. Rainey slid her arm around Katie and pulled her in tight.

She whispered, "I'm sorry, Katie."

"Shhh. We'll talk about it in the morning."

Rainey closed her eyes more in love with Katie than she had been just hours ago. If she could only see the world like Katie did, the whole glass half-full thing, Rainey would enjoy life more. Katie, it seemed, could even see the good in Rainey.

CHAPTER SEVEN

Rainey awoke to the smell of bacon frying and coffee brewing. Her arm shot to the empty side of the bed, even though she knew Katie wasn't there. That was another reason she was glad the doors were replaced. Before Katie, the slightest sound or movement could rouse her from a deep sleep. Now she slept so soundly she probably wouldn't hear an army marching through the room. As much as she assumed the role of protector in their relationship, it was Rainey that truly felt safer now. Katie gave her peace.

The clock said eight thirty. Rainey's head said too much bourbon. She crawled out of the Laura Ashley floral print sheets. She was still trying to get used to all the frilly stuff Katie had added to the décor. Rainey and her dad had been more the bland, solid color types. Katie was anything but bland. Rainey appreciated Katie's talents for decorating, but right now the flowers were swimming, causing her stomach to roll over.

She was seated on the toilet, head in hands, when she heard the top on a Coke can pop open and fizzle. Rainey raised her head to see Katie standing in the doorway of the bathroom. She held the red can with its familiar logo out for Rainey.

"Thought you might need this. I saw the evidence of foul play on the coffee table. I do believe this is the standard southern cure for over indulgence."

Rainey said nothing. She took the Coke from Katie and downed it without stopping. She could feel the sugary cold liquid as it made its way through her body. Rainey hadn't really had much to drink since she met Katie. They drank wine with dinner or had an occasional beer, but liquor as a sleeping remedy or stress reliever had gone by the way side. She was getting too old for this. The alcohol took so much more out of her now than it did when she was younger. Back then, she could hold her own with most anybody and pop back up the next day unfazed. This morning she felt like shit. Knowing she had to finish the conversation from the night before with Katie did nothing to improve her condition.

Katie was her perky self, as usual. She was already showered and dressed, looking unaffected by their late night. She took the empty can from Rainey's hand and said, "Take a quick shower. It'll help. Breakfast is almost ready."

"Katie, I..." Rainey stammered.

"Honey, right now you are hung-over, naked, and sitting on a toilet. You're quite defenseless. It just wouldn't be fair."

"Are you still mad?" Even Rainey thought she sounded like a scolded child.

"No." Katie stepped over to Rainey and kissed her on the forehead. "Now, get moving."

Rainey showered and dressed in an old pair of jeans. She threw on a tee shirt and an old University of Virginia sweatshirt. She was going to be late to work and stopped in the bedroom to call Ernie and let her know. When Rainey turned the corner into the kitchen, Katie was feeding Freddie by the back door.

She smiled up at Rainey. "He brought me a mole. He just laid it at my feet while I was cooking."

Rainey's eyes darted around the kitchen. "What did you do with it?"

"Relax. I threw it away already. I still can't believe a big ol' FBI agent is scared of rodents." Katie giggled.

"I'm not afraid of them. I just don't like them." Rainey sat down and immediately began to guzzle the glass of orange juice beside her plate.

Katie placed bacon and eggs, along with cut fruit, and fresh baked biscuits on Rainey's plate. She brought the pitcher of orange juice and a cup of coffee for Rainey to the table and then sat down. Rainey dove into the food and began to feel better as the caffeine did its magic. Her head cleared of fog and she thought she might actually recover before noon.

Katie waited patiently, having learned that Rainey wasn't the most social person before her first cup of coffee. She ate her breakfast, watching Rainey's every move. Rainey was conscious of the looks from across the table.

"What? Do I have food on me somewhere?" Rainey finally asked.

"No. I'm just waiting for you to finish so we can talk, because I've obviously misunderstood you."

Rainey leaned in closer. "Look, if this is about my comment concerning your husband last night, I truly am sorry. That was totally out of line."

"No, that isn't what this is about, but it did get me thinking. We jumped into this thing without getting to know each other."

Rainey didn't like where this was going. Her heart sounded the alarm. Katie must have seen something in Rainey's expression that triggered her next statement.

"Honey, don't panic. I'm not breaking up with you. I'm trying to understand you. We skipped the dating and went straight to mating. There is so much we don't know about each other. I know I love you, I know you love me, but I don't know what shaped you into the person you are. I know some of it, but not enough."

"Katie, you don't need to know all of it. You should never have to know what I know. You've seen enough, as it is."

"I don't want the details. I want to know what you think and why. You of all people should realize your childhood, your abandonment issues, your FBI career, have all made you what you are."

Katie wasn't finished talking, much to Rainey's displeasure. She stood up and went to the counter, producing a thin book Rainey recognized from her reference collection on the bookshelf. Maybe she should have locked those books up, too.

"I read this report from the Symposium of Serial Murder, before you got up. Your unit of the BAU sponsored that event and finalized the report, correct?"

"Yes, that's correct." Rainey was always entertained when Katie questioned her like an attorney questions a witness. Hours of coaching JW through Law School had made her quite adept at this method.

"I was particularly interested in the section called Causality of the Serial Murder."

Rainey knew instantly where this was going. She let a bit of a sly grin cross her lips when she said, "I bet you were."

"It said, and correct me if I get this wrong, that serial murderers, like everybody else are a product of their heredity, their upbringing, and the choices they make during development, but there really are no single identifying factors."

Rainey nodded. "You're doing well so far. Now for the point I believe you're about to make, the part where you throw my own words back at me."

"Didn't you, Special Agent Rainey Bell, say that the most significant factor is the serial killer's personal choice to pursue his or her crimes?"

"Yes, I believe those were almost my exact words."

Katie put the book down on the table, her hands going to her hips. Here comes the point, Rainey thought.

"When we were discussing sperm donors did you not consider that the parents help shape the child's decision making process?"

"Touché. You win. You're right. Every parent is faced with a crapshoot of genetics. I concede and bow to your positive influence."

Katie hugged Rainey tightly, saying, "I know that's huge for you. Thank you."

"You are very welcome," Rainey said, smiling. She couldn't help it. Katie was so happy it was contagious.

Katie returned her smile. "One step at a time. I'm going to let you get used to the idea, before we do anything else. I'm learning to let you mull things over. You're much more pliable that way."

"I'm being handled by a master manipulator. I see that now."

Katie threw her head back and laughed. "I prefer to call it persistent."

"You are that, darlin'." Rainey's laughter joined Katie's, as she repeated, "Yes ma'am, you are that."

Rainey stood up, sweeping Katie into her arms, kissing the breath out of both of them. When they broke for air, the look that passed between them rapidly changed from passion to desire. They may not have known all of each other's thoughts and dreams, but they definitely knew each other's bodies. They spent the last nine months exploring them thoroughly. Within seconds, Katie's long sleeved tee shirt hit the floor, followed quickly by Rainey's sweatshirt and several other clothing items. Several minutes later, a spent Katie leaned into Rainey chest. She began to giggle.

Rainey swept the stray hair from Katie's damp forehead, and asked, "What's so funny?"

"If that's going to happen every time we have a fight, I think we should fight more often."

#

Rainey decided to take the morning off and spend time with Katie. They were measuring out the ground plan for their new house on the lot beside the cottage. She checked the local media reports this morning and found nothing new about the body found yesterday. Rainey was lost in thoughts that the police would probably find the missing woman's case was related. A small dirt clod hit Rainey in the back as she bent down by the one of the corner stakes. Rainey turned to see a smiling Katie armed with a hand full of small dirt clods.

"What the hell?" Rainey stood up, grinning at Katie who had another projectile cocked and ready.

Katie let fly with the next clod. It hit Rainey in the thigh, sending a small cloud of dust into the air. "You need to loosen up," Katie said, reloading and nailing Rainey in the shoulder.

Rainey dropped the tape measure and reached for ammunition. The ground had been turned over and the clods were easy to find. Katie continued to blast her repeatedly, the whole time taunting Rainey.

119

"When's the last time you walked in a room and didn't scan for the exits?" Pow! A cloud of dust blew off Rainey's arm. "When's the last time someone did something for you and you didn't look for ulterior motives?" Smack! That one hit her in the head.

Rainey stood up and pegged Katie in the abdomen, moving to avoid the next onslaught, and saying, "A few hours ago in the kitchen, I think."

Puff! She got Katie in the butt. She wasn't throwing as hard as Katie. She didn't want to hurt her. Splat! A clod hit Rainey in the cheek.

"Damn, Katie that hurt."

Katie laughed. "Oh, did the little girl hurt the big ol' FBI Agent?"

Rainey dropped the clods and took off for Katie.

"Oh shit!" Katie exclaimed and ran away laughing.

Rainey caught her with no problem. She wrapped her arm around Katie's waist and pulled her down, cushioning Katie's fall with her own body. They were laughing so hard neither could speak. Every time they made eye contact, they laughed harder. They stayed there, Katie lying across Rainey's chest, until they caught their breaths and then lay still for a moment longer, listening to each other breathe.

They were startled into sitting position by Mackie's Escalade barreling toward them. He slammed on breaks and jumped out quickly, well as fast as a more than three hundred pound man can jump out. He shouted, "I thought you were dead!"

Katie looked at Rainey. "See, you are all paranoid as hell."

At that moment, Ernie came out of the office and shouted up the hill, "When y'all get through rolling around on the ground, somebody needs to go bail Derrick out of jail."

\#

Rainey looked at the young man handcuffed to the chair. Derrick thought about stealing Rainey's car last summer, but changed his mind when the cold steel of her nine-millimeter met his chin. She gave him her card, sure that he would need bailing out sooner or later. Since then, Derrick's mother called Rainey whenever he got into trouble, which seemed to be frequently. This time he was with a bunch of guys in a stolen vehicle. He swore he didn't know the car was hot, but there he was in handcuffs facing felony charges.

"Derrick, I think you need to find a better class of friends. You're just not a good criminal and I don't know how many more times your mom is going to be able to come up with the premiums on these bail bonds."

The lanky seventeen-year-old squirmed in the chair. "Rainey, I'm trying to stay out of trouble. I just keep being in the wrong place at the wrong time."

"Like I said, get some new friends. Now, how are you going to make this money to pay your mom back?"

"I don't know."

Rainey smiled. "I do. You're coming out to my house and digging a foundation. That ought to keep you out of trouble. You got a lawyer?"

"No."

"I'll give your mom a number. This is your last chance, Derrick. After this, we're done if you're going to continue to be a low life thug. This is your fork in the road, young man. Make the wise choice. Now, let's go over it one more time... If you don't show up to this court date..."

Derrick answered in rote singsong, "Then you'll come knockin'."

"And if I come knockin'..."

"I better not run."

"And if you run..."

"You won't knock next time."

"And if you give me any shit..."

"You'll shoot my ass."

Rainey smiled and patted Derrick on the shoulder. "Good, we understand each other. Wait here. I'll sign the papers and they'll release you to your mother. Sit tight and keep your mouth shut." Rainey started away.

Derrick stopped her. "Hey, Rainey."

She turned back around. What she saw was a scared kid, not a gangbanger. He had potential. She hoped he got out of "the life" before it killed him. "Yeah, Derrick?"

"Thanks, man. I'll do a good job on that foundation. Just send Junior after me. I'll do you right."

Rainey smiled. "I know you will."

#

Once Derrick was taken care of, Rainey took the opportunity to go over to the courthouse. The missing woman and the recent body discovery had her curious. She knew she could find out something from her old cop buddies. Rainey decided to leave her car and walk from the Durham County Detention Center to the Judicial Building. She left her weapon in the trunk of the car before she went in to see Derrick. She was not law enforcement anymore and was not allowed to carry a weapon on government property. The temperature outside had reached the low seventies and the sky was clear of clouds. Taking her jacket off, she slung it across her arm, and walked up South Mangum Street.

Crossing the railroad tracks that ran down the middle of Pettigrew Street, Rainey turned off the sidewalk between lawyers' row and the parking garage, emerging in front of the hub of law enforcement in Durham. The mirrored windows of the huge building reflected the bright sunlight, giving the structure a golden glow. The Judicial Building was a buzz of activity. In addition to the County Sheriff's offices, it housed Criminal District and Superior Courts, the District Attorney's offices, Family Court, the State Judiciary Court, Superior Court, and Judges' Chambers. It was humming with activity as usual. Rainey was glad she left her car at the Detention Center. She never would have found a parking place.

The female officer at the front desk buzzed her through the keycard lock. Rainey didn't need directions. She and Danny had been in and out of the Sheriff's department for weeks during the initial Y-Man investigation. The task force in that investigation included officers from all branches of law enforcement in the triangle area. They gave the profile together to a room full of officers, some of whom later saw her naked, staked out on a bed, with a Y-incision slashed across her torso. She had not interacted with them since and she had no way of knowing which officers saw her. She was too out of it to see or recognize faces the night Danny found her half-alive. When she pushed through the doors of the homicide division, Rainey instantly knew who had been there and who hadn't. Faces went slack and turned away, before turning back with a weak smile and wave. At least three of the men in this room and one woman had seen her that night.

Rainey crossed the room, heading straight for the woman she knew witnessed her torture chamber rescue. She knew because Detective Sheila Robertson stood sentry over her in the hospital, fiercely guarding Rainey's privacy from nosey officers who just wanted a peek at the nearly dead FBI agent. Detective Robertson took care of Danny too, making him eat and sleep, and promising to watch Rainey while he did. The sharply dressed African American woman was smiling openly as Rainey approached. Sheila extended her arms and wrapped Rainey in a hug, before pulling back and speaking.

"Rainey Bell. Lord girl, you're gorgeous. Retirement looks good on you."

"Sheila, it's so good to see you."

Sheila noticed Rainey look around the room. "Oh girl, don't let them staring bother you. You're still somewhat of a fascination around here. They've all read the files. They won't soon forget your name."

Rainey shook her head and laughed. "Sometimes I wish my name was Jane Jones, Rainey just sticks out."

"Honey, you're famous. You might as well get used to it. I for one am glad to have you around. Still available for a consult sometime?"

"Anything for you, Sheila."

"Follow me. I need to show you something." Sheila said.

Shelia headed for a conference room Rainey recognized as the one she and the team had used before. It would be two years in May since that night, when Rainey's life changed forever. She wondered what Sheila was about to show her.

"Does this have anything to do with the body you found yesterday?" Rainey asked, as they approached the door at the end of the hall.

Sheila pulled open the door to the room. "Yes, as a matter of fact, it does."

Rainey followed Sheila into the room. She froze after only a few steps.

Sheila continued talking. "We put the specifics in NCIC. I'm just waiting on the results. If he did something like this somewhere else, I'm sure it will pop up. I just want to get your take on..." Sheila stopped talking when she saw the look on Rainey's face.

Someone had taped photos on the wall, opposite the door. Rainey scanned the photos, starting at the far left. The first photo showed a large object wrapped in black plastic, with duct-taped remnants of hands the only part of the body showing. The next photos were of the woman laid out on the autopsy table. The black plastic was cut away, but still visible under the headless corpse. A long slice down her abdomen exposed what was left of her intestines. The decomposition was slowed by the coldness of the water and the plastic, but it was still very advanced. This woman had been dead for nearly a month. Her tissue was beginning to liquefy.

Rainey stared at the photos, taking a step closer. Her heart began to race. She had seen photos like this before, and it brought the memories rushing back. She looked at the hands still incased in duct tape.

When Rainey finally spoke, she said, "I'm assuming you did not find her head with the body."

"No, we found it in the plastic with her."

Rainey's eyes darted to the picture of the skull further down the wall and breathed a sigh of relief, but it was short lived.

"Did you find anything in her hands?" Rainey asked, all the while hoping the answer would be no.

Sheila answered, "Yes, we found a bible verse typed on computer paper. The plastic kept her dry, but the decomp made it hard to read. The lab is cleaning it up so we can be sure, but we think it's Deuteronomy 32:42. We put the words we could read in a bible search engine and that's what we got."

Rainey could not take her eyes away from the photos. She asked, "What does that verse say?"

Sheila dug around on the table, producing a sheet of paper. She read, "If I whet my glittering sword, and mine hand take hold on judgment; I will render vengeance to mine enemies, and will reward them that hate me."

Rainey looked away from the wall and focused on Sheila. She asked, "Nothing about virgins?"

"No," Sheila responded.

Rainey kept taking in the facts as fast as she could, weighing the information carefully. "Was there anything else on the paper, anything at all?"

"There were these smudged symbols. See." Sheila handed Rainey the paper. "The tech drew out what he thought it looked like. He's still processing it, trying to bring out the image more."

Rainey looked at what the tech had drawn out. "_שׁ_ח" A few of the symbols were missing, but she recognized it. "It says, Messiah, in Hebrew."

"You can tell from that what it says?"

"What about a cross? Did you find one with the body?"

"Yes, it's right here." Sheila lifted an evidence bag from the table and handed it to Rainey. "The asshole taped it to her chest. Guess without the head it wouldn't stay on the body."

Rainey looked at the cross. It was just a simple gold cross, mass marketed, with no way to trace it. It was impossible that someone recreated this much detail without intimate knowledge of the previous cases, especially the Messiah symbol. Only a handful of people knew about that and one of them was locked up forever in Virginia.

Sheila continued to talk while Rainey surveyed the photos again. "The M.E. said the victim was on her knees for some time, just before she died. There was evidence that she was bound, possibly to a tree. He found bark in her hair and abrasions to her back consistent with his theory. She was sexually assaulted with an instrument, no semen present. It's hard to tell from the pictures, but there was a lot of violence perpetrated on her. She had two cracked ribs. She was alive when she was decapitated by a long slender blade, possible a sword or machete. She saw it coming."

"Dammit!"

"What, Rainey? What do you see?"

"I see a copycat serial murderer. There've been no more bodies with similar injuries?"

Sheila looked surprised. "No, this is the only one."

"You haven't located them yet, or he's just getting started. Do you know who the victim is?" Rainey said, reaching for her cell phone.

"We're pretty sure it's Lisa Jones. We're waiting for the DNA results, but there was a tattoo on her shoulder. She designed it herself, so it's unique enough to use for an initial ID. The Doc could see it, even with the decomp. She went missing from Chapel Hill about a month ago."

Rainey dialed a number and held the receiver to her ear. She continued to pepper Sheila with questions. "The missing girl from Durham, are there any similarities between her and this victim?"

"I looked into that and yes, same personality and body type, and more importantly, they were both lesbians."

Rainey was shocked by this new information, but did not have time to react. A voice on the other end of the phone got her attention.

"Rainey Bell, how the hell are you?"

"I'm fine Danny, but we have a problem."

Danny changed to a more serious tone. He knew her well enough to recognize the anxiousness in her voice. "What's wrong?"

"I'm in the Durham County Sheriff's Office looking at autopsy photos. I think they have a serial killer and he's a copycat."

Danny seemed relieved it wasn't something to do with Rainey personally. The worry left his voice, replaced by his investigator tenor. "What makes you say that? Who's he copying?"

"I'm looking at praying hands duct taped together and they found a bible verse with Messiah in Hebrew drawn on it."

"Son of a bitch," Danny exclaimed.

There was no doubt in Rainey's mind who was involved. "You need to toss Dalton Chambers' cell. He's talking to someone."

Danny paused for a second. Rainey heard the hesitation in his voice when he finally spoke. "Uh, Rainey, they moved Chambers to Central Prison, in Raleigh, three months ago. They've decided to prosecute him for the kidnapping, in case something goes wrong in Virginia with his appeals. So far they've kept the move quiet. They are going to arraign him on the sixteenth. I was going to call you before the media broke the story."

"Fuck, Danny. You didn't think I needed to know a psychopath that promised to have someone kill me was in my backyard?"

"I'm sorry, Rainey. I should have told you. Look, I'll get to Raleigh as soon as I can. Should only take me a couple of hours. I'll call you if I find anything. Does Durham want to make my involvement official?"

Rainey looked at Sheila, who was staring back, open-mouthed. "Do you want this to be an official request for BAU help?"

The words shot out of Sheila's mouth so fast and loud, there was no question how she felt. "Hell yeah! Bring the cavalry if you have to. We're in deep shit here, if I hear you right."

Rainey returned to the phone. "Yes, make it official… and Danny, plan to come by the house when you're done at the prison. I think we need to talk."

CHAPTER EIGHT

Rainey stayed with Detective Robertson for an hour more, relaying what she knew about Dalton Chambers. Sheila was familiar with the news stories, but not the facts. There were differences in the murders, but only someone talking to Dalton would know so many details. Since there was no trial, the Messiah signature was never made public. The lesbian angle was a new twist, but Rainey hoped that had more to do with the new killer than Dalton's fantasy. He preferred virgins. This UNSUB obviously had a thing for lesbians. The fact that Rainey was in a relationship with a woman did not escape her attention. If it wasn't the UNSUB's preference, then the question was how much did Dalton know about her life now?

Rainey was barely present during the discussion with Sheila. Her thoughts were on not going into a panic. She could feel it beneath the surface and it frightened her. The panicked feeling was a new experience for Rainey. The closest she had ever come to the sensation was the drive to find Katie, after she was kidnapped. Not even during her own attack and recovery did she ever feel so out of control. Katie was the common denominator. Rainey wasn't with her, she wasn't sure Katie was safe. She had to leave. She had to find Katie, now!

She excused herself. "Sheila, I've told you all I know at this point. You need to wait and see what Danny comes up with in Chambers' cell. If he's communicating with someone locally, you should find out fairly soon. Until then, if he's really a copycat, you have a partial profile to work with. It should be enough to get your investigation rolling. I'm sure Danny will call you the minute he knows anything and the rest of his team should be here soon."

Sheila wrinkled her brow, questioning Rainey, "You don't want a piece of this? I can get you on as a consultant."

Rainey took a deep breath, trying to quell the growing anxiety threatening to overwhelm her. She exhaled slowly, and then said, "Right now, I have a much bigger problem to deal with."

Sheila tilted her head to one side, looking even more puzzled. When she spoke, the concern for Rainey showed in her voice. "You know this lesbian angle is not by chance. There are no coincidences. You taught me that. What could possibly be more important than finding the man that may have been sent by some maniac to kill you?"

Rainey started for the door, saying, "I have to go tell Katie that a piece of crap I put away is probably trying to have me killed. How do you say, hey babe, another serial killer is after me, how was your day?"

#

On the drive home, Rainey tried to think how she would tell Katie about this new development in their lives. Rainey resigned from the FBI last summer, telling Danny, "I know what I want to do with the rest of my life and chasing serial killers is not on the list. I'm going to spend my time being happy, with Katie." Rainey spent the last nine months doing just that, being happy. So blissful, in fact, that she began to think that maybe the life she led before would fade away someday. She knew now it would never be possible to forget. The lids on her mental boxes, where Rainey compartmentalized her life, began to fly open. Her worlds were crashing into one another. There would always be serial killers and sexual sadists coming out of the woodwork, some who knew her personally. As Katie said earlier, Rainey was paranoid, but it was for a good reason.

Rainey brought Katie into this world of constant threat. Now, she had to protect her. Rainey did what she could, teaching Katie how to use the weapons in the house, always reminding her to be vigilant and cautious, but none of that would stop a determined killer. If Dalton's minions were coming after Rainey, Katie was in real danger. Rainey really didn't want to tell Katie that part. It was hard enough keeping Katie from freaking out over the bail bonds business. They agreed that Rainey would call before she went to apprehend a particularly dangerous skip, and then call Katie back when the capture had been completed. It was the least she could do to keep Katie from worrying every minute. It minimized the amount of time Katie thought Rainey's life was in danger. With the turn of events today, that was a luxury Rainey could no longer grant. They were both possible targets of a serial killer, again.

Rainey thought about sending Katie away, somewhere safe. Maybe Katie and her mom should go to Europe for a while. At least, until Danny caught this latest UNSUB. The lid on the box where she kept the foreboding thoughts slid off. Those thoughts were the voices in her head that told her she should never have brought Katie into this sphere of twisted killers. She slammed her hands on the steering wheel in an uncharacteristic loss of control.

"Fuck!"

Out of the box flooded the feelings she ignored, the warnings she dismissed. In the beginning, Rainey's instincts told her dragging Katie into this life was a mistake. Ernie knew what kind of business they were in and exactly what kind of people might be coming after Rainey. Mackie chose the life long ago. Katie had only discovered the enormous stresses of being in a relationship with someone like Rainey after she fell in love. It had been Rainey's responsibility to tell Katie what she was really getting into. She had, up to a point, but she was also afraid to tell Katie too much. Rainey selfishly had not wanted to lose Katie, so she held a substantial amount of information back, stuffing those feelings in the little mental box, and putting it away. She told herself that she could keep Katie safe. Rainey didn't know if that was really possible anymore.

Rainey was happy to find Katie's car in the driveway. She said she was going to clean out the closet in the master bedroom today, but Katie went off on little sudden trips all the time. She always told Rainey or Ernie where she was going, but sometimes she just had to get out of the house. Rainey thought it was because they were so isolated out in the woods and a social butterfly like Katie needed to talk to people. Rainey encouraged Katie's continued work with her literacy centers, but insisted that the centers hire security. The thought of Katie in that rundown strip mall in Durham made Rainey cringe. Katie only went two nights a week now, usually when Rainey had to work, and some Saturdays. Katie seemed content to live out on the lake, away from the hustle of the city, but a woman with that much energy had to focus it somewhere. Today, the closet was her planned project.

Rainey opened the front door of the cottage, happy to have found it locked. She punched in the alarm code to quell the incessant beeping. She was surprised to find the room empty. Katie was usually right there to greet her when she came home. She shut the door, locked it, and re-armed the alarm. She hung her jacket, took off her holster, and opened the gun safe. In the act of putting the gun away, her systems went on high alert. Rainey's instincts were telling her something wasn't right. Katie should have appeared by now. Maybe she was in the closet and didn't hear Rainey come in. Maybe she was under a pile of boxes and couldn't get up. Rainey told her not to move the heavy boxes from the top shelf, for two reasons. The boxes were too heavy for Katie to move, and she didn't want Katie to see what was in them.

She stood there with the gun safe open, her hand on the Glock still inside the holster, observing her environment. She could not smell supper cooking, which was always the first thing Rainey noticed when she walked in the house. It was eerily quiet, the hum of the refrigerator motor the only sound she could make out. She carefully pulled the Velcro retaining strap open. In the quiet, the ripping sound was excruciatingly loud. She took the gun, leaving the holster in the safe and shut the door. Glock in hand she peeked into the kitchen. No Katie. She checked the back door. It was locked. She surveyed the rear deck through the glass in the door.

Rainey wasn't in a panic, yet, but the beating of her heart was beginning to pick up the pace. She told herself Katie was fine, just distracted, anything but that something was wrong. Rainey knew she was overly cautious, and yes even a bit paranoid, but she had good reason to be before today. After what she found out in Durham a few hours ago, her paranoia triggered a survival instinct she listened to very attentively. Rainey chose to look at how she lived her life as not so much in a perpetual state of fear, but more a constant vigil of readiness. Her guard had been down once. That sure as hell wasn't going to happen again.

She crossed the main room, hugging the wall to her back. At the corner, where the wall met the hallway to the master bedroom, Rainey could see into the home office. The computer monitor was dark, gone to sleep from at least an hour of inactivity. Peeking around the corner, she could see the bedroom door was half open. If she called out Katie's name, she would give away her position. She saw no movement and heard only the sound of her own heartbeat, picking up its pace. Slipping around the corner, Rainey kept her eyes on the crack between the doorframe and the hinged edge of the door. She was about to enter the bedroom when she heard something inside the walk-in closet, the entrance of which was obscured behind the half open door. The next sound turned her blood to ice.

"Hello, Agent Bell, so nice of you to join us." The Virginia accent was unmistakable.

Chill bumps erupted over Rainey's entire body. She took a step closer to the opening, then froze again as the voice continued. "I told this pretty blond lady here that it was you that I really wanted to talk to. She's really nice to spend time with, but then she's not you, is she? I've waited so long for this. Come on in and sit a spell. We have a lot of catching up to do."

Rainey took a deep breath, let it out slowly, clasped her pistol in front of her, and crashed into the door. The bedroom door and the closet door smashed together. In the briefest of seconds, Rainey saw Katie sitting in the closet floor, pictures and notebooks scattered around her, and then the door slammed shut. The next voice she heard stopped her in her tracks.

"Hello Dalton. You asked to see me and now I'm here. What is it you want to talk about?"

It was Rainey's own voice. Katie was listening to the tape of her first interview with Dalton. Rainey stored the tape in one of the boxes she had asked Katie to leave on the top shelf. Apparently, Katie did not listen.

"Rainey, what the hell?" Katie's voice cried out from inside the closet.

The rush of adrenaline crashed into Rainey's heart with the full force of the fear she had held at bay. The fear turned to anger instantly. She snatched the closet door open so forcefully it banged into the other door and slammed shut again. She snatched it back open, this time holding on to it, and shouted, "What the fuck, Katie! I thought that asshole was in here. What the hell are you doing?"

The tape continued to play in the background. Dalton's sickly sweet drawl echoed on the walls of the closet. "Well, Rainey, may I call you Rainey, what an unusual name. Your parents were hippie freaks, I guess. Bet your momma was pretty. Bet you look like your momma, all tall and dark with those green eyes…"

Rainey took two long steps into the closet and hit the stop button on the old cassette recorder. Katie must have also found it in the boxes. Rainey still had the Glock in her right hand.

"Oh my God, you scared the shit out of me," Katie said.

"I could say the same about you. I repeat; what in the hell are you doing?" Rainey's anger boiled just below the surface. She pointed at the crime scene photos and notebooks opened on the floor around Katie.

Rainey kept a Murder Book for each of the cases she investigated or researched. When she left the BAU she brought some of them home with her, the rest she gave to Danny. They contained the detailed elements of each crime, copies of reports and photographs, among Rainey's personal notes. Dalton Chambers had been one of the cases she felt the need to hang onto. Along with Dalton's Murder Book, Rainey had placed accounts of other unimaginable deeds in the boxes and stored them in the top of the closet. People turn away from the screen when they show crime scenes on TV shows. They would never come out of their houses again, if they saw some of what was in the boxes Katie had emptied onto the closet floor.

Katie began closing notebooks and putting them back in the boxes. "I'm sorry, Rainey. I tried to get one of the boxes down and I dropped it. Once I saw what was in them, I couldn't stop myself." She paused and looked up at Rainey. "Oh God, what time is it? I can't believe I've been in here this long. You must be starving." She started throwing things back in the boxes faster.

"Leave it," Rainey said, sternly.

Katie stood up. "Are you mad because I didn't listen to you or because I scared you?"

Rainey tried, but did not succeed, to control her anger. She glared at Katie. "You need to listen to me when I tell you that you don't need to know everything I've seen and done."

"Rainey, I... I had no idea..."

"That's kind of the point. You don't have any idea. You and most of the world have no clue what's out there. I believe that's a good thing, don't you? There are all kinds of reasons you shouldn't be looking at these files, but the most important one is, because I asked you not to."

Katie's hands shot to her hips. "Oh, come on. You told me the boxes were too heavy for me, not to leave them alone because they had your life secrets in them. I had no choice but to try, just to prove I'm not some shrinking violet. All this stuff poured out when I lost my balance on the stepladder. At least, the first one happened that way."

"So, if I specifically said leave the boxes alone, because I don't want you to know what's in them, would you have done as I asked?"

"Of course I would," Katie said defensively. "I respect your privacy. You said nothing about privacy and don't use that tone with me."

The walls in the closet begin to close in on Rainey. She closed her eyes against the pictures of bloody crime scenes scattered on the floor. With the sound of that maniac's voice still ringing in her ears, she could almost smell him. Rainey turned and walked out of the closet. She crossed to Katie's big reading chair, by the window. She sat down and took the clip out of her gun, cleared the chamber and placed it on the table by the chair. She put her elbows on her knees and dropped her face into her hands, the rush now leaving her body weak with its ebbing. Katie followed her out and sat on the ottoman in front of her.

Katie tried to lighten the mood. "How ironic. We just came out of the closet together, again."

Rainey laughed despite her desire to remain angry with Katie. She looked up to see Katie's big blue eyes inches from her face. Katie was smiling at her, but her brow was knitted with worry. She reached out and touched Rainey's knee.

"Honey, I'm sorry. But honestly, I'm glad I did it. I found out something about you that I needed to know."

Rainey sat back. Still not completely able to lose the anger in her tone, she said, "Yeah, and what was that?"

"I read your writings. Your depth of understanding is... well, simply over my head. How you did what you did is beyond me. I listened to those tapes and I heard a completely different person in that room. Your voice was so detached from emotion. If I didn't already know you, I would have described that person as unfeeling and cold."

"I did what I had to do to survive being exposed to sadistic criminals like that. The colder I was the harder they tried to shock me. They told me their sickest secrets trying to break that ice. Sitting for hours listening to them drone on about their inhuman behaviors takes a level of dispassion few can achieve. The ability to understand the incomprehensible, that's what my specialty required, and I was damn good at it. You're trying to reconcile the person you love with a person who could sit there unfazed by a sociopath."

"That's not it at all," Katie interjected.

Rainey didn't let her explain. She launched into, "It's me Katie, that's who I am, but what you don't hear is me throwing up afterwards. You weren't there in the early years when I struggled until I could be that detached, until I could turn it off at night when I came home, until I could focus all my energy on locating and locking them up without paying a toll for each one. That's what my training required of me. That's what my humanity demanded of me."

Katie tried again to speak, "I know…"

"No, you don't know. You have no point of reference for me to explain the depravity I've witnessed. I put those things in a box and put them away. I'd like to put the memories away too, but Katie there are just some things you can't un-see. So sometimes I come off cold and unfeeling. I can be cautious, suspicious, even a bit paranoid, do you blame me?"

Katie didn't say anything. She just shook her head from side to side. She seemed to comprehend Rainey just needed to talk, without interruption.

"Katie, I'm not going to be the happy go lucky, throw caution to the wind kind of person you are. Falling in love with you is the only unplanned, spontaneous thing I've done since I was a teenager and didn't know any better. I've been reckless with you and it's been good for me. You make me think all things are possible. I may balk, seem initially too cautious, but I work through my reservations most of the time. I took a chance with you and that is so not in character with the person I grew up to be. You remind me of being young and innocent. I'd like to hang on to that feeling. I'm giving you everything I can... but there is probably always going to be a part of me you can't have access to. I'm respectfully asking you to leave it alone."

Katie leaned into Rainey, placing both hands on her knees. "What I wanted to say is that I read your notes, I listened to your voice, I saw some of what you've seen. That's enough for me. I thought I knew everything, because of what I went through last summer, but I didn't. You're right. I couldn't possibly grasp the depth of horror you've seen. I appreciate where your fears and doubts come from. I understand now, Rainey."

"Do you believe me when I say I'm not holding anything back from you that is yours to have? Do you understand how hard it was for me to let you in, to love you?" Rainey's voice shook and she wished it wouldn't. "I know life can be completely changed in an instant. I didn't want to care about you, because I didn't think I could take another loss in my life. But I confronted that fear and I'm dealing with it every day. If I ask you to lock the door, be aware of your surroundings, don't park your car in certain places, it is not because I think there's a serial killer around every corner. I'm not paranoid or uptight, Katie. I just can't bear the thought of anything happening to you."

Katie climbed up into Rainey's lap and wrapped her arms around her neck. She looked deep into Rainey's eyes and said,

"I will never doubt your instincts again. I will not call your paranoia or wariness silly. I will respect your knowledge of things I don't need to know or want to understand. I will be patient when you are cautious, but I reserve the right to plead my case. Is that workable for you?"

Rainey leaned in to Katie's lips, because she could no longer resist. She cupped the back of Katie's head in her hand and pulled her tight against her.

Katie broke free and breathed whispered words against Rainey's lips, "I'll take that as a yes."

Rainey smiled. She kissed Katie and then hugged her close, saying softly into her ear, "I love you, ya' know."

"Yeah, I know."

Now that Rainey's anger had ebbed, she knew she had to tell Katie about Dalton's copycat lurking out there somewhere. Maybe it was good that Katie had seen the Murder Book on Chambers. It would help Rainey get across the seriousness of the threat. Just as she started to broach the subject, Rainey's cell phone rang.

Katie stood up, so Rainey could remove her phone from her pocket. She looked at the screen. She couldn't ignore it. It was Ernie. Rainey flipped the phone open. Before she could speak, Ernie began talking.

"Rainey, Mackie needs you. He wants you to meet him in an hour. Chauncey is about to bolt. Mackie set it up where Chauncey thinks he's coming to pick up some money, so he can disappear. If everything goes as planned, we're off the hook for two hundred grand failed appearance. You know if you don't stop this guy, you'll damn near bankrupt this place."

Rainey answered, "Now, Ernie, do you really think I would bail out a felon without keeping an eye on him? One of his homeboys has been on the phone with Junior, twenty-four-seven. That's how we knew he was going to run. Probable

141

cause, we're revoking his bail. My prerogative. All I have to do is deliver him into custody."

"Don't get cocky, Rainey," Ernie scolded. "Will you have back up?"

Rainey didn't mind Ernie's scolding. Ernie knew this business, she knew these criminals, and she loved Rainey. Her thoughts were always on Rainey and Mackie's safety.

"Mackie was going to arrange for some of the fugitive squad to go in ahead of us. Chauncey's armed. I know that. The police know that, too, so if he flinches he's probably a dead man. I hope he just comes out peacefully."

Ernie responded, "From your mouth to God's ears. I'm going back to work now, in case the great detective loses her man. Somebody has to pay the bills."

Rainey thought about Katie, home alone. She said, into the receiver, "Ernie, I need you to come to the cottage. I'll explain when you get here... and bring your gun."

Rainey hung up. She said, to Katie, "I have to go meet Mackie. We're taking Chauncey Barber into custody."

"Why does Ernie need to come over here? You're not taking her with you are you?"

Rainey dropped her eyes to the floor. "No, that's not the reason." She glanced up at Katie's puzzled expression. She had no choice, but to tell her the truth of their circumstances. "Katie, I'm so sorry to have to say this. You have no idea how I wish it wasn't true."

Katie began to look more worried than puzzled. "What is it, Rainey? What's happened?"

Rainey pointed at the ottoman in front of her. "Please, sit down."

Katie was frightened, now. Rainey could see it in her eyes. She sat down, without saying a word.

"Katie, after I bailed out Derrick, I went to see Sheila Robertson in the Durham Sheriff's office. While I was there, she asked me to review her latest case. I did, and I recognized the signature. I called Danny, he's on his way."

"What does that have to do with you or me? Why does Ernie need to come over here with her gun?"

"That tape you were listening to when I came in, did you listen to anymore of that particular killer?"

Katie thought about it, and then answered, "Yes, one more. I got them out of order, so I listened to the second one first. I'd just started the first one when you came in."

"So, you didn't hear my last interview with him?"

"No," Katie answered. "Why?"

"That was Dalton Chambers. I saw the pictures on the floor, so you know what he did to his victims."

Katie shuddered. "Yes, he was really sick."

"Katie," Rainey paused, looking for the right words. "The last time I saw him he threatened to kill me."

"So, he's in prison in Virginia, isn't he?" Katie asked, innocently.

"Not anymore, he's in Central Prison in Raleigh. They're going to prosecute him here."

Katie relaxed. "Lord, I thought you were going to say he escaped."

"It's not that simple. Dalton promised to have one of his "fans" hunt me down. He knows where I live. The case I saw today is a copycat of Dalton's murders. Dalton has a connection here in the triangle and I'm afraid he's coming for me."

The color drained from Katie's face. She gasped, "Oh, my God."

Rainey leaned forward and took both of Katie's hands in hers. "Honey, you are in danger, too. He'll lash out at the people I love, if he can't get to me… and he's killing lesbians. That's another reason you aren't safe."

Katie was speechless. The terror in her eyes spoke volumes. Rainey had been so wrong to bring this fear back into Katie's life. She knew all along that this was a possibility, and yet, she let Katie walk into this without all the facts.

"Katie, I'm sorry. I should have been honest with you about the risks you were taking being with me. I'm so sorry."

Katie said nothing. She appeared to be too scared to speak. Rainey tried to reassure her.

"Danny is on his way to Dalton's cell. He'll tear it apart until he finds out who Dalton has been talking to. The BAU is sending a team. They will catch this guy."

Katie finally spoke, "Are you going to help them?"

"No, my priority is you and keeping all of us safe. I'm not in the FBI anymore. They can handle this without me. I just need to keep us alive until they arrest him."

Katie began to cry, softly. Rainey, who could investigate horrific crime scenes, stare down a serial killer, and pull the trigger on a criminal without blinking, could not handle seeing Katie cry. Her heart was breaking when she pulled Katie off the ottoman and into her lap. She held Katie close and whispered in her ear.

"I'm so sorry. You don't deserve to have to go through this again."

Katie sniffled, and then said, "I'm not worried about me. I can't lose you."

Rainey felt the tears welling in her eyes. Her voice cracked, when she said, "I can't lose you either."

The knock on the front door, followed by a "Yoohoo," startled both of them. The alarm beeped a warning, and was quickly silenced. Ernie had let herself in.

Katie stood up and wiped the tears from her eyes, calling out, "We're back here. Be there in a sec." She looked down at Rainey. "Promise me, you'll be careful when you take this guy down and then hurry home, okay."

Rainey's voice cracked again. "Okay."

Rainey stood up. Katie hugged her, saying, "I love you too much, Rainey Bell."

Rainey brushed her lips on Katie's, whispering back, "No, you love me just enough."

CHAPTER NINE

Chauncey Barber, whose bail Rainey was about to revoke, was a suspect in some gang related shootings, but he was on bond for charges relating to criminal enterprise. Rainey didn't really care. She just wanted him locked up. She knew he'd run when she bailed him out. That's why she paid someone to watch him. If she revoked, more than likely no one else would pick up the bond, and the judge might raise the amount anyway. Either way, Chauncey would be out of Rainey's hair, back in jail, and she had his non-refundable premium of $20,000.

Chauncey was a former basketball star at a local high school that couldn't shake the gang life. He already spent several years in prison for armed robbery. He was six-feet-five-inches tall and used his time inside the walls of Central State Prison to become tattooed and thickly muscled. He was known to have a quick temper and an even swifter trigger finger. He was armed, according to her informant. There were also several guns in the house they were going to raid. She was very happy the fugitive squad was willing to lend a hand on this one. Chauncey had, like so many before him, sworn he was not going back to prison.

Rainey concentrated on putting her emotions back in their proper boxes, while she sped to Mackie's side. She left Katie to explain to Ernie what was happening. Rainey never had anyone worry about her the way Katie did. It was an awesome responsibility to take someone's hopes and dreams with you when you went out to do the job. Her dad had worried, but she never thought of his concerns as she did Katie's. This thinking was a distraction and she needed to be focused on the task at hand, bust this guy, and get back home as quickly as possible, without getting dead in the process. By the time she reached the scene, she was back in control.

True to her word, Rainey took all precautions. Four blocks away from the target house, she stood at the back of the Charger gearing up. Her Sarkar IV, bulletproof vest came with removable attachments. She rarely wore the extra protection, but considering the amount of firepower that was going into this situation, she feared being shot in the crossfire more than she feared Chauncey. She added the upper arm and throat pieces, along with the collar. She even put on her helmet, which she never wore. Mackie helped her get the collar to stay on right. He wore his normal vest, but he made Junior wear the collar on his, and borrowed a helmet for him from the fugitive apprehension team.

In order to make this work, Rainey had to take custody of Chauncey. The police could go in first, if he broke a law, but could not enter the house without a warrant. He had not violated his bond, yet. Rainey needed to get him to come out the door voluntarily. The plan was for Junior and Mackie to go around back with two guys from the fugitive team, while Rainey knocked on the front door. She would have four officers with her. The police presence could convince Chauncey to surrender peacefully, or send him over the edge into the "going out in a blaze of glory" mentality. Rainey hoped everything went easy. She sure didn't want to shoot the guy.

Junior's cell rang. He answered it, listened for a few seconds, and then said, "All right, we're comin' in." He hung up and looked at Rainey. "Chauncey's getting' antsy. He don't want to wait. Says the boys can bring him the money later. Bobo says he's messed up on somethin'. There's three people in the house. Bobo says don't fuck up and shoot him, he's wearin' a NC State hoodie."

"Okay, I guess we better go. He'll be in the wind if we don't." Rainey pointed at Junior. "Let the other guys know Bobo's a good guy and what he's wearing."

When they were alone, Mackie got Rainey's attention. "You don't have to do this. Let me go in the front."

Rainey had not told Mackie about the copycat, yet. She wanted him focused on the task at hand.

"No, he'll probably run out the back. I doubt he'll come at me with four cops on my hip. Let's just try and talk him out of there."

"It's your call, but if he flinches…"

Rainey nodded. "Chill out, big guy. I've been face to face with worse than Chauncey Barber."

"Don't get cocky," Mackie warned.

"You're the second person to tell me that in the last hour."

Mackie stared down at her. "Then, I guess you better heed the warning."

Three minutes later, Rainey stood at the end of the walkway leading up to the little white house. The place belonged to Chauncey's grandmother, who was at Bingo for the moment. On either side of Rainey, two officers with rifles, trained on the front of the house, kept pace with her as she walked up to the porch. She stopped on the top step, watching for signs of movement. Her pistol was drawn and secured with both hands. She listened for a moment before moving closer to the door. She could hear male voices coming from the front room on her right. She moved to the left of the door and waited for the four officers to take positions.

"Chauncey!" Rainey yelled. "Chauncey come on out. It's Rainey Bell... I got to take you in ... Back on out this door with your hands in the air... You hear me Chauncey?"

There was movement behind the door. A scared voice said, "Hey man, don't shoot my ass. I'm comin' out. I ain't Chauncey, but I don't want to get my ass shot. You feelin' me?"

"Yeah, I feel ya'," Rainey yelled back. "Open that door nice and slow. Back out with your hands clasped behind your head. You flinch and four of Raleigh's finest are going to light you up. You got it?"

"Okay man, here I come."

One of the cops grabbed the storm door and held it open. The wooden door creaked open slowly, revealing Bobo in his red hoodie. He backed out and went to his knees on the porch, hands quickly placed on the back of his head. The wooden door slammed shut again.

Bobo looked up at Rainey. "Man, he's nuts. Y'all better call some more cops. He ain't coming out of there."

One of the cops patted Bobo down and then told him to get across the street. Rainey looked at the four men holding rifles on the front of the house. Each man nodded it was time to make a move.

"Chauncey, don't make me have to shoot you," she tried one more time. "Come on out and we'll go straighten this out at the courthouse. You could be back on the street by suppertime."

"Fuck you! You come in that door, bitch, and I'm going to blow you up," Chauncey shouted from behind the door.

"Is that a threat, Chauncey? You packin'? You know that's a violation of your bail. Now the cops can come on in. Are you sure that's what you want?"

Rainey moved as she talked. She slid down by the door handle, with the wall protecting her back. She signaled the cop to her right, who in turn said into his headset, "Go, go, go."

They heard the back door splinter, as Mackie and the others gained access rather rapidly. Rainey turned the handle on the door and the four cops entered one behind the other. By the time Rainey made it into the house, Chauncey was face down in the floor. He had been too drugged up to take the safety off his gun.

Rainey was standing in the hallway, holstering her weapon, when Junior said, "Where's the third guy?"

She heard the distinct click-click of a revolver being cocked behind her. She looked up at the top of the small staircase to see a young boy, probably thirteen or fourteen, with the barrel of a gun pointed squarely at her.

"Chauncey, who's this young man with the weapon aimed at me?" Rainey said, as calmly as she could muster.

"That's my sister's boy. Don't shoot him."

"I'm more worried about him shooting me at the moment, and you know these guys are going to blow him away after that, right?"

"Darnell, put that gun down fool," Chauncey said. The cuffs seemed to have cleared his mind some.

Darnell was trembling, the gun barrel wavering in the air. He looked like a child with a toy, but the voice that spoke was not childlike. "I'm going to pop this bitch. I'll make my bones and be out in seven years."

One of the cops peeked around the corner at Darnell and Rainey. He tried to reason with the kid. "Son, that 'bitch' is a former FBI agent. You don't know the world of hurt that's going to come down if I let you shoot her, so I'm not going to let you do that. You'll be dead before you can pull the trigger. Now drop the weapon and no harm done."

"Shit, I'll be famous if I pop a FBI bitch and if you shoot me I'll be a legend."

"Then dead it is," the cop said.

Rainey saw the grin creep across Darnell's face. She saw his finger twitch and knew she was about to be shot. It all happened so fast. In one move the cop stepped in front of Rainey, as she dove for the floor. He fired his weapon at the boy. The bullet from his gun crashed into Darnell's leg milliseconds before the bullet from his revolver smashed into Rainey's right shoulder. The force of the bullet rolled her. She lay there taking stock of her condition. Her shoulder hurt like hell, but when she looked she could clearly see the end of the bullet sticking out of the ballistic material on the shoulder pad she had added.

"Thank God for small miracles," she said under her breath.

Darnell was in a pile at the top of the stairs. He dropped his gun and was now screaming like the kid he was. The cop stood over him.

"Shut up. You'll live a long and happy life in prison. Maybe your uncle there will teach you the ropes when you get to the big house."

Mackie was suddenly standing over Rainey. "You all right?"

"Yeah, the shoulder pad caught it. Gonna bruise like hell. What the fuck? I thought one of those guys was supposed to clear the upstairs."

"That young one was supposed to, but I think he got excited," Mackie said, nodding toward the young cop being chewed out by an older one.

Rainey could hear the sirens coming. "Shit. Katie."

Mackie looked confused. "What about Katie?"

"You know this hit the scanner. The news trucks will be here in a minute. I have to call her, before she sees this."

Mackie helped her to her feet. She walked out onto the porch and dialed home. Katie picked up on the first ring.

Rainey spoke quickly, "It's over. Everything's all right."

"Then, why do I here sirens in the background?" Katie asked.

"Cause the guy's nephew decided to shoot at me and one of the cops shot him." No sense in lying, she would see the news.

Katie's voice was strained with worry. "Are you okay? Did he hit you?"

"Just a graze on the shoulder. It hit the vest, so no harm done. I wanted you to know I'm okay, in case the news trucks show up. You good?"

"Rainey, can we seriously talk about you getting shot at all the time? I mean is this normal?"

"Honey, we'll talk when I get home, okay? I love you. I have to go."

"Okay, but we're going to talk about this."

"I gotta go, Katie. Bye."

Rainey didn't want to talk about it now. She wanted to get this asshole booked, along with his wanna-be gang banging nephew, and get home. Her boxes were coming open, and her walls were crashing in.

\#

Paperwork and interviews with the police about the incident took up the whole afternoon. When she wasn't dealing with the police, she explained to Mackie who Dalton was and how his copycat might be after her. Mackie did not appear surprised; in fact, it seemed he had been expecting it.

"Baby girl," he said, his big bass voice rumbling in the narrow hallway, "We knew this day could come. You got a plan?"

"I had a plan, but that went out the window when I met Katie."

"Sounds like your plan was, "bring it on, let the assholes come," but now that you have Katie, your life means more to you."

Rainey's father had been killed just weeks before the attack that nearly killed her. From that moment until she met Katie, Rainey was prepared to challenge all comers. She didn't care if someone from her past came looking for her. If she survived the next attempt on her life, great, if she didn't, then so be it. That type of thinking did not jive with the added responsibility, for not only Katie's life, but also their lives together.

"Mackie, I've never been accountable for someone else's hopes and dreams. It's overwhelming sometimes. I'm afraid I can't protect us both."

Mackie lowered his voice. "You'll be surprised at what you can do when you love someone. Loving someone gives you strength. Your daddy didn't survive the jungle because he was some badass. Nobody was going to kill him, because he had to get back to his baby girl."

"Dad was never afraid of anything."

"Not true. He just channeled his fear into action. As smart as you are, you should know that fear can do two things. It can paralyze you, or it can be a powerful motivator."

"Everything is happening so fast. I can't think."

"Let your instincts kick in. It's like when you are in an accident, how everything slows down. You see it all happening in slow motion."

Rainey nodded in agreement and added, "That's your brain shutting down all the processes it doesn't need to survive the threat."

"Then clear your mind. Let your training take over. The only thing you need to be thinking about is how to catch this fucker, before he makes his move."

"I'll have a better idea what I'm dealing with after I talk to Danny."

Mackie was making his own plans. He said, "I'll look after Ernie and the business. Use your training. Profile him and send Danny after his ass." He put his bear paw size hands on her shoulders. "You call me, I come running. You don't go nowhere alone. Day or night, you call me. You got that?"

"Yeah, I got that." Rainey could barely reach around Mackie's giant shoulders when she hugged him. She whispered, "You stay safe."

Mackie squeezed her tightly. "You too, baby girl."

"Always."

#

Three and a half hours after being shot, Rainey pulled the Charger under the cottage. She checked her shoulder in the bathroom just before she left the police station. It was already deep shades of purple and black. The throbbing heat from the bruise was becoming distracting. When she got out of her car,

Rainey saw a black SUV, typical of the BAU team, coming down the road toward her. Damn, she still had to meet with Danny. All Rainey wanted was an ice pack and some Ibuprofen. She certainly was in no mood to deal with Dalton's copycat, or Katie's reaction to her being shot. She sighed loudly, knowing the chances of avoiding either one of those things was slim.

Katie was standing on the deck, looking down at Rainey when she emerged from under the cottage. Rainey smiled for the first time in hours.

"That's Danny coming now," Rainey called up to Katie, as she began to climb the stairs. "I'm sorry, I forgot to tell you he was coming."

Katie rushed Rainey when she reached the deck. She wrapped her arms around Rainey and hugged her tightly, too tightly. Rainey wriggled loose.

"Ouch!" She exclaimed, and rubbed her bruised shoulder.

Katie stepped back. "Oh, I'm sorry. Are you hurt? You said you weren't hurt."

"Calm down. It's just a bruise," Rainey said a little sharply, still smarting from the pain.

Katie tilted her head and looked at Rainey. "I'm going to assume that tone is because you are hurt and hungry. Have you eaten?"

Rainey felt stupid. Near-death experiences tended to make her short tempered and cranky. Katie didn't deserve the attitude. "I'm sorry. I am hungry and I want to change my clothes."

"Ernie's still here. Just walk through, be nice, and I'll explain that Danny's coming and you need to change. I'll even make you a sandwich, okay?"

"Come here," Rainey said. Making sure her arm was on the outside this time, she hugged Katie and kissed her. "Thank you. That would be fantastic."

Rainey followed Katie into the house. She detoured into the kitchen long enough to grab an ice pack from the freezer. Ernie tried to question Rainey. Katie interceded, which she greatly appreciated.

"Rainey wants to put on a clean shirt and Danny is on his way in."

"I love you, Ernie, but I know you have a thousand questions, and I just can't answer them right now," Rainey added.

Ernie looked at Rainey with concern, but she didn't push the issue. She said, "I'm going to go on home, now." Then uncharacteristic of their usual teasing banter, she added, "I love you, Rainey. Be safe."

"Watch your back, Ernie. I love you, too." Rainey bowed out and went to the master bedroom.

She pulled off the black turtleneck she was wearing, careful of her bruised shoulder, and tossed it into the hamper. She looked in the mirror at the swelling contusion and winced. The bullet may not have pierced the skin, but an object in motion stays in motion until acted upon by an unbalanced force. A thirty-eight caliber bullet could travel anywhere between six hundred and ninety to upwards of eleven hundred feet per second, depending on the load. The law of inertia was clearly visible on Rainey's skin. She reached down to pick up the icepack from the bathroom sink just as Katie appeared in the doorway. Katie saw the bruise and reacted.

"Jesus Rainey, that wasn't a graze was it? He shot you."

Rainey covered the bruise with the ice pack, flinching when the frosty plastic hit her tender skin. "It hit my vest. No harm done."

Katie turned pale and looked sick. She backed up and sat down on the trunk at the end of the bed. Rainey followed her into the bedroom. She knelt down in front of Katie, still holding the ice to her shoulder.

"Hey, it's okay, really. It's not as bad as it looks."

"Three inches higher and I'd be picking out your funeral clothes," Katie snapped. She looked into Rainey's eyes and said, "I can't live like this."

The statement hit Rainey hard. She stood up and took a step back. After a moment, she went back to the bathroom. Katie remained silent. Rainey taped the icepack to her upper arm with athletic tape, splashed water on her face, and then stared in the mirror as she dried her skin. "Fuck it," she said, to no one. She walked into the bedroom where Katie sat, still stunned. Finding a sweatshirt in the drawer of the dresser, Rainey eased it on, careful with her shoulder. She turned to Katie finally.

"Katie, now is not the time to have this conversation. Danny is here and I have to talk to him. So, if you think you can live with it just a little bit longer, I'll be available to have this discussion in about an hour." The sarcasm was intentional.

"Rainey, I didn't…"

"Save it. You said what you meant."

Katie protested, "Hey, wait a minute."

"No, you wait a minute. I've bent over backwards to insulate you from what I do for a living. This has nothing to do with my FBI career. You can hold me responsible for not telling you someone from my past might come after me, but you knew this was my job. I don't know what else I can do about that." Frustrated, Rainey stormed out of the bedroom and went to the living room to fix a drink.

By the time Rainey walked in the room, where Danny and Ernie were waiting, she was mad as hell. Ernie took one look at Rainey and did not say a word, just picked up her purse, told Danny goodbye, and exited the cottage. Rainey poured a drink without speaking to Danny. She hadn't been this angry in a very long time. The waves of fury just kept coming. A voice in her head said this was more than an argument with Katie. This rage was coming from everything that happened today and long before. She walked by Danny, going into the kitchen, disarmed the alarm on the backdoor, and stepped out onto the deck. She slammed her fist on the deck railing.

"Fuck! Fuck! Fuck!"

A light tap on the door alerted her to Danny's presence. She turned to see him in the doorway.

"May I come out there or would you rather continue to abuse the woodwork a bit longer?"

Rainey glared at him, unspeaking.

"Let me see, either you're mad cause you got into a fight with Katie or you're mad cause you almost got killed. Which is it?"

Rainey was off on a much-needed rant. She didn't have them often. In fact, she once heard herself referred to, by a fellow agent, as having ice water in her veins. She remained tight vested with most of her feelings, but on rare occasions she would vent. When she finally blew up, Danny was often the sounding board. He was probably expecting it.

Rainey turned and shouted at Danny. "I am pissed that I didn't climb those stairs and strangle the shit out of that kid for almost shooting me in the head. I could kill that fucking cop that didn't do his goddamn job and got me shot. I am livid that I let that happen, because I wasn't focused enough to do my job. And most of all, I am really fucking pissed that you didn't tell me about Dalton Chambers being moved to within twenty miles of me. Jesus Christ, Danny, what were you thinking?"

Danny remained silent. He sensed she wasn't finished.

Rainey paused, took a deep breath, and then continued with less venom and volume. "I terrified Katie, not once, but twice today. Once, by telling her that a serial killer is again threatening our lives and then nearly dying shortly after. And to top it all off, she says she can't live like this. She's scared that every time I walk out the door it will be the last time."

Danny who never took it easy on Rainey, said, "I can't believe you didn't see that coming."

"She knew who and what I was when she met me. I'm not giving up the bond business. It's all I have left."

Danny spoke softly, "You have her. Isn't that enough? Let someone else do the criminal catching. Sit in the office, go fishing, enjoy your life."

The words left Rainey's mouth, before she really thought them, "What if that is not enough? What if I can't live like that?"

"I was wondering when your feet were going to come back to the ground. You know our relationships rarely work. It's not a bed of roses for Katie, either. Welcome to the real world."

"What does she expect from me?"

Danny tilted his head and wrinkled his brow in question. "You really don't know, do you?"

"No, enlighten me," Rainey shot back.

"Rainey, everybody is not like us. They can't turn their emotions on and off."

"That's funny. I can't seem to turn them off these days."

Danny pointed a finger at Rainey. "You know damn well what I'm talking about. Something horrible happened to you. You dealt with it and now you're moving on. You may have some residual fears and distrust, but you put the big hurts and terrors in a box and filed them away for future study."

Rainey interrupted, "I'm not as cold blooded as everybody thinks."

"I didn't say you were. I, of all people, know what you went through."

"I had to let it go, Danny. When I met Katie that was easier to do."

"You've had more training and time, than Katie, to come to that conclusion. Nine months ago, her world was turned upside down. Is it too much to ask for her to want some safety and security for a while? You're out there kicking in a major violent felon's door, and for what, twenty grand? You know you shouldn't have bailed him out in the first place. You did it for the money. Why, because of Katie wanting a new house."

Ernie had obviously been shooting her mouth off. Rainey had the money to build a house without Katie's help. She invested well and had her Bureau severance, but it was all tied up in accounts with penalties if she touched it. So she took Chauncey as a client when no one else would. She knew he was a risk, but she wanted to pad her bank account a bit with all the expenses they were about to have with the house and a baby. Danny was right. She'd taken a lot of sketchy clients lately. It didn't matter to Rainey that Katie could finance it all and not put a dent in her trust. It was just part of Rainey's character that she needed to pull her own weight. Rainey tried to speak, but Danny wouldn't let her.

He continued his analysis of Rainey's situation. "Rainey, you jumped into this relationship during the worst possible time. You were already traumatized and then you were re-victimized by the same attacker. In the middle of a fight for both your lives, you found each other. You've studied human behavior as much as anybody. You know the adrenaline of new love is wearing off. The glasses of romantic illusion are losing their power. The day-to-day realities of what you did and do for a living are finally hitting home with Katie, and you are realizing that maybe you made a mistake subjecting her to this. I think the question is, what do you expect from her?"

The doggie door popped opened, startling both of them. Freddie ran by, as if something were chasing him. Rainey looked in through the kitchen window. Katie was loading the dishwasher rather forcefully. Rainey thought Freddie had the right idea in running. Rainey looked back at Danny, whose attention had been drawn to the blonde slamming pots and pans around. They couldn't see her face or hear her voice, but her body language strongly suggested that Katie was mumbling under her breath. Rainey knew most of what Katie was saying had her name spattered in it a few times, probably with, "Fuck you," in front of it.

"Hell hath no fury..." Danny said, chuckling.

"How would you know? You haven't kept one long enough to make her that mad."

"So, are you going in there?"

Rainey shook her head from side to side. In her best Carolina hick accent, she said, "No. That there, Danny, is an extremely angry little ball of fire. I'm not touching it until it burns down to an ember." Rainey rubbed her aching shoulder, before adding, "Let's go down to the office. I have some bourbon down there, and I'm thinking I'm going to need a whole lot more to drink, before this night is over."

Danny laughed and followed her down the back steps. "You stay gone too long, and those embers might turn to ashes."

"Danny, why do you think you know so much about women? I am one, and half the time I can't figure her out."

Danny retorted, "I don't have to know much about women. I know you and what a pain in the ass you can be."

#

161

"So, what did you find?" Rainey asked, pouring them both a drink.

Danny sat in one of the old leather chairs in front of Rainey's desk. Rainey had calmed down considerably and was now focused on finding out what Dalton had been up to. Danny pulled a small notebook from his inside coat pocket and began flipping pages. Rainey approached with his drink and put it on the table. She sat in the chair beside him, took a drink, and laid her head back.

While Danny organized his thoughts, Rainey organized her mental boxes. She closed the one where she put Katie, and all that came with her, when she needed to focus elsewhere. The box for the bail bond business, another one where her fears and doubts resided, and all the boxes not needed for the task of the moment were snapped shut. Then she opened the one containing her behavioral analyst tools, along with one of the other dusty containers in the corners of her mind, Dalton's box. Rainey was the expert on Dalton Chambers. If anyone knew his motives, it was Rainey. This old box had been closed for three years. She was preparing herself to do battle with Dalton, again. If she let her emotions run wild, she wouldn't be able to process the information Danny needed to nail this fucker once and for all.

Danny took a sip of his drink, before he began. "Rainey, I tossed his cell. I mean we tore it apart. There was no obvious communication between Chamber's and his copycat. I found lots of correspondence, but none that jumped out at me as anything other than the basic serial killer fan bullshit. There were church bulletins from several churches, a few books on psychology, and a bible, of course. We took it all, every shred of paper we could find. I sent it all to Quantico."

Rainey did not open her eyes when she asked, "What are you not telling me? I hear it in your voice and you've never needed to read from that damn notebook the whole time I've known you. You could recite whole crime scenes by heart. So, you were just killing time, trying to figure out how to tell me they screwed up and let stuff get through to him that he should not have."

Danny cleared his throat. "I found a bunch of newspaper articles. They were all from last summer. All the details he would need to find you were in those articles. He highlighted your address, Katie's name, her parents' names, your mother's name, Ernie, and Mackie's, too. He had the pictures that went with the articles, as well. He also had the stories on your father's murder. These were all copied on computer paper from the originals, and stuck inside his legal papers. It would have been easy to miss them. If it came in a package marked legal, all they could do was search for contraband, they couldn't read any of it."

Rainey remained perfectly still. "Does he still have that female lawyer, the one who wanted to marry him?"

"Yep. She saw him on the day he left 'The Onion.' Someone from the Roanoke field office has been sent to pick her up. A night sitting in an interview room should loosen her tongue. We'll know if she gave him the information on you, by morning."

Rainey's eyes remained closed. "What exactly did Dalton say when he saw you?"

Danny didn't sugarcoat his answer. He repeated the conversation verbatim. "He said, 'Agent McNally, what a distinct non-pleasure. So, Rainey Bell is a dyke. I guess that makes you a faggot. Come to save the dyke's ass, have you? I can't see why. She prefers pussy. Now, you really don't stand a chance."

Rainey remained still. She did not react to Danny's statement.

Danny was quiet for a few moments, and then he said, "Rainey, the team is here in Durham. We're going to stay on this until we find this guy. Trust me when I say, I will not rest until you and your family are safe."

Rainey finally raised her head from the back of the chair. She finished her drink in one big gulp, before she spoke. "I will never be safe, as long as people like Dalton are out there; I will continually be looking over my shoulder. You and I both know there will always be Daltons to contend with. The best thing I can do is hope I see them coming. Other than that, my life is forever fucked."

Danny tried to placate her mood, somewhat. "You put yourself in the line of fire for the greater good. It is unfortunate that the events of last summer made you vulnerable. Everyone knows who you are and what you look like. Some asshole is always going to want to challenge you. I know you didn't ask for this and I wish it hadn't happened, but you are a highly skilled former FBI agent. You can survive this. Look what you've already lived through. Your training saved your life and Katie's. Trust your instincts Rainey. You have one of the best minds of all the agents I know. You can figure out how to live without fear."

"It's Katie, Danny. When she gets in my head, I don't think straight. Pardon the pun. I'm afraid I won't hear my little voice telling me what to do, because my focus is on keeping her safe. My being shot today was a direct result of not paying close attention to the details. She blurs the details. I'm afraid she can't stay with me. I'm afraid I'll have to let her go, because I love her too much to let her stay."

"Fear is freezing you, don't you see that? Stop being afraid of losing her and start making sure you can keep her. Go proactive. Help me find this guy. You know Dalton better than anyone, who are we looking for?"

"I can't actively be involved in the investigation. That would scare Katie to death, but I will give you my opinion, and then you and the team are on your own. My job is to keep my family alive."

In Rainey's mind, Ernie and Mackie were part of her family. They were really all she had left, except for Katie, and she wasn't sure how much more of this Katie would take. She would have to call her mother, which she dreaded immensely, but it was the right thing to do. Her mother and stepfather were in danger, just like the rest of them, even if Rainey never really spent any time with them.

Danny picked up a pen from Rainey's desk, poised to take notes. He said, "Okay, fair enough. Just tell me what you think and I'll share it with the team."

Rainey stood up, walked to the counter, and poured another drink. She offered the bottle to Danny. He put his hand over his still full glass and waited for her to begin.

Rainey didn't sit back down. She walked over to the window and peered into the darkness at the lake. She watched the tiny lights on a small boat, as it slowly passed the end of the dock, headed to the boat ramp just south of Rainey's property. The lake closed to boat traffic at nine p.m. She let her mind wander, while it sorted through her encyclopedia of Dalton Chambers knowledge. When she was ready, she turned to Danny and began.

"The differences in the case, here in Durham, and Dalton's crimes are what sticks out to me. The body was left in the death position for some time, before it and the head were packaged and thrown in the river. Why did he move the body? Was he trying to conceal it, or was he making sure it would be found, or did he panic and lose focus? The kill sight was probably on public land like Dalton's. There isn't much privacy here in the triangle, unlike where Dalton committed his murders. In order to have the seclusion he would need, for the amount of time he spends with the victims, he chose a place where he was positive no one would find him. That makes me think of avid hikers, hunters, even farmers in the area around the river, someone who knows the lay of the land."

Rainey took a drink and began to pace. Her mind focused on the details. Things began to click. "I don't think this guy is a controlled killer like Dalton. He may develop into one, but right now he is learning. He followed his instructions to create a copycat crime, but somewhere along the way I think he panicked, probably when the head came off. He is not a practiced killer. I think this victim may have been his first. When the next body is found, I think you will see signs of more control. The first kill didn't turn him off. I'm sure he killed the woman that is still missing. There are too many coincidences in how the victims were taken, who the victims were, and where they were last seen. The most obvious difference in these victims and Dalton's is they were not virgins, or even attempting to appear that way. From the reports I saw, I gathered these were staunch lesbians. How does a man get that type of woman to go willingly with him? He must use a ruse similar to Bundy. The 'man in need of help' con is my bet."

Danny asked, "This bar where the women were last seen, I am assuming it's a lesbian or gay bar."

"Feme Sole, it's a lesbian bar."

"Have you been there?"

Rainey thought about her promise to Katie to take her dancing. "No, but I planned to take Katie, Saturday. That's one more promise I'll have to break."

"Yes, you will break that promise," Danny said. "If he's hunting you and you show up in his territory, he won't be able to resist coming after you. He wants to please Dalton and you are all that piece of shit thinks about."

That didn't make Rainey feel any better about the situation. She tried to move on. "Physically, I think this guy is like Dalton. Good looking, charming, you know, the boy next door. He gets these women isolated and then he strikes. The victims' cars were parked, untouched, near the bar. So, he must lie in wait for them near there. Durham police and the Sheriff's department are patrolling the area now, but I don't think they will be able to spot him. He will blend in with the crowd. There are several bars in the area, so he could appear to be a young man leaving a bar. He won't be sporting a flannel shirt and chewing tobacco, that's for sure."

Rainey felt as if the years melted away and she was back on the team when Danny jumped in. It was just like old times. "He definitely has a working vehicle. He transports the victims to remote locations, so it's probably an SUV or truck. After "Silence of the Lambs," no woman is going to follow a guy to the back of his van to lend a hand. He hunts on the weekends, so he probably has a nine to five job during the week. If he's in a relationship, he is able to be gone for many hours without suspicion."

Danny's phone rang. He answered, "McNally."

Rainey watched Danny's facial expressions as he carried on a conversation with someone, apparently a member of the BAU team that accompanied him.

"Uh huh, yeah, I'll be right there... No, Rainey is not consulting on this case... Yes, I will. See you in about thirty minutes... Yes, send the coordinates to my phone... Yeah, okay and make sure the locals don't touch anything until I get there." He hung up and turned his attention back to Rainey. "Glad I didn't drink that booze. It's going to be a long night. They found the missing girl."

Rainey asked, knowing the answer before she did, "Is it him?"

"Looks that way. This one was still tied to the tree. And before I forget, Curtis says hello."

Curtis joined the BAU four years before Rainey resigned. He was still young and new enough not to be jaded. Rainey had liked him and his young wife. They were such a cute couple. She wondered how their marriage was holding up under the stress of his job. If he had a secret, she wished he'd share. Rainey's only real friends had been co-workers. She suddenly felt some of the isolation and loneliness Katie must be experiencing.

Danny looked at Rainey with his eyebrows raised. "You're sure you don't want in on this?"

Part of Rainey did want to go with Danny, but she knew she couldn't. She had her own mess to deal with over at the cottage, and besides she was well on her way to getting drunk. Rainey was not an agent anymore; she would never be again, not as long as Katie was in her life.

"No, Danny. I can't. I need to go home. Keep me informed and call me if you want more of my insights, but no, I can't work this case. It would be too much to ask of Katie."

They started for the door, Danny saying as they moved, "Okay, but if you change your mind, you know you are welcome to step in at any time." He paused, put his arm around her shoulder and said, "I miss you, Rainey. I really do."

"I miss you, too Danny."

#

Danny waited while Rainey locked the office, then they walked back up the hill together. They said goodbye at the SUV and then Rainey made her way to the front steps. She watched until his taillights disappeared into the trees covering the road. Her shoulder was pounding again, the ice having long since melted. She approached the door, hoping Katie had calmed down by now. She looked around once more, taking in the property with a trained eye. Nothing looked out of place. Freddie joined her on the deck. She petted him on the head.

"I don't know if you want to come in here, now. She might still be mad." Freddie rubbed up against her, purring loudly, and meowed. "Easy for you to say. You have a doggie door to escape out of." Freddie looked up at Rainey and meowed, louder this time. "Okay, if you think it's safe, we'll go in."

Rainey took a deep breath. Reaching for the handle, she discovered the door was unlocked. A small act of rebellion on Katie's part, Rainey was sure. Of course, Katie knew Rainey and Danny were only a few feet away, and would come running if anyone approached. Katie did leave the alarm on, which was loudly announcing Rainey's presence. She peeked in and saw the living room was empty. Rainey locked the door behind her, reset the alarm, and went in search of the fuming little blonde. She found Katie in the bedroom, reading on her Kindle, by the window. Katie looked up for a second and then went right back to the screen. Okay, this was how Katie was going to play this, the silent treatment. Rainey could do that easy enough. She turned around and went to the kitchen in search of food. The alcohol had not landed well in her hollow stomach.

She found Freddie waiting by his empty bowl. "Looks like I'm not the only one being neglected. We're on our own tonight, Bud."

Rainey fed Freddie and then opened the refrigerator, looking for something to feed herself. On the top shelf, Katie had placed a sandwich wrapped in cellophane and a glass of milk. So Katie wasn't so mad she wanted Rainey to starve. She took the sandwich and milk out to the living room. When she lived alone she always ate in front of the TV. Katie insisted on eating at the table. This was Rainey's little act of rebellion.

She turned on the flat screen and settled into the couch. Katie would come out of the bedroom eventually. Rainey could wait. Right now she was looking for a basketball game to watch. It wasn't basketball season, to Rainey's chagrin, but she found a replay of the Duke – Carolina game from this past season, on one of the sports channels. Avoiding the problem wasn't going to make it go away, but a little food and ACC basketball would make it easier to face. If she were lucky the fight would come and go before the second half.

Her stomach growled as she unwrapped the sandwich. Since Katie had her on a regular eating schedule, when she missed a meal Rainey felt like she was starving. She used to go a whole day on one quickly grabbed hamburger. She took a huge bite out of the sandwich just as Katie came into the room. Oh God, Rainey thought, could she just swallow this before the fighting started?

"I see your basic needs are being met," Katie said, sarcasm dripping from her words.

"wthawnk yuuu fo thw san wooch," Rainey tried to say, the sandwich hanging out both sides of her mouth. She swallowed and tried again. "Thank you for the sandwich."

"I made it before you ran off with Danny for your secret meeting."

"I didn't run off with Danny to have a secret meeting. You were slamming pots around, so I thought you needed some space." That sounded like a plausible answer. Rainey didn't want to admit that she was afraid of Katie's anger, and ran like a scared little girl to the safety of her office. She thought about taking another bite of the sandwich, but that might send Katie over the edge.

"You don't think I need to know what's going on, here? Is this something I don't," Katie made quotation marks in the air around her next words, "need to know?"

"No, you should know everything, but Danny didn't have much on this guy, yet. I know Dalton, but he's locked up. They found the missing girl. That's why Danny left. I'm sure we'll know more tomorrow."

"You could have included me in the conversation with Danny. I have a right to know who's trying to kill me," Katie argued.

"You didn't give me a chance." Rainey threw the sandwich down on the plate and stood up. "Jesus Katie, what the hell is wrong with you? First you tell me you can't live with my job, which is the reason we met in the first place, and now you're accusing me of keeping something important from you. You were angry and not in a talking mood, from what I could tell. I'm sure the dishwasher can testify to that."

"You weren't exactly in a cheerful mood yourself." Katie hesitated and then said, "I don't know why you insist on chasing down criminals. This isn't any safer than your FBI job, maybe even worse. You said you stayed at Quantico doing research most of the time, and at least you weren't the first to go in when you were in the field. Haven't you faced enough life and death situations to last a lifetime? What is it Rainey? Do you need the thrill?"

"I resigned to be with you."

Katie shouted, "Then be with me! Not out risking your life on a daily basis."

Rainey was angry, Katie was angry, and this conversation was going nowhere unless they figured out what they were angry about. Rainey knew anger was usually a symptom of a deeper emotion, like fear. The analyst in Rainey watched Katie's body language. She listened to the tone of Katie's voice. Rainey needed to be calm and rational, in response. As long as they remained standing and confrontational, nothing would be accomplished.

"Katie, sit down," Rainey said, in her best soothing voice.

Rainey learned something at that moment about women, for which her behavioral analyst job did not prepare her. Never tell an angry woman to sit down. She had faced off men twice her size and told them to sit their asses down, she had taken control of drug crazed bond skippers, but she would never again tell Katie to sit down during an argument. It had the same effect as throwing water on a grease fire. Katie stood on her tiptoes and let fly with everything that had been bothering her since they met. Rainey could only stand by and watch.

"I will not sit down! I have a few things to say and I intend to stand here and say them. First of all, yes, I did know what you did for a living and I have done my best to accept the fact that every time you walk out that door could be the last, but you take unnecessary risks and that is selfish. Do you ever think about how I feel? You walk around fully armed and alarmed, but you put yourself in situations that are dangerous for no reason. Do you have a death wish? If you do, tell me now, so I can try to fall out of love with you."

"Katie, I..." Rainey tried to say something, but it was no use.

"Second, if you think for one minute I'm going to live the rest of my life in fear, you are sadly mistaken. I will not live like that and you don't have to, either."

Rainey saw her opportunity to respond. "I don't take unnecessary risks and I don't want you to live in fear. I just want you to be cautious and aware."

"Bull shit, Rainey. You want me in this cottage where you think you can protect me. I see the apprehension in your eyes every time I get in the car. I have accommodated your fears

R. E. BRADSHAW

and stayed close to home, most of the time, but I have been alone about as much as I intend to be. I'm re-entering my life and I won't be looking at every person I meet as a potential threat."

"So, this really isn't about me, is it?" Rainey shot back. She could remain calm in the worst of situations, but Katie could make her crazy. Like now, when Rainey should have shut up, but didn't. "Now that the fog of your trauma is lifting, you can see the future, and you don't like what you see. Is that it?"

"Don't analyze me. I did not say I didn't want a future with you. I said I don't want to live in fear. We don't have to. We could leave here and never look back. I have enough money for both of us. You don't have to risk your life every day... I'm not good cop wife material, Rainey."

Rainey had this conversation, albeit a bit differently, with Bobby. She knew where this was going and the pain caused her to lash out. "You picked a fine time to come to that conclusion."

"We can't bring a child into this environment of fear and mistrust," Katie said, emphatically.

"Then don't!"

That was the deal breaker. Katie left the room. Rainey did not follow her. She grabbed a bottle of bourbon from the cabinet and went to the kitchen for a glass, to await what she knew was coming next.

A few minutes later, Katie came out of the bedroom carrying a suitcase. Rainey couldn't stop her if she tried, so she didn't. Rainey stood in the archway to the kitchen, as Katie passed without a word. Katie turned at the door, looking back at Rainey. Katie started to say something, but changed her mind. With tears streaming down her face, she disarmed the alarm, opened the door, and walked out of Rainey's life.

173

CHAPTER TEN

Rainey didn't fall apart when Katie shut the door, at least not right away. She sat on the couch, the open bottle of bourbon on the table in front of her, shot glass in her hand. She knocked back another shot and watched the minutes tick by on the DVR display. When enough time had passed, she picked up her cell phone and dialed Katie's parents. This was not a phone call she wanted to make, but she had to. After the third ring, Katie's father answered the phone.

"Hello," said the now familiar voice of Timothy Meyers.

"Mr. Meyers, this is Rainey." He had asked her to call him Tim, but it didn't seem appropriate at the time.

"I suspected you would be calling when Katie arrived here in a puddle of tears. Would you mind telling me what's going on? We can't get anything out of Katie, she's so distraught."

Rainey felt her own tears just below the surface. She was relieved that Katie was safe at her parents' home in Durham, but the magnitude of Katie's leaving was tearing at Rainey's heart. She told herself she only had to hold it together a few more minutes. She focused on her mission, and said. "Mr. Meyers..."

He interrupted her, "Please, call me Tim. You're family, now, even if there appears to be a problem with that, at the moment."

Rainey began again, "Tim, I need to tell you a few things. I'll let Katie tell you why she left me, but I need you to know that your family isn't safe."

Suddenly more serious, Tim said, "I'm listening."

"A man I put in prison has information about you and your wife, as well as Katie. He now has a man on the outside who may be coming after me and the people I care about. He has killed two women so far, but I believe, and so does the FBI, that I am his main target. I was informed this evening that he knows who you all are and most likely where you live."

Rainey heard Katie's voice choked with tears. "If that's Rainey, just hang up," she shouted, "I don't want to talk to her."

A searing knife of pain cut through Rainey. It was all she could do to keep from losing it.

She heard Tim say, "Katie, I know you are upset, but I need to talk to Rainey. Please, go back in the kitchen with your mother."

Rainey had to get the rest out, before she lost control. "I'm going to ask the police to put a car in front of your house. I don't want anything to happen to any of you, because of me."

She could hear Tim breathing on the other end of the phone. She let him absorb the information.

Finally, he spoke, "Rainey, do I need to get my family out of town?"

"That wouldn't be a bad idea," Rainey answered.

"What about you? Is someone watching you?"

Rainey genuinely liked Katie's father. His concern for her welfare was characteristic of the kind of man he was. Rainey tried to sound reassuring, when she said, "I'll be fine. My main concern is Katie and the rest of you. Please watch over her. She doesn't want anything to do with me right now, and that makes it difficult for me to protect her."

"I'll keep her safe, Rainey, and I also want to offer a piece of advice. Having been through a few of Katie's meltdowns in the past, if you will be patient, her brain will re-engage in a day or two. My Katie is a bit hot headed when she's scared or hurt. Just give her time. She'll come around. She must care about you deeply to be this upset."

A tear slid down Rainey's cheek. Her throat tightened and her voice cracked when she tried to speak. "I... I don't know how to fix this."

Tim spoke to Rainey, as her father would have, with tenderness and knowing in his voice. "This too shall pass. I wasn't all that happy when Katie chose to live with you, but I see how you two love each other, and I know whatever caused this temporary separation will work itself out. My advice to you is to catch this guy and then try to fix your relationship. You can't do both at the same time."

"Yes, sir," was all Rainey could muster. Her tears flowed freely now.

"Don't worry about Katie. I will make sure the house is locked up tight and the alarm is on."

"Thank you," she choked out. "I'm sorry this is happening."

"This guy after you isn't your fault. Maybe you were just too good at your job." Tim suddenly chuckled. "And another thing you should know, I've been dealing with these emotional Meyers women for a lot longer than you have. Trust me, there will be a calm after the storm."

Rainey was near the end of her ability to hold her tempest of emotions at bay. She had to get off the phone. "I'll call you when I know something… and Mr. Meyers, load your gun."

"I will. You stay safe."

"Always," was Rainey's familiar reply.

Tim hung up. Rainey had one more call to make, if she could just hold on. She dialed Danny's number. He picked up on the first ring. When Rainey heard his voice, the dam broke and all attempts to make a comprehendible sound failed her. Instead, she began to sob.

"Rainey… Rainey… What's wrong?" Danny asked, alarm in his voice. He received no answer and tried again. "Rainey, are you hurt? Is Katie all right?"

She managed to sputter, "She… she left."

"Where did she go? Is she somewhere safe?"

Rainey took a gasping breath and said, as fast as she could, because it was probably going to be the only coherent words she would mutter for a while, "She's at her parents' house in Durham. Could you put a patrol car on the house?"

"Yes, I'll do that right now." Rainey heard Danny turn to someone, barking orders. "I need you to get a patrol car outside of Timothy Meyers' house… No, I don't know the address. Look it up… Yes, Timothy and Melanie Meyers, Durham… Don't stand there. Do it, now!" He returned to Rainey. "Rainey, do you need me?"

She stammered out a response, "No… I'm okay… Danny, I didn't know… I didn't know it would hurt like this."

Rainey closed her phone and fell into one of the big pillows on the couch. She could smell Katie's perfume on the fabric, which only made the racking sobs that shook her body more intense, but she couldn't pull her face from the pillow. The last time she indulged in such self-pity was the day she met Katie, after learning the Y-Man was back. Katie had held her while she collapsed in a shower of tears. This time there was no Katie to soothe her breaking heart. Rainey hugged the pillow to her tightly and completely fell apart.

#

Rainey was startled awake by a knock on the door, followed shortly by the sound of the door opening and the alarm going off. She jumped off the couch, unable at the moment to understand what was happening. She reached for her gun on the table, where she placed it before passing out. A searing pain, from the deep muscle bruise left by the bullet, jolted her from her stupor.

"Stand down, it's just me."

Ernie's voice penetrated the fog in Rainey's hung-over brain. She fell back to the couch and buried her head beneath a pillow.

"Good Lord, what in the hell happened here?"

She was near Rainey now. She could see Ernie in her mind, probably standing over her with her hands on her hips. The table in front of the couch was scattered with the remnants of Rainey's dance with the bourbon devil. The now dried out sandwich lay uneaten beside her Glock. Several glasses were on the table, progressing from a shot glass to the tea glass that had done her in. The only positive thing Rainey could think, at the moment, was thank God the bottle had not been full.

"I see you've been up to your old tricks." Ernie began cleaning up while she reprimanded Rainey like a wayward teenager. "I thought we were past all this. Liquor is not your friend, Rainey. It might have helped in the moment, but look at you now. Bet your head hurts like hell."

Ernie carried the empty bottle and glasses to the kitchen. She continued her one sided conversation, while Rainey remained immobile on the couch.

"You are not a bit of good to anybody in this state. When are you going to grow up and find a different way to deal with problems? So, she left you. Do you think getting drunk is going to get her back? Thank the Lord, Mackie slept in his truck outside. Anybody could have walked up on you last night."

"Getting walked up on," was how Rainey's father expressed being unaware. He had been walked up on more than once in the jungles of Vietnam. He and Rainey shared the same feral cat defenses, cautious and suspicious, constantly checking the surroundings. Maybe it was because he raised her that way, but those characteristics had served her well. She had forgotten his first rule of defense last night. He would remind her often, "Rainey, *always*, always be aware. If you see them coming, you got a chance." Rainey wasn't even aware of what time she finally succumbed to the alcohol.

"You're one of the smartest people I know, but you don't have a lick of sense." Ernie was suddenly standing over Rainey again. "Get up. I brought you a Coke. Go take a shower. I'll fix you something to eat." Rainey remained motionless. Ernie kicked at Rainey's foot. "I said get up. You've wallowed in self-pity long enough."

Rainey's muffled voice came from under the pillow. "Go away."

"Rainey Blue Bell, I said move!"

Rainey was tall and strong enough to snap this little woman like a twig, but even as Rainey approached the age of forty-one, Ernie intimidated her as if she were still a child. Ernie raised four boys who all grew to be over six feet tall, and mothered Rainey most of her life. She took no crap from them as kids and she wasn't about to take it now. Rainey knew she was fighting a losing battle. She sat up, glaring at Ernie from underneath her now matted mass of hair.

"You got no one to blame but yourself for the mess you're in. Stop feeling sorry for yourself and fix it."

Rainey's voice was scratchy and dry, when she asked, "How did you know Katie was gone?"

Ernie handed Rainey the Coke, saying, "She called me, balling. Neither one of you has the patience God gave Job to work out your problems. She's hot headed and you are like a snake when backed in a corner. You always lash out, say things you don't mean. You've been that way your whole life. I called Mackie and he came over here."

The Coke disappeared from the can into Rainey's mouth; the sugar began to course through her body. She vaguely remembered seeing Mackie's Escalade show up on the security camera feeds. She was coming around and said, "You haven't known me my whole life and I stopped acting like a hormonal teenager long ago."

"I know you must have said something hateful. That poor girl is all kinds of torn up."

Rainey remembered what she said to Katie about not bringing a child into this environment, the one thing Katie wanted more than anything. A pang shot through her chest, her stomach rolled over, and she was up and off the couch in a flash. She ran to the bathroom and threw up.

When she could speak again, she gasped out, "Fuck my life!"

She climbed into the shower, careful with her shoulder, and let the water wash away the salty trails of tears from her cheeks. She had to wash her hair with one arm. If Katie were there, she would have done it for her. Katie. What was she going to do about Katie? She tried a dozen different scenarios in her mind, but none of them seemed plausible. She needed to apologize for saying such a hurtful thing, but perhaps it was the truth. Maybe Katie was right not to want to live like this, and certainly bringing a child into Rainey's life would scare anyone. Rainey was once again faced with the choice of her job or her relationship. After the way Rainey reacted to Katie's apprehension, there was no way Katie would compromise, now.

Katie wanted a child more than she wanted Rainey. She came as a package deal. Rainey knew that from the start. Katie had been upfront about having a child. She discussed it with Rainey before they committed to a relationship. Rainey said yes, without even thinking. Truly content for the first time in her life, she would have said anything to keep Katie. Rainey remembered holding Katie in her arms and promising they would be happy. They had been, until this week. The stress of building a house, Rainey's job, Katie trying to get pregnant, and now this asshole out there hunting them had been too much. The polish on Rainey's perfect world had begun to tarnish.

She climbed out of the shower and dressed in her favorite button fly jeans, worn thin in all the right places. Her shoulder was stiff and achy, even the water in the shower hurt when it bounced off the now fully bloomed black bruise. The blood just below her skin was already being pulled down her arm by gravity, enlarging the discoloration. She looked in the bottom drawer, where Katie hid all Rainey's tattered tee shirts, found an old Kitty Hawk Pier shirt, and pulled it on slowly. The tee shirt made her feel close to her father. Fishing all night on the pier was one of their favorite things to do together. She missed him every day. She more than needed him today.

When she arrived in the kitchen she found dry toast, two ibuprofen, and a glass of orange juice on the table with a note from Ernie. The note said:

> *If you can keep this down, we'll talk about*
> *a real meal. You need to do several things*
> *and I suggest you do them in the following*
> *order:*
>
> 1. *Eat your breakfast.*
> 2. *Focus. There is a killer after you, or did you forget?*
> 3. *Call Katie, and apologize for whatever bonehead thing you did.*
> 4. *Re-focus, because you can't think when you talk to Katie.*
> 5. *Come to the office. Danny will be here in an hour.*

Numbers two, three, and four were the tough ones. Rainey had no chance of clearing her head and calling Katie was going to be a challenge. What could she say? She thought about it while eating her toast. She was still thinking when she finished the last piece of crust. She put food and water down for Freddie, who she presumed was out on his morning stalk. She then wrestled her still damp hair into a ponytail. When there was nothing else she could do to delay the inevitable, she picked up her phone and dialed Katie's parents' home. She was relieved it was not Katie's mother, but Tim who answered. She wasn't up for twenty questions from Melanie.

"Good morning," she said, trying to sound better than she felt.

Tim answered in a cheerful voice, "And good morning to you. I suppose you would like to speak to my daughter, or has something else happened?"

"No, everything is the same as when we last talked. I just need to talk to Katie, if she'll speak to me."

She could hear Tim moving around. She supposed he was going to ambush Katie with the phone.

"I'm taking the phone to Katie, now. Oh, by the way, the police car is outside. Thank you."

Rainey was relieved. "Good. I'm glad they are there."

She heard Tim tap lightly on a door and then say, "Katie, honey, Rainey's on the phone. She wants to speak to you."

Rainey heard Katie's muffled voice, but she couldn't make out what she said.

Tim spoke again, "Katie, I'm not going to relay messages. Be an adult and come to the door."

There was sound of rustling around and then Katie's voice came over the line. "I don't want to talk to you."

"Katie, I'm sorry."

"Sorry for what, Rainey, that you finally said what you really think, instead of what you thought I wanted to hear?"

"Well, I can tell you're still angry. I guess a rational discussion is out of the question, at this point."

Rainey called that one correctly. Katie shouted into the phone, "You're damn right!" Katie took a breath and gathered steam. "Go play FBI agent. That's what you want to do. Go be a hero, get your thrills."

"Katie, I don't want to be an agent I didn't ask for this."

"No, you didn't, but you knew there was a distinct possibility that this would happen. Something you didn't think was necessary to share with me. Now, I really know why you are the way you are. Your paranoia, the nightmares, it's not because of what you've seen and done. It's because you knew someone was coming. How many more men are going to come hunting you?"

Rainey could only answer, "I don't know."

"Well, you should know. Instead, you stay out there on the lake like bait, just waiting for them to come for you. You might not have a death wish, Rainey, but it's as if you don't think you should have survived the first attack. You put on a show of moving on, but you haven't. I survived nearly being murdered and look at the rest of my life like a bonus. You look at it like borrowed time. I'm not going to sit around and watch you wait to die."

The connection terminated relatively quickly after that. Rainey held the phone in her hand, staring down at it. Katie was right. Rainey could know more about the criminals that might come after her. She did just sit back and wait. Rainey could have been more proactive about their safety. She could have had Danny checking these guys' mail, if they were in prison, or keep her posted on the unsolved cases she was involved in. She simply closed the box and prayed it stayed closed. But what Katie did not understand was, even with all her training and precautions, Rainey would never know for sure if, or when a psychopath was coming for her.

The phone rang in her hand. It was Katie's parents' number. Rainey flipped the phone open and put it to her ear.

Katie began talking right away. She was much calmer than before, when she said, "Rainey, I'm not coming home until you catch this guy. So, you go get him. I don't want you distracted worrying about me or us. When this is over, we'll talk."

"Will you promise me you'll be careful? Don't go anywhere by yourself." Rainey pleaded. "Why don't you and your parents leave town?"

"My sisters will be here tomorrow. My mom suggested we go back to L.A. with them."

"That would be great," Rainey said, relieved that the Meyers family, at least, appeared to have discussed it. Then quickly, before Katie could hang up again, she said, "Katie, I don't want to lose you. Just let me deal with this and I will spend the rest of my life keeping my promise to you."

All the wind had gone out of Katie's anger, now. In a hushed voice, she asked, "What promise are you talking about?"

"I promised you we'd be happy."

Katie sniffled. Rainey knew she was crying again.

"I love you, Katie."

"I love you, too, Rainey. Please, be careful."

"Always."

Rainey heard the call lost tone and knew Katie was gone. She flipped the phone shut with a mission to accomplish, so she could have her life back, a life with Katie, children, and a happily ever after. She understood why Katie didn't want to come home. The distance between them made it easier for Katie to deal with the fear and worry. Katie recognized that she was a distraction and she wanted Rainey focused on the killer, not her. Rainey had a job to do, and if given the chance, she would kill this bastard. He would be one less asshole Rainey would have to worry about in the future, and before this was over, she would make sure Dalton Chambers was sitting on death row, where he belonged. If they would let her, she would insert the needle.

#

When Danny arrived, shortly thereafter, Rainey met him at the door of his SUV. She had already filled Ernie in on her plans. Before leaving the cottage, she redressed, digging out her former work clothes from the closet in her old room. That's where she kept the FBI jackets and hats, the dark suits, and other echoes of her former life. Now, she looked like the poster girl for the FBI; white blouse, black slacks, and blazer to match, with her Glock clipped to her hip. Her hair hung in a thick braid down the back of her neck. A few loose curls framed her face. She wasn't going to sit back and play defense any longer. She was in offensive mode, focused, and ready to do battle for her life.

Before Danny could get all the way out of the vehicle, Rainey said, "I'm in. Get me my credentials."

Danny asked, "For good, or like on the Y-man case, temporary reinstatement?"

"It's temporary. I'm never going back full-time."

Danny smiled. "I processed the paper work for your temporary reinstatement before I left." He reached back into the vehicle, producing Rainey's credentials in the leather case she recognized as her own. A long, deep scratch in the leather was a reminder from a particularly hairy arrest. He smiled when he handed it to her. "I had a sneaking suspicion you might be needing this."

Rainey took the case, opened it, and saw her official badge number on the gold shield. The picture on the ID was at least two years old. It was taken just before her father was killed. Rainey barely recognized her former self. Too much had happened since then. She thought she left all this behind her. Rainey put the credentials in her blazer pocket and looked back at Danny.

"When this is over, I want to sit down and come up with a plan to keep this from happening again. Katie pointed out that I've been sitting around waiting, instead of getting ahead of these guys. If one of these assholes breathes my name, I want to know about it."

"Are you and Katie all right?"

"As all right as we can be, right now." Rainey kicked at the ground. "She's staying with her parents until this is over."

Danny must have sensed Rainey's mood accurately, because he let the subject of Katie drop. He pointed to the office door. "Okay, let's get you caught up." He started for the door.

Rainey grabbed his arm. "Danny, I want to see Dalton."

"Right now? I need to tell you what we found at the last crime scene."

"Now, Danny. You can catch me up on the way."

"Are you sure that's wise? This could be his whole reason for doing this, to see you scared."

Rainey narrowed her eyes. "Do I look scared to you?"

CHAPTER ELEVEN

In 1870, North Carolina began construction on Central Prison, the first institution of its kind in the state. The castle-like building, complete with parapet walks and conical spires, took inmates fourteen years to build, using granite quarried just outside the prison's east wall. The prison underwent many renovations over the years, the last in the 1980's, losing its Gothic dark looks for a more modern façade. Only a few of the older buildings remained on the prison's twenty-nine acres, located near downtown Raleigh.

Central Prison housed the Tar Heel state's worst criminals, along with Death Row where inmates awaited appeals and the ultimate punishment a jury of their peers prescribed for them. Velma Barfield, the first woman in the United States to be executed since 1962, and the first woman to receive a lethal injection, said her re-born Christian final prayers there. Rainey hoped this was the last place Dalton Chambers would draw a breath.

A long corridor stretched the length of the prison, connecting all the buildings. Command stations and secure entryways controlled access into each building along the passage. When Danny left the prison yesterday, he asked that Dalton be moved to "Cell C," where Death Row inmates spent the hours just before the state exacted its retribution. There were no executions scheduled, making it the most isolated area in the prison. Danny wanted to know every person that came in contact with Dalton. This was the easiest way to control that. Besides, Rainey thought it was an excellent way to give Dalton a glimpse of the reality of his future.

Since the door on the cell holding Dalton had only a small narrow window, the guards placed him at a little stainless steel table attached to the floor outside the cell. He waived his right to council, which would have delayed the meeting until arrangements could be made. Dalton was anxious to see Rainey, too eager to do the smart thing and wait for his North Carolina attorneys to be present.

When Rainey entered the room, Dalton appeared to have been staring at the door, awaiting her arrival. He broke into a smile of self-satisfaction when he saw her. He was handcuffed and chained, wearing a stun belt, just like the last time Rainey was at "The Onion," in Virginia. A few feet away a guard held the control box, with his finger on the button, ready to light Dalton up. He was three years older and was starting to look more like the man he would have grown into, if he were not a sadistic killer. He would die long before his cherubic looks turned him into a distinguished looking older man. Even with the appeals process, Dalton would be dead years before he turned forty. Rainey was going to see to that.

Rainey walked straight to the table and stood over Dalton, just within his reach. She hoped he would make a move towards her. She wanted one good punch to his pretty face, before the guards could get to him. Dalton sat absolutely still, but his eyes travelled up her body. He made no effort to conceal his leering look at her chest, while he spoke.

"Well, hello Rainey. I can call you Rainey, can't I? Can't call you Agent Bell anymore. I hear you've left the Bureau."

Rainey stepped back and took a seat at the table opposite Dalton. She smiled, saying, "It's Agent Bell again. I got my credentials back, just so I can testify at the death penalty stage of your upcoming trial."

"Well, tried and convicted in your mind already, is it? They have nothing on me, but what I told you after I made a deal. My lawyers tell me they'll have all that thrown out. I'll be back in Virginia within the year."

Danny sat down. He spent the drive to the prison filling Rainey in on the details of the recent body find, and a bit of information that made Rainey ecstatic. He now repeated it for Dalton.

"I'm surprised your lawyers haven't told you why North Carolina is so interested in prosecuting you, now. Maybe they don't know, yet. They'll find out at the arraignment on the sixteenth, I guess. No harm in telling you now, though." Danny paused to let Dalton sweat a bit. "You weren't such a careful killer on that first one. We found DNA on the head, in the mouth to be exact. It was too little to test back then, but tests became available, making it possible to identify you positively as the killer. You're toast, Chambers."

Dalton's reaction was typical of his previous behavior when caught. He turned his frustration on Rainey. He leaned forward, placing his cuffed hands on the table. "I can see the top of the scar where he cut you. Were you scared, Agent Bell? Were you terrified? Do you dream about what happened? Do you scream at night when he comes for you?"

Rainey answered with no emotion, "No, actually I have very little memory of the attack and he's dead. So no, I don't dream about him."

"Yeah, I read about that, how your girlfriend stepped in to save your life."

Rainey laughed. "Don't believe everything you read in the paper, Dalton."

Dalton smirked. "But that stuff about you being a pussy licker, that's true, isn't it?"

He was trying to make Rainey lash out at him. His whole game was to try and shock her into losing her cool. She didn't take the bait. She leaned in closer and whispered, "Is that why you're so obsessed with me, cause I'm getting some pussy and you're not?" She ran the tip of her tongue across her upper lip.

Dalton had not expected that response. It startled him. This was a different Rainey Bell than he had dealt with before. The Y-man assault *had* affected her, but not in the way he wanted. He sat back away from her and turned his attention to Danny, while Rainey was sure he was plotting his next attempt to break her. "You tossed my cell yesterday and got me put in isolation. What else can I do for you, today?"

Danny answered, "I want to know who you've been talking to. We have your Virginia lawyer in custody. After spending the night in jail, she should be spilling her guts, about now. She'll bargain a deal with anything we want to know, or go to prison herself for slipping you those newspaper articles."

"I have a right to read the paper," Dalton shot back.

"Yes, you do, but within the limits set by the court, which specifically stated that you could not possess any information of a personal nature concerning the law enforcement officers who investigated you. Once you threatened Agent Bell here, you lost your right to have that information."

"I don't have to tell you who I have been corresponding with."

Danny shook his head in disagreement. "You really don't get it. You're a felon. You don't have many rights left. The prison, however, does have the right to know who you talk to. You need to have your lawyers explain that to you."

Dalton ignored Danny, refocusing on Rainey. "Before they moved me in here, I heard they found a body. They say it's my copycat. Did they find the head, yet?"

Rainey knew Dalton did not have the details of the crime. He was arrogant enough to believe his copycat would have followed his instructions to the letter. She returned his volley.

"As a matter of fact, we did. Seems the master doesn't have total control of his puppet. He couldn't leave her tied to a tree. He covered her with plastic and threw her in the river, head and all. "

Dalton sneered at her. "Why do you think he's killing lesbians?"

She ignored his question. She looked over at Danny. "I don't think this guy is copying Dalton at all, too many dissimilarities. It's obvious he's communicated with Messiah here, but this UNSUB covered the victims eyes."

Dalton's whole motive for his crimes was seeing the terror in his victims. Rainey just ruined Dalton's fantasies. He could no longer sit in his cell and daydream about his copycat's crimes. She put the image of the blindfolded victim in his mind, even if it wasn't true. Dalton would never know, at least, until they had caught the other killer. He was isolated and the only information he could get was from the investigators that came to see him. Rainey used that to her advantage.

"And there was that other glaring difference..." She paused and watched Dalton lean forward a little. He was predictably intrigued. "This UNSUB doesn't seem to have Dalton's taste for playing with the body after death. No evidence this guy even got much blood on him. He never touched her after she died. Doesn't have the stomach for Dalton's real depravities."

Dalton reacted by going on the attack. "One less dyke in the world. No great loss. Or is that two? There is another perverted cunt missing. He must be ridding the world of abominations like you. I'll pray for your soul, Agent Bell."

Rainey sneered back at him. "And what, pray tell, does the good book say about men who get off having sex with dead bodies?"

Danny jumped in the conversation. "We can prove that you and only you could have told your boy on the outside some of the aspects of your crimes. Conspiracy to commit murder, I think that's a death penalty charge in this state, isn't it? For a guy who thinks he's so smart, that was a stupid ass thing to do."

Dalton laughed loudly. "You have no clue who committed this murder, and without the killer being caught, you'll never prove a thing."

"What makes you think we won't catch him?" Danny asked.

"Because, you're here asking me who it is. Agent Bell came to talk me into giving the killer up. No chance of that happening. I'd rather take the needle and know this dyke is looking over her shoulder every minute."

Rainey slammed her hand down on the table to get his attention. "Look at me, you piece of shit. The only thing I'm looking over is the sight of my gun. When I find your little boyfriend he'll talk or he'll die, it's that simple."

Dalton's head snapped back to focus on Rainey, his facial expression one of pure hatred. When he spoke, his words were pure venom. "When the time comes, I've given special instructions on what to do with you. Still out at your dead father's lake cottage, I understand. Shouldn't be hard to get to you out there. This one's going to practice on the little blonde first."

The words hit their mark, but Rainey did not show any reaction to Dalton. Instead, she said, "I hope he's ready to die then, because that little blonde is prepared and willing to put a bullet in him."

"She'll never see it coming," he paused, leaning forward again, smiling with evil intent, "and neither will you. I wish I could be there to see the surprise on your face."

Rainey kicked Dalton's leg, where she splintered his bone with a bullet four years ago. He screamed in pain. She smiled wickedly. "Oh, I'm sorry. Is that where I shot you? That scar tissue builds up in there and hurts like hell, doesn't it?"

Dalton glared at her. "You bitch. If you came here to make a deal, so I would tell you who the killer is, then you just fucked that up. When your pretty head comes off, I want your last thoughts to be of me. I told you I would get you, Rainey Bell, and now the time has come."

Rainey let loose with a fury. "Deal? Who said anything about a deal? I would rather die knowing you're on death row than make a deal with you. That's what this is all about. You thought you could threaten me with one of your sick puppets and make a deal to give him up, so you could avoid the needle. We both know you get no satisfaction from these murders. You can't get off without a dead body to abuse, you fucking twisted freak. "

"You won't live long enough to testify," Dalton hissed

Danny had remained silent until now. "Come on, let's go. We're not going to get anything out of this guy we don't already know."

Rainey wasn't finished. "You better hope I die before I get to tell the world about all your perversions. I hope your momma will be there. I want her to know just what kind of inhuman animal she raised."

That got under Dalton's wall of psychopathology. He may not feel remorse, but he didn't want his momma to know the level of depravity he had stooped to. Rainey knew that from her previous interviews. Dalton's face flushed red.

"She won't believe a word of what you say. My mother will know you for the whore you are. She will know your sin of lying with a woman. God knows it, too. You and me, we're going to fry in hell together for eternity and that gives me great peace, that and knowing you will die with your precious Katie Meyers' head on a stake in front of you. Oh, darn, I let part of the plan out of the bag. I so wanted that to be a surprise."

Rainey stood up to leave. Danny was right. They had all they were going to get out of Dalton. If she stayed in the room much longer, she'd be up on charges for assaulting a prisoner in chains. She knew he wasn't going to tell her anything before she arrived. She just wanted to show him that she wasn't sitting at home, in fear for her life.

She had one more thing to say before she left. "I promised you I would be at your execution, but I'm going to take that back." She placed her hands on the table and leaned in to within an inch of Dalton's nose. Very softly, so no one else could hear, she said, "If anything happens to Katie, I will come back here and kill you myself. Don't be afraid of God's punishment. Be afraid of me."

He lunged for her, but the guard with the box in his hand was faster. Dalton let out a roar, when his body went rigid. He fell off the stainless steel stool and landed on the floor. Rainey squatted down beside him.

"You picked the wrong person to fuck with. See, I've already faced death. It doesn't scare me. You, on the other hand, are scared out of your mind of the hell fire you will roast in. That, Dalton, gives *me* great peace."

#

On the way to Durham, after leaving the prison, they stopped to feed Rainey's hangover and grab a Coke at a drive thru. Once back on the road, Danny started laughing unexpectedly.

Rainey looked over at him and asked, "What's so funny?"

This made Danny laugh harder. When he regained control, he blurted out, "When you said that thing about getting pussy and licked your lips, I thought I was going to lose it."

Rainey started chuckling and then fell into all out laughter with Danny. Once again, she was reminded how much she missed him. They had survived their stint in the BAU by making each other laugh.

"I'm not sure where that came from," she said, once her breathing returned to normal. "I swear it just popped into my head."

Danny's body shook again with another round of snickers. "The look on Dalton's face was priceless. He sure as hell wasn't expecting that. It was certainly a side of you I had never seen."

"It's a side of me I've never seen. I think I might really be losing it."

"Those guards will be reviewing that piece of security tape for years. Bet it ends up on YouTube."

"Oh, my God," Rainey exclaimed. "You have to make sure that doesn't happen."

Her expression of horror made Danny laugh harder. When the laughter subsided, Danny grew serious.

"You know I should take your shield for threatening to kill him."

"You heard that? I thought I was whispering." Rainey wondered aloud, "Did the guards hear me?"

"No, I don't think so, but you need to rein it in a little bit. I don't want you accused of being a loose cannon."

Rainey turned in the seat so she was facing him. "I would, you know."

Danny took his eyes from the road and gave her a warning look.

"Don't look at me like that. If anything happens to Katie, I'll kill him. I don't care if you have to testify that I said it. I wouldn't care what happened to me after that."

"I'm sorry, I didn't hear you." Danny reached down and turned the radio on and the volume up, adding, "The radio is too loud."

Rainey knew it would destroy him to have to testify against her, so she took the hint and let it drop. She turned the radio off and changed the subject. "The first woman went missing a month ago. The second went missing two weeks ago this Saturday. That makes his timeline ripe for another murder this weekend."

"Yeah, that's what I've been thinking. We need to stake out that bar and maybe get some cops on the inside."

"I'll go," Rainey said. "At least, no one would suspect anything. It was plastered all over the local news that I am living with Katie."

"Not a good idea," Danny stated, categorically.

"I'll take Sheila with me."

"She's a little old for you, don't you think?"

"It's not a fucking date, Danny."

"Damn, I was just kidding. Anyway, I think you should get Sheila to provide officers to go in undercover."

Rainey ignored Danny's not too subtle objection to her going in undercover. "I think we should go by the bar and talk to the owner, before we go in Saturday. I would like a look at the place in the light of day."

Danny looked at his watch. "Okay, but first we have to go to the Sheriff's office. Sheila set us up in the conference room. I have some things I need to tell the team and I have to talk to Quantico. I want to know if they've found anything in the stuff I took out of Dalton's cell."

"Did you make copies before you sent it off?" Rainey asked.

"Yeah, the team is going over them now. I sent copies to Brooks, too. She's scanning them and running them through one of her magic programs. She'll call if she finds anything."

"I'll take a look. There may be something there that would be meaningful to me." Rainey paused, then asked, "So, what did we learn from talking to Dalton?"

"He's still a narcissistic puke."

"Well that, but what else? Let's see. He said I would be surprised at who the killer is. Why would he say that? Does that mean I know this person?"

"Or Katie does, possibly," Danny answered. "He also made it clear that she is this guy's first target, not you."

"He did repeat that several times, but I think it was to scare me. He couldn't get a rise out of me by threatening my life, so he tested the water to see if that would work."

"It worked all right. I could see your jaw muscles tighten every time he mentioned her. I'm sure he noticed, too."

Rainey was surprised. "I thought I covered my reaction pretty well, until the end when I threatened to kill him."

"Even if you think it's a threat to get at you, I'm going to talk to Katie. She needs round the clock protection. Do you want to go with me when I talk to her?"

Rainey thought about it and answered, "No, she doesn't like me much right now. I think she still loves me, but I said something I shouldn't have. I'd rather she listen to you than be sitting there thinking about how mad she is with me."

Danny didn't pry. He knew if Rainey wanted to tell him what happened, she would. He changed the subject. "If Dalton thinks you or Katie know this guy, then it has to be somebody from here. They didn't follow him down here from Virginia. That narrows it to what, nearly one million males in the Triangle area."

"You can narrow the search by age. I think this guy is probably Dalton's age or close to it. He's twenty-eight now. So, let's say mid-twenties to mid-thirties on the UNSUB. He isn't as smart as Dalton. He's been manipulated into becoming a killer. He's not a psychopath. He felt remorse on the first one. I think that's why he covered her in plastic. He couldn't look at her. I don't think he has the social skills that Dalton had with his victims, either. We should get the word out before the weekend."

"I'm going to talk to the media this afternoon, after we present the profile to Sheila's people. We'll warn the lesbian community to be on alert," Danny said. "How many more do you think he'll kill, before he comes for you or Katie?"

"He's cut off from communication with Dalton, his master. He's more likely to make a mistake, if he's stressed. He may panic and go for me sooner than he anticipated. That may be how we catch him."

Danny took his eyes from the road, gluring at Rainey. She pointed at the cars braking in front of him. He slammed on brakes, avoiding a rear-end collision by inches. Neither spoke until the traffic began to move again.

Danny gripped the wheel tightly, keeping his eyes on the cars in front of him, his tone somber when he spoke. "You want me to let you set yourself up as bait."

Rainey could see she was going to have to sell him on the idea. "Let me draw him out. I won't be alone. Put a tech truck on me. Watch and listen. See who I see, listen to what I hear. You can help me find him. If what Dalton suggested is true, I might not see it coming, but you will."

Danny quickly replied, "I'm a little bit like Katie on this one. I've already witnessed enough of your near death experiences. You keep tempting fate and it's going to catch up to you one day. Setting yourself up as prey should be our last resort. Give us time to work the profile, before we do anything that risky."

Rainey stared straight ahead. "I don't have the luxury of time. People I care about are in danger. I'm not setting myself up as prey. I'm assuming the role of predator and I'll do the hunting, this time. You can either help me, or take my credentials back and get out of my way."

CHAPTER TWELVE

Danny's team was waiting in the conference room Rainey visited with Sheila, yesterday. Crime scene photos from the newest body find had been added to the wall with the previous victim's photos. Rainey scanned them quickly as she entered the room, before she began greeting her former teammates. The second victim bore a striking resemblance to Katie, which caught Rainey off guard. Danny had not mentioned the victim's description. She was taller and more muscular, but her hair and facial features were very close to Katie's. It shook Rainey a bit, and then she closed her Katie box. She had to focus and Katie had no place in this room.

Roger, the team member she had known the longest, was the first to reach her. He was a strong, quiet man, who looked a lot like Harry Belafonte in his older days. He hugged Rainey, saying, "It's good to have you back."

"Thank you, Roger, but it's just temporary. Good to see you."

James, the tech guru that usually traveled with the team, looked up briefly from his laptop screen and smiled. "Nice to see you, Rainey."

"You too, James."

Paula, a tall, Nubian beauty approached next. Rainey was surprised to see she was extremely pregnant.

"I guess you got busy after we last saw each other," Rainey said, indicating the other woman's protruding belly.

Paula rubbed her hands across the bulging fabric of her top. "Yep, this is my last case before I go on leave."

Rainey looked at her deliriously happy former colleague. "It's true what they say. You look positively glowing. I'm very happy for you."

"Thank you, Rainey. It's good to see you, again. Sorry it's under these circumstances."

Young Agent Curtis stepped forward, grinning from ear to ear. He captured Rainey in a bear hug. "So good to see you, Rainey. We missed you."

"Good to see you too, Curtis. How's your wife?"

"She's as fantastic as ever. She said to tell you hello."

Danny broke up the reunion, before Rainey could speak to Eric, the young trainee she met last summer. He nodded in her direction, which she returned, and everyone took a seat at the long conference table. Danny stood at the head of the table.

"Rainey and I just visited Dalton Chambers. Our suspicions were correct. He has communicated with this UNSUB. Rainey and Katie Meyers are the ultimate targets. That's about all we got out of him."

Roger asked, "Any idea if the UNSUB followed him here from Virginia?"

Danny answered, "No, we believe he's from the triangle area. This last body was found on a very remote trail. It would be hard for a person unfamiliar with the area to find the scene.

Men, clearing the trail of winter debris for a riding club, found the body by chance."

Rainey picked up one of the folders on the table. She wanted to familiarize herself with the information again. James slid a tablet computer in front of her. A sticky note was attached to the top, saying, "This is a clone of your old computer. Your sign in and passwords restored, change them. File on desktop – Chambers' Copycat."

Rainey flipped the cover open, typed in her information, and opened the file. Her mind and body remembered rooms like this, these people, and walls covered in pictures of victims. She felt very alert, which was surprising considering her hangover. Even so, Rainey poured a cup of coffee from the carafe, sitting in the center of the table, to ensure she stayed that way. She found the scanned documents removed from Dalton's cell in the desktop file. Rainey lost herself in Dalton's correspondence while the others talked.

Rainey quickly went through the news articles written last summer. The story the Y-Man gave to a reporter detailing her attack was there. Dalton read it so often the smudges and worn spots showed up on the copy. There were dozens of pictures and print articles in Dalton's possession. The news media had taken the tragedies Katie and Rainey experienced into the realms of sensationalism. There had been a frenzy of coverage that died away only with the approach of Hurricane Earl. Rainey had never been so glad to know a hurricane was coming in her life. Reporters lost interest in her and Katie's personal lives and they were finally left alone.

Rainey read Dalton's fan mail and looked over the church bulletins and newsletters. She was reviewing the autopsy report on the second victim, when she heard Danny say her name. She looked up to see the admonishing look on his face.

"Rainey, I need you to engage here. What's your opinion? Who are we looking for?"

In an instant, she was back in the game, her mind clear. She knew the profile. The information she absorbed while the others were talking fell into place. She felt the rush of knowing this was the one thing she did really well. Behavioral analysis was Rainey's calling. She studied crimes of human wickedness and read them like a book, picking out the main player's motives. Rainey stood up and moved to the wall of pictures. As if the last two years had not happened, Supervisory Special Agent Rainey Bell commanded the room.

"Look at this first victim, Lisa Jones. She was 31, a nurse, not a big woman, but she was well built and from what I read, a regular visitor to the gym. Her friends described her as flirtatious, outgoing, and always willing to help others. The pictures we received from those friends show a socially adept, attractive, young woman. It's the same with the second victim, Kim McNatt; similar body types, personalities, habits. Without the heads, these pictures could be of the same woman. These were alpha females, high-risk victims for the UNSUB; they would fight for their lives. This matches Dalton Chamber's preference for victims."

Curtis interjected, "You left out they were lesbians." He was immediately embarrassed, looking away from Rainey to his iPad.

Rainey smiled. "Yes, they were lesbians, which is different from Dalton's victims. There are two possibilities here. Either the copycat was directed by Dalton to kill lesbians as some sort of message to me, or it means something to the UNSUB. My guess is, the UNSUB's fantasies already included killing lesbians and Dalton exploited that."

"The second crime scene is more organized than the first," Paula commented. "From reading your murder book on Dalton, it appears the UNSUB got more of the details correct."

Rainey moved to the area with pictures of the first body. "Look here, see these shallow cuts on the neck. I think this is when he started to panic. He followed Dalton's instructions to the letter, up to the moment he had to kill her. Then he hesitated. Afterwards, the panic consumed him. He could not complete the tasks assigned to him. He left the body for some time and then returned to dispose of it and the head. It was imperfect. The kill had not gone as he fantasized it would. He failed the master."

Roger spoke up. "So it was probably more the failure than remorse that compelled him to get rid of the body."

"Yes, I believe so," Rainey answered. "He would have preferred we did not find that one. Look at his second victim." Rainey moved to the photos of Kim McNatt's headless body. "This victim is almost exactly as Dalton would have left her."

Curtis, recovered from his earlier embarrassment, asked, "You say almost. What's different?"

"He didn't play in the blood. He has no taste for it. Once she was dead, he disposed of the head, probably in the river, and left the scene."

"But he completed the task assigned to him by his master," Danny added.

James looked up from his laptop, where he had been viewing the crime scene photos. "What's this hole in the ground in front of the second victim? It looks like a pole or something was shoved in there."

Danny answered quickly, "That's part of Dalton's instructions. He's practicing."

"What's he practicing for?" Curtis asked.

Rainey showed no emotion, when she replied, "That's where he plans to stake out Katie's head, when he kills me."

"Oh, my God," slipped from Paula's lips.

Eric's youth prevented him from having the couth not to say, "Wow. What did you do to this Chambers guy? You must have pissed him off, big time."

Roger was usually the quiet voice of reason, but he snapped at Eric. "You stay around long enough, you'll piss someone off, too. Right now you're pissing me off."

Eric slumped back against his chair.

Rainey continued the profile. "We might want to look at this UNSUB as the subservient partner in a serial tandem. The crimes have both organized and disorganized behaviors, suggesting two minds at work here. One partner who is highly intelligent with psychopathic tendencies. The other, of average intelligence with psychological problems, rather than an antisocial disorder. If we look at it that way, then we're looking for an UNSUB who is approximately Dalton's age. He is physically fit and strong enough to control these women. He is not as socially adept as Dalton. He will have used a con to get these women to go with him, probably the "man in need of help" ruse. I don't think you'll find him unattractive, but he will not think he's good looking. He will be shy around these women, until the moment he takes control. He could display a tough exterior, but he is insecure on the inside. He has low self-esteem. He could not have done these crimes without his partner directing him."

Danny expounded on Rainey's train of thought. "The UNSUB would then be the disorganized partner. He will not have had a happy childhood and probably a missing or abusive parent. These types are drawn to groups like the military, looking for acceptance and guidance. They are rarely successful. He is easily manipulated by strong personalities.

He'll have a job where he is never in charge, always following someone else's directions. If he is in a relationship, he does everything to please his partner, and most likely feels disappointed in his efforts. When he discovered Dalton Chambers, he found his soul mate. The one person who could relate to the fantasies that plagued him his entire adult life."

Paula interrupted, "If he fantasized about murders before he met Chambers, what does he get out of copying someone else's crimes?"

"He's pleasing the master," Rainey replied. "That's his satisfaction. Dalton Chambers represents to this kind of mind the type of person he wants to be. It's hero worship. The closer he comes to mimicking Dalton, the better his release, which he more than likely achieves reliving his successes while having sex with his wife/girlfriend, or manually. That's why the first crime was different. It didn't hold up to the standards set for him, so he wasn't able to use it for relief of his frustrations."

"Okay," Roger said, "how do we proceed?"

"We recommend the locals canvas the area where the victims disappeared, extensively," Danny explained. "I'll make a statement to the media warning the lesbian community to be vigilant. We'll send in undercover officers and patrol cars at night, as well. Someone has seen this guy. Someone knows him. We just have to find that person."

There was a knock at the door. Sheila stepped in. "I've assembled everybody in the bull pen."

Danny looked around the room, before he answered, "We're ready. Just give us a minute."

Sheila left the room. Danny leaned down, placing his hands on the table, making eye contact with each team member, except for Rainey, when he said, "Rainey has asked to place herself in the line of fire, to use her presence to draw out the UNSUB. After what you've heard about her personal interests in this investigation, do any of you have any objections to her remaining involved?"

No one spoke. They all looked at Rainey. She stood in front of the backdrop of horrifying pictures. She eyed each individual. The look Rainey gave was meant to reassure them she knew what she was doing.

Danny waited the appropriate amount of time for responses. When none came, he said, "All right then, let's go give this profile."

Rainey hung back as the team filed out of the room. Danny started for the door last. He turned back to her.

"Are you coming?"

"No, I'm a distraction. Too many people out there know - even saw - what happened to me. I don't want them thinking about that while you give the profile. I'm going to call Brooks, see if she found anything."

"Okay... Hey Rainey, give Katie a call. Set up a time after the press conference when I can go see her."

"Sure," Rainey said, softly.

Katie flooded back into her mind. Those emotions had been in their appropriate box while she was in agent mode, but now rushed forward with a vengeance. Danny opened the door to leave.

"Danny, if something happens, will you make sure Katie knows what she meant to me?"

Danny didn't say, "Nothing's going to happen," the usual reaction when someone hears an appeal like Rainey's. He knew it was more than a possibility that he would be required to fulfill that request.

"Yes, Rainey, I'll tell her."

Danny closed the door behind him. Rainey returned to her seat. She opened the file with the bulletins and newsletters from churches around the country. Rainey learned from the fan mail that Dalton requested his fans put him on their church mailing list. Most of his correspondents were church people. Some were honest Christians, trying to save his soul. The others were the type of sick, demented, women and men, who find serial murderers attractive.

Rainey was drawn to one bulletin in particular. On the cover, a color picture of a stained glass window depicted a woman on her knees praying. At first glance, Rainey thought it was a man with long hair, a disciple or a saint, but now she could clearly see breasts under the long cloak. She used the zoom feature on the tablet to look at the picture more closely. The praying hands of the woman were wrapped with a gold braided chain, resembling rope. A small, gold cross dangled from the chain.

Rainey quickly punched Brooks' number into her cell phone.

"CITU, how can I be of service?" Brooks sounded extremely professional.

"Oh, you must have done something really bad to be answering the phone like that."

"Rainey Bell, is that you?" Brooks asked enthusiastically, and then just as quickly changed her tone. "I am not happy with you. Can't even call or email an old friend. Just take off with not so much as a goodbye or kiss my ass."

"Last I checked those particular lines of communication work both ways, and don't tell me you don't have my number or my email address. You probably have a satellite image of my house. How far is it from my front door to my office?" Rainey asked, teasing.

"Thirty yards. By the way, I love the Mountain Dew hillbilly sign, but don't try to distract me..."

Rainey cut her off. "See, I could feel you watching me. I knew it. And under what official guise did you gain access to that image, oh great one?"

Brooks laughed. "Okay, you got me. I had to see where you were. How are you? Is life good there in the countryside?"

"You should come and see for yourself."

"Honey, you know my black ass ain't going no further south than it already is. You feel me?"

"That is such a crock of shit and you know it. You can't tear yourself away from that computer room. You're afraid it will die without you."

"Girl, you know I can't leave my babies here alone, they need me."

Rainey could just see Brooks looking around her room filled with monitors and whirring fans. "All right then, put your babies to work for me."

"McNally filled me in on this copycat down there. I saw your temporary reinstatement paperwork go through yesterday. I assume you are working the case?"

"Yes, and I found something I need you to look into. Can you pull up the documents Danny sent you, the ones from Dalton Chamber's cell?"

Brooks responded, "I'm running the documents through a word recognition program. So far no hits on anything remotely connected to you or the Raleigh-Durham area."

"Look at the church bulletin from the House of Holy Redemption, in San Diego."

Rainey heard fingernails rapidly tapping on a keyboard. Brooks followed quickly with, "I got it up on my screen. What am I looking for?"

"Find out everything you can about the church. I see it has a return P.O. Box instead of a physical address. It's probably bogus."

"I'll dig around. Should I call you or McNally with what I find?"

"Call Danny. He's the lead on this." Rainey paused and then added, "Thanks, Brooks. When this is over, we'll have a nice long chat."

"Rainey Bell, I know this Chambers guy promised to have you killed. As of now, I'll have a program running twenty-four hours a day. If someone so much as breathes a word about you in the future, you will know it. We should have done this years ago. I should have thought of this."

"I have a degree in computer forensics. I should have thought of it myself," Rainey answered, disappointed that she hadn't had the forethought to write a simple search program. She continued, "When this is over, I'm going to do a lot of things differently. I am thankful that you are one of the people that will be watching my back... I love you, Melatiah Brooks."

"I love you, too, Rainey Blue Bell. You be safe."

"Always."

Next, Rainey called Katie's cell phone. She got no answer. She left a message, and then dialed the Meyers' home phone. Katie's mother answered.

"Hello, Mrs. Meyers, this is Rainey. May I speak with Katie?"

Rainey felt like a teenage boy calling his girlfriend's house late at night. It was early afternoon, but still, she would not have been surprised if Melanie Meyers hung up on her. Of the women in Meyers family, Katie was most like her mother. She was the source of Katie's good looks and her temperament. Joyously happy to be alive every day, but fiercely protective of her family, Melanie was as much a force to be reckoned with as her youngest daughter.

"Rainey, I'm sorry, but Katie's asleep. I took her cell phone and made her lie down. She was up all night."

"Could you have her call me when she wakes up? Agent McNally wants to set up a time to meet with her this evening."

"Yes, I'll tell her... and Rainey, I'm sorry this happened. You were good together."

The statement stung Rainey. It sounded like Melanie believed Rainey and Katie's relationship was over. She wanted to say she was fighting to keep that from happening, but she said, "I'm sorry I brought this killer into your lives."

"It's not your fault, Rainey. You couldn't have known this would happen. You take care of yourself and I'll give Katie your message."

"Thank you."

Rainey hung up. Melanie had meant to make Rainey feel better, but she only made the guilt worse. Rainey had known this could happen. Hoping it wouldn't was not been the best course of action. She could see that now, and if given the opportunity, she would do her best to keep it from ever happening again.

#

When the team returned to the conference room, Detective Sheila Robertson returned with them. Rainey asked her to set up a meeting with the owners of Feme Sole for the next day. It was already close to 4:00 p.m. and Rainey was beginning to feel the drain of her previous night's indulgence. She had to make plans with James, so he could prepare the surveillance equipment Rainey would be wearing when she entered the bar Saturday night.

There was still the press conference to get through before she could go home. Danny thought it was a good idea to have Rainey in front of the cameras, in case the UNSUB was watching. He would be, Rainey had no doubt about that. Her presence might agitate his already stressed puppet mind. His master was locked away where he could not communicate with him. The UNSUB was on his own.

The press conference was held outside the courthouse on the front steps, just before the six o'clock news. Rainey and the rest of the team stood behind Danny, as he explained to the public what was happening and warned the lesbian community to be on alert. The reporters listened quietly until Danny finished his statement, and then they began to hurl one question after another in his direction. Most of the inquiries had something to do with identifying the UNSUB, but one voice rang out above all others. It was Cookie Kutter, the television news reporter that dogged Rainey and Katie incessantly for weeks last summer. Rainey hated her, and her parents too for giving her such a stupid name.

"Agent McNally, why is Rainey Bell here? Has she rejoined the FBI?"

Danny responded, "We asked Agent Bell if she would help on this case, and she has been reinstated temporarily."

Cookie wasn't about to let up. "Is it because she worked on the Dalton Chambers case or because the UNSUB is killing lesbians and Agent Bell is one?"

Danny was growing agitated. Rainey heard it in his voice, when he answered, "Agent Bell's expertise in the Chambers' case is unequalled. The UNSUB we are searching for is copying Chambers' crimes. Agent Bell's insights are paramount to this investigation."

A wall of sound erupted at Rainey. It seemed that all the reporters began shouting questions at once.

"Agent Bell, are you thinking about returning to the BAU full-time?"

"Have you visited Dalton Chambers since he's been at Central Prison?"

"Is your connection with Dalton Chambers the reason this UNSUB is killing lesbians? Are you a target of yet another serial killer, Agent Bell?" That was Cookie. Rainey recognized her superior tone.

Danny stepped aside when Rainey moved in front of the bank of microphones.

"I'll make a brief statement," Rainey began. "I do not want my presence to sidetrack you from the real story here. There is a person out there hunting young women in this community. There are two families grieving the loss of a daughter. There are heartbroken friends of the victims. These young women, Lisa Jones and Kim McNatt, deserve justice for the crimes committed against them. Do not lose focus on what's important today. Get the word out about this UNSUB. Someone knows him, somebody has seen him. Help keep this community safe. My involvement should not be a distraction. I am here simply to assist the local police and the FBI in finding justice for these young women."

Cookie's voice rang out. "Where is Katie Myers? Is she still living with you? Is she still a lesbian?"

Rainey glared at Cookie. She wanted to strangle the bottled blonde. Instead, she smiled, and answered, "She's somewhere safe." She started to walk away, but the devil got the better of her. She added, what Rainey was sure would be the sound bite of the day, "Be sure to have that man of the hour draped on your arm there, Cookie. Wouldn't want people to think your continued interest in my personal life means you are anything but heterosexual, would you?"

#

Two hours after the press conference, Rainey got a ride home from a deputy. She planned to go home, soak in the tub to help with her sore shoulder, and then spend the evening processing all the information she gathered so far. Danny got a call from Katie's mother. He was invited to dinner, where he could talk to Katie and her parents, together. Rainey was not invited. Although she had stated she didn't want to interfere with Danny's discussion of Katie's safety, she was hurt by the exclusion.

The sun had been down about an hour when Rainey arrived on her front deck. Ernie was long gone. She waved goodbye to the deputy and entered the cottage. It had never felt so lonely to enter the quietness of the cottage. The warning, beep - beep, from the alarm bounced off the walls. Rainey lived alone most of her adult life. She welcomed the quiet of her home all those years. Now, the stillness in the air felt heavy. The life had gone out of the house. Katie was not there to breathe it back again.

Rainey disarmed the alarm and heard Freddie's doggie door pop open and shut. At least she was not completely alone. She hung up her jacket, put away her weapon, and set the alarm. She went to the kitchen, flipping on the light as she entered. Freddie squinted up at her and meowed loudly. Rainey reached down to get his empty food bowl, when she noticed Freddie was leaving muddy tracks on the floor. He regularly tromped through the swamp surrounding the property. This wasn't the first mess he'd made.

"Look at your feet. You're leaving paw prints everywhere. Katie would not be pleased."

Rainey pulled some paper towels from the dispenser under the cabinets. She wet a couple and knelt down to clean up the mess.

"You know what this means, don't you? You have to have a bath."

Freddie meowed, doing donuts around her arms while she cleaned.

"No arguments. If you get this on the comforter, Katie will kill us bo…."

Rainey froze in mid-word. Looking down at the paper towel in her hand, she saw that it was not mud, but blood she was wiping up. She dropped the towel and grabbed Freddie up from the floor. She checked him from head to toe. No wounds were present, but his paws, legs, and face were wet with blood. Rainey dropped the cat and ran for the gun safe, by the front door. She pulled out the Glock, still in its holster, and clipped it to the belt at her waist. She moved to the bedroom, opened the gun safe in the wall, and pulled out her father's twelve-gauge shotgun. Rainey loaded it quickly, and then racked one of the five shells into the chamber. She grabbed a flashlight from the bedside table and headed out of the room, before catching a glimpse of herself in the mirror.

Now, this is the part of the movie where Rainey always shouted at the TV, "Don't go out there alone, you idiot. Call for back up and wait." Instead, she carried the shotgun to the closet in her old room. Rainey yanked her FBI windbreaker from a hanger, and used it to cover her blood stained white blouse. She kicked off her low-heeled pumps, and slipped into a pair of boots. Prepared to do battle, she picked up the shotgun, and went back to the kitchen.

Rainey stopped in the living room, turned on the TV, and brought up the security cameras. Nothing looked unusual. She pulled her cell phone out, and dialed Danny's number. When he answered, she said, very quickly, "My cat just tracked blood into my house from outside. It could be a dead animal, but it's fresh. Someone could be hurt."

"Rainey, I'm on my way to Katie's. Don't go out there alone. I'll turn around. Do you want me to send a car?"

Rainey's heart was pounding. The hair on her scalp and arms was tingling. Something bad was happening. "No,

Danny! You go to Katie. Make sure she's safe. Send a car. I'm going out there."

"Rainey, wait!"

She slammed the phone closed and put it back in her pocket. She closed her eyes to calm her mind and body. She heard her father's voice, "Remember your training, Rainey. Don't let anyone walk up on you. You make sure you see them coming."

Rainey whispered, "Always."

#

Rainey shut off the lights in the kitchen, so her silhouette wouldn't show in the doorway. She opened the door slowly and peered into the now black night. She clicked on her flashlight, probing the deck for the source of Freddie's footprints. There was nothing there but more paw prints, leading her down the back stairs. When she reached the ground, the prints were harder to see. She put the shotgun to her shoulder, holding the flashlight to the barrel and went hunting.

Rainey checked under the cottage and around her car, stopping to grab her ballistic vest from the backseat, and squatted by the car. She put the vest on quickly, fastening the Velcro straps tightly to her torso. This was war and she wasn't going in totally unprotected. She listened for sirens, and hearing none, proceeded down the driveway to the road. She trailed the light around the perimeter. Still, there were no signs of blood or a body. Freddie stepped out of the darkness in front of her. With his black fur, he was impossible to see unless he wandered into the light. He walked about ten steps in front of her, as she made her way down to the office, scanning her surroundings constantly. Tiny gravel, on the surface of the road, crunched beneath her feet. She moved to the shoulder to lessen the sound of her approach. Freddie sauntered down the road, as if they were out for an evening stroll. If there was danger lurking, Freddie was unaware of it. That was a good sign.

Rainey approached the office, crouching down to make herself a smaller target. She swept the ground under the Mountain Dew painting with the flashlight, seeing nothing there but dried grass in need of cutting. She moved to the front of the building, checking all the windows and the door. Everything was locked up tight. Rainey shined the light in the windows. Nothing looked out of place.

She was running out of places to look without going into the woods, which Rainey was not prepared or stupid enough to do. If the source of the blood were in the thick woods and swamps, they would need to bring dogs to find it. She crept around the corner, toward the lake. The beam of her flashlight bounced off the surface of the water and into the trees. She searched the shoreline, as she eased down the side of the building. She ran the beam of light over the ground behind the building. She saw no traces of blood anywhere. Freddie followed her and danced around her legs.

"Where did you get that blood all over you?" She whispered to the purring feline between her legs.

Still cautious, but relieved at not having found a body on her property so far, she headed back around the building, scanning the surface of the lake by the dock. Rainey's father had installed motion detector lights on the dock to discourage people from using it as a make-out haven. If anyone had crossed the motion detector barrier, the dock would have been lit up like a landing zone. Rainey continued toward the parking lot in front of the building. She stepped too close to the sensors and the dock burst into view, startling her down to one knee, shotgun poised to take aim, trying to adjust her vision to the sudden brightness. She blinked several times against the blinding glare of the lights. That's when Rainey saw the blond hair.

For a moment, she was frozen in time. Everything stopped. Her heart, her breathing, her ability to move, all ceased to function. She was suspended there on one knee, while her mind tried to make sense of what it was seeing. A sudden rush of adrenaline seized her and thrust her legs and arms into action. She ran down the dock, falling to her knees in front of a bloody piling. Staked out, in a macabre cannibalistic scene, was a decapitated head. A mass of blond hair covered the face. Rainey reached up with trembling hands, parting the hair gently to the side. She saw the woman's startled expression and fell back. Rainey's arms slid to her sides, her chin dropped to her chest, and she began to sob. Gasping breaths of air burned her lungs. Waves of sadness washed over her, juxtaposed with her immense relief. It wasn't Katie, but Rainey had just located Kim McNatt's missing head.

CHAPTER THIRTEEN

Rainey put herself back together before the first police car arrived, with Mackie hot on its tail. She waited at the end of the dock. The deputy leapt from his car and ran toward her. She pointed at the head on the dock. When the deputy saw it, he gagged, covering his mouth with one of his hands.

"Don't puke on my crime scene," Rainey said.

The deputy went over to his car, leaned on the hood, and lost his dinner.

Rainey called out to him, "When you're done, call it in," and then turned her attention to the panting Mackie at her side.

"I'm all right. I guess you heard the call go out on the scanner. Sorry, I didn't call to warn you."

Mackie began to calm down. "I wish you'd called me before you went outside."

"I know, but I didn't have time. Someone could have been bleeding to death out here. I couldn't wait."

"That's just the excuse you're using to justify such a stupid move. Rainey, you know better than that."

Rainey defended her decision. "What if it was you laying there, bleeding? Would you want me to wait twenty minutes for the cops to get here, before I came out of the house? Would you have waited, if you thought it was me?"

"No, I wouldn't have waited, but then there isn't a killer stalking me, leaving heads on my dock."

With a little more emphasis than was called for, Rainey said, "I took a vow to protect and serve. I've known from day one that my life may have to be given for someone else's. You need to consider that I have been trained to stay alive, before you judge my actions."

Mackie turned his head quizzically. "Who was that meant for, baby girl, me or Katie?"

The newly recomposed deputy walked up with a roll of crime scene tape, ending that part of their discussion. Mackie helped the deputy seal the scene, while Rainey called Danny, letting him know everything was okay, and what she had discovered. Rainey walked over to Mackie when she was finished

"Hey, I'm sorry. I was still in a bit of shock. You didn't deserve that."

"It's okay, baby girl. You got a lot on your mind."

Rainey remembered Ernie. "Look, you better call Ernie. Tell her what's happened so she won't hear it some other way." Mackie was already pulling out his phone. "And tell her the crime scene guys will be back in the morning, so she won't freak when she sees them."

"Anything else?" Mackie asked, poised to dial his phone.

"You should go on home, too. It's going to be a while before they finish processing the scene. Danny is on his way. He won't let me stay out here by myself, so don't worry." Mackie started to say something. Rainey interrupted, "Really, I'll stay in the house."

Mackie would worry, but he agreed to go home. Danny arrived exactly an hour after Rainey's call. The rest of the team, Detective Robertson and her officers, the Medical Examiner, and crime scene investigators were already there when Danny pulled into her driveway. Rainey sat on the stairs, alone for the first time since the first officers arrived. Freddie perched on the step beside her, watching all the activity down at the dock, somehow aware that he needed to be close to her.

Danny approached, trying to force eye contact. "Rainey, are you okay?"

Rainey looked him straight in the eyes, because she knew he was looking for her reaction. Danny wanted to know if she could remain on the job. She was rattled, but Rainey wasn't backing off.

"I'm fine, Danny. Pissed, but fine."

Danny sat down on the step just below her. He leaned back on one elbow so he could see her face. Danny knew her, maybe even better than Katie did. He knew what to say.

"You know, they keep running that part where you questioned Cookie's sexuality on the news. That's pretty funny stuff. Katie clapped when I showed it to her."

"Is she okay? Does she know what happened?"

Danny patted Rainey's knee. "That's a strong girl you're hooked up with. She's more worried about you than herself, at this point."

"Did you convince her that she's in more danger than me? The plan is her first. Did you tell her that?"

"I did, and I also forced her to accept an armed guard at all times. She'll be outside the door when Katie goes to the bathroom. She'll sleep on the floor in Katie's bedroom. Katie will not move inside the house without protection, and if she leaves the house, which I totally objected to, a male officer will accompany her, as well. Two patrol cars are in the driveway."

Rainey perked up. "She? Who is guarding Katie?"

Danny smiled. "The biggest, baddest woman I could find. She's from vice. She's been around. Detective Robertson says no one will get by this cop, not even you."

Rainey was unsettled by the news another woman would be sleeping in the same bedroom with Katie. It took her mind away from the scene at the dock, which was exactly what Danny had calculated it to do. She smiled down at him.

"She's safe then?"

Danny stood up, extending his hand to Rainey. "She's locked down tighter than the President. The Secret Service doesn't get to sleep with him."

Rainey took his hand and raised her eyebrows. "On the floor, right? You said she's sleeping on the floor."

Danny laughed, pulling her to her feet. "Well, now, I guess that's entirely up to Katie. We all know what happened the last time she had a female bodyguard."

#

At midnight, Rainey's cell phone rang. She was still down at the dock, waiting for the crime lab to finish collecting evidence. They were packing up to leave for the night, but would come back first thing in the morning. Daylight could reveal more evidence. Rainey pulled the phone out of her pocket. She saw Katie's name on the caller ID, flipped the phone open, raising it to her ear rapidly.

"Katie, is everything all right?"

"Yes, I'm fine," Katie replied, softly.

Rainey stepped to the other side of the building, away from Danny and the few others still talking under the bright halogen lights brought in by the investigators.

"Katie, what's wrong?"

"This is all wrong, Rainey. Me over here and you there, people getting their heads cut off, a strange woman watching me sleep, it's all wrong."

"She's really watching you sleep? Where are you? Is she watching you, now?"

"No, I'm hiding in the bathroom," Katie said, laughing.

It did Rainey's heart good to hear Katie laugh. She smiled into the phone. "Well, you can't sleep in there. You're going to have to come out sometime."

"I will... I just missed you. I wanted to hear your voice, know that you were okay, before I try to sleep, which seems to be impossible without you next to me."

Rainey's throat tightened, her voice hushed, when she said, "I miss you, too."

"You do know last night was the first night we've been apart since July?" Katie asked.

Rainey kicked at the ground. "Yes, I'm well aware of that."

"I saw you on TV." Katie changed subjects, as she often did, forcing Rainey to pay attention whenever she was talking to her. If she didn't, she could end up completely lost. Katie continued, "That was so good, what you said to Cookie. I laughed."

"Yeah, Danny told me you clapped."

"Oh, she deserved it. That was fabulous... You looked great, by the way."

Rainey never took compliments on her looks well. She said, shyly, "You're biased."

"No, really Rainey, you looked fantastic, confident. The FBI Agent persona looks good on you. I never saw it before, but you looked... I don't know, comfortable maybe."

"I wasn't. The shoes were killing me."

It was quiet for a moment, and then Katie said, "Do you miss it? Is that what you really want to do? Am I keeping you from your passion?"

"No, Katie. I was gone from the Bureau long before I met you. I just didn't know it, yet. I don't have to be in the FBI to do what I do. I would like to consult on cases from time to time, if you can live with that, but I don't want to be submerged in this anymore. It's just not a good place for me to be."

"Are you sure, Rainey? I don't want you to wake up one day and be sorry. I don't want to be the reason you gave up such an important part of who you are."

"But it's not all I am."

"I know that," Katie responded, quickly. "You are a cop at heart, though. I don't think you would be happy if you weren't chasing bad guys."

"Katie, I... I know I'm not the ideal person to have a relationship with. My job is scary sometimes. My past catches up with me occasionally. I respect that frightens you. I can do more to make you less fearful, but I can't promise you that something bad won't happen. I could be killed in a car accident, just as easily as on the job. I trained for this, just like you did to be a teacher. I can handle myself out there. The question now is, can you learn to respect that?"

Rainey hadn't meant to speak so freely. The silence on the other end of the phone suggested it might have been too much.

Katie cleared her throat. Her voice sounded dry and tense, when she answered, "I know I love you more than I've ever loved anything, but I can't answer that now. We jumped into

225

this relationship under similar circumstances. I don't want our decisions concerning the future to be clouded by all this. Do you understand, Rainey?"

Rainey saw Danny coming toward her. The last of the investigators pulled away in a county van.

"Katie, I have to go now. Danny's coming." She was wriggling out of answering the question posed to her. The doubt that their relationship would ever work out was quite evident in Katie's voice. Rainey couldn't deal with that possibility at the moment. "Promise me, you'll do what the deputy says, okay?"

"I'll make sure to stay with my escort. I don't want to worry you, Rainey. You focus on catching this guy. Like I said, it's who you are."

Rainey heard the edge in Katie's voice. She could tell Katie was trying to control it.

"I love you, Katie. Don't give up on me."

The phone went silent.

#

As predicted, Danny slept on the couch. This became a problem for Rainey soon after she went to bed. She couldn't sleep, tossing and turning in the big bed for more than an hour. Rainey pounded on the pillows, changed sides of the bed, and even lay across it sideways at one point. She could smell Katie everywhere, and she felt the empty space where Katie should be. Rainey thought she might have been able to fall asleep on the couch, but then Danny was there. She ended up on the futon in the home office and finally slept a few hours.

Now, Rainey was standing in the closet, looking at shoes. In the two years since she last dressed in suits to go to work, Rainey wore tennis shoes, hiking boots, even tactical boots, but not heels. Yesterday had nearly done her in. She was dressed in dark blue slacks and blazer, with the obligatory white blouse, the other "uniform" of her FBI days. Katie had rows of brightly colored heels. Rainey had the blue and black variety of low-heeled calf boots and the smallest heeled pumps she could find. She owned one really nice pair of high-heels that went with the black dresses she wore on rare occasions. Rainey's clothes fit on half of one of the long racks that ran along the walls of the large, master bedroom closet. Katie's wardrobe filled the rest.

Rainey stared at her shoes, wondering if anyone would notice if she just put on a pair of Nikes. The thought then occurred to her that she wasn't really an agent anymore. She slipped back into that skin yesterday with ease, but despite what Katie said about her looking comfortable, it didn't quite fit anymore. Rainey left the suit and blouse in a pile on the closet floor, not even bothering to hang them up. She wouldn't be needing them anymore.

Danny was waiting in the kitchen when Rainey emerged from the bedroom dressed in black jeans, a black silk shirt, black linen blazer, and her favorite black tennis shoes. Her hair was pulled back in a ponytail, hanging out the back of her FBI ball cap. Danny poured a cup of coffee for her, before sitting down at the kitchen table.

"I have to say that is the most comfortable couch I've ever slept on." Danny smiled cheerfully.

Rainey peered out from under the bill of her hat. "I'm glad someone got some sleep."

Danny eyed her up and down. "I see we're done following the FBI dress code."

"I've never understood how we are supposed to chase down criminals in heels," Rainey protested.

"You're not required to wear heels." Danny grinned.

"Yeah, try wearing dress slacks with flats. Not a good look."

Danny sipped his coffee. Then he said, "Besides, you aren't supposed to be chasing them. That's for someone else to do. We profile them, they catch them, that's how this works."

Rainey stared down at her coffee cup. "I'm not waiting for someone else to catch this guy."

"I know, 'you're hunting and I'm to stay out of the way,' but Rainey, you know the way we do it works. The cop with a score to settle storyline rarely works out for the best in real life. You're ignoring years of experience that tells you I'm right. I'm going to ask you one more time, please don't paint a target on your back. We'll catch this guy."

"I am using my experience. You know we would be trolling for this type of UNSUB. We'd have undercover all over this, hoping one of them would attract his notice. He wants me; more specifically he wants Katie, then me. I need to be right in front of him. I have to draw his attention from Katie and any other woman in his path. At least, I'm prepared for him. I'm afraid these other women, including Katie, would be dead the moment he said hello."

"Okay, I see your point." Danny leaned forward, placing his freckled forearms on the table. "Here's the other thing, if we blanket this one bar, what's to say he doesn't move to another one?"

Rainey had thought about that. "He hit the same location twice on purpose to draw us in. He had to involve me in the case, somehow get close to me. This type of UNSUB needs to control the situation, so he's studied this location. We might find a personal connection to this particular place, after we catch him. The location of the abductions, my involvement in the case, this is all part of his fantasy."

"You are ignoring the obvious conclusion here, Rainey. He's also fantasized about the trap he's set for you. He knows you won't be alone. He's not going make a move in front of all those people and the cops he knows are there. His strategy has to include getting you alone. How has he planned to do that?"

"It's going to come in transit. I don't think he wants to confront me on my own turf, here at the cottage. When I'm in my car is the only time I'm alone."

Danny hammered home, "Again, you've missed another way he gets to you. He draws you to him, using Katie."

Rainey narrowed her eyes. "But you promised me, she is safe. Danny, I can't do this if I should be with Katie. If there is any doubt in your mind about her welfare, then I'm not leaving her side, period."

Danny tried a lighter tone, when he said, "As long as she doesn't try to elude her body guards, I have a hard time believing anyone could even speak to her without a well trained officer in very close proximity."

Rainey smiled at Danny's use of the word "elude." Katie had not attempted to elude her last set of bodyguards; she simply forced them to do what she wanted.

Rainey stood up and walked to the sink, while saying, "I made her promise to go nowhere without an escort." Rainey started laughing, while rinsing her coffee cup.

Danny joined her at the sink. "What's so funny?"

Rainey chuckled, under her words. "Her sisters are coming today. I think I'd much rather be bait for a killer than have to stay in that house with those women."

\#

Danny's cell phone rang, as they were walking down the steps of the cottage. He saw the caller ID and turned on the speakerphone. "Good morning, Miss Brooks. I have Rainey here with me. She can hear you, so don't talk about her like you usually do."

"McNally, you are not nearly as funny as you think you are." Brooks' voice cracked into the morning air. She didn't give Danny time to respond. "How's my girl, this morning? I saw the crime scene photos when I came in - Gruesome - Just some fucked up people in this world, I'm telling you, just fucked up. And most of them know your name. You need to get a new name like Jane Smith or some shit..."

Rainey had to distract Brooks from her diatribe. She had obviously had too much coffee. "I've thought about that," Rainey interrupted, then quickly asked, "Hey, did you find anything on that church?"

It worked. Brooks was redirected appropriately. The information Rainey sought came through the speaker in Brooks' highly caffeinated voice, "You were correct about the bogus P.O. Box, but not like you think. There was a box rented two years ago by a John Paul Pope. Of course, there is no such person connected to the San Diego area. I did find several though, which amazed me. Anyway, the place is a mail service, mostly dealing with military personnel. That's why they did not find it unusual to have been forwarding the mail to another box in Raleigh for the last eighteen months, where the mail was picked up regularly until the first body was found. The mail has stacked up there and is being held for you at the main downtown post office."

Brooks took a much-needed breath and continued, "The Church does not actually exist, as you might have guessed. To pass a simple security check in the prison mailroom, the church listed a physical address, email address, and contact person - the same Mr. Pope - all of which is one big fairy tale. The address is an empty lot. The email address is Gmail that can be accessed from anywhere in the world, from multiple devices, and bounced through several filters and additional mail servers. The address has only received mail, except for the spam we all must endure, from the two prisons Dalton has been housed in."

Rainey interrupted again, "Has there been any activity on the account?"

"No activity, if you don't count the regular clearing of said spam, and a monthly mailing of the bulletin to another Gmail account that bounces back to this one. That's just to keep the account active. No other outgoing mail except to verify the address for prison security; once, two years ago when the bulletins started arriving in Virginia, and three months ago when Dalton was moved to Central Prison."

Danny asked, "Did you trace the monthly uploads of the bulletin?"

"Yes, I did. They were uploaded from Internet hot spots starting in San Diego, two years ago. Then at the same time his mail began to be forwarded the UNSUB started using networks in the Raleigh-Durham area, on the coast, in the mountains, really all over the state of North Carolina, and up into Virginia. Your boy is a sightseer. He uploads at different times of the month, so no pattern there. He trolls through neighborhoods until he finds an unprotected network. I checked out the families. No leads. He never hits the same place twice. There is literally no way to trace him, unless he tries to upload now. I got his ass, if he even peeps into that account."

Rainey thought back on what Brooks said about no mail since the first body was found.

"Danny, he must have another way to communicate with Dalton. He knew we would search his cell. Why didn't he get rid of the evidence? Why give us this line of communication to his pupil?"

Brooks chimed in. "You might think I'm crazy, but Charles Manson had a cell phone and a Facebook account. I'm just sayin'."

Danny was adamant. "I would have found a cell phone. He's been moved, anyway. He certainly doesn't have it now."

Rainey didn't miss a beat. "Did they do a cavity search?"

#

Danny drove away, headed for Durham. Rainey walked down to the office, where Ernie was waiting for her to sign the weekly checks. Rainey would join Danny and the others, as soon as she was finished. The crime scene guys had come and gone by the time she and Danny came outside. Rainey glanced at the dock. The crime scene tape had been cleared away and someone made an effort to wash the blood off, but there was still a dark stain where the head had been. Entering the main office, she found Ernie sitting on the couch, an unusual place for her.

"What? Are you lounging on the couch already? I suspected that's what you did when I wasn't here," Rainey teased.

"How did he get that close, Rainey?" Ernie was in no mood for playful banter.

Rainey sat on the couch beside the older woman and told it plain, the way she knew Ernie expected it. "We think he came up on a boat. The motion detectors only work when you cross from land to the dock, or vice versa. If he never came down the dock, he would have remained in complete darkness."

Ernie turned to look at Rainey. "How would he know that?"

"Because he's been here before. People come up here all the time in boats, thinking we're still a bait shop. If he came on

the water at night, then set off the motion detectors, I wouldn't
have paid much attention if the lights went right back off. It's
such a common occurrence."

"Katie might be right," Ernie began. "It's not safe out here,
you two alone, so far away from help and exposed."

Rainey stared out the window toward the cottage. "I don't
know what I can do to make this place safer, short of building
a compound and that's no way to live."

Ernie patted Rainey's leg. "You'll think of something.
Right now, you have to return a call to 'the Hill.' She's called
three times since the newscast yesterday."

'The Hill' referenced Chapel Hill and Rainey's mother.
She had forgotten to call her, not thinking she was in real
danger. Rainey had so little contact with her mother that she
doubted the killer was interested in her or her stepfather, but
she should have called. Having her mother find about Rainey's
involvement in the case from the news was sure to bring down
the wrath of Constance Herndon.

"Oh God, please tell me I don't have to talk to her today."
Rainey pleaded with Ernie. "You call her back. Tell her I'm
fine and I'm sorry I didn't call her."

"No, ma'am. I've already had the pleasure twice this
morning. I'm good for another year or two."

Rainey cringed. "That bad, huh?"

Ernie pushed off Rainey's knee and stood up. "Constance
is on the warpath, honey. Stick your head up and let her take
her best shot, before she gathers any more steam."

Rainey fell back against the couch, exasperated. "Can my
life get any more complicated at this moment?"

Ernie had reached her desk when she turned to face
Rainey. "Sure honey, Katie could call and tell you why she
reacted the way she did the other night. She's been taking

hormones for the last month and is scheduled to be inseminated next week."

Rainey popped up into a rigid sitting position. "You're making that up."

"No, darlin', I'm not. She wanted to surprise you. Surprise!"

#

"Hello, mother," Rainey said into the receiver.

She was seated at her desk, signing checks, and praying this conversation would be as brief as possible.

"Caroline Marie, I cannot believe you were on the news and did not warn John and me."

John Herndon was Rainey's stepfather. He adopted her, which Rainey had demanded reversed when she discovered the existence of her real father. He was a nice enough man, but he was no match for his wife, and no source of comfort to Rainey. She ignored her mother's insistence on calling her by the name she was given, after her grandmother, who thought "Rainey" was base and uncivilized, had changed her birth-name. Once she knew her real name, she had insisted on being called "Rainey," to her grandmother's severe disapproval. Her mother called her Rainey most of the time, unless she was in trouble. She called her "Caroline Marie" when she was in really big trouble.

Rainey talked fast, so her mother would have no time to comment. "Mother, I did not call you because I didn't want to alarm you. Just so you're caught up, I have been temporarily reassigned to the Bureau and I may appear on TV several times before this is over. I appreciate your concern, but I'm surrounded by good officers that won't let anything happen to me."

Constance leapt in with both feet. "I am not talking about your career choices. Quite frankly, I'd rather have a daughter in the FBI than one who chases lowlife bail jumpers for a living. What I am calling about is your announcement to the world that you are a lesbian. Do you have to continue to rub it in our faces? I won't be able to go to the club, until John Edwards gives them something else to wag their tongues about."

The truth was out. Her mother cared more about her bridge club than Rainey being hunted by a serial killer. She barely remembered the years when her mother was kind and loving. That was before Rainey's grandmother fully sunk the teeth in and changed Connie into Constance forever. It did not surprise Rainey that her safety was the least of her mother's concerns.

Rainey took a breath and let it out slowly. Then, as calmly as she could, said, "I did not make an announcement about my sexuality. I answered a few questions and told off an obnoxious reporter. I assure you, attracting your attention to my personal life was the last thing on my mind."

"Don't take that superior tone with me," Constance shot back. "I think that attack on you did something to your brain. Your father would be so disappointed in this leap into sexual debauchery. Living in sin, in his house. Bill would never have approv..."

Rainey, who for the most part tried to be, at least, respectful of her mother on the rare occasions that they spoke, launched into her mother with all the built up frustrations of the last week for fuel.

"I may not be the daughter you wanted, but my father was proud of me and loved me for who I am. Don't presume to speak for him, not now, not ever. Do you understand? Shut up now, or I'll never speak to you again, or is that what you want? If so, lose my number, disown me, claim you found me in a ditch and did what you could, but alas, I was just too common to fit into your world. Fuck you, Connie. Is that clear enough for you?"

Rainey slammed the cell phone shut and threw it down on her desk. She stood up, grabbed two fists full of hair, and roared at the ceiling, "Ahhhhhhhhhhhhh!"

She heard slow clapping at her office doorway. Rainey turned to see Ernie standing there, smiling, and continuing to clap in a slow deliberate rhythm.

"Now that, baby girl, was a long time coming."

#

Every possible button that Rainey Bell possessed was being pushed. Rainey's boxes were coming uncapped at an alarming rate. On the way to Durham, the hands-free device in her car began to speak.

"You have a call from Katie. Please press the call button to answer."

Rainey glanced at the mirror, where the call button was located. "Not now, Katie, not now," she said aloud, but she pushed the button anyway.

"Hey honey," Rainey said, trying to sound upbeat.

"Don't 'hey honey' me. I know exactly what you're planning to do and it's just plain nuts."

Oh my, God! The UNSUB might be under stress because he couldn't communicate with his master, but Rainey had the exact opposite problem. She couldn't keep people from talking to her. Was a minute alone to gather her composure too much to ask? How was she supposed to out-think Dalton Chambers, who, although he was a complete narcissist, had an extremely high IQ? Rainey couldn't put the lids back on the boxes fast enough.

"What are you talking about, Katie?"

Playing dumb did not work. "Rainey Bell, you are not going to that bar Saturday night. That's it! I'm putting my foot down. Let the team do the work. Consultants don't wear body wires and set themselves up as bait."

"Well, I can see we need to tighten up security at the police station. Did one of the cops tell you?"

Katie was almost hysterical. "No, Danny told me. He thought I should talk to you, while you still had a chance to change your mind. Rainey, you can't go through with this."

Rainey made a mental note to tell Danny to fuck off, too. "Did he also tell you why I'm doing this? I'm not going in there alone. I will be wired with both video and audio, so the team can see what I see. If the UNSUB is in that bar, he will have to get close to me. He won't be able to resist. If I can't spot him, maybe the team will. We have to be proactive on this guy. We can't sit around and expect him to make a mistake. He could make us wait a long time, but he will come for us, Katie. Have no doubts about that."

"Why does it have to be you? Can't some other lesbian cop go in there? I mean, I'm sure they would spot a straight one right away, but there has to be someone else."

In that high moment of stress, Rainey found Katie's comment hysterical and began to laugh.

"Are you laughing?" Katie was incredulous.

Rainey tried to control her amusement, when she said, "So, what you're saying is, that because I have slept with a woman for nine months of the forty years I've been alive, these women will be able to tell within seconds that I have crossed over to their ranks."

"Rainey, I hate to inform you, but you are a famous lesbian around here. You're not only a famous lesbian; you're a hot FBI agent with a gun. You are the quintessential lesbian icon."

They both laughed for a moment and then a hush fell over them.

Rainey spoke first. "I will not be alone in there, Katie. There will be five other armed women in the bar with me, and a dozen cops outside. Saturday night, Feme Sole will be the safest place in Durham."

"How will you recognize him?"

"A lot of it has to do with body language, eye contact, things like that. The team will look for people watching me. How they watch me is more important than the fact that they are."

"What about afterwards, when you go home?"

Rainey suspected, if they didn't locate the UNSUB at the bar, Danny would not allow her to go home alone. He was giving her rope, but he wouldn't let her hang herself. "I'll be covered then, too. Danny will make sure of that."

"I still think this is crazy." Katie would not let up.

Rainey made a fatal mistake. She responded without thinking, "That's because your hormone levels are jacked up and you can't be rational."

There was a deadly silence on the line, followed by, "Your call has ended. If you would like me to reconnect your call, say, 'Yes,' or press the call button to hang up."

CHAPTER FOURTEEN

Rainey managed to make it through the rest of the morning without making anyone else mad or telling them off. She could feel herself near the edge of a roaring tempest. If one more person dropped a load on her, Rainey was going to show everyone just how hot the ice in her veins could run. Nobody really knew Rainey's thoughts and desires. No one knew the weight she carried. They were all about to find out, because Rainey Bell had reached her limit. God help the person that tipped the scale.

Rainey leaned with her back against the wall of the conference room, arms crossed over her chest. Her body language said, "Stay away." She eyed Danny from across the room, still sweltering beneath the surface because he shot his mouth off to Katie. They had been with the team all morning, planning and re-checking the evidence. The opportunity to confront Danny had not presented itself. When it did, he was going to get an earful.

"Rainey, I need to put this video camera on your jacket."

It was James. Rainey had been so engrossed in her thoughts of kicking Danny's ass, she did not feel James approach. She stood up straight and turned to the shorter man, presenting the lapel of her jacket.

James talked while he pinned on the button size camera. "This is real simple. See, it has a clasp, just like a tiepin. Tomorrow night, wear black if you can. It won't show up, especially if you put it in place of a button, or something like that. It has a built in microphone, but I want to add an extra one for backup, and you'll have an earwig so we can talk to you. " He stepped back. "Great. You don't notice it at all on that jacket. Now, we can see and hear everything you do." He moved back toward his computer on the table. "You just wear that around for a few minutes, so I can check the feed."

Rainey looked down at the small black camera. "How far away can you be?"

"About 1000 feet, clearly. I'm going over to the bar this afternoon to check for interference possibilities. The jail is very near there, so I don't want to get mixed up in their bandwidth. I think we'll be okay, unless they all start talking at once. If we need to, one of the other officers can wear a transmitter to receive and boost your signal."

"I'm going over there this afternoon. You can test it then."

"Great, just let me know when you're ready to leave. I'll get the van ready."

James went back to work on his computer. The rest of the team was making plans for lunch. There was nothing left to do, except Rainey and Detective Robertson's visit to Feme Sole. When the others began moving toward the door, Danny walked over to Rainey.

Keeping his voice low, he said, "Your body language suggests that your mood soured since I left you this morning. I assume Katie called you."

Rainey glared at Danny. Between gritted teeth she responded, "It was not your place to tell her."

"She had a right to know, Rainey."

Rainey raised her voice slightly, the anger apparent in her tone. "That may be true, but she should have heard it from me, not you. You don't know what she's like, how wound up she can get. You scared her."

Danny lowered his voice more, apparently trying to get Rainey to do the same. "I think we should continue this conversation in private." He turned to the others, who had stopped at the door to watch the fight. "Could you give us a moment, please?"

The room cleared. Danny sat down on the edge of the table. He lowered his shoulders and smiled calmly. Rainey recognized the non-confrontational technique they used on agitated suspects. It did nothing to quell her anger.

As soon as the door closed behind the last gawker, she said, "What you did was far outside the bounds of our personal and professional relationship. I've stood by and watched you screw up one relationship after another and not once did I stick my nose in your business."

"Maybe you should have," Danny answered, candidly. "Be mad at me if you want, I did what I thought needed to be done. Lying to her, about the danger you are putting yourself in, is not going to fix your relationship."

Rainey's anger flared. "I did not lie to her!"

Danny's calmness was in stark contrast to Rainey's temper. "It's a lie of omission. I know you don't want to hear this, but that's the root of all your problems with Katie."

"Now you're going to profile my relationship? That'll be the fucking day…"

"The fucking day, what, Rainey? The fucking day you listen to someone other than yourself. Since your father died and then the assault, you quit listening to anybody. You stopped trusting people. You became excessively cautious, constantly vigilant, and overly protective of the people you care about. That's classic post traumatic stress."

"What, now you're going to tell me I need a shrink? I did my Bureau required time on the couch, thank you."

"A few more sessions couldn't hurt. Maybe you and Katie should go together. You might learn what is really behind her concerns. You haven't told her what you're really afraid of and the not knowing is terrorizing her."

Rainey continued to scowl at Danny. "She doesn't need to know the details."

"It's not your job, Rainey, this one or the bail business. I don't think you give her enough credit. Katie knows she fell in love with a cop. She knows what dangers are out there, but she sees your fear, and it doesn't have a name. Katie can't process it and deal with it until she knows."

Rainey took a step closer to him. "Back off, Danny."

Danny stood up. Non-confrontational strategies went right out the window. "Why not tell her what really lurks out there, the thing that drives the fears of Rainey Bell?"

Rainey seethed. Her hands were clinched in fists, her jaw muscles contracted.

Danny stared into her eyes, calculating his chances of getting away with what he was about to say.

He softened his tone, and said, "You're not scared of someone coming after you. You are more than prepared for that. You're afraid of losing someone else. You're terrified of being left behind, broken hearted, and alone."

"You don't have a fucking clue what I'm afraid of," Rainey spat.

"You're the one pushing Katie away, not your job, not the boogey-men out there. You're obsessed with protecting her and in so doing you are smothering her. You're going to lose her, because of it."

Rainey turned on her heels and stormed out the door. She passed the rest of the team in the hall, staring at the open laptop James held up for them. Rainey realized they had been watching the fight on screen. From the looks on their faces, she could tell the lapel camera caught it all. Rainey unpinned the camera from her jacket and handed it to James.

"Here, take this. It's obvious that it works," Rainey snapped.

She continued down the hall and entered the bullpen. Rainey found Detective Robertson at her desk.

"Come on, Sheila. I'm taking you to lunch."

#

On the way to the car, Rainey called Feme Sole, hoping to reach one of the co-owners, Phyllis Rowan. Rainey found the name of the bar appropriate for a lesbian club in the middle of judicial central. In the past, women had few individual rights of their own. A woman was designated feme sole in order to conduct business and own property independent of a man, a right that had to be bestowed upon her by the state. The name of the bar was a reminder of just how hard women had to fight for independence. The bar was located down the block from the Detention Center, on Pettigrew Street.

On the third ring the husky female voice of a long-time smoker said, "Feme Sole."

"Hi, I was wondering if Phyllis was around?"

Rainey heard the distinct intake of a drag on a cigarette and then the exhale, before the voice said, "Yeah, this is Phyllis. What can I do for you?"

"I'm Agent Bell with the FBI. I believe Detective Robertson has been in contact with you. I know we're set up to come to the bar later this afternoon, but the detective and I would like to come earlier, if that's okay with you? We were going to grab a quick lunch first."

The voice brightened on the other end. "We serve lunch, if you want to come on now. Tell me what you want and I'll get it going."

Rainey imagined a cheeseburger dripping with grease and deep-fried fries, but Katie would have a fit if she knew Rainey ate that much fat. Rainey had to admit she was healthier since Katie made it her mission in life to feed her, but healthier meant more food and extra miles to run. Katie distracted her from running too many mornings and Rainey worried about the pounds that would slow her down. With that in mind she said, "How about a chef salad? Do you have that?"

"One fresh chef salad coming up. Sweet tea?"

"Sweet tea would be fantastic." Rainey looked at Sheila, who nodded that was fine with her. "Make that two of everything. See you in a few minutes."

Rainey was quiet on the way to the bar and Sheila must have sensed it was best to leave her alone. When they exited the car, in the big dusty parking lot next to Feme Sole, Rainey turned to Sheila.

"When we go in there tomorrow night, I don't want you near me. Find a spot today, where you can see the whole dance floor. I'll ask the owner to reserve the table. I want to know where to look for you, if I need you."

"I gotcha' back, girl. Don't you worry about that."

Rainey examined the bar's typical tobacco warehouse architecture, prevalent in the old "Big Tobacco" district. Durham once held the largest tobacco company in the world, American Tobacco, formed when the five biggest rivals in the industry became one company in the late eighteen hundreds. The city began extensive urban renewal back in the nineties. Now the old abandoned warehouses and factory buildings, with their elaborate red brickwork, were commercial and residential spaces. A bar in this district probably did very well. At least, the real estate was worth a bundle.

Large windows occupied most of the front of Feme Sole. The old warehouse was two stories tall, with huge six-paned black iron windows equally spaced down the exterior walls. The windows toward the back of the building were bricked over on the bottom floor, but the top windows were still paned with the original swirling antique glass. A finely tailored, black canopy lined the sidewalk in front of the entrance. Above the second floor windows, hung a giant LED screen almost the length of the façade. At the moment the sign spelled out "Feme Sole" in cursive purple letters. It certainly looked classier than most of the dive bars Rainey had experienced during investigations.

Rainey walked beyond the entrance, to the adjoining alley. Sheila was by her side. A small deck area sat at the back of the building. Rainey could just see the edge of it. She walked to the back. The deck contained chairs and tables, with ashtrays everywhere. A sign on a small door leading back into the bar read, "Extinguish all smoking materials before re-entering." The deck was obviously the smoking area for the bar. The old tobacco barons would be surprised to see that even on Tobacco Road you could no longer smoke inside. Rainey turned around and studied the alley once more.

"What are you thinking?" Sheila peered down the passage. "Are you looking for a good place to park the van?"

"No, actually, I was thinking Katie's ancestors probably owned the ground we're standing on, or at least some of it. The Meyers clan made its fortune in tobacco."

"Shit, my people probably worked the fields," Sheila joked.

"And mine probably cleaned the house." Rainey was talking about her father's family. She never considered herself part of her mother's world, on the other side of the tracks.

Sheila slapped her hip, where her gun was holstered. "Look who's got the gun, now."

Rainey slapped a high five with Sheila, saying, "We've come a long way, baby."

"Speaking of coming a long way..." Sheila placed her hand gently on Rainey's arm. "Your new life has been good for you. I saw it, when you walked in the other day. You were sparkling."

Rainey chuckled. "Sparkling? Come on, I don't sparkle. I don't even twinkle."

"Say what you want, that woman rocks your world."

A smiling Rainey nodded in agreement. "She does that. She can also make me crazy."

"That's love, honey. My husband is lucky to be alive. I remind him often that I do carry a gun, but like Billie sang it..." Sheila broke into song, "My man, I love him, so."

Rainey laughed for a moment, and then turned serious. "How does he handle your job?"

"He knew I was a cop from day one. I met him when I pulled him over for no taillights."

"Katie knew what I did for a living. It doesn't mean she likes it."

Sheila stopped just outside the entrance. "Rainey, I'm going to give you one piece of advice. It worked for me. You need to put what you do in perspective for Katie. Remind her that soldiers leave their families every day, firefighters risk their lives, scientists study deadly diseases... the list goes on. Is my family's happiness more important than the families of those men and women? What about the woman killed on the highway, coming home from her second job with groceries for her six kids? Would my death in the line of duty somehow be more tragic? That woman was doing her duty, too. It's all in the point of view."

"Sheila, you are a wise woman."

Rainey opened the door and the two women walked into a large room, brightly lit by the sun streaming through the many windows. Most bars were dark, smelling of old beer and stale cigarettes, not Feme Sole. The room was big and airy. The only aroma came from the food on the tables in front of the patrons. The interior walls were exposed red brick like the exterior. On both the left and right walls were wrought iron black staircases leading to a balcony that looked over the room and presumably into the dance area beyond. Gigantic, heavy wooden doors, old and darkly stained, dominated the wall directly ahead of Rainey. To the left of those doors stood a bar made of wood, matching the doors. To the right, overstuffed couches and chairs were grouped together in conversation pits.

They made their way to the bar, through rectangular tables filled with women, ranging from construction worker to hot lawyer. Some were alone, eyes focused on computers or e-readers. A large table group laughed over baskets of sandwiches and chips. A few obvious couples sat lost in their own conversations. This wasn't Rainey's first experience in a lesbian bar, but this time her perception was altered. She had convinced herself her own sexuality would not matter, but Rainey felt all the eyes on her and knew Katie had been right. There wasn't a single lesbian in the bar that didn't recognize her, if not as the famous FBI agent, as one of them.

Rainey ignored the stares and walked up to a large shouldered woman with very short gray hair. The woman had to be Phyllis. She looked like someone who would sound like the voice on the phone, with deep wrinkles around her lips from years of drawing in the nicotine-enhanced smoke. Phyllis Rowan looked like she'd been around the block a time or two. She stood behind the bar, drying glasses. From what Rainey could see, she was five seven or eight, and two hundred and fifty pounds. Phyllis was a big woman.

Rainey stepped up to the bar and took a seat on a tall wooden stool. Sheila remained standing beside her. Phyllis sauntered over, throwing the towel across her shoulder. She was dressed in a dark blue, crisply ironed, button up shirt. The words "Feme Sole" were embroidered over the pocket, in neon purple. She smiled and turned her head a little to one side, peering at Rainey curiously.

"Agent Rainey Bell in my bar. I am honored."

Rainey stuck out her hand to receive Phyllis' thick grip. "You must be Phyllis."

The large woman grinned. "Yes, ma'am, that's me."

Sheila extended her hand for a paw shake from Phyllis, saying, "Detective Robertson. Nice to finally meet you, Ms. Rowan."

"It's Phyllis and it's nice to meet you, as well." Phyllis looked over the other patrons. "Let's go in the other room so we can talk without the gawkers." She pointed at the big doors. "I'll go through the kitchen and pick up your salads. Meet ya' on the other side."

Rainey and Sheila followed Phyllis' instructions, entering the vast hall located behind the doors. Only the support beams, brick pillars, and black steel balconies remained of the former tobacco warehouse. As Rainey suspected, the balconies extended along both walls over the dance floor. A stage was set up at the far end of the room. Tables sat under the balconies near the windows. Heavy black curtains were pulled back to allow the sun into the room. Two long bars were centered on each side of the space where the windows were bricked in.

Phyllis appeared carrying the salads and tea. She stopped at a small table set with silverware and a basket of crackers. Phyllis motioned to the waiting women. "Come on over here."

Rainey pulled out a heavy wooden chair and sat down across from Phyllis. Sheila sat next to her. Rainey took a big drink of the cold iced tea. "Oh, thank you. I needed that," Rainey said, an attempt at putting Phyllis at ease.

Phyllis smiled. "Go on, eat your lunch. I can talk while y'all eat. I pretty much know what you're going to ask."

Rainey unfolded her silverware from the white cotton napkin, while pushing Phyllis in the right direction. "I know you've already talked to the police, but could you tell me what you know about the victims?"

Phyllis avoided the apparent painful topic, by saying, "I didn't ask you what dressing you wanted so I brought ranch out, but I can get you something else."

"Ranch is just fine," Sheila said. "Thank you."

Rainey had not waited and was already drenching the mound of sliced ham, turkey, eggs, cheese, and bright red tomato wedges nested in deep green lettuce. If it tasted as good as it looked Rainey was going to be impressed. She was starving and hoped the food improved her mood.

She prodded Phyllis again. "I realize how difficult it can be to talk about people you obviously cared about, but it will be helpful to the investigation to know these women, who they really were. Not Cookie Kutter's version of things."

Phyllis leaned back, letting out a string of chuckles. "What you said to her was priceless. I record the news so I can catch up when I'm home. I played that sound bite over and over. Good one!"

Sheila chimed in, "I think the hair bleach has affected Cookie's brain. She wasn't such an ass when she was still a brunette."

After a good laugh from the three women, Phyllis started spouting information. "I knew Lisa Jones very well. She started coming to my old bar when she was still wet behind the ears. Lord, in her younger days she was a lesbian on a mission, hell bent on sleeping with as many women as she possibly could." Phyllis chuckled at her memory. "I watched her grow into a responsible young woman over the years, but she still had that wild streak. It got her in trouble sometimes."

Rainey wiped her mouth with her napkin. "How so?"

Phyllis chuckled more heartily. "Let's just say, her girlfriends overlapped on occasion. I loved her, but she ran amok when the girls started taking their clothes off in front of her and they did, often. She was one of those rare breeds. She could charm the clothes off a woman without even intending to."

"Did she leave a trail of broken hearts?" Sheila asked.

Phyllis smiled, again. "Not broken hearts per se, but changed by the experience. That was the thing about her. She could piss them off, but she always left them smiling in the end. My partner in the bar, Dara Thomas, had a taste of that. She's not here right now, but I can give you her number."

Rainey drained her tea. Phyllis rose to get a pitcher by the kitchen door. She continued to talk, returning with the tea and filling their glasses.

"Now, this other girl, Kim McNatt, I don't know much about her. I've seen her in here. Never made any trouble. I would remember her if she had. In this business you learn to recognize the bad apples." ·

Rainey took a break from eating to ask, "What would it take to get one of these women to go with a complete stranger, no struggle, freely follow him to his car?"

Phyllis rubbed her gray hair into short spikes, sticking out in all directions. "I don't know about Kim, but Lisa was a nurse. She would have helped anyone in trouble. That's just the kind of person she was."

Rainey switched from the victims to the UNSUB. "What can you tell us about the men that come in here?"

"Well now, you got your gay boyfriends who like to party with the ladies sometimes. Then there are the straight couples that join their friends. Dara puts on a hell of a light show. This place has every lighting gadget she could squeeze in here. That's what she does for a day job. She runs a lighting equipment rental shop. Got a nice little business. It made her enough money to help me buy this place."

Rainey was interested in the men that frequented the establishment, not how the two women financed their dream bar. She redirected Phyllis. "Do you get many straight men alone?"

Phyllis darkened. "No, we discourage their patronage, if you get my drift. This is a lesbian bar. The women here need to feel safe. If a guy comes in here hitting on women, I know about it. If it becomes a problem, well then, I have a right to refuse service."

Sheila finished eating and slid her half-eaten salad away. "Whew! That was a huge salad. Thank you, it was delicious."

Rainey wasn't finished with her plate, but she paused to ask, "What about bi-sexual couples, trans men, other members of the gay community that may not fit the mold of typical lesbian?" Rainey saw Phyllis' eyebrows shoot up. "Phyllis, I'm not interested in the politics of who belongs where. I'm looking for a killer that doesn't belong *here*. You've seen him, maybe even talked to him."

Phyllis' body language registered she understood what Rainey was driving at. "The only thing that sticks out in my mind was a bi couple about six weeks ago. They got plastered and the guy started suggesting things to some of the girls that didn't go over very well with the alpha crowd."

So Phyllis was a student of human nature. Rainey believed that to be an asset. She stopped eating and leaned forward. "The couple - who was in charge, the man or the woman?"

"Oh honey, that girl was just along for the ride. She didn't want to be here. You could tell he made her come. Don't get me wrong. I'm not the sex police. Plenty of consenting adults, happy couples for the most part, party here with us. What goes on outside this bar is none of my concern."

Rainey made eye contact with Sheila, verifying that the detective knew the man's behavior didn't fit the profile. Their UNSUB would seek to please his mate, not force her to participate in something against her will.

"Phyllis, let's narrow the scope. Were you here the night Lisa Jones went missing?"

"I'm here every night except Monday and Tuesday. Those are slow nights."

"Could I ask you to close your eyes?" Rainey asked, softening her voice. Phyllis complied. "Now, I want you to think back to the very last time you saw Lisa. Was it that night?"

Phyllis nodded, answering, "Yes. I talked to her, before she went home."

Sheila pulled a pad and pen from her purse and began to take notes. She remained silent, letting Rainey probe Phyllis' mind.

"Okay," Rainey began, "I want you to focus on that conversation. Can you see her?"

Phyllis only nodded this time.

"Focus on Lisa. What is she wearing?"

"It was warm out. She had on a tank top tucked into ratty jeans. She was happy. She just got a raise at work."

"Do you remember what time you talked to her?"

"I teased her about going home before midnight. I told the police I thought it was around 11:45."

Sheila acknowledged she had that information, by nodding to Rainey.

"Let's go back a few minutes before you see Lisa. What are you doing? Where are you in the bar?"

Phyllis opened her eyes and pointed toward the long bar on the left side of the room. "I was leaning over there, just watching for a minute."

Rainey stood up. "Let's go stand by the bar."

Phyllis and Sheila followed Rainey across the room. Sheila sat on a stool, pad in hand, while Rainey stood near the dance floor.

Rainey asked Phyllis, "Could you stand exactly where you were that night?"

Phyllis moved to the end of the bar, leaning on it with her left elbow, one leg crossed over the other at the ankles.

"Now, close your eyes again. What song is playing?"

Phyllis smiled broadly, her eyes remaining closed. "It was 'Redneck Woman' time. We play it most nights when the crowd gets going. Everyone was singing and dancing with no one in particular. It's one of those rowdy bar songs women go crazy over."

"I want you to pick out one woman in the crowd, no one special, just really focus on that one person. Do you see her?"

"Yes, she's young, too young. I'm thinking about checking her ID again."

"What is she wearing?"

"She's dressed like a teenage boy, long shorts, Rugby shirt, ball cap."

Rainey had the woman focused. She was counting on Phyllis' skills of observation, honed from years behind a bar.

"Zoom out, Phyllis. Take in the whole room... Freeze that image in your mind... Now, scan that photo. The women are into the song. What are the men doing? Where are they?"

Phyllis moved her head around as she examined the picture in her mind. "There are just so many people. I see some of the regular guys by the bar. I've known all of them for years." She moved her head, indicating the southeast corner by the entrance. "A few guys are with the big birthday party in the back, most of them are singing. I can't see much for the bodies in front of me and I was watching that kid. I just don't see anyone that jumps out at me as not belonging."

Rainey learned one thing. Whoever this guy was, he blended in here, or this woman would have noticed him.

"Okay, you can open your eyes. You did great."

Phyllis blinked her eyes several times, adjusting to the light. "I've racked my brain, run through that night over in my head. I don't recall a single thing out of the ordinary."

Sheila spoke up. "When did you first see Lisa? Which direction did she come from?"

Phyllis swung her head to the right, pointing at a six-seat table, larger than the rest, placed near the end of the bar with a great view of the stage. "She came from Dara's table."

"Who was sitting there?"

"Dara was with her flavor of the month. Dara's sister, Chelsea, and her boyfriend, and one of Dara's exes and her new girlfriend were also there. A bunch of girls were around the table, but that isn't unusual. Dara draws a crowd. That's why it was odd when she and Lisa had that fling. They were too much alike to make it work."

The information clicked in Rainey's brain. Dara Thomas was Chelsea's sister, the teacher who took over Katie's classroom. Rainey let the thought pass and asked Phyllis, "Was anyone watching Lisa walk toward you?"

Phyllis smiled and shook her head from side to side. "You don't understand, a lot of eyes were watching Lisa every minute she was in here. Just like they watched you walk in that front door. Women like you get noticed. It's not about looks, although you certainly don't fall off in that department. There's something about you girls that women cannot resist."

Before Rainey could respond, the big doors opened. Another woman, wearing a shirt like Phyllis', stepped in the room. "Sorry to interrupt, but there are some FBI folks out here, said they were here to meet Agent Bell."

The three women started moving toward the door.

"One more question, Phyllis," Rainey said as they walked. "Did Lisa smoke? Would she have been out on the deck?"

"No, Lisa didn't smoke. Didn't like to be around people that did. She tolerated me, but I didn't smoke around her."

Sheila asked, "Does someone watch that door?"

"Yes," Phyllis pointed at another door on the opposite side of the back wall, "and that one, too. When this room is opened those doors have to be unlocked. Same with the ones upstairs leading to fire escapes out back. Fire Marshals rules. But no one comes in without a stamp from the front door. We change the stamp slightly every night. My bouncers know what to look for only after they show up for work."

"Sounds like you run a tight ship," Rainey commented.

"Been corralling women for a lot of years. I've seen every trick in the book."

"My...uh..." Rainey was suddenly at a loss for what to call Katie. She was certainly more than a girlfriend, wife didn't sound right, and partner or lover just didn't cut it. Rainey settled on simply using her name. "Katie and I planned to come here before all this. I hope the publicity hasn't hurt your business."

"Are you kidding me? I've had more business since this started happening. Had to turn people away last Saturday night. The women of this community are taking a stand against fear and hate. It's like they are daring someone to come get them."

They were almost at the door, when Rainey replied, "I can understand that feeling."

"When this is over, you bring that pretty little Miss Meyers in here. I'll make sure you have a good time," Phyllis said, and then punched Rainey playfully in the arm. "Nice catch, by the way."

In a moment of unusual personal sharing, Rainey replied, "Everyone thinks it was me, but I assure you, I was the one that got caught. Sweet, innocent, Little Miss Meyers is a handful."

Phyllis slapped Rainey on the back hard, chuckling loudly. "Ain't they all, sista', ain't they all?"

Rainey felt comfortable enough with Phyllis to say, "I had no idea."

Phyllis laughed louder. "Welcome to the drama filled world of women, Agent Bell. Glad to have you."

Rainey responded with, what she realized in that very moment was true, "I'm glad to be here."

CHAPTER FIFTEEN

"Move only when there are advantages to be gained. Cease when there are no advantages to be gained," Mackie loosely quoted Sun Tzu, while lowering himself onto the couch in the office.

Rainey sat on the other end of the couch, her feet up on the coffee table. Ernie pecked away on her keyboard at her desk. Rainey had just lamented to Mackie that she felt useless just sitting there. She was in the office rather than with the rest of the team, because she just didn't want to talk to Danny. Rainey told everyone she had some business to take care of and she would see them all tomorrow, before she was to walk into Feme Sole in search of the man who wanted her dead.

Rainey's tattered copy of "The Art of War" was on the bookshelf at the cottage. She retorted, "Sun Tzu also said, 'Opportunities multiply as they are seized.' I could be doing something, I just don't know what."

Mackie's bass voice rumbled. "Pretend inferiority and encourage his arrogance."

Ernie slapped her hands down on her desk. "You two stop spouting Chinese war strategies, or go somewhere else. Some of us are working."

Rainey stood up. "Come on, Mackie. We're not wanted here."

"I never said I didn't want you." Ernie paused to add more drama and then added, sarcastically, "I want you. I want you to go through those files I sent to your inbox." She turned to Mackie. "And I want you to turn in your receipts from last week."

Rainey was in no mood for paperwork. "I'll have the files done by noon, tomorrow. I promise. I'm going home, now. I need to think. You comin' Mackie?"

Mackie hesitated. "Uh… let me get those receipts for Ernie and then I'll be over."

Rainey chuckled. "Big as you are and you're scared of that little old woman."

Mackie's deep belly laughs shook the air. He winked at Rainey. "I seem to remember she's armed and it's almost legal."

Rainey winked back. "Yeah, well that might be the biggest mistake I ever made."

Ernie was not to be played with lightly. Her stinging tongue was legendary and usually had an element of comedy, but not today. "Stand around and joke if you want. You found a head outside this office last night. You're trying to draw a maniac to you. Laugh it up! You only live once."

Rainey exchanged looks with Mackie and he went out to his truck, leaving the two women alone.

"Okay, Ernie, let me have it. Everybody else has had their shot at me today."

Ernie came out from behind the desk, arms crossed over her chest. "Henry was here earlier. He made it very plain and as my husband, he does have a say in this. Rainey, I've never been afraid of being out here alone most of the day. It was always kind of peaceful, after living in a house with five men. I looked forward to coming here, but today I've looked forward to going home every minute. Driving up this morning and seeing that blood on the dock..."

Rainey tried to interrupt, but Ernie wouldn't let her.

"What came here last night was not human, it was pure evil. I'm a strong woman. You know I don't back down easy, but I talked to Henry. Honey, I can't stay out here anymore. Either we move in closer to civilization, or I'm quitting. Evil has found you, Rainey. Even if you catch this one, there will be another. You can't protect all of us."

She was too stunned to speak. Every piece of Rainey's foundation was crumbling, brick by brick. Was Mackie growing tired of life with her and all that entailed, as well? His admonishment was sure to come next, the way things were going. Rainey grasped at the bricks, trying to hold everything together. It was no use. Life, as she had known it, was coming to a close. There were so many problems to solve, people to please, it was all just too much. She felt like George in "It's A Wonderful Life," about to jump off the bridge. She was waiting for the bell to ring. She needed her angel to get his wings.

Ernie was losing patience with Rainey's long pause of self-reflection. "Well, are you just gonna stand there?"

Rainey stammered, "I... I don't know how to respond."

"I'll make it easy for you," Ernie said, lifting a stack of papers from her desk. "You can either go through these ads for a place to move this business, or you can find another office manager. Rainey, you might be prepared to die out here alone, but I'm not."

Rainey took the papers from Ernie's hand. She looked down at the pages and all she could see were dollar signs. She raised her head and refocused on Ernie.

"Can I afford this? With the house and the baby, can I afford to move the office, too?"

"Honey, there won't be a house or a baby, if you don't move us away from here. She isn't going to stay out here with you, don't kid yourself." Ernie let that sink in, before adding, "It's time you touched your daddy's money. It's what he would want you to do. He never moved the business to town, because he always said, 'Rainey can do that when it's hers.' He made the sacrifices so you didn't have to. Don't hold onto this place because of memories. Go make some new ones somewhere else."

Rainey's father left her a 350,000-dollar life insurance policy. She paid off his few debts, which wasn't much, and put the rest in the bank. The business was in great shape. She didn't need the money, so she buried it in an account, along with the pain it represented. It had crossed her mind to use the money for the house, but she couldn't bring herself to spend it. Ernie read her mind.

She walked over and placed her hand on Rainey's elbow. Calm and gentle now, she said, "Baby girl, you think holding on to that money lessens the pain of his loss. The real problem is you didn't have the chance to grieve him, before you had to fight for your own life. You haven't healed from either event. Let go of the past and begin again. That's what Billy would have wanted for you."

Rainey enveloped the small woman in her arms. She cried softly for a few minutes. Ernie held her and patted her back.

Rainey whispered, "I miss him, so much."

"I know you do, honey. I know you do."

The next whisper was barely audible, when Rainey said, "I can't lose you, too. Promise you'll stay. I'll work this out."

Ernie pulled out of Rainey's grasp. She looked up into Rainey's face and smiled.

"Well, Henry did say, if worse comes to worse, you can set up shop in the old barn on our place. I doubt seriously anyone would come on a place with five grown men totin' shotguns."

#

Mackie came over to the cottage, after he turned in his receipts. He saw the real estate ads on the kitchen table where Rainey had tossed them, before grabbing a beer out of the refrigerator. Ernie had also included a list of houses to look at. The hint was not subtle. Mackie found her standing at the sink in a daze. He opened the refrigerator, took out a beer, and joined her at the counter.

"Your daddy and me, we discussed moving into town several times. He worried about you out here, when you were younger."

Rainey looked up at Mackie. "But I loved it here."

"He knew that, but there were other things to think about. Being twenty minutes from help if there was an accident, you being out here alone sometimes, and no other kids to play with, he worried about those things."

"I guess it never bothered me. I never thought about it much," Rainey said, taking another swig of beer.

"Rainey, if you want to sell the property and move to town, I have no objections. I'll tell you straight, if something like this had happened when you were younger, Billy would have moved to protect you."

Rainey crossed the floor and stared out the back window. Very quietly she said, "This is all I have left of him."

"That's not true, baby girl. This place doesn't hold your father's spirit, you do. And whether you know it or not, you are Billy Bell through and through, more than's good for you sometimes. Take care of your family, Rainey. That's what he would have done."

Rainey didn't turn around. She continued to stare out into the coming darkness. "I never imagined living anywhere else. This was always the place where I planned to live out my days. When things were at their worst, I would close my eyes and come here."

Mackie put his empty beer bottle on the counter and walked over to Rainey. He put his giant arm around her. "Baby girl, this is your decision. You have a lot to think about. I'm going home. If you need to talk or want me to come back out here tonight, you call me."

"Okay," Rainey whispered. She was already lost in the myriad of thoughts swimming in her head.

Mackie left through the front door, arming the alarm as he went. Freddie came in from his evening romp. His greeting trills and the tapping of his claws on the floor were the only sounds. Rainey fed him and made a sandwich for herself, a robot going through the motions. She had to force herself to eat. The ache in her gut was not hunger pangs. She ate at the table in deference to Katie's rules, even though she wasn't sure Katie was ever coming back. When she finished, Rainey cleaned up the kitchen and took the ads and the tablet computer out to the couch. She spent about two hours going over all her assets.

If Rainey sold her property, she could manage purchasing a house like Katie wanted, closer to Chapel Hill in a gated community, with security patrols already in place. That didn't mean some psycho wasn't already living within the gates, but Rainey would have a better chance of seeing him coming. The lots were big and wooded, close to Lake Jordan. Freddie could stalk small animals in a new territory. She would simply be on the other end of the lake. The interstate was close by, Chapel Hill minutes away, a mall located just up the road. It was a thriving community geared toward families and children. It would suit Rainey's need for seclusion and Katie's desire to be in the middle of life.

Of course, committing to this meant Rainey was giving up her last vestiges of independence. Even with Katie living there, it was still Rainey's house. If she gave into this, Rainey would be binding herself to Katie forever. In theory, she had already done that, but to really depend on Katie to hold up her end of the bargain was taking a big step. They had not even shared a checking account, up to this point, and now Rainey was thinking about dumping the majority of her life savings into the pot. If this didn't work out, where would she go? When the house was being built on her property, she figured Katie would let her buy her out if things went south.

Rainey realized suddenly that she never really thought it would last with Katie. Something would happen. It had been too good. Things like that never survived long in Rainey's life. She was a happy-go-lucky kid until she turned ten, found out she'd been lied to from birth, and became bitter because of it. She recovered from most of her trust issues, with the help of her father, and succeeded at her life's ambitions. Rainey lost her father too soon, her career followed shortly after. Her life, she thought, was like that Robert Frost poem. "Nothing gold can stay."

Rainey's cell phone rang. Danny's name was on the caller ID. She narrowed her eyes at the phone. The anger from earlier flashed to the surface, but she had to answer. If she didn't, he would drive out there to make sure she was all right.

"What?" She asked, curtly, when she answered.

"Still pissed, I see."

"What do you want? I'm busy." Rainey wasn't up for anymore of Danny's crap today.

Danny's voice took on a formal tone. He evidently was tired of Rainey's crap, too. "Your suspicions were correct. Dalton was hiding a prepaid cell phone, charger and all. It never ceases to amaze me what these guys will shove up their asses. Brooks pulled the records. Chambers made calls and texts to another prepaid number, up until we confiscated the phone. We called the other phone, got an answer, but no voice, just a hang up. We traced the call to an area south of Chapel Hill, but it's turned off now, probably in the trash somewhere."

Rainey forgot about being mad. "We assumed the UNSUB was on his own, making decisions and possibly mistakes. If Dalton has been in his ear this whole time, then this is a trap. Dalton orchestrated my involvement and guessed correctly that I would appear at this club. The UNSUB will be there Saturday night. Now, we just have to figure out what Dalton's plan is."

"We aren't going to be able to ask him for a while. It seems there was a bit of a scuffle when they did the cavity search. Dalton has been moved to the hospital wing, with a severe concussion. The medical staff and his lawyers are preventing us from talking to him."

"He's not in isolation, anymore?" Rainey was concerned.

"He's under twenty-four hour guard and separated from the other patients. Don't worry; he's not going anywhere. They worked him over pretty good."

Rainey ignored Danny's reassurances. "Check out every single one of the people in the hospital and the trustees. If he gets a chance, he's gone and he'll kill anyone in his path to freedom."

Danny tried again to calm her fears. "He's chained to a hospital bed, with four guards on him. Relax Rainey, Dalton is not your biggest problem right now."

Rainey sighed. "I have more big problems than I care to have, at the moment."

By now, Danny's tone had become more compassionate. "I know you have a lot going on. You need to get some rest and focus your attention on the one problem you can do something about. We catch this guy tomorrow night and then you can deal with the other things. Is the cop car outside?"

"Yes."

"Good." Danny said, at a loss for what to say next.

Rainey asked, "Have you checked on Katie, tonight?"

"Yes, she's fine. Her sisters are there."

Rainey would have tolerated Maria to see Katie. She missed her that much.

"Okay, well..." Rainey said, looking for a way to end the conversation. "I guess there's nothing to do, but stick with the plan. I'll see you tomorrow."

Before he hung up, Danny made one last comment. "You do know I have your back, don't you? You do trust me?"

Rainey might have been angry with Danny, but she trusted him with her life. She replied, "Always."

#

Rainey spent the next several hours planning. She tackled one problem at a time. Finally she concluded there was no other way, but to take a leap of faith with Katie. She sent detailed emails to several people with instructions on what to do. Rainey had to convince Katie they could have a life together. This was a step in the right direction. She trusted Ernie to make it all happen. Rainey didn't have time to take care of things personally; she had a killer to catch and another to see strapped to a gurney with a needle in his arm.

Once the email was sent, Rainey switched gears. She went into the closet, taking down one of the heavy boxes from the top shelf. She carried it to the living room and emptied its contents onto the coffee table. Reflexively, she checked the security camera feeds on the TV and then immersed herself in the world of Dalton Chambers. She reread the bulletins from the House of Holy Redemption and then set about looking for some clue to the code in which it was written. Somewhere in that pile on the coffee table was the key to catching the UNSUB. Rainey just had to find it.

At one a.m., the clue remained elusive, but her tired eyes blurred the words beyond recognition. Rainey had resisted getting reading glasses, but her age was beginning to catch up with her. She also didn't think she could stand to listen to another word from the interviews she had playing in the background. Rainey had enough of Dalton Chambers' perversions for one evening. She petted Freddie, who had curled up beside her on the couch.

"The eyes are the first things to go, little man. I guess I am getting old. Come on; let's go to bed. We'll try again in the morning."

Rainey checked the security cameras, again, reconfirmed that all the doors and windows were secured, and took Freddie into the bedroom with her. She locked and bolted the bedroom door, took the still loaded shotgun out of the gun safe, along with her father's .45 pistol, and placed them by her bed. She crawled between the sheets, hoping that she would be able to sleep there without Katie. She needed a good night's rest. She lay there for a few minutes, before reaching for her cell phone on the nightstand. Rainey hit a few buttons and placed the receiver to her ear. She got Katie's voicemail and knew Katie was looking at the phone, refusing to answer.

When prompted, Rainey simply said, "I wanted you to know, I really do love you. No matter what happens, I needed you to know that. Good night, Katie."

#

Emotional and physical exhaustion finally caught up with Rainey. She fell asleep, and woke almost seven hours later, the most she'd slept in days. She may have dreamed, but she was too tired to remember. Rainey was thankful for that, sure that Dalton crept about in her mind while she lay slumbering. She put on shorts and a tee shirt and went to the kitchen. She consumed some juice and one of the breakfast cookies Katie forced on her when Rainey didn't want eat. Rainey hadn't run in a week and was in desperate need of a good sweat, but she wasn't going unprotected. She stopped at the gun safe, putting on her shoulder holster and a windbreaker to cover the Glock. She zipped her cell phone into a jacket pocket and stepped into a gorgeous Carolina spring morning.

Once she had assured the deputy that his presence wasn't needed anymore, he drove away. It took a while to get moving, but once she was warmed up, the running relaxed her. She took the well-worn two-mile trail through the woods that she and her father cleared for her, back in high school days. After she went away to college, he kept it cut back so she could run it when she was home. It was one of the things she was going to miss when she moved, but that decision had been made last night. Some of Rainey's anxiety diminished when she finally decided to commit to a life with Katie. Still, parting with the only real home she'd ever known was going to be hard. Rainey took in her surroundings, and was reminded how lucky she

267

was to have had a place like this in her life. She vowed she would come back and run this trail, if the new owners would let her.

When Rainey rounded the final bend, she saw what appeared to be a piece of paper stuck on the side of the last tree, before the path broke out of the woods. As she grew closer her strides slowed, until she stopped abruptly, a few feet from the tree. Someone had printed a picture on computer paper and stapled it to the tree. The paper was damp from the morning dew and curled up on the edges, but it had not been there long. Rainey took a step closer, unable for a second to see the image in the photo or read the sentence typed below it. A cloud moved above, allowing the sun to penetrate the shadows. Light spilled across the trunk of the tree. The image came into focus. Rainey sprinted toward the house as fast as she could, punching numbers into her cell phone as she ran. Danny picked up on the first ring.

"Hope you got some rest last night and are in a much better mood," he said, jovially.

Rainey bounded up the steps to the cottage, saying breathlessly, "Danny, move Katie and her family, now! He knows where she is and he's watching her."

"Why? What's happened?"

"He left me a message. He took a picture of Katie and her family in their backyard. It had to have been yesterday. Her sisters were in the picture."

Danny grasped the seriousness of the situation immediately. He turned from his phone and spoke, "Roger, get over to Katie Meyers parents' home. Tell them to pack an overnight bag and then bring them here... Move! Curtis, go with him!" He spoke again to Rainey, "Where did you find the picture?"

Rainey answered, while she fumbled with the key, trying to get into the house. "He stapled it to a tree on my running trail. There was a message typed under the picture."

"I'll send a tech team out there to collect it. What did it say?"

Rainey closed the door and rearmed the alarm. With her back against the door, she slid down to the floor, the panicked breathing beginning to subside.

Danny waited for her to catch her breath and asked again, "What was the message, Rainey?"

Rainey repeated what she read. "It said, 'I thought she was in a safe place.' He watched the newscast."

"Rainey, Katie is safe or I would have known about it. I'll go on and call her now and explain what's happening. You wait for the tech team. I'll take care of Katie and her family and then I'll call you." He paused, and then asked, "Are you okay? Do you still want to go through with this thing tonight?"

"I want this over with," Rainey spat, the anger and fear for Katie's safety welling up, before she said, "I'm ending this tonight, one way or another."

"Calm down, you need to get your head on straight, or I'm not letting you go in there."

Rainey did not hesitate when she said, "Try and stop me!"

CHAPTER SIXTEEN

The crime tech unit arrived and took the picture back to the lab. Rainey busied herself cleaning her gun and cooking lunch. She hadn't had a hot meal in days, so she warmed up some frozen ravioli from the last batch Katie made. Danny called back after a while, exasperated. It seemed he had a taste of the Meyers women, and what Rainey was up against in dealing with them, especially Katie.

"Damn, Rainey. How do you get a word in edgewise?"

Rainey laughed. "I take it your conversation with Katie did not go well."

"I've never been so tongue tied in my life. She should have gone into politics. Katie could teach them a thing or two about debating."

"I guess you lost," Rainey said, concerned, but still amused.

"I guess you knew today was the big party for Mr. Meyers. Those women are not budging. I did get them to agree to more security and to leave at the conclusion of the party."

"Well, at least you got them to move out for the night. I've never won a single concession from one of them, most especially Katie."

"Rainey, that woman is a little ball of fire, way too hot to handle. Are you sure you're up to it?"

"You know, Danny, when we were kids we did things we knew we weren't supposed to do, because the joy of doing it was worth the punishment we took later. Some things are just worth the pains you suffer. Katie is worth the trouble."

Danny softened his tone. "I hope it all works out for you, Rainey. I really do. I wasn't sure this relationship would last, but you two are like moths to a flame. You belong together."

Rainey smiled into the phone. "Yeah, well, if I get burned, I'll remind you that you said that, while you're telling me, I told you so."

Danny's voice was hushed when he asked, "Are you ready, Rainey?"

She knew what he meant. Was she ready to go get this guy? Was she prepared to spot him? Had she thought of everything?

"Katie's safe, right?" Rainey asked.

"They'll be staying in the Center City Hotel, a block from the Sheriff's Office. In addition to the deputy on duty now, I sent for another female agent to stay with her. She's about to graduate and I think you'll like her."

"You put a trainee on protective duty? What makes you think I'm going to like her?"

"You recommended her for the job." Danny's laughter filled the air, just before he hung up the phone.

Rainey had written so many letters to the agency on behalf of applicants, she spent the next several hours trying to guess who the trainee could be. Danny wasn't going to tell her. He enjoyed knowing something she did not and watching her squirm while she tried to figure it out. She would no doubt find out soon enough, if things went the way Rainey wanted. If they could catch this guy, the first thing she was going to do was go get Katie.

She took a long, soaking bath, and mulled the question over. The bruise on her shoulder was beginning to show hues of yellow and variants of purple, the deep black beginning to fade. The warm water relaxed her. She got out after an hour, combed through her hair, and waited for it to dry. Rainey hung out on the couch looking at Dalton's correspondence, still searching for the key to the code. She called Ernie to make sure she got the email and the files Rainey reviewed, as promised. She checked in with Mackie, who wanted to come on the stake out, but Rainey convinced him a man of his stature was not good for undercover work. People were bound to notice him. All afternoon, no matter what she was thinking about or doing, in the back of her mind she played out the coming evening's events. At six o'clock, she repacked Dalton's files and tapes in the box and put it back in the closet. Then she went to get dressed.

"He's coming for you tonight," she said, to her naked image in the mirror. Her eyes travelled down the white scar. Flashes of memory from that night flooded her mind. She let the box lid fly open and remembered the terror and the pain, but it did not make her weak. It made her stronger. Rainey used those memories to fuel her fire. She stared at her reflection in the mirror, tracing the scar with a fingertip. Rainey knew a new fight for survival was imminent. This time she was ready.

Her father's voice echoed in her head. "See him coming, Rainey. Nobody can get you, if you see him coming."

"I'm banking on that, Dad. Stay with me. I might need you."

"Always," came the reply.

\#

Rainey slid on her favorite boots. She could run in them and better yet, she could fight in them. A properly placed thick wooden heel could do a lot of damage. She already had on blue jeans and a black tank top. To accommodate the tech equipment and hide her weapon from view, she had to wear her jacket. Being inside the hot, packed nightclub necessitated she wear as little as possible underneath. She let her chestnut waves hang down over her shoulders. On the outside, she looked like many of the women that would be innocently wandering the bar, looking for a good time. There was nothing innocent about Rainey's intentions.

Rainey made sure Freddie's food and water bowls were filled. The sun wasn't down yet, so he was still off exploring the grounds. Rainey checked the holster clipped to the belt at the back of her pants. She pulled the Glock from the holster, just to make sure it was in the proper position. Holstering the weapon, she put on her jacket, giving the cottage one last sweeping glance. The days here without Katie had been long and lonely. Maybe it was time to start over. She left the cottage knowing tonight could be the beginning or the end.

She stopped at the back of her car, opening the gun safe in the trunk. Rainey suspected she would be in or near her car when the UNSUB made his move. She took out the Sig and Beretta 9mm's and slipped full magazines into them. She loaded the Mossburg shotgun with nine shells, racked one into the chamber, and added a tenth. Rainey started to pick up the Taser, and then left it behind. She had no intentions of taking this guy in. She closed the trunk and opened the driver's side door. She put the Sig under her seat, the Beretta in the console, and laid the shotgun on the floor in the back. Someone was going to die tonight, Rainey hoped it wasn't her, but she was going down in a blaze of gunfire if she did.

Rainey thought about calling Katie again, and then realized she would be in the middle of her father's party. She'd call her later, before she went in the bar. Rainey didn't want Katie saddled with the memory of how their last conversation ended, if indeed it was the last. She drove to the judicial building, listening to a Jason Mraz CD Katie had given her. When the song "I'm Yours" played, Rainey sang along and meant every word. It was her turn to win some or lose some. Rainey may have taught Katie to protect herself, but Katie taught Rainey a lesson or two about living life like there's no tomorrow.

Her mood was surprisingly upbeat, while James hooked up his surveillance gear.

"So, James, when I go to the bathroom, are you going to turn this thing off?"

James continued working, as he answered her question, "If you need a moment of privacy, just say so. I will kill the video feed. I'll have to leave the audio on, so you can tell me when to reactivate the camera."

"That's great. Everybody will hear me pee."

James smiled up at her. "It won't be the first time we've listened to someone go to the bathroom. Trust me, peeing is my least concern."

The hubbub around her ceased, while the team went over the plans once again. Danny and Paula would stay in the van with James. Their job was to watch the people watching Rainey. Roger, Eric, and Curtis would split up and join the uniformed cops at both the front and back entrances. Detective Robertson reserved a table on the balcony where she could see most of the floor. She would also be carrying a signal booster for Rainey's equipment. The other women would go in as couples stationed around the bar. Rainey was covered like a blanket.

She knew the UNSUB wasn't going to take her in the bar, it was the ride home she worried about. Danny planned to follow her with the surveillance van, but it was still risky. The goal was to identify the suspect inside the bar, and pressure him into giving himself away. That was Danny's plan, anyway. Rainey's plan was to get him to follow her home, where she would dispense with him in short fashion. No trial, no jail time, no serial killer fans of his to come after her. No, this time she wouldn't be aiming for a leg.

#

At nine o'clock, Detective Robertson and the others left to go to the bar. Rainey was to follow an hour later. Danny remained behind. He would ride over in Rainey's car with her. Rainey paced around the room and fiddled with the earwig James gave her.

"You know this is going to be useless with all the loud music," she complained.

Danny, who didn't look up from his computer screen, said, "We've used that model before in loud settings. We got them after you left the Bureau. They work very nicely."

Rainey ignored him and stuck the earwig in her pocket. She continued to pace. Danny called her over to his computer. He pointed at a satellite image on the screen.

"Brooks sent me the winter satellite images for the area around your house. It makes it easier to see the farm paths into the woods that connect to the road you'll be driving. Make sure you are aware of their locations. Now that the leaves have come in, he could hide in there and come out at you unexpected."

Rainey glanced at the screen. "Most of those paths have chains or gates across them to keep people out."

Danny looked up from the computer. "You just watch those paths. Anybody can get a bolt cutter."

"I got it, Danny. I could drive that route with my eyes closed. I know what to look for."

"Let's get him before it goes that far. Come on, it's time to go."

"Give me a minute, will you? I need to call Katie."

Danny stood and put his hand on Rainey's arm, as she reached for her phone. "I'd advise against that. I talked to the agent with Katie when they moved the family to the hotel. It seems Katie and her sister Helena had quite a bit to drink at their father's party. Nothing good could come of you calling her now."

Rainey thought about it and decided Danny was right. If Katie was still mad, the alcohol would definitely free up her tongue. Rainey didn't need Katie's stinging retorts in her head right now.

"Okay, let's do this," she said, heading for the door.

Danny hesitated to move. He stopped Rainey at the door by saying, "I know you're going to kill him if you get the chance. Just make it righteous, Rainey. Don't give me a reason to lock you up."

"It will be a clean shoot," Rainey said, smiling. "Don't I look scared for my life?"

"No, you look hell bent on someone dying tonight," Danny said, still not moving.

Rainey opened the door. She turned back to Danny. "Well, then your job is to make sure it isn't Katie or me."

#

The area around the bar was packed with cars. Rainey was lucky Roger had staked out a parking place for her, in the lot next to the bar. She and Danny got out of the car and went their separate ways, he to the van at the end of the alley and Rainey to the front entrance. She slipped in the earwig and checked the feed.

"James, can you hear me?"

"Loud and clear, Rainey."

The LCD sign above the entrance flashed the Feme Sole logo, interspersed with the announcement that all proceeds from tonight's door went to the families of Lisa Jones and Kim McNatt. From the looks of things, the lesbian community was more than willing to support their own. The line at the door disappeared around the corner.

"Okay, folks, let the show begin," Rainey said, as she stepped through the line and walked up to the front door.

One of the girls taking up money and stamping hands was the same one Rainey saw yesterday. She nodded at Rainey, beckoning her to come on through. Rainey wasn't trying to hide who she was. It was a good thing, too. Heads all around the front room started to turn, as women poked each other and pointed. The lounge area was covered in lesbians of all sizes, shapes, ages, and colors. Women were draped on the staircases, leaning against the walls, eating at the tables, and crowded around the bar. Music poured over the balcony, thumping so loud, Rainey could feel it against her chest. Rainey took a second to let her eyes adjust to the darkness of the room and the flashing multicolored lights above her head. A thick haze hung in the air, not from cigarette smoke. Theatrical effect machines pumped artificial fog from the rafters. Laser beams sliced through the atmosphere, spilling over from the dance area beyond the doors.

Rainey scanned the room. She recognized one of the couples against the wall, as cops from Sheila's team. Rainey heard voices in her earwig. She pushed it down further in her ear in time to hear Sheila's comment.

"Agent McNally, we have a problem. If you'll check the feed on the door, just before Agent Bell entered the bar, you will see what I mean."

Rainey covered her mouth with a fake cough. She asked, "What is it, Sheila? I'm making my way to the doors now."

"Don't come through the doors, yet," Sheila said, quickly. "Stop at the bar and get a drink. You're going to need it."

Rainey moved toward the bar, saying, under her breath, "Why? Who's in there, Cookie Kutter?"

She heard Danny exclaim, "Fuck me."

"Come on guys, who is it?" Rainey implored, not worrying about people seeing her talking to herself anymore.

Danny spoke hurriedly, "Rainey, get out of there. I'm coming in."

"What the hell, Danny? I'm not afraid of Cookie Kutter."

Sheila butted in, "Listen to him, Rainey. Walk away."

"Who the fuck is it? Tell me now, or I'm coming through those doors... Danny?"

Paula's voice joined the fray. "He's on the move, Rainey. He's coming to you. Come out and let him deal with this and then you can go back in."

"I don't understand," Rainey said, frustrated.

Phyllis Rowan came through the large doors from the other room. The sound amplified and then muffled again, as the doors closed behind her. She spotted Rainey and made her way over to her. She slapped Rainey on the shoulder and laughed loudly. Phyllis leaned in close, but still had to shout.

"Damn girl, that's a handful you got there. I didn't know you were bringing her with you tonight."

It suddenly dawned on Rainey who was in the other room. She shot around Phyllis, yanked open one of the wooden doors, and stormed into the dance hall.

She heard Sheila say in her ear, "Okay guys, I have eyes on Agent Bell. She's moving across the room toward the northwest corner. I think she sees the problem."

Rainey neared Dara Thomas' private table. A blonde, with her back turned to Rainey looked extremely familiar. She was going to read Katie the riot act for this stunt. Rainey reached out and grabbed the blonde's shoulder, whirling her around. She was shocked when the recognition hit her. Gillian Knox wore a surprised look, immediately replaced by consternation.

"Agent Bell, I wish someone had warned me that alcohol and these two don't mix."

Rainey looked at the table in front of Knox. Katie and her equally beautiful sister, Helena, were holding court, with all eyes on them.

Knox continued to defend her actions. "I tried to keep them at the hotel. They just walked out. Short of handcuffing them, I wasn't sure what to do, so we just followed them here." She pointed at the female cop in plain clothes and the two uniformed officers behind the table.

Danny was in Rainey's ear again, "Let me handle this Rainey. Remember he's watching you."

"I am well aware of that," Rainey said.

Knox looked puzzled. "You knew she was here? I just now called it in."

Rainey pointed at her ear. Knox got it and quit talking, just about the time Rainey quit listening and stepped up to the table. Katie was drunk and loud.

She was saying, "Rainey said this would be the safest place in Durham tonight, so here we are."

"Yes, here you are," Rainey shouted over the music.

Helena saw Rainey first. She sprang from her chair and hurried around the table. She hugged Rainey, while saying, "Our hero has arrived. Rainey, we were looking for you and Katie said you would be here."

Rainey made no move to hug Helena back. She stared at Katie, who was trying to stand up, unsuccessfully, until the female deputy steadied her. Katie slurred when she said, loudly, "Well, hello. Don't I know you?"

"Maybe not well enough," Rainey shouted back.

Katie waved her arm to get people's attention, calling out, "Look, everybody, Agent Bell is here, never fear."

Rainey undraped Helena from her neck and started around the table. Katie took a few steps backward, falling up against the deputy. She smiled up at the officer, saying, "Ooo, Agent Bell looks mad."

"Agent Bell is mad," Rainey said, grabbing Katie by the elbow. "Come on, you're going with me."

Katie snatched her arm back. "I don't have to go anywhere with you."

By this time, everyone else at the table was on their feet. Other people were watching. Rainey tried a different tack. "Katie, I would very much like to talk to you in private."

Helena was suddenly at Rainey's side. "From what Katie's been telling me, she'd very much like to get you in private, too."

Katie slurred, "Not when she's like this, all mad and bossy."

Chelsea Thomas spoke next. Rainey recognized her from seeing her at Katie's school. "Rainey, I'm sorry. Katie invited us to her father's party and when she found out we were coming here, she insisted on accompanying us."

R. E. BRADSHAW

Rainey responded, "It's not your fault, I understand how unreasonable she can be." She aimed that last part at Katie, who now was leaning on the female cop.

The look on the cop's face was priceless. If Rainey hadn't been so mad, she would have laughed. Gillian wore the same expression. They had both been Katietized, unable to redirect the little blonde from her desires. Rainey knew the feeling well.

"I came here to have a drink and dance. That's what I intend to do. You go off and hunt your man, Rainey Bell. I'm going to have a good time."

"Why don't we all just sit back down? We're drawing a crowd," a dark haired woman said. She extended her hand to Rainey. "Agent Bell, it's an honor to meet you. I'm Dara Thomas, Chelsea's sister."

Rainey shook Dara's hand, while the deputy helped Katie back into her chair. "It's nice to meet you," Rainey managed to say, still watching Katie out of the corner of her eye. "Please, call me Rainey."

"All right, Rainey," Dara turned to the others retaking the seats at the table, "this is Rhonda and Barb, friends of mine, and this is Chelsea's boyfriend, Jared."

It was the first time Rainey noticed the man beside Chelsea. Rhonda and Barb shook Rainey's hand and then Jared stood up, extending his hand for her to shake. He was tall and had a military bearing, but seemed shy just the same.

He smiled and said, "Nice to finally meet you. I've heard a lot about you this evening."

Rainey looked at Katie and said, "I'll bet you have."

Jared laughed. "Look, I'm just the designated driver. I had nothing to do with how we got here."

"I'm more interested in getting you out of here at the moment."

Jared sat back down, saying, "I understand. If you can pry them out of here, I will make sure they get home. We're surrounded by cops. Nothing's going to happen to them."

Rainey squatted down by Katie's chair, so they were eye to eye. She put her hand on Katie's knee and with all the sweetness she could muster at the moment, she said, "Katie, honey, it's not safe for you to be here. Please, let Agent Knox take you and Helena back to the hotel."

Katie went from obstinate to mushy in seconds. She put her arms around Rainey's neck and said, "I missed you."

Katie then proceeded to kiss Rainey in front of the gathered crowd. Rainey saw flashes going off and knew they were going to be on Facebook pages around the triangle in moments. She wrapped Katie in her arms and stood up, pulling Katie with her.

"Katie, come with me, please."

Rainey got no resistance this time. She tucked Katie under her arm and made her way toward the back door. She saw that Danny was now present and paralleling her movement out of the bar. Rainey looked back over her shoulder at Knox.

"You get the other one," Rainey said, indicating Helena, who was now draped on the befuddled female deputy.

Katie leaned into Rainey heavily, her arms tightly gripping Rainey's waist. When they reached the back door, Danny was waiting. He opened the door for them and they stepped onto the deck. Curtis was there leaning on the railing. He smiled at Rainey.

"Got yourself a spitfire, did you?"

Rainey couldn't help but laugh, looking down at the almost passed out Katie. "Yes, I did," she said, leading Katie off the deck and into the parking lot.

Danny followed with the rest of Katie's entourage. Rainey looked at him and said, "Give me a minute with her, okay?"

"Take your time, I think this mission is blown anyway."

Katie came around a little more, when Rainey leaned her up against the building so she could look at her.

"Rainey, please take me home with you. I don't want to stay away anymore."

Rainey steadied the leaning Katie with both hands on her shoulders. "Honey, I can't take you home, not yet. I need you to go back to the hotel with Agent Knox. I promise I'll come get you as soon as I can."

Katie threw her arms around Rainey. "I don't want to sleep alone. I need you."

She reached up and pulled Rainey's lips to hers. Drunk out of her mind and oblivious to their surroundings, Katie kissed Rainey passionately, which Rainey couldn't help but return. Rainey heard the voice just before they were bathed in a blinding white light.

"There she is!" Cookie Kutter shouted. She rushed at Rainey, microphone in front of her mouth and a television camera on her heels. "Agent Bell, the rest of the lesbian community is on high alert and you're in the alley making out with the former wife of Representative J. W. Wilson. Are you on duty or here socially? What do you have to say for yourself?"

Rainey didn't have time to answer. She felt Katie slip out of her arms and didn't react fast enough to stop what happened next. Katie stepped up to Cookie, balled up her fist, and popped Cookie in the jaw, sending the reporter backwards onto her butt. Katie stood over her with the cameras running.

"That's for all the crap you put us through last summer... and this is for being named after a kitchen utensil."

Rainey grabbed Katie by the waist and lifted her into the air before Katie landed the kick she was about to administer to Cookie. Danny rushed forward, getting between the camera and Rainey, who was trying to wrestle the furious Katie into submission. Rainey ended up carrying Katie to the waiting patrol car, where Knox had finally wrangled Helena into the back seat. Rainey shoved Katie into the seat beside her sister. She buckled Katie in, most of the fight having now left the feisty blonde. Rainey looked at Knox in the front passenger seat.

"Warn her parents that she's going to be on the news." She turned back to Katie, lifting her chin so she would make eye contact. "Honey, you go with these officers and be good. I'll come get you as soon as I can… and Katie, if they have to, I'm telling them to handcuff you to the bed. Do not come out of that hotel room, again."

Katie had not heard a word. She was long gone and barely aware of where she was. She grinned at Rainey. "I love you, Rainey Bell."

"I love you, too."

Katie slumped over on her already passed out sister. Rainey brushed the hair from Katie's face. Knox turned around in her seat. Rainey was aware that they were not alone, but she leaned over and kissed Katie on the cheek.

Without looking away from Katie, she said, "Gillian, I'm trusting you with the most precious thing in my life."

Knox said, softly, "I know that, Rainey. You can depend on me."

"I meant what I said about the handcuffs. Lock her down. I don't need to be worrying about where she's run off to." Rainey never took her eyes off the sleeping Katie. "Keep her safe, for me. I know she's trouble, but she's my trouble."

"Consider it done," Knox replied, adding, "I haven't forgotten you saved my life. I owe you one."

Rainey stood up and closed the car door. She watched until the brake lights disappeared. Danny stepped up beside her.

"Cookie decided not to press charges when I told her I would need to take the video into evidence before she could air it. I kept Katie out of jail, but not off the eleven o'clock news."

"That's good," Rainey said. "Maybe Katie will be too embarrassed to come out of the hotel room until this is over."

Danny chuckled. "I'll say it again, that woman is a handful."

Rainey finally looked away from where the patrol car had driven off. She smiled at Danny. "Yeah, but I think I'll keep her."

"God bless you, my child," Danny said, making the sign of the cross.

Rainey laughed. "He already did."

#

Rainey went back inside the bar. Danny resumed his position in the van. The excitement over Katie's exit had died down and only a few heads turned when Rainey re-entered. She made her way back over to Dara Thomas' table. The women surrounding Dara cleared a path at Rainey's approach. Dara looked up at Rainey with a knowing smile.

"She's cute, but I bet she drives you crazy."

Rainey pulled out a chair and sat down, saying, "You have no idea."

Dara's blue eyes sparkled against her dark skin and hair. Her toned muscular arms indicated a woman who worked out, or worked hard for a living. When she grinned both cheeks dimpled. She wasn't gorgeous, but cute, and apparently quite popular with the ladies.

A waitress came by and Rainey ordered a double shot of top shelf bourbon. Danny's voice crackled in her ear.

"Don't forget you're driving."

"Shut up, I need it," Rainey said, quietly.

"I'm sorry, did you say something?" Dara asked.

Rainey covered her remark. "I need a drink."

Dara laughed. "I understand. Does she get like that often?"

"Obstinate, yes. Drunk, no. Actually that's the first time I've ever seen her drunk. Under different circumstances, it might have been entertaining."

"I guess she's under a lot of stress. Chelsea was telling me about all that's going on. I'm sorry you're both having to go through this."

Rainey wondered just how much Katie had told Chelsea. She and her boyfriend were no longer sitting at the table. Rainey looked out on the dance floor. She didn't see them.

Rainey asked, "Where did Chelsea and Jared go?"

"They went on home. They never stay very long. Chelsea has Sunday school to teach in the morning. I'll give it to her, she shows up here, but lesbians don't really jive with her upbringing."

Rainey's drink arrived. She tried to pay, but Dara waved off the waitress.

"Thank you," Rainey said, and took a sip of her drink. "I thought you and Chelsea were sisters. Did you not grow up in the same house?"

Dara leaned forward so she wouldn't have to shout. "I am an only child, biologically. My mother was unable to have more children after I was born, so they fostered kids. Chelsea came to live with us when she was five-years-old. I was fourteen at the time. She had been bounced around from home to home, within the same dysfunctional extended family. She was shy and quiet, but my mom coaxed her personality out. Mom and Dad adopted her officially, after convincing her drug crazed mother to give up parental rights."

"Sounds like it worked out for the best," Rainey said, taking another drink.

While she listened to Dara, Rainey surveyed the room. There were very few men in the bar. Rainey looked up at the balcony where Sheila was still sitting.

Sheila saw her and her voice came on the earwig, "I see you, Rainey."

Rainey acknowledged her with a nod.

Dara continued her story. "My mother became a fundamentalist Christian, shortly after Chelsea moved in. Her newly found faith did not sit well with my coming out at sixteen. My father supported me, but my mother hit the roof. Chelsea was young. The only stable home she had known became a war zone, ultimately ending with my father and me moving out. Chelsea was left with my mother and raised in that doctrine. We lost touch for years, but she moved here two years ago and we reconnected. She's trying to accept my lifestyle, but it's hard to get through that many years of hate being spewed at you."

The buzzwords fundamentalist, hate, and faith, got Rainey's attention. "When did you move to Durham?"

"Oh, I was born and raised here."

Rainey wanted clarification. "But you said, Chelsea moved here. Did your mother move away, after the split?"

"Chelsea and my mother moved to Oklahoma and lived in the Elohim City sect, until my Dad was able to get Chelsea out and in college. She taught for a couple of years on the west coast and then moved back here after Dad sent her a job application. I haven't seen or heard from my mother in years. Chelsea still keeps in touch with her, but I'd rather not deal with her at all. I'm proud of Chelsea for overcoming all that crap she had to listen to."

Elohim City was the home of a religious sect made up of radical Christians. Some still believe the residents had something to do with Tim McVeigh and the Oklahoma City bombing. A former sect guest, Richard Snell, taunted guards that something big was planned for the day of his execution. He was put to death in Arkansas on April 19, 1995, just hours after McVeigh brought down the Alfred P. Murrah Federal Building in Oklahoma City, killing 168 people, including nineteen children under the age of six. Rainey was more than intrigued by Chelsea's connection to these people.

Rainey tried not to sound too interested, when she asked, "Chelsea taught on the west coast?"

"Yes, near San Diego. She met Jared at Elohim City, too. He joined the Navy when she left the sect. He was stationed out there and she wanted to be near him. When he got out he moved here to be with her. They are very sweet together. He obviously worships the ground she walks on. They are getting married in August."

Rainey dug deeper. "He seemed like a nice guy."

Dara grinned. "He is. She hasn't slept with him. Won't even go to his house without a chaperone. He has much more patience than me."

"What does he do, now that he's out of the navy?"

"Jared works for a computer tech company. He's the guy that comes around to solve your software problems. He's a wiz with computers. He does all the graphic designs for my business and the bar."

Rainey hoped Danny was reviewing the video on this guy. She realized they had no last name, so she asked, "I didn't catch his whole name. I need to look him up. I could use a new logo."

"It's Jared Howard. He's really good. If you want, I could give you his number."

Rainey wanted everything she could get on this guy. "Sure, that would be great."

Dara picked up a pen and a small rectangular card, from a decorative mug in the center of the table. Feme Sole provided blank "Call Me" cards for their patrons. While Dara wrote down Jared's information, Rainey looked around the room again. It wasn't wise to focus on one suspect until all the other options had been eliminated. In the corner, opposite Rainey's table, a small dark man was watching her. When he realized she was looking, he quickly diverted his attention to the dance floor. Dara handed Rainey the card and dropped the pen back into the cup.

Rainey held the card so it was visible on the camera. She was sure a background check was in progress, and that was confirmed when Danny's voice sounded in her ear.

"We're running Howard now, Rainey. Turn back to the man in the corner. We need a close up if you can get one."

"Thank you," Rainey said, pocketing the card. "Dara, do you know that man in the corner over there?"

Dara followed Rainey's gaze. It wasn't hard to pick out a man in this crowd of women. Dara shook her head from side to side. "No, I don't know him."

Rainey stood up. "Well, I'm going to go get a better look at him. I just wanted to ask you one more question. I know you knew Lisa Jones. Phyllis told me. Did you also know Kim McNatt?"

Dara studied Rainey's face. She answered cautiously, "Yes, I knew Kim, intimately if that's what you're getting at."

Rainey smiled to ease Dara's anxiety. "Just trying to connect all the dots. Both women were seen here with you, then, at this table?"

Rainey's question was as much for Danny as it was for the woman in front of her. It didn't help Dara's apprehension.

"Do you think these murders might have something to do with me?"

"The victims were connected to this club and you are part owner. It's just a piece of the puzzle." Rainey started to turn away, but looked back at Dara. "Watch your back, Dara. He's close."

Rainey crossed the floor toward the man in the corner. He was on his cell phone, pretending to be in deep conversation, but he was watching her approach. A tall, statuesque, redhead, nearly half Rainey's age, suddenly obstructed her path. She smiled seductively at Rainey.

"Hi, my name is Ashley." The redhead's drawl was pure central North Carolina. "I certainly know who you are. Could I interest you in a drink, Agent Bell?"

Danny said, in Rainey's ear, "Oh good, lord. That woman is a lesbian? No wonder I can't find a woman like that. They're all at the gay bars."

"Thank you," Rainey said, "I appreciate the offer, but I'm a little busy right now."

Ashley smiled and leaned closer, slipping a card in Rainey's blazer pocket, and whispering in her ear, "I'd like to keep you busy for a couple of hours. Call me."

The earwig erupted with different voices.

"Oh, good God," was Danny voice.

Rainey was sure it was Sheila that said, "Steady, girl."

James let out a quiet, "Oooooo."

Paula was the voice of reason, "Settle down, boys."

Rainey realized her camera was level with the Ashley's cleavage. She smiled and leaned into the redhead, giving the boys in the truck a close up. More gasps and whoops quickly followed.

"I'm flattered," Rainey said, "but I'm taken."

Ashley was not fazed. With a big beauty queen smile, she said, "Well, variety is the spice of life. If you get tired of that little blonde, you give me a call. By the way, I'm a natural," Ashley winked, "redhead that is."

Rainey laughed and shook her head from side to side. "I bet you are, Miss Ashley."

Ashley went back to a laughing table of girls. Rainey continued toward the corner. The guy wasn't there. Rainey was alarmed.

"He's not there anymore. Sheila, do you see him?"

"No, he was under me. He could only have gone out to the lobby."

Rainey went through the doors and ran into Phyllis coming the other way.

"Phyllis, did you just see a guy with dark hair come through here? He was alone."

Phyllis, ever observant, said, "Yeah, he's over there by the window."

Danny was in Rainey's ear again. "Sheila, move to the balcony over the lobby. I want more eyes on this guy. Couple two, he's right behind you, dark hair, khaki slacks, burgundy shirt."

Rainey moved toward the man. He was typing into his cell phone and didn't see her until she was right on top of him. He was about her height, clean cut, not bad looking, but his body language suggested he was timid. That was confirmed when Rainey said, "Hello," and he nearly jumped out the window.

"Hel...Hello, Agent Bell."

"You know who I am? Now, who are you?"

The guy's eyes darted around the room. He stammered, "Mike, Mike Hopkins."

Rainey took a step closer and Mike shrank from her. She pressed him, "Well, Mike-Mike Hopkins, why were you staring at me? You were taking pictures, too. Give me that phone."

Mike handed over the phone without a word of protest.

Paula's voice said, "He's not our guy. Look at that body language."

Rainey was looking at the pictures on Mike's phone and becoming increasingly angry. Mike had been taking shots of Rainey since she walked in. He had shots of her talking to Katie and a very compromising looking picture of the buxom redhead whispering in her ear. She began to delete the photos as fast as she could.

"You're just some creep taking pictures, aren't you? What, do you go home and plaster your walls with them? Where do you live? I'm sending a car over there to see just what kind of a pervert you are."

Rainey thought Mike might wet his pants. He started to cry. "I live in Wake Forest, but please don't send a car to my house. My mom would kill me. I'm just a photographer, a runner really, for Cookie Kutter. I want to be a journalist. I'm studying at State. Honest, I just take pictures and send them to her."

Rainey continued to delete the photos, more forcefully now. "Well, she won't get these pictures."

Mike wiped his cheek with the back of his hand. "Don't be mad, okay, but I already sent them. That's what I was doing when you walked up. I'm sorry. Are you going to arrest me?"

Rainey stopped deleting the photos. It was futile, now. Cookie would plaster as many shots of Rainey as she could in a thirty-second sound bite. Katie was not going to like the redhead shot, but maybe she would miss it cowering from the images of her flying on Cookie in a drunken rage. Rainey handed the phone back to Mike.

"Mike, if I see you again, you'll be pulling that phone out of your nether parts. Lose Cookie's number. Find a real reporter to work for. Got it?"

Mike snatched the phone from Rainey's hand and was already moving toward the door, when he said, "Yes, ma'am."

Rainey watched him leave the club. "Scratch that guy off the list," she said, "He's probably going to change his pants."

James answered, "We're running him anyway, just in case. Danny sent a car to follow him."

Danny came on. "We just heard back from Brooks. Howard fits our timeline in San Diego. He moved here eighteen months ago. No criminal record. We're working on his military records."

Rainey looked out the window, turning her back to the room, so they couldn't see her talking. "Danny, he knows where Katie is."

"Already on it. His picture is being circulated to Katie's detail and I've doubled the guards on her room. No one is getting to Katie. You just watch your back."

Sheila spoke next, "Rainey, there is a man at the bar. He's been watching you. He hasn't looked away since I spotted him. Blue oxford button down, brown hair, your six-o'clock."

Rainey turned, surveying the room. She saw the man leaning on the bar. He had his head back, drinking from a beer bottle. He smiled at the woman beside him and appeared not to even notice Rainey, until he peeked. They always peek. His face slackened, the smile leaving him. He turned back to the bartender, and signaled for another beer. Rainey watched as he paid for the beer, and then left it sitting on the bar. He turned to the woman beside him. Rainey could tell he was asking the woman to watch his beer. She distinctly read the words bathroom on his lips.

Sheila saw it, too. "He's on the move. Heading into the big room, I believe toward the men's room. Agent Bell is following him. I'm moving... and have eyes on the suspect. Rainey he's five yards in front of you, heading toward the stage."

The crowd had thickened considerably. Rainey followed what she thought was the back of the guy's head, but the strobe lights, firing rapidly, made keeping track of him almost impossible.

"He's rabbiting," Rainey said. "He's not going to the bathroom, he's headed for the southwest exit. Is there anybody on that door?"

Sheila's breathless voice said, "I'm moving to the fire escape over the rear door."

Danny's tenseness was clear in his tone. "Slow down, Rainey. We're moving people into position."

Rainey pushed her way through the crowd. She could no longer see the suspect. "I've lost him, Danny. He's too far in front of me."

Rainey burst from the throng and saw the door just ten feet in front of her, the blue-oxford nowhere in sight. She ran to the bouncer at the door.

"Did a man just leave through this door in a blue button down shirt?"

The large woman shook her head. "Nobody's been out that door in the thirty minutes I've been standing here."

Rainey pushed the door open, surprised to see Roger standing there. He shrugged. Rainey turned back to the dance floor, quickly.

She shouted now, not worried about someone knowing she was wired, "Sheila, he backtracked. Find him. He's headed for a different exit."

Danny called out orders, moving his chess pieces into place. Every exit, out of the dance hall, was immediately covered by the undercover cops on the inside and uniformed cops on the outside. Rainey headed for the lobby. She finally reached the bar where he left his beer in care of the woman. The woman was still there, but the beer was not.

Rainey shouted over the din of voices and music, "What happened to the guy that was standing here?"

The woman looked puzzled. "Who? That guy? He just tipped the bartender and left a full beer on the bar. Guess he got what he came for. I saw him leaving with a bunch of girls."

Rainey picked her way through the throngs of women to the door. "He left, Danny. He's with a bunch of girls. He used them as a smoke screen. I'm coming out the front door."

Danny motivated his troops. "Let's move people. Fan out. Khaki pants, blue oxford shirt, brown hair. Find this guy. Rainey, don't you go off alone."

Rainey ran out the entrance and into the street, searching the crowd exiting and entering the bar. Two uniformed cops joined her, the description of the suspect loudly blaring out of their walkie-talkies. Rainey pointed west, toward the alley.

"You go that way," she said to the cops.

Then Rainey turned and ran in the opposite direction. She stopped at the corner of the building, slowly leaning out until she could see the activity in the well-lit parking lot. A woman sat on the hood of a car, smoking a cigarette, while another stood in front of her, hands on her hips, domestic dispute in progress. A couple leaned against the next building, groping each other feverishly. Two cars sat side-by-side, windows down, with a woman in each. They appeared to be having a conversation through the open windows, rather than either giving up their independence and leave her car.

Roger and Curtis walked up the center of the parking lot. Rainey stepped into view.

"Did you see him?" she asked.

"No, he didn't come this way."

Rainey looked behind her. This guy didn't just vanish. He was here somewhere. She jogged past the entrance to the other side of the building. She found the same results. No one saw which way this guy went.

"Un-fucking-believable," Rainey said, in frustration.

#

Danny found her seated at the bar in the lobby, nursing a shot of bourbon.

"You took your earwig out."

Rainey looked up at him. "Yep, needed a moment alone."

Danny sat on the stool next to her, surveying the room. "I had no idea there were so many beautiful lesbians. No wonder you jumped ship."

His attempt at humor fell on deaf ears. "How did that guy get out of here?" Rainey asked, followed by her knocking back the remainder of the shot.

"I don't think it matters." Danny stood up. "Come on, I want to show you something."

Rainey followed Danny out of the bar to the van. The back doors were open. They stepped up and James turned a monitor toward them.

Danny pointed at the screen. "Watch this."

The video started to play. It was Rainey's perspective on discovering Katie in the bar.

Danny leaned in closer. "Don't watch Katie. Look at the people at the table."

Rainey directed her attention to the table and stopped on Jared. Before she ever cleared Gillian, and made her way to Katie, he was watching Rainey. He came in and out of the shot, as Rainey moved around, but he was always watching her. At one point, the camera caught him taking a picture surreptitiously with his phone. Everyone else's attention was on Katie and Rainey, so no one noticed.

Jared's expression changed when he was introduced to Rainey. He forced a smile and maintained it until Rainey's attention was drawn back to Katie. The video continued for a few seconds and then James stopped it.

"That's all there was of him on the feed. We have him on surveillance from the door camera leaving with his girlfriend right after you went out the back with Katie." James hit a button on the keyboard and the image changed to the man in the button down shirt. "We also have a good shot of oxford man leaving. We're running it through facial recognition software."

Danny stepped away from the back of the van and Rainey followed. Lightning flashed far off in the distance. A storm was coming.

"Rainey, that's not all we got on Howard. He was dismissed from the military for striking a female officer. They let him resign, calling it stress related. He did use several slurs against her sexuality during the assault."

"Do you have enough for a warrant?"

Danny scratched his red five o'clock shadow. He'd had a very long day, as well. "I have a car on his house. His Jeep is in the driveway. Someone is in the house. The surveillance team saw the TV come on. Not sure if it's him, but he lives alone. Could be the girlfriend."

"No, Dara told me Chelsea would not go to his house without a chaperone, remember."

"We can get a warrant to match his tire prints to the ones we found at the last scene. It's a crapshoot though. There were so many tracks in there before we got to the scene. We can sit on him, wait for him to make a move, keep running his info until we find enough, but no, I don't think I can get a warrant because he took your picture and he happened to live in San Diego."

"Bring him in for questioning," Rainey suggested. "He's the weak partner, he'll break."

Paula waddled over to them, cell phone to her ear. She hung up and told them, "We have the connection. Brooks came in tonight and ran Howard's name through her 'magic machines,' as she calls them. Howard was the tech the prison's new software company sent to trouble-shoot the install. He's been inside Central Prison. They're not sure how he gained access to Dalton, but they're looking into it."

Danny sprang into action. "That's enough. I'll get the warrant." He pointed at Paula. "Get the team together and coordinate with Detective Robertson on the arrest."

"What about me? What do you want me to do?" Rainey asked.

Danny didn't answer. Paula stepped away, as if she knew this wasn't going to go well. It seemed the team had discussed it without Rainey present, which was obvious when Danny spoke.

"Go home, Rainey. I don't want you on this bust. You've been drinking and you're looking for a fight. Come in tomorrow and I'll let you question him, but right now, you are to go home, or better yet, go stay with Katie in the hotel until we have him in custody."

"Are you fucking kidding me, Danny?"

"No, I'm not, and if I see you anywhere near the bust, I'll have you arrested. One of these nice deputies is going to follow you home. I'll call you when it's over."

Rainey was livid. "I had one shot and a couple of sips of the first drink. You're just looking for an excuse to keep me out of this."

"And you gave it to me," Danny answered, adding, "Now, go home and stay out of trouble. We know who he is. It's over, Rainey. Just go home."

Rainey stormed off in the direction of her car.

Danny called after her, "Don't follow us, Rainey. I told them to pull you over if you did."

Danny conveniently never said where Jared lived, so Rainey couldn't go there ahead of them. She wasn't going to the hotel at this hour. Katie was probably still passed out. She thought maybe in the confusion of the moment, while officers were moving to their cars, preparing to leave, she could slip out of the parking lot and avoid the tail. Rainey didn't need anyone to follow her home if Jared was under surveillance. It felt like an intrusion and a punishment, one she did not deserve.

Rainey reached her car, pushed the button on the remote, and reached for the door handle. She pulled the door open, just as a man stood up from the shadows, behind the car. It happened so fast Rainey didn't have time to react consciously. Her gun was in her hand and pointed at the man in a split second.

She screamed, "Freeze, asshole!"

Mr. Blue Oxford took several steps back, his hands flying into surrender position. "Whoa! Whoa! I just wanted to talk to you."

The commotion at Rainey's car drew other officers' attention. In a flash, Blue Oxford was surrounded by cops, with weapons drawn.

Rainey took a step closer to the frightened man. She shouted, "Get on your knees! Hands on the back of your head!"

The man complied, but kept on pleading with Rainey. "Jesus, man! I just wanted to talk to you."

"Shut up!" Rainey shouted at the man, making eye contact with the closest cop. "Cuff him and search him."

Danny appeared at Rainey's side. "Where'd he come from?"

Rainey holstered her weapon, and said a bit accusatorily to Danny, "Behind my car. He was waiting for me in the middle of all these cops."

The officer finished cuffing the man and stood him up at the back of the car. Another officer pulled on latex gloves and began asking the man questions.

"Do you have anything in your pockets that might injure me? Are you carrying any weapons?"

Blue Oxford realized how much trouble he was in. He explained in earnest, "No, I don't have any weapons. There's a pen in my right pocket. I just wanted to talk to Agent Bell. Really guys, I'm not some creep, I'm just a writer."

The gloved cop handed Rainey the man's wallet. She looked at his ID. "Martin Douglas Cross," she read aloud. "Martin, what did you want to talk to me about?" Rainey continued to go through Martin's wallet.

Martin looked scared to death, when she glanced up at him. He apparently lost the ability to speak.

Rainey prodded him. "You wanted to talk to an armed FBI agent bad enough to spring up out of the darkness and scare the shit out of her, so talk. What's on your mind?"

Martin sputtered, then got on a roll, "M... m... my name is Marty Cross. I write crime novels. I'm writing about the Y-Man murders. Cookie Kutter said you were in the bar on Twitter. I've been dying to interview you, but I can't get around that woman in your office and your numbers are unlisted. She reads your mail, you know, that woman, Ernestine... I think that's her name...anyway I saw you in the bar and I decided to go up to you, but first I had to go to the bathroom. Then I changed my mind halfway there, and came back to the lobby. I couldn't find you so I found your car and waited... I wasn't..."

Rainey waved her arms. "Stop! Just stop.

"But I..."

"Zip it, Mr. Cross," Rainey commanded.

Martin clamped his mouth shut like a kid in trouble, sucking his lips inward.

"Let me get this straight, you came to this bar to talk to me, because Cookie tweeted about me being here." She folded the wallet, and dropped it on the trunk of the car. "Martin Cross, this is your lucky day. Agent McNally seems to think I'm a loose cannon. Good thing I didn't fly out of control and shoot you. Oh, and here's my statement on the Y-Man case - you're going to want to write this down, Marty - No comment!"

Rainey opened the door to her car, got in, and slammed it shut. The engine roared to life. She threw the Charger into gear and punched it. Rainey looked in the rear view mirror to see the gloved officer snatch the wallet off the trunk just before she sped away. One last glance behind her revealed Danny pointing and shouting while officers ran in all directions. Rainey smiled.

"Catch me if you can."

CHAPTER SEVENTEEN

Rainey took the Boulevard out of Durham and around Chapel Hill. By the time she joined the 15/501 highway, she was positive no one was following her.

"You have a call from an unlisted number, please press the call button to answer, or say…"

Rainey hit the button on the mirror. "What?"

"Girlfriend, you need to chill," Brooks' voice enveloped the interior of the car.

"Brooks, I'm sorry. I thought it was Danny."

"No, Agent McNally thought you might talk to me. He said you were in a 'mood.' I asked him which one and he said, 'The bitchy one.' Have we forgotten how to play well with others, Agent Bell?"

"He sent me home, Brooks."

"That asshole, trying to protect you from yourself. How dare he?"

"Now, don't you start on me. He didn't have to pull me off the bust. I wasn't going to shoot the guy in front of everybody. I'm not crazy."

"He's just looking out for you, Rainey."

"I know, but it still pisses me off not to be there."

Brooks' voice brightened. "How about the next best thing? We can listen to the feed. James is my homeboy. Taught him everything he knows."

"Hook it up. I want to know the second that piece of shit is in cuffs."

"Okay, hang on and be quiet, while I talk to James. He won't be able to hear us after I cut off my mic."

Rainey enjoyed the feeling of conspiracy. She listened as Brooks talked to James, scanning the road out of habit while she waited. The lightning flashes were growing closer and more frequent. Rainey heard the feed go live and then Brooks was back.

"Okay, Rainey Bell, you have a front row ear to the action."

"Thank you. I really appreciate it."

Rainey heard Danny's voice in the speakers, giving instructions as to who was going where. The SWAT team would do the knock. The BAU team would follow with the warrants for Jared Howard's arrest and the search of his property and vehicles. His instructions were followed by silence. Then one by one each group of officers called in their ready positions. Rainey's heart rate quickened, even though she was miles away. She turned on her signal light and pulled onto the road, leading to the cottage. She heard the blam, blam, blam of an officer banging on a door with his fist.

"Jared Howard, this is the police. We have a warrant for your arrest."

Blam, blam, blam.

"This is the police, open the door and come out with your hands in the air."

Danny's voice came out strong. "Go, go, go!"

A door splintered in the air around Rainey. She heard voices shouting.

"Clear, right."

"Clear, left."

"Clear, upstairs."

"All clear, nobody's home."

Rainey slammed on brakes, loudly screeching to a halt. It wasn't because of what she was hearing; it was what she saw in her headlights in front of her car.

Brooks heard the brakes lock up. She shouted excitedly, "Rainey, are you okay?"

The feed from Howard's house mingled with their conversation.

"Agent McNally, there's no one in the house."

Rainey, staring straight ahead, said softly, "There's a cat run over in the road. It looks like my cat."

Danny said, "Dammit. Somebody get me Rainey on the phone."

Rainey told herself Freddie never came this far up the road, but she really didn't know where he went.

Brooks echoed Rainey's next thought, "You know that's a trap, don't you?"

"Agent McNally, can you come to the basement?"

"Be right there," Danny answered.

"Let me shut this feed off." The white-noise from the audio disappeared from the speakers. Brooks continued, "I'll say again, you do know that's a setup, right? This is when you scream at the hero, 'It's a trap! Don't do it.' Listen to your gut, Rainey."

Clouds moved in, shutting out the moonlight. A flash from a far off lightning strike announced the rain as it began to fall in sheets around the car. Rainey peered into the darkness. The rain forced her to turn on the windshield wipers.

She shouted over the rain drumming on the roof of the car, "Yeah, Brooks, I know it's probably a setup, but if that's my cat, I can't let him lie out there in the rain."

The sky lit up again. Rainey could clearly see it was a black cat. She couldn't see its tail the way it was positioned. She spoke to Brooks as she slowly began to pull the car forward.

"I'm going to pull up beside it and open my door. If it's not him, I'll know very quickly. Freddie doesn't have a tail."

The drumming became a roar, as the wind buffeted the car, blowing the rain sideways. The noise was deafening. Rainey heard the call waiting tone and knew Danny was calling her. She ignored him.

Brooks shouted over the din, "Sounds like the skies opened up on you. There's a big storm on the radar down there."

Lightning struck nearby, followed by a loud clap of thunder. Rainey kept her eyes on the cat in the road, careful to pull just to the side of it. She stopped the car and sat still for a minute. Checking the mirrors and looking in the woods on both sides of the road, she realized she was perpendicular to a one-lane dirt road on her left. A metal gate across the entrance denied access. Rainey couldn't see anything out of place, but it was pouring down rain. She dug out a flashlight from the console and shined the beam down the dirt road. The rain was coming down so hard it reflected the light back at her.

"Okay, Brooks, I'm going to open this door now. Let's hope for the best."

"I'm with you. You just keep talking to me."

Rainey pulled the door handle and pushed the door open a few inches. Rain blasted her in the face. The wind roared amid the torrent of water, while thunder rumbled through the trees. She put the flashlight in her left hand, pointing it down at the road. Holding the door open, she slowly pulled the car forward. The body of the cat came into view headfirst. It looked like Freddie, but so many black cats looked like him, she wasn't sure. Lightning flashed. A loud slap and deafening rumble followed. Her heart began to break, but stopped abruptly when a long tail came into view.

"It's not him," she exclaimed, shutting the door, one second before the truck slammed into the driver's side of her car.

#

"Rainey, Rainey Bell, answer me!" Brooks' voice rang in Rainey's ears.

The airbags had deployed and smoke filled the air. Rainey was disoriented. The rancid smell from the airbag propellant burned her nose.

"Rainey, I'm starting people to you, hang..."

Brooks was cut off by, "OnStar emergency, this is Nancy. I have your airbags deployed. Can you respond?"

Rainey tried to breathe but a sharp pain on her left side restricted her intake. She gasped out, "Send... help."

Brooks' voice broke back in, "Oh no you don't, OnStar bitch. Rainey, I'm back. Can you hear me? Help is on the way."

Rainey's senses began to come back. The howling wind and rain continued. The storm was directly overhead now. Lightning strobes lit up the sky repeatedly, one thunderclap overlapping the next. Out of the corner of her eye, she saw the grill of a truck through the spider-webbed driver's window. Her circumstances rushed at her and the flight or fight instinct registered the alarm. A jolt of adrenaline jump-started her heart into a racing rhythm.

Rainey could hear the truck engine roaring as the driver tried to crush the Charger. The passenger side was smashed into the embankment of the ditch she'd been slammed into. The truck pinned her door shut. She had to get out of the car. Rainey released her seatbelt. Holding her left arm close to her side, where she thought her ribs might have been broken, Rainey climbed over the console and into the backseat. She pulled the Glock from the holster on her waistband and took the Beretta from the console. She laid the pistols on the seat and pulled the shotgun from the floor. All the while, she managed to grit her teeth against the pain and take a breath, so she could talk.

"Brooks, it's him. Send everybody. I have to get out of this car. I'm a sitting duck in here."

Rainey saw the light in the cab of the truck come on and go back off. He was out of the truck. A bolt of lightening illuminated his silhouette in front of the car, aiming a pistol directly at her. He fired three times. Luckily he never hit the same place twice and the armored glass did its job.

Brooks screamed through the speakers, "Oh my God! Help her. Help her."

The pain in her ribs had to be ignored. He was out there and she couldn't see him. Rainey pulled herself across the seat and reached for her keys. She yanked the remote off the chain. She dug into the console, pulling out a pocket knife.

"I'm getting the hell out, now!"

Brooks yelled, "But he's out there."

Suddenly, shots exploded above Rainey's head in the rear windshield. Again, the glass held.

Rainey shouted back, "It won't be long before he's in here with me."

Brooks was talking again, but not to her. "I repeat shots fired! Shots fired! Agent in distress. Move your asses! McNally! James! Anybody! Rainey's in trouble!"

Rainey dug the knife into the center of the seat back. She installed the computer equipment in the car. Rainey knew what was behind the seat, access to the trunk. She smelled something burning and looked up to see the man standing behind the flames that were now engulfing the front of her car. She tore at the fabric and foam with the knife, as he put one shot after another in the windshield, chipping away at the high security glass. Thank God he had not realized the roof was unprotected.

Once she had a hole in the seat large enough for her body, Rainey lifted the shotgun and used the butt end to break away the fiber board blocking her exit. She shoved the shotgun in before her, put the remote in her teeth, and lifted the two pistols from the seat, putting them in her waistband. She laid on her back, kicked off the console and pulled herself into the trunk. Rainey located the shotgun and grasped the remote with two fingers. She hit the trunk release and came up out of the trunk like Rambo, firing over the lid at the front of the car.

She turned and jumped out of the trunk, blindly firing the shotgun behind her, as she landed on the ground. She lost her breath with the pain of the jolt, but kept moving. Rainey fired the shotgun again and scrambled over the embankment, into the cover of the woods. Brooks was screaming her name, her cries faded as Rainey ran for cover, while her car went up in flames.

#

Rainey lay on the ground behind a fallen tree. She tried to calm her breathing, so she could reduce the pain in her ribs and listen, but the rain and thunder were too much to overcome. All she could do was wait for the next lightning flash and hope she saw him. Rainey raised her head slowly, peering into the blackness. He could be right on top of her and she wouldn't have seen him. The rain soaked her, running into her eyes, making it even harder to see. Still, she focused on the abyss in front of her. Three strobes of lightning lit up the area. A tree exploded about a hundred yards away. Rainey had to fight the instinct to duck and took the opportunity to see where she was. Rainey had one advantage. She knew these woods.

Another lightning strike revealed the silhouette of a man running to her left. Rainey stood up and fired one of the pistols in his direction. She immediately moved from that position, because the muzzle flashes would have given her away. She ran further from the road, heading for the lake. With the water at her back, she could lie in wait for him. The rain slowed. Rainey dropped down behind a tree, listening. This guy was military trained. He would be moving with her, stopping when she stopped, listening, as Rainey was, to every sound.

Rainey knew she had to keep moving. If he had night vision, he couldn't use it now. The lightning would blind him, but the storm was moving fast. She couldn't count on the lightning hanging around and he struck her as the kind of guy that probably owned night vision goggles. The thought kept her head down, as she crept closer to the lake. A streak of lightning revealed the lake just a few yards away. It also revealed Rainey to the man chasing her. She heard the pistol fire behind her and she hit the ground. Two more shots whizzed over her head. Rainey began to crawl.

The ground started getting soggier, as she inched through stumps and brambles to the water's edge. She slid on her stomach down the muddy bank, disappearing into cypress knees and the blackness of the water. Behind a large tree stump, Rainey put the shotgun down in the water. She pulled out the pistols, taking the bullets from the Beretta magazine and filling up the one for the Glock. She now had fifteen chances to take Jared Howard down. Leaving the shotgun behind, Rainey slithered between the stumps and waited.

She didn't have to wait long. Jared emerged from the trees, just as a flash lit up the woods around him. Rainey fired three times, hitting him in the shoulder with one. He stumbled back into the cover of the trees. He was wounded, but not dead. Rainey ducked behind a stump and waited, again. The rain subsided and then abruptly stopped. Rainey listened to the sudden quiet. For the first time, she heard sirens, lots of them.

Jared heard them, too. He called out to her from the darkness. "I'm hit. Help me."

Rainey didn't answer. He was trying to get her to give away her position. The sirens were very close now. She heard movement near the shore to her left and fired. She heard him scream in pain and her car blow up, just before her head went under water. Rainey emerged about ten feet away. Jared had fallen back behind the curtain of bushes lining the bank.

She heard him moaning. He cried out, "Fuck, my knee is shattered."

Rainey thought he could have been bluffing, to get her out of the water, but he sounded truly hurt. The cold of the water caused Rainey to shake uncontrollably. She couldn't stay in the water much longer and still be able to shoot her gun accurately. The sound of tires screeching and sirens abruptly shutting off alerted Rainey that help was near. She needed to let them know where she was. Thinking quickly, she turned away from shore to help cover the muzzle flash, aimed the gun at an angle so the bullet would fall harmlessly to the bottom of the lake, and fired. Quickly she slipped under the surface, hearing what sounded like an echo of her shot, just before her ears filled with water.

Rainey skimmed under the surface of the shallows, until she could no longer hold her breath. When she raised her head, she saw flashlights and heard her name being shouted from the shore. Still she remained quiet. Calling out now might get her killed. The lights grew closer and the shouts louder. Jared could be lying there waiting to take her rescuers down when they emerged from the woods. Rainey weighed her options, deciding to take a chance on getting shot, rather than watch someone else walk into a trap.

"Watch out! He's on the bank. He's hit," she shouted toward the shore. Rainey waited for the shots to come her way, but none came. The flashlight beams stopped coming forward and began to search more slowly, moving toward the shoreline. Her teeth were chattering loudly now, she called out again. "I'm here, in the water. He's on the bank to your right."

A silhouette, formed by a glowing flashlight, stopped where Rainey thought Jared had fallen. The beam examined something on the ground and then began searching the water.

A familiar voice called out to her, "Rainey, where are you?"

More flashlights searched the surface of the lake. Rainey tried to stand, her frigid muscles unable to push her out of the water. She clawed at the surface for balance and managed to stumble forward a few steps.

She called out weakly, "I'm here, Danny. I'm here."

Several beams of light lit up the water around her. She heard splashes and then Danny's strong arms lifted her to her feet. He cradled her against him, bringing her to the shore.

Through chattering teeth, Rainey asked, "Wh... Where is he?"

Danny sat her on the ground, took off his jacket, and draped it over Rainey's shoulders. He stood up, shouting at someone. "Get those EMT's down here. Tell them to bring warming blankets."

Rainey asked, again, "Wh...wh...where is he?"

Danny looked down at her. "He's dead, Rainey. Looks like he shot himself in the head. It's over."

#

Rainey stared at the clock, as the minutes passed by. She was on a bed, in the distant corner of the emergency room of Wake Memorial, wearing a hospital gown. She could hear activity all around her, but because the nurse had pulled the privacy curtain closed, Rainey was isolated and beginning to wonder if they forgot about her. She had been deposited in the corner bed, after x-rays showed no broken ribs, just deep bruising. Warm blankets and a saline drip took care of her hypothermia. Playing with the bed's remote control, trying to find a comfortable angle to accommodate the pain in her ribs, had grown futile. She settled on forty-five degrees and tossed the control on the table. Rainey wanted to go home, but there was no one there to take her. Her clothes were soaked and stuffed in a plastic bag on the chair against the wall. Her cellphone was in her pants pocket, probably forever ruined. It was six a.m. and she was contemplating how to get to a phone without exposing her ass to everyone in the hall.

Danny's voice called to her from the other side of the curtain. "Hey, you decent?"

"As decent as I can be in a hospital gown. Who designed these things, a voyeur?"

Danny parted the curtain and stepped inside Rainey's "room."

Her spirits brightened. "God, I'm glad to see you. I thought everyone forgot where I was. Can you get me out of here?"

Danny looked at her closely. "Well, your lips aren't blue anymore. Guess you'll live."

"I'll be fine. The doctor said it's just bruised ribs and I didn't go too far into hypothermia. He was going to release me, but that was an hour ago."

Danny took the bag of clothes from the chair and sat down. He looked tired and worried. Rainey saw that look many times when she was in this very emergency room almost two years ago. It was one of the few memories she had of that night.

"Really, Danny, I'm all right. Like you said, it's over."

He leaned forward, placing his elbows on his knees, hands clasped in front of him. "That's the thing, Rainey, it isn't over."

Rainey sat up too quickly. Pain radiated out from her bruised ribcage. Wincing, she wheezed out, "You said he was dead."

"He is dead. Jared Howard was the man in the woods tonight and he died of a gunshot to the head, like I said."

"Then why isn't this over?" Rainey asked, holding her side and taking quick breaths.

Danny dodged the question with one of his own. "Did you see anyone else in the woods?"

Rainey squirmed around in the bed, until she could sit up straight without the searing pain. "No, I barely saw *him*."

Danny rubbed his face in his hands, vacillating. Then he dropped his hands and turned to look at Rainey. "The M.E. says Howard was shot while lying on his back. The gun in his hand was placed there. The person who shot him was standing over him."

Rainey's jaw dropped open. She wasn't sure how to respond. Rainey knew she didn't shoot the guy in the head. The M.E. must have been wrong. At that moment, the curtain was thrown back and a very hung over Katie appeared. She had tried to clean herself up, but the alcohol had taken a toll only bed rest and hydration could cure. Crossing the few steps to the bedside slowly, Katie's eyes moved over Rainey, checking her for signs of injury. Satisfied that Rainey would live, Katie let out the breath she seemed to have been holding.

"Are you okay?" she asked, reaching for Rainey's hand.

"Yeah, I'm good," Rainey answered, just before Katie spontaneously bear hugged her. "Ouch! Except for the bruised ribs."

Katie released her grip on Rainey. "I'm sorry, did I hurt you?"

"A little," Rainey replied through gritted teeth, fighting off the stabbing pain.

Katie went back to just holding Rainey's hand. "We'll put ice on it and then climb in that big bed and sleep for days. I'm so tired, Rainey. Let's go home."

Rainey's staccato reply was interspersed with quick intakes of breath. "If they… would… give me… release papers… I will… gladly go home with you."

Danny interrupted the reunion, "Katie, I need to talk to Rainey. Could you wait outside?"

Katie glanced at Danny and then turned back to Rainey, a look of confusion on her face. Rainey squeezed Katie's hand. She took a deeper breath so she could calm Katie's fears.

"It's okay. Go find someone to get me out of here."

Katie's color began to fade. "Rainey, is everything all right? He is dead, isn't he?"

Danny answered, "Yes, Jared Howard is dead and he was the UNSUB we were looking for. There was enough evidence to convict him in his basement, alone."

Rainey watched as Katie focused her blue eyes on Danny. She was a smart woman and she heard the "but" in Danny's tone. "Then what do you need to talk to Rainey about? What are you not telling me?"

Danny's eyes darted back and forth between Rainey and Katie. Rainey hoped the expression on her face said, "Yeah, answer her."

He must have realized they were standing together on this one, because Danny didn't ask Katie to leave, again. He replied, "There is some question as to the manner in which Howard died. I'm sorry, but Rainey is now a suspect in the investigation."

Rainey fell back against the mattress, causing shards of pain to affect her exclamation of, "Are you... fuc... king...kidding... me?"

Katie took matters into hand. "As someone who could probably pass the bar exam, I am informing you that Rainey has been in a trauma. She will not be making any statements for forty-eight hours and then only with an attorney present. Unless you have reason to hold her, I am respectfully asking you to leave us alone. The FBI has gotten the last pound of flesh out of Rainey Bell." Katie pulled on Rainey's hand. "Come on, honey. We're going home."

Rainey gasped out, "I can't."

"Why not?" Katie asked. "He can't make you stay here."

"I know... but... I don't... have any... pants."

#

Katie managed to talk a nurse out of a pair of scrubs for Rainey. With Rainey in the passenger seat, she drove through the drive-up window at the pharmacy for Rainey's pain meds, stopped for a biscuit and a drink so Rainey could take the meds, and then headed to the cottage. Rainey fell asleep on the way home, finally able to relax and let someone else be in control. Katie's gasp brought her out of dreamland abruptly.

"Oh my, God! Look at your car."

Rainey lifted her head to see her sleek, black Charger being loaded on the back of a flatbed. The driver's side was smashed in, windows blown out, a dusty sooty remnant of her beloved Dodge Charger.

"Damn, I loved that car."

Katie patted her hand. "I know you did, honey. We'll get you a new one. Maybe a tank next time."

They slowed passed the flatbed on the other side of the road. An old farm truck was chained down on the bed, with pieces of the gate still embedded in its smashed grill.

"You're lucky you survived the impact," Katie was saying. "I still can't believe it was Jared. I've seen him several times with Chelsea. I was shocked when they told me. You're right, Rainey, I just don't see the bad in people."

Rainey adjusted in the seat, sitting up straighter. "It took a lot of trained professionals to pick him out." She paused and then smiled over at Katie. "I'm glad you don't see the bad in people. We make a good team."

Katie smiled back and reached for Rainey's hand. "Yes, we do make a good team."

Rainey squeezed Katie's hand. "I'm making some changes I hope you will approve of. I'm going to sell the property and move us closer to Chapel Hill. Would that make you happy?"

"You don't have to sell it. We can keep it, use it as a summer cottage or something."

316

Rainey laughed. "I'm not the summer cottage kind of girl. We're just moving to the other end of the lake."

Katie turned into the driveway at the cottage. She shut off the engine and turned in her seat to face Rainey. "Whatever it takes to make this work, I'm willing to do. I'll try not to worry so much and trust that you know what you're doing. If it means waiting on the baby, then I'll wait."

"Keep your appointment, Katie."

"What appointment?"

"Ernie let the cat out of the bag. I know you were scheduled for insemination this week. I'll go with you. We might as well start this parenting thing together, don't you think?"

Katie strained against her seatbelt to kiss Rainey. She put both hands on Rainey's cheeks, pulling back and saying, "I love you. I don't ever want to be apart from you again."

Rainey chuckled. "Well, since I am selling my home and just liquidated most of my assets to buy you a house, you're stuck with me."

"I'll pitch in my half," Katie said, still holding Rainey's face.

"Don't worry, you'll be pitching in. I hear kids cost a bundle."

Katie let go of Rainey and released her seat belt, saying, "There you go with that plural kid thing again."

Rainey unbuckled herself and opened her door. She turned back to Katie. "Honey, with my luck, you'll have six the first go around."

CHAPTER EIGHTEEN

Katie did as she promised. She and Rainey climbed the stairs and went straight to the bedroom. After Rainey was iced down, Katie curled up next to her, and they slept like the dead for hours. Rainey only roused for a moment, when Freddie jumped on the bed. He found his usual spot next to Katie and joined them in slumber. All was right with the world in the little cottage.

Rainey awoke to the smell of sautéing onions. Katie was home. The cottage once again breathed to life. She stumbled from the bed to the bathroom, holding her ribs. In her experience, the soreness would continue to multiply for at least three days. Rainey planned to spend those days as immobile as possible. Curled up in the bed with Katie sounded like a good way to pass the time.

She stripped off the scrubs and stepped into the shower. Rainey kept her injured side protected from the spray. Still sporting a tender shoulder, her left ribcage was just turning a light shade of purple, the bruise having not fully made it to the surface yet. The impact of the truck into the side of the car had jolted her entire body. The pain in her neck and back was competing with her ribs for top billing. Rainey was so close to the door when the truck hit, her side took the impact nearly full force. If she hadn't sat up when she did, her neck would probably have been broken. For that reason alone, Rainey was thankful for the pain radiating down her spine. She was also very thankful when the naked blonde climbed in the shower with her. Too injured to do anything but hold Katie against her, it was enough.

#

They were eating the spaghetti Katie prepared when her phone rang. Katie looked at the caller ID.

"It's Chelsea. I know she must be devastated."

Rainey agreed. "Go on, answer it."

Katie slid her finger across the screen of her phone and put it to her ear.

"Chelsea, are you all right?"

Rainey figured if anybody understood what Chelsea was going through, it was Katie. Rainey continued to eat while Katie talked to the distraught woman on the phone.

"You don't need to apologize to me or Rainey. We certainly understand finding out someone you care about was not who you thought they were... Yes, Rainey's fine. We're back at the cottage. She just needs to rest for a few days... Are you alone? Where's Dara... You shouldn't be alone right now. When is Dara coming back?"

Rainey could see the wheels turning in that little blonde head.

Katie listened and responded, "Well, have you eaten? At least let me bring you some food... Yes, I know where that is.

Ernie, Rainey's office manager, lives on that road... Uh huh... Let me get Rainey settled back in and I'll come over and bring you some spaghetti... Oh, it's no trouble at all... No, she'll be asleep anyway, after I give her some more pain medication... Okay, see you in a bit."

"You're going to leave me here, alone?" Rainey whined, when Katie hung up the phone.

"You won't even know I'm gone."

Rainey put her fork down. "Trust me, I will know."

"Okay, then ride with me. She's at her father's farmhouse, about a mile before you get to Ernie's. You know the barn with the shiny red roof."

"I didn't know her father lived out this way," Rainey said, standing slowly. "Thank you, for the food. I've been starving since you left." She reached for her plate, to take it to the counter.

Katie took the plate. "I'll get that." She talked while she cleared the table. "I didn't know Chelsea's father lived out here, either. She said he's gone fishing in the mountains and she's been house sitting. Dara's due back there before dark. I just want to check on her, make sure she's all right. I know the questions she's asking herself right now."

"Ahhhh," Rainey moaned, using the chair for support to push herself upright. It was painful, but rewarding when she completed the move and took the pressure off her ribs.

"You need another pill," Katie said, heading for a bottle on the counter.

"No, just some ice, please. I'm going to go sit on the couch, if you don't mind."

Rainey hobbled into the front room. About halfway there, she realized the more she moved the better she felt. She walked to the big bay window, stretching her torso slightly as she went. It was a beautiful day. The rain left everything crisp and clean. Rainey panned from left to right, stopping on the Sheriff's car parked where the road disappeared into the trees.

"Son of a bitch. He's put a tail on me."

"What, honey?" Katie appeared with a bag of frozen peas, handing it to Rainey, who pressed it to her side immediately. "What tail are you talking about?"

Rainey pointed out the window. "That one. It's like they're saying, 'we're watching you.' Does Danny really think I'm going to run?"

Katie placed her fingers under Rainey's chin and pulled her eyes into focus. She searched Rainey's face for the truth. "I'm only going to ask you this once. I don't care what the answer is. I just want to know the truth. Did you do what Danny thinks you did? Did you execute Jared Howard?"

"No. I shot him twice, but not in the head. I was never that close to him, ever, even after he was dead. I would have killed him if I could, but no, Katie, I did not cold-bloodedly stand over him and pull the trigger on a helpless man."

With absolute honesty, Katie responded, "I did."

Rainey let the confession of past sins go without comment, before she said, "The Medical Examiner is wrong. It was pouring down rain, he was covered in mud. Any number of things could have skewed his findings."

"I don't care what they say. I believe you. Maybe we should call a lawyer, a real one."

Rainey couldn't believe she was in this situation, but she had to agree with Katie. She knew she hadn't shot Howard while he was down, but if the medical examiner was willing to testify that someone had, Rainey would have a hard time convincing a jury that it wasn't her. She'd shot her mouth off enough to bury herself in circumstantial evidence. Danny would be forced to reveal what he knew about her state of mind. Rainey tried to kill Howard and probably would have stood over him and pulled the trigger, but she didn't. Would she be convicted for simply admitting the truth about what she might have done?

"You're right," Rainey said. "I'll call Molly Kincaid in the morning. I've worked with her before on a few of her cases."

Katie laughed. "I know her. I used to see her at charity events. You know she's a lesbian, right?"

Rainey stared out the window. "I hadn't really thought about it. Damn, that pisses me off."

Rainey had switched gears too fast for Katie. She was still stuck on Molly Kincaid's sexuality. "What, that Molly is a lesbian? Would that make a difference to you?"

"No, not Molly," Rainey pointed at the car again, "the cop outside my house."

Katie looked at the patrol car and started to giggle. "Hey, want to have some fun?"

#

Rainey left the cottage and walked down to the office. She waited inside and watched through the blinds, as Katie came down the steps carrying a box. She put the box in her car, got in, and backed out of the driveway. Rainey laughed when Katie pulled up next to the patrol car. She couldn't hear what was being said, but she was sure Katie was charming and sweet, while she handed the officer a plate and a bottle of water she pulled from the box. Katie got back in the car and put it in reverse. She backed all the way to the office, stopped the car in front of the door, and came inside.

"He's headfirst in that plate by now. Go on, get moving," Katie said, to the smiling Rainey.

"You and your sisters played hell with your parents, didn't you?" Rainey asked.

"It's the art of misdirection. Now, go."

Rainey went out the backdoor and around the side of the office building. She hunched over to avoid being seen, slipping into the back seat of Katie's car undetected. Rainey was having so much fun the pain was worth it. Katie came out the front door of the office, making a show of saying goodbye.

"I'll be back in a little while, Rainey. Bye."

Rainey sprawled across the backseat, trying desperately not to laugh, because it hurt so much. Katie got in the car and they drove right by the cop.

Katie waved at him and said to Rainey, conspiratorially, "He's got spaghetti hanging out of his mouth. He never saw a thing."

From the back seat, Rainey replied, "I'll remind you of these evasive maneuvers you're so good at, when our son or daughter slips away from you."

"Won't happen. If my sisters and I haven't done it, then it probably hasn't been done, yet. I'm prepared for the worst."

Rainey held her sides, fighting off a chuckle. "Oh, this is going to be fun, watching you wrangle a kid just like you."

"That's the same thing my father said," Katie replied.

Rainey lost control of her laughter and gave into the pain, looking forward to laughing through the hurts with Katie, for the rest of her life.

#

Katie pulled her car to a stop in the shade of an enormous pecan tree and rolled all the windows down.

She told Rainey, "Now, you just sit here and relax. Here, take my phone." She dug inside her purse, producing headphones. "You can listen to music while I'm in there. I'll tell her you're waiting, so I can get out of there fast."

Katie had stopped to let Rainey get in the front seat, after they were clear of the cop. She took the phone from Katie, but left it on the seat beside her. Rainey just wanted to listen to the quiet. Her eyelids were heavy and she thought she would just nap while Katie visited with her friend. Rainey wasn't being antisocial. She wouldn't be good company in her current state. The sneaking around had drained her energy. Katie grabbed the box from the back seat.

"I'll be right back. I can't wait to see that guy's face when we drive back up with you sitting in the front seat."

Rainey smiled. "You're really enjoying this."

Katie stuck her head in Rainey's window. "Yes, I like sneaking around with you." She kissed Rainey on the cheek. "I'll hurry, I promise."

"No rush. I'm going to close my eyes for a minute. Take your time."

Katie bounded off toward the front door of the old two-story farmhouse. The yard was swept clean of leaves and the buildings looked well kept. The big barn at the back of the property appeared freshly painted. Rainey noticed a newer model pickup truck with the logo for a lighting company on the door. It was probably a truck Dara used for her business. A silver sedan was parked next to it. A breeze drifted through the car. Rainey laid her head back on the rest and closed her eyes.

Her brief moment of peace was disrupted by Katie's phone ringing. Rainey picked it up and saw Danny's number on the caller ID. She dropped the phone back on the seat. Closing her eyes again, she listened to the breeze washing through the leaves of the ancient tree. The phone rang again. This time it was Ernie. Rainey wasn't up for relaying all the events of the previous evening to a curious Ernie. She ignored the ringing until it stopped. She settled down again, just before the phone started to ring a third time.

"Oh, for crying out loud!" Rainey exclaimed, grabbing the phone up off the seat. It was Mackie this time. She answered, "Why is everybody calling Katie? Can't we just have a day where we don't talk to anyone else?"

"Rainey," Mackie's voice rumbled, "Danny is trying to reach you. He said you evaded the cop watching you."

"Yeah, well, tell him to go fuck himself. I didn't shoot that guy in the head."

"That's not why Danny is looking for you. They were going through the evidence and found a video on his computer of Howard with one of the victims. The camera was moving. Someone else was there. He had a partner."

Rainey suddenly realized she did not have a weapon with her. The police had her Glock and Beretta. She told them where to look for the shotgun. The Sig was probably in evidence, after someone fished it out from under her smoldering seat. Rainey hadn't thought to take a gun from the house for the first time in years. She had been too wrapped up in Katie's escape plan and just didn't think about it. Thinking the danger was over, she had relaxed, and now Rainey was in a panic. She needed to get both of the women out of the house and back home, where she could protect them.

"Mackie, I'm with Katie at Chelsea Thomas' father's house, the one with the big red barn roof, near where Ernie lives. I'm going to go in the house and get them both. I'll take them back to the cottage. Meet me there."

Rainey hung up, throwing the phone down on the seat. She moved as fast as she could in her condition, gripping her arm close to her injured side. The pain didn't matter. Rainey had to get them somewhere safe. She knocked on the door. She saw Chelsea coming toward her through the lace curtains of the door window. Chelsea turned the handle, pulling the door open. She smiled at Rainey.

"Decided to come on in, huh?"

Rainey stepped into the hallway, speaking rapidly, as she did. "Where's Katie? We have to get out of here. Grab your keys, lock up, you're coming with us."

Chelsea closed the door behind them. "Why, what's wrong?"

Rainey's eyes darted around, looking for Katie. "I'll tell you on the way. Where's Katie? We have to go, now."

Chelsea looked alarmed. She pointed down the hall. "She's back there, in the kitchen."

Rainey started toward the open door at the end of the hallway. "Hurry up, grab your stuff. I'll get Katie."

Chelsea was right behind Rainey, when she asked, "What's happened? Jared's dead. What are you afraid of?"

Rainey reached the doorway, saying, "He had a partn…"

Rainey froze. Katie was seated at the kitchen table with Dara Thomas. Both women were tied to chairs. Dara had been beaten severely and was barely conscious. Katie was crying, blood trickling from the corner of her gagged mouth. Rainey turned quickly, coming face to face with a pistol, extended from the hand of Chelsea Thomas.

"Back up, Agent Bell. Don't try to be a hero. I'm going to kill you. We can do it now or later, though you might want a chance to tell your precious Katie goodbye."

"Chelsea, stop it," Dara said, weakly.

"Shut up! I told you to shut up!" Chelsea screamed.

Rainey started running scenarios through her head. A seriously deranged woman was holding a gun on her. Negotiating strategies flew through her mind. What did Chelsea want, besides the obvious murderous intent? Chelsea was the kind of killer with a perceived injustice. Rainey had to keep her talking. If she could identify what Chelsea needed to talk about, maybe Rainey could stall her long enough to figure out how to get the three of them out of there alive. She backed away from Chelsea, hands in the air, submissive as she could appear.

"Chelsea, what do I need to do for you put down that gun?"

Chelsea was a pretty, petite blonde on every other occasion Rainey had seen her. Currently she had the look of a mental patient, severely in need of medication. She glowered out from under her brow, facial muscles slackened into a sneer.

"Put down *your* gun, Agent Bell. I know you never go anywhere without one. Katie told me. She's been a fountain of knowledge as far as you're concerned. You're all she talks about, you know."

"Chelsea," Rainey needed to repeat the woman's name, keeping her grounded in reality as much as possible, "I'm not carrying a gun today. The police have my weapons. They took them last night."

"Katie informs me you have a house full of weapons. You should know she's worried about the baby getting hold of one of them."

"Pat me down. I'm not wearing a weapon."

"Pull your shirt up," Chelsea growled. "Turn around."

Rainey did as she was told.

"Now, pull up your pants legs. Let me see your ankles."

Once again Rainey complied, showing both ankles, and then returned to standing with her hands in the air. She had managed to get closer to Katie, whom she could hear breathing fast on her left. Dara was coughing out blood and moaning now. The rope binding her to the chair was the only thing keeping her upright.

"Chelsea, I need to tell you the police will be coming, soon. Let's resolve this before they get here."

"You're lying. You didn't know I was Jared's partner. You wouldn't have come in here unarmed if you did."

"You're wrong, Chelsea. I would have come in here even if I knew you had a gun and I didn't. I wouldn't leave Katie like that."

"Lesbian abominations, that's what you are. Just like my worthless sister."

Rainey ignored the taunts. "I just told Mackie where I was. I'm sure Katie's told you about Mackie. If I don't call him back in a few minutes, he'll bring the cavalry down on this place."

Chelsea let out an evil laugh. "Then they'll find a bunch of dead dykes when they get here."

Rainey only gave Mackie a rough idea of her location. She needed to keep Chelsea busy long enough for him to realize something was wrong. Maybe he could figure out where they were. Rainey could only hope.

"Dara told me about your upbringing, how her coming out ruined the only good family you had known. She feels bad about that. She told me she was glad you moved back here, so you could be a family again."

"I'm not her family," Chelsea bellowed. "I share no blood with her. I came here to root out the evil she does and slay her and her kind. She is going to burn in hell for her debauchery, just like you and the perfect Miss Meyers over there."

Logic and reason were of no use in Rainey's bag of tricks. She tried another distraction. "Where does Dalton Chambers fit into all this?"

Chelsea brightened at the mention of Dalton's name. "I'm carrying on his work, ridding the world of sinning women. Whores, lesbians, they all deserve to die. He helped me see the way."

"And Jared, he was just your servant?"

"He was a tool, an instrument of God, sent to help me with my calling."

"Jared did what he did to those women for you. He loved you and you killed him. How does that sit with your God?"

"He was a soldier in the war for morality. He knew I had to kill him. He knew he was too weak to take the torture the police would put him through."

"Chelsea, I don't know what you were told out there in Oklahoma, but the police don't torture people. They'll get you the help you need, if you just put down the gun. I promise I won't let anything happen to you."

Chelsea's evil laugh bounced off the old wooden walls. "You aren't going to be around long enough to keep that promise. Get my sister on her feet. We're going to the woods. I have a place prepared for you."

Rainey didn't move. Letting Chelsea take them to the woods would sign their death warrants. "What's the plan, Chelsea? Did Dalton lay it all out for you? How do you expect to get away with this?"

"Oh, it's genius really. I'll escape the mad partner, while he's chopping your heads off. At least, that's what I'll tell the cops. I'll come out of the woods and direct the police to your mutilated bodies. Everyone will be so sad and nobody will suspect me. You didn't."

"That's a lot of forensic evidence to hide. Are you sure you've thought this through? I think Dalton is setting you up to take the fall for all of this."

"Then I'll take my punishment and join him in heaven, where we will be as children of God, forever young, frolicking on streets of gold, while your souls roast in hell."

Rainey forced a laugh. "Oh, Dalton has no intentions of joining you in heaven. He told me we were going to fry together in hell. I think that's closer to true, don't you?"

Chelsea's face flushed blood red, aiming the gun at Rainey's head. "Get her up. Move! You too, Katie, stand up."

The sound of the front door opening startled Chelsea. Rainey hoped it was someone who could help them and not someone that would send Chelsea into firing away at all of them.

"Yoo-hoo, Mr. Thomas. It's Ernestine, from down the road. Are you home? I'm looking for Katie Meyers. She's a friend of your daughter Chelsea. I saw her car out front. Mr. Thomas, can you hear me?"

Chelsea aimed the gun toward Katie and whispered, "You say a word and Katie gets it first."

Ernie's voice grew closer. She was headed straight into a slaughterhouse, still calling out, "Yoo-hoo, anybody home? Chelsea?"

At the sound of her name, Chelsea turned her head toward the door. The instant Chelsea took her eyes off her, Rainey's fight reflex kicked in. She flew at Chelsea, sending all her weight into the smaller woman, smashing her into the wall. The pistol flew from Chelsea's hand and skittered across the floor in Katie's direction, but Chelsea wasn't giving up. With the strength of a madwoman she clawed at Rainey and kicked her in the ribs with her knee.

Instead of buckling her, the shards of pain brought forth a rage from the depths of Rainey's soul. Combined with the time spent with her father, learning how to survive with her bare hands, it proved to be a nearly lethal combination. She slammed her forearm down on Chelsea's throat, forcing an instant choking cough out of the smaller woman. Rainey leaned down harder, as Chelsea clawed at her arm, gasping for a single wisp of air.

Rainey bared her teeth. "When you get to hell, save Dalton a seat. He's going to be right behind you. You sick twisted fuck!"

Rainey pushed down harder. The blood vessels in Chelsea's eyes began to swell. Tiny spider veins appeared just below the surface of the skin on her cheeks.

"Rainey, let her up," Ernie said, calmly.

Rainey held fast.

Ernie spoke again. "Rainey, it's over. Let her up."

Rainey suddenly became aware of the other people in the room, again. She let go of the gagging woman and crawled across the floor, picking up Chelsea's gun. She stood up, tucking the gun in her waistband and ran to Katie's side. She pulled the gag down and started untying Katie from the chair.

"Are you hurt, Katie?"

"I'm sorry, Rainey. I didn't see it coming. I couldn't warn you."

"I didn't see it coming either." Rainey released Katie from the chair. "It's okay, we're all right now."

Chelsea continued to clutch at her throat, sucking in air.

Ernie moved to Dara. "What is this child's name?"

"Dara, Dara Thomas," Rainey replied, still checking Katie for injuries.

"Dara, honey, wake up," Rainey heard Ernie say, but she was too concerned with Katie to listen for a response.

Rainey dropped down on one knee in front of Katie. The jolt of hitting the floor doubled her over, wincing in agony. The adrenaline was subsiding and her body now remembered the pain.

Katie leaned over her, grubbing her shoulders. "Rainey, are you all right? Ernie, call 911. Rainey, answer me."

Rainey couldn't answer. She didn't have the breath. She could only look up at Katie, helplessly. Katie's expression of concern instantly changed to horror as her eyes locked on something behind Rainey. Recognition hit Rainey after her instincts had already taken over. Her hand was on the grip of the gun, before she even thought about it. In one move, she ripped the gun from her waistband, swung around and fired, at the same time another firearm discharged in the room.

Chelsea Thomas staggered, a large knife in her hand, poised to strike. A pool of crimson formed on her blouse, where the two bullets entered her heart. She took one more step forward. Rainey saw the moment of recognition in Chelsea's eyes, the second it dawned on her that she was already dead. There was a short intake of breath, and then she was suspended in motion, before dropping as if someone cut the strings on a marionette. Dalton's puppet would dance no more.

The noise of the shots startled Dara awake. She screamed. Rainey looked over the table to see Ernie, still holding her revolver.

Comforting the frightened woman, Ernie said, "It's okay, Dara. She's gone. She won't hurt you anymore."

Katie slumped to her knees in front of Rainey. She put her arms around Rainey's neck and started to cry. Rainey dropped the gun on the floor and held Katie. She heard Ernie calling 911.

Rainey whispered into Katie's ear, "It's okay, baby. We're safe now. It's okay."

Through her tears, Katie said, "People keep trying to kill us, Rainey. Why can't they just leave us alone?"

Rainey lifted Katie's chin so she could see her eyes. She smiled down at the beautiful blonde that was hers and hers alone.

"You know what they say, 'What doesn't kill us makes us stronger.' We're stronger today than yesterday, and we'll be stronger yet, tomorrow. As long as I have you, I don't care what comes. We'll make it Katie, I'll keep my promise."

There was one beat of understanding between Katie and Rainey. One moment, when they both knew, beyond a shadow of any doubts either may have once harbored, whatever they encountered in the future they would go through it together. Time stood still. The room around them fell out of focus. All Rainey could see was Katie's blue eyes... no sounds... and all was right with in Rainey's world, once again...

... ...

"Oh for Pete's sake! Can we at least get out of the room with the dead body, before you two go all goo-goo-eyed?"

CHAPTER NINETEEN

Dalton waited in the hospital bed, chains draped around his waist and locked to the bed. When Rainey and Danny entered the room, the self-satisfied smile slid off his face. Dalton had been informed that he was being moved out of isolation, which he was happy about, but seeing Rainey meant his plan to kill her had failed. She smiled as she approached the bed, concealing the pain in her ribs with each step.

"Surprised to see me?" Rainey asked.

He glared back at her, nostrils flaring, dark bruises under each eye from the beating he had taken. His right eye was swollen shut, but it was still twitching.

"You're little plan to kill me didn't work, as you can see. By the way, we found a phone at Chelsea's house, yesterday. She kept every text message you ever sent. We have you on conspiracy to commit murder that resulted in several deaths. If you don't get the needle for killing that little girl, and I can't imagine a jury not sentencing you to death for that piece of work, you'll definitely get what's coming to you on this one.

You'll be on death row, pretty soon. Since your co-conspirators are dead, you're the only person left to exact revenge upon."

"They won't give me the death penalty for killing two dykes," Dalton snarled.

Rainey laughed. "You just keep telling yourself that."

Dalton flushed with anger and shouted, "There will be more. You'll never be able to rest. They'll find you and that whore you live with. I'll haunt you till the day you die, Rainey Bell. You'll never forget about me."

Danny remained quiet and let Rainey do all the talking. Rainey figured he just came with her to make sure she didn't do anything to disgrace the badge she was still carrying. She continued to smile at the creature in the bed. He was not a man, but an abomination in the truest sense of the word.

She leaned in a bit closer. "Dalton, I may not forget you, but I will not live in fear of you. You, on the contrary, will think about me every moment for the rest of your miserable life. I'm going to testify against you at your trials. The penalty phase will be the most fun. You wouldn't believe the testimony they'll let in during that part. When I'm done, there won't be any doubt about the punishment you deserve. Trust me, you will draw your last breath soon enough."

"I might be on death row, but I'll live another ten or fifteen years on appeals. All that time you will be looking over your shoulder and even after I'm gone, they'll keep coming."

"No, they won't," Rainey answered, quickly. "They'll know what happened to the last ones you sent and I assure you the same fate waits for the rest of them. Keep dreaming, Dalton. It's all you have left to do. I, however, will be living my life, free of you."

Rainey turned to go. Dalton strained against his chains. The guard holding the little black box flinched. Rainey raised her hand to stop him from pushing the button.

"Wait," she said. "Let him speak."

Dalton glanced at the guard and then turned back to Rainey. "God will exact his punishment on the wicked. Your lying with a woman is against God's law. You'll join me in hell fire after death. I'll wait for you, Rainey, and we will be together forever."

Rainey met Dalton's glare with another smile. "If loving Katie is what I'm called to answer for at the end of my life, then I have no fear. You may have read the bible cover to cover, but you're no Christian, Dalton. People like you give religion a bad name. You twist things around to make them say what you want them to say. I don't believe you're a truly religious man, but I do believe you understand the concept of retribution. You chose the path you're on and now you shall reap the seeds you sowed. Burn in hell, Dalton Chambers." She leaned in and whispered, "You're going to get there, sooner than you think."

#

Rainey walked with Danny out of the prison. On the way, she bumped into Bobo, wearing his State red hoodie again, heading for the visitors' lounge. She nodded at him as they passed.

Danny asked, "Who's that?"

"An informant I've used from time to time. He helped me catch the guy whose nephew shot me."

"Did I hear right, when you were on the phone with the DA this morning? Are you asking them to drop the charges against that kid?"

"Chauncey said he'd plead guilty to the enterprise charges and save them a trial, if the DA dropped the charges against his nephew. They asked me what I thought."

Danny started shaking his head back and forth. Rainey cut him off before he could voice his displeasure.

"Look, he's just fourteen. I said yes, under some conditions. I pay for military school after he attends disciplinary boot camp this summer. If he doesn't hold up his end of the bargain, he goes back to court to face the charges."

Danny asked. "What does Katie say about it?"

Rainey smiled. "She says we're saving the world, one child at a time. She is, however, a little upset about the picture of me and the redhead they keep showing on the news."

"Just keep showing her the clip where she belts Cookie. She'll forget about the redhead."

Rainey laughed. "I bet you won't forget that redhead anytime soon."

Danny flushed red and changed the subject. "Is Ernie okay? It's not everyday that you shoot someone."

"You're assuming that's the first person she ever shot." Rainey grinned.

Danny was taken aback, before Rainey let him off the hook.

"I was just kidding. Yes, she's going to be fine. She actually argued with me over who shot first. She isn't happy about having to kill someone, but Ernie is damn sure I would never have survived if she hadn't shown up."

"So..." Danny hesitated and then rushed the question, "Are you going to stay in the bond business or are you coming back where you belong?"

Rainey reached in her coat pocket and pulled out her credentials. She handed them to Danny. "I belong here, with Katie. I'll change the way I do business to make her feel more comfortable, but I have a life with her now and the BAU just doesn't fit in that future."

"But, Rainey..." Danny started to say and then smiled. "I guess you know what you want and I am happy for you. I hope I can find that kind of love one day."

"You will, Danny."

"So, you're really going to do this family thing. I just never pictured you changing diapers."

Rainey grinned. "I never imagined my life would be like this, but you know, I'm really looking forward to it. Besides, I heard godfathers change diapers, too."

PART III

Revenge is an act of passion; vengeance of justice. Injuries are revenged; crimes are avenged. ~ Samuel Johnson

CHAPTER TWENTY

Monday, August 22, four months later.

"Come on, Rainey, it's six o'clock already. I don't want to be late," Katie called from the other room.

Rainey sat on the couch in the den of their new gated community home, on the north side of Jordan Lake. She stared at the sonogram image in her hands. She worked all day at the new office on Franklin Street, in Chapel Hill. Ernie had her moving boxes and cleaning for hours. Katie met her at the door with the sonogram, all smiles and giddy. Rainey's body was tired, but her mind was numb. She looked at the fuzzy image in her hands and tried to take it all in. All those years of trying to have a baby with her former husband had failed time after time, but with healthy sperm and hormones Katie got pregnant almost instantly. They were having a baby. Rainey knew that before today, but this news was still a bit shocking.

Rainey was supposed to be leaving in a few minutes to go to the old lake property. When the land sold right away,

Rainey asked no questions. She took the money and put it down on the new house. It wasn't until a month later that she realized Katie's foundation had purchased the property. Katie hired Derrick and his mother to oversee the camp she put in place and helped Derrick, who turned out to be quite bright, get his GED. He and his mother moved into the cottage away from Derrick's bad influences. He would start Junior College in the fall, studying to be a social worker.

The camp offered literacy courses at night and on the weekends. Katie also provided a safe haven for women, who had been victims of violent crimes, and their children to come enjoy the lake several weeks out of each month. Counseling was available, but it was mostly a place for them to relax and feel safe. Rainey was tasked with providing security, which she did by hiring armed off-duty cops, who happened to all be women.

Tonight, they were supposed to attend a big party, where Katie was to dig up the first spade of dirt on the foundation of the new battered women's safe house she was building beside the cottage. It would have the latest security measures, as prescribed by Rainey. The state finally agreed, with Katie's father's influence, to allow the road to be gated near the lake. A guard house would be built where the road disappeared into the woods. Katie now had something to keep her busy during Rainey's work hours. She had a purpose, which kept her from concentrating on what Rainey was doing. Katie still worried, but seemed to have come to terms with her fears concerning Rainey's chosen occupation. All the pieces of the puzzle fell into place and their life together seemed to be heading in the right direction.

Rainey's attention was torn from the sonogram by the mention of Dalton's name from the blond newscaster on the television. Dalton's trial for the murder of the young girl was

RAINEY NIGHTS

scheduled to start next week. Rainey worked all summer with the prosecution team, preparing the case against him. There was no doubt in anyone's mind that Dalton would get the death penalty. Still, Rainey had seen stronger cases than this one fall apart. A second trial for the deaths of the women in Durham was years down the road. Despite what she said the last time she saw him, as long as Dalton Chambers was alive, Rainey retained an acute awareness of the danger he represented.

Rainey focused on the woman with the perfect hair and makeup, trying to sound like a serious reporter, as she said, "In breaking news, there will be no need for the upcoming murder trial of convicted serial killer Dalton Chambers, who attended a pretrial hearing today in downtown Raleigh. While being transported back to Central Prison, Chambers was attacked and killed by another inmate, Chauncey Barber. Barber, who was taken to the courthouse today for arraignment on charges of murder, in connection with several gang style killings, is already serving thirty-five years to life on criminal enterprise charges. No word on what caused the attack."

Rainey heard Katie beside her. She wasn't sure how much Katie had heard until she saw the look in Katie's eyes. For a moment, there was a question, unspoken, hanging in the air. Rainey wasn't sure how to answer that question. Katie must have decided not to ask it. Her expression changed and she smiled sweetly.

As if she hadn't heard a word, Katie said, "Honey, are you still in shock?"

Rainey didn't know what to say.

Katie's smile grew at Rainey's helplessness. "I see you still have not regained your powers of speech." She knelt down in front of Rainey and took the sonogram from her hands. "You know this is all your fault. You just kept insisting on children."

342

Rainey looked into those sparkling crystal blue eyes and felt a wave of contentment wash over her. She could deal with anything life had to throw at her, as long as Katie was there, of that she was absolutely positive. She was about to tell Katie how much she loved her, when they were both drawn back to the blond on the TV screen.

"In other courthouse news, Cookie Kutter, a local news reporter was arrested last night for drunk driving, after police picked her up for leaving the scene of an accident in the parking lot of a well known lesbian bar in Raleigh."

Katie started laughing and turned to Rainey. "Damn, you nailed that one. You said she was way too interested in your private life."

Rainey chuckled at the picture of Cookie on the screen, being led away in handcuffs. "Yeah, I guess I did." Standing, Rainey helped Katie up from the floor. She pulled her close and whispered in Katie's ear, "Do you have any idea how much I love you?"

Katie leaned back and smiled up at Rainey. "You just remember that when you're changing three babies' diapers at four in the morning."

Made in the USA
Lexington, KY
11 April 2012